PIRATE KING

LAURIE R. KING

First published in Great Britain in 2011 by
Allison & Busby Limited
13 Charlotte Mews
London W1T 4EJ
www.allisonandbusby.com

Published by arrangement with Bantam Books,
an imprint of The Random House Publishing Group,
a division of Random House, Inc., New York., NY, USA.
All rights reserved.

Map copyright © 2011 by JEFFREY L. WARD

Interior photo credits:
Fernando Pessoa: found in *Circuilo de Leitores, Fernando Pessoa—Obra Poetica, Vol. I*
The brigantine *Romance* by Gloria Cloutier Kimberly: courtesy of Jane Meyer
Moroccan house: courtesy of the photographer, Zoe Elkaim

Permission to reprint lines from
Fernando Pessoa's 'Maritime Ode'
as translated by Richard Zenith.

A CIP catalogue record for this book is available from
the British Library.

10 9 8 7 6 5 4 3 2 1

ISBN 978-0-7490-4091-8

Typeset in 12.5/17.4 pt Adobe Garamond Pro by
Allison & Busby Ltd.

Paper used in this publication is from sustainably managed sources.
All of the wood used is procured from legal sources and is fully traceable.
The producing mill uses schemes such as ISO 14001
to monitor environmental impact.

Printed and bound by
CPI Group (UK) Ltd, Croydon, CR0 4Y

This one's for Gabe:
Welcome to the madness.

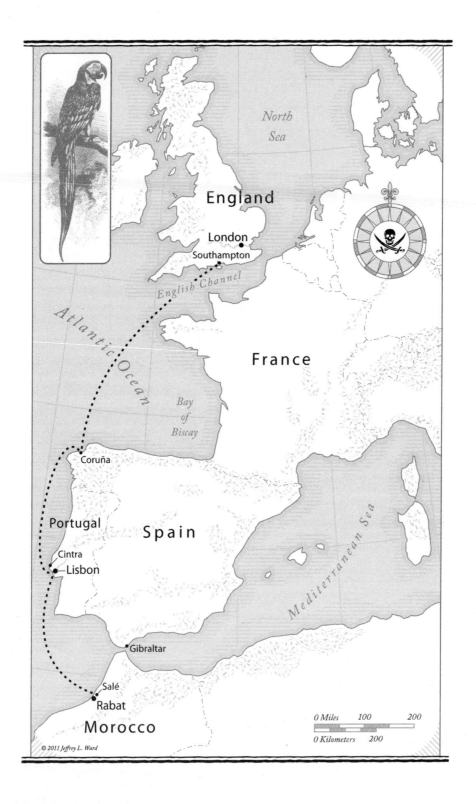

North
Sea

England

London
Southampton

English Channel

Atlantic Ocean

France

Bay
of
Biscay

Coruña

Portugal   Spain

Cintra
—Lisbon

Mediterranean Sea

Gibraltar

Salé
Rabat

Morocco

© 2011 Jeffrey L. Ward

0 Miles   100   200

0 Kilometers   200

PIRATE KING

a Moving Picture in Three Acts

Director:
Randolph St John Warminster-Fflytte

Assistant director:	Geoffrey Hale
Assistant's assistant:	Mary Russell
Cinematographer:	Will Currie
Choreographer:	Graziella Mazzo

The Cast:

Major-General Stanley played by Harold Scott
Ruth played by Myrna Hatley
Mabel played by Bibi
The Pirate King played by Senhor M.R.X. La Rocha
His Lieutenant, Samuel, played by Sr La Rocha's Lieutenant
Frederic played by Daniel Marks

The Sisters:

Annie	Ginger
Bonnie	Harriet
Celeste	Isabel
Doris	June
Edith	Kate
Fannie	Linda

The Pirates:

Adam	Gerald
Benjamin	Henry
Charles	Irving
David	Jack
Earnest	Kermit
Francis	Lawrence

The Constables:

Sergeant played by Vincent Paul

Alan	Donald
Bert	Edward
Clarence	Frank

AUTHOR'S FOREWORD

I FIND MYSELF OF MIXED mind about this, my eleventh volume of memoirs concerning life with Sherlock Holmes. On the one hand, I vowed when I began writing them that the accounts would be complete, that there would be no leaving out failures or slapping wallpaper across our mistakes.

Nonetheless, this is one episode over which I have considerable doubts – not, let us be clear, due to any humiliations on my part, but because I fear that the credulity of many readers will be stretched to the breaking by the case's intricate and, shall we say, colourful complexity of events.

If that be the case with you, dear reader, please rest assured that for this one volume of the Russell memoirs, you have my full permission to regard it (and alas, by contagion, me) as fiction.

Had I not actually been there, I, too, would dismiss the tale as preposterous.

– MRH

BOOK ONE

Ship of Fools

November 6-22, 1924

Chapter One

RUTH: I did not catch the word aright, through being hard of hearing . . . I took and bound this promising boy apprentice to a *pirate*.

'HONESTLY, HOLMES? PIRATES?'
   'That is what I said.'
'You want me to go and work for pirates.'
O'er the glad waters of the dark blue sea, our thoughts as boundless, and our souls as free . . .
'My dear Russell, someone your age should not be having trouble with her hearing.' Sherlock Holmes solicitous was Sherlock Holmes sarcastic.
'My dear Holmes, someone your age should not be overlooking incipient dementia. Why do you wish me to go and work for pirates?'
'Think of it as an adventure, Russell.'
'May I point out that this past year has been nothing but adventure? Ten back-to-back cases between us in the past fifteen

months, stretched over, what, eight countries? Ten, if one acknowledges the independence of Scotland and Wales. What I need is a few weeks with nothing more demanding than my books.'

'You should, of course, feel welcome to remain here.'

The words seemed to contain a weight beyond their surface meaning. A dark and inauspicious weight. A Mariner's albatross sort of a weight. I replied with caution. 'This being my home, I generally do feel welcome.'

'Ah. Did I not mention that Mycroft is coming to stay?'

'Mycroft? Why on earth would Mycroft come here? In all the years I've lived in Sussex, he's visited only once.'

'Twice, although the other occasion was while you were away. However, he's about to have the builders in, and he needs a quiet retreat.'

'He can afford an hotel room.'

'This is my brother, Russell,' he chided.

Yes, exactly: my husband's brother, Mycroft Holmes. Whom I had thwarted – blatantly, with malice aforethought, and with what promised to be heavy consequences – scant weeks earlier. Whose history, I now knew, held events that soured my attitude towards him. Who wielded enormous if invisible power within the British Government. And who was capable of making life uncomfortable for me until he had tamped me back down into my position of sister-in-law.

'How long?' I asked.

'He thought two weeks.'

Fourteen days: 336 hours: 20,160 minutes, of first-hand opportunity to revenge himself on me verbally, psychologically, or (surely not?) physically. Mycroft was a master of the subtlest of poisons – I speak metaphorically, of course – and fourteen days

16

would be plenty to work his vengeance and drive me to the edge of madness.

And only the previous afternoon, I had learnt that my alternative lodgings in Oxford had been flooded by a broken pipe. Information that now crept forward in my mind, bringing a note of dour suspicion.

No, Holmes was right: best to be away if I could.

Which circled the discussion around to its beginnings.

'Why should I wish to go work with pirates?' I repeated.

'You would, of course, be undercover.'

'Naturally. With a cutlass between my teeth.'

'I should think you would be more likely to wear a night-dress.'

'A night-dress.' Oh, this was getting better and better.

'As I remember, there are few parts for females among the pirates. Although they may decide to place you among the support staff.'

'Pirates have support staff?' I set my tea-cup back into its saucer, that I might lean forward and examine my husband's face. I could see no overt indications of lunacy. No more than usual.

He ignored me, turning over a page of the letter he had been reading, keeping it on his knee beneath the level of the table. I could not see the writing – which was, I thought, no accident.

'I should imagine they have a considerable number of personnel behind the scenes,' he replied.

'Are we talking about pirates-on-the-high-seas, or piracy-as-violation-of-copyright-law?'

'Definitely the cutlass rather than the pen. Although Gilbert might have argued for the literary element.'

'Gilbert?' Two seconds later, the awful light of revelation flashed through my brain; at the same instant, Holmes tossed the letter onto the table so I could see its heading.

Headings, plural, for the missive contained two separate letters folded together. The first was from Scotland Yard. The second was emblazoned with the words *D'Oyly Carte Opera*.

I reared back, far more alarmed by the stationery than by the thought of climbing storm-tossed rigging in the company of cut-throats.

'Gilbert and *Sullivan*?' I exclaimed. 'Pirates as in *Penzance*? Light opera and heavy humour? No. Absolutely not. Whatever Inspector Lestrade has in mind, I refuse.'

'One gathers,' Holmes reflected, reaching for another slice of toast, 'that the title originally did hold a double entendre, Gilbert's dig at the habit of American companies to flout the niceties of British copyright law.'

He was not about to divert me by historical titbits or an insult against my American heritage: This was one threat against which my homeland would have to mount its own defence.

'You've dragged your sleeve in the butter.' I got to my feet, picking up my half-emptied plate to underscore my refusal.

'It would not be a singing part,' he said.

I walked out of the room.

He raised his voice. 'I would do it myself, but I need to be here for Mycroft, to help him tidy up after the Goodman case.'

Answer gave I none.

'It shouldn't take you more than two weeks, three at the most. You'd probably find the solution before arriving in Lisbon.'

'Why—' I cut the question short; it did not matter in the least why the D'Oyly Carte company wished me to go to Lisbon. I poked my head back into the room. 'Holmes: no. I have an entire academic year to catch up on. I have no interest whatsoever in the entertainment of *hoi polloi*. The entire thing sounds like a headache. I am not going to Lisbon, or even London. I'm not going anywhere. No.'

CHAPTER TWO

PIRATE KING: I don't think much of our profession, but, contrasted with respectability, it is comparatively honest.

MY STEAMER LURCHED into Lisbon on a horrible sleet-blown November morning. My face was scoured by the ocean air, I having spent most of the voyage on deck in an attempt (largely vain) to keep my stomach from turning inside-out. My hair and clothing were stiff with salt, my nose raw from the handkerchief, I had lost nearly half a stone and more than half my mind, and my mood was as bloody as my eyeballs.

If a pirate had hove into view – or my husband, for that matter – I would merrily have keelhauled either with a rope of linen from the captain's table.

My only source of satisfaction, grim as it was, lay in the knowledge that several of the actors on board were every bit as miserable as I.

The eternal, quease-inducing sway lessened as we left the open sea to churn our way up the Rio Tejo towards the vast harbour – one of Europe's largest, according to someone's guide-book – that in the days of sail had made Portugal a great empire. The occasional isolated castle or fishing village along the shore slowly proliferated. Our view panned across a lighthouse, then picked up an odd piece of architecture planted just offshore to our left, a diminutive fort in an unnecessarily exuberant Gothic style. (Was that the style the guide-book – Annie's? – had called 'Manueline'?) Someone in the crowd of shivering fellow passengers loudly identified it as the Tower of Belém; my mind's eye automatically supplied the phrase on an internal subtitle:

> 'That's the Tower of Belem!'

I shook my head in irritation. I had watched more moving pictures over the past few days than in the past few years: My way of seeing the world had changed dramatically.

Beyond the Manueline excrescence rose Lisboa itself – *Alis Ubo* to the Phoenicians, *Ulissipont* to the Romans. Our first indication of the city was the spill of masts and belching smoke-stacks that pressed towards the docks. As we drew nearer, a jumble of pale walls and red tile roofs rose up from the harbour (it looked like a lake) on a series of hills (the guide-book had claimed seven, on a par with Rome) punctuated by church spires (a startling number of those) watched over by a decaying castle.

Pirates, I sniffed as I eyed the castle gun-ports. Any sensible member of the piratical fraternity would have steered well clear of this place.

I pulled my thick coat around me, made a fruitless attempt to clean my spectacles, and went below to assemble my charges.

My job – my official job – was to shepherd, protect, nurse and browbeat into order some three dozen inmates of a mobile lunatic asylum. I was the one responsible for their well-being. It was I who ensured the inmates were housed and fed, entertained and soothed, kept off one another's throats and out of one another's beds. I was the one the inmates ran to, sent on errands, and shouted at, whether the complaint was inadequately hot coffee or insufficiently robust lightbulb. On the first night out from England, I had been roused from a fitful sleep by a demand that I – I, personally – remove a moth from a cabin.

A fraternity of actual pirates could not have been more trouble. Even a travelling D'Oyly Carte company would have been less of a madhouse.

But I was working neither with buccaneers nor with travelling players: The letter with the heading of the firm responsible for the Gilbert & Sullivan performances had merely been by way of introduction. Instead, I found myself the general coordinator and jack of all trades for a film-crew.

In the early years after the War, Fflytte Films had appeared to be the rising star of the British cinema industry: From *Quarterdeck* in 1919 through 1922's *Krakatoa*, Fflytte Films ('Fflyttes of Fancy!') seemed positioned to challenge the American domination of the young industry, producing a series of stupendously successful multi-reel extravaganzas with exotic settings and dashing stories. Then came *Hannibal*, which ran so far over budget in the preliminary stages, the project was cancelled before the second reel of film was fed into the cameras. *Hannibal* was followed by the wildly popular *Rum Runner*, but after that came *The Writer*, which took eight months to make and ran in precisely four cinema houses for less than a week. *The Writer*'s failure might have been predicted – a three-reel drama about a British novelist in Paris? – except that Randolph St John Warminster-Fflytte ('Fflyttes of Fantasy!') was a director famous for pulling hugely successful rabbits out of apparently shabby hats (*Small Arms* concerned the accidental death of a child; *Rum Runner* was about smuggling alcohol into the United States; both had returned their costs a hundredfold) and a movie about a thinly disguised James Joyce might have been as successful as his other ugly ducklings, particularly when one threw in the titillating appeal of the *Ulysses* obscenity ban.

However, since the film had skirted around the actual depiction of the obscene acts in question, it went rather flat. So now, with three costly duds on his hands and the threatened loss of his aristocratic backers, Fflytte was returning to the scene of his three previous solid successes ('Fflyttes of Fanfare!'): the sea-borne action adventure.

This one was to be loosely based on the Gilbert & Sullivan operetta. *Loosely* as in wobbling wildly and on the verge of a complete uncoupling. Not an inch of film had gone through the cameras; the Major-General was drunk around the clock; the cameraman's assistant had a palsy of the hands that was explained to me, *sotto voce*, as the result of a recent nervous breakdown; the actress playing Mabel had taken the bit into her teeth with this, her first starring rôle, and was out to prove herself a flapper edition of Sarah Bernhardt (if not in talent, then in imperious attitudes and a knack of fabricating alternative versions of her personal history); and the twelve other young ladies playing the Major-General's daughters – yes, thirteen daughters altogether –

formed a non-stop cyclone of lace, giggles and yellow curls that spun up and down the decks and occasionally below them – far below, to judge by the grease stains on one pink dress thrust under my nose by an accusing maternal person. Even the eldest of the 'sisters', a busybody of the first order, had blinked her big blue eyes at me in practised innocence from more than one out-of-bounds state-room.

We had not left the Channel before I felt the first impulse to murder.

'Producer's assistant', then, was my official job. My unofficial one – the one Holmes had manoeuvred me into – was given me by Chief Inspector Lestrade in his office overlooking Westminster Bridge. He had stood as I was ushered in, but remained behind his desk – as if that might protect him. A single thin folder lay on its pristine surface.

'Miss Russell. Do sit down. May I take your bag?'

'No, thank you.' I dropped the bag I had thrown together in Sussex – basic necessities such as tooth-brush, clean socks, reading material, and loaded revolver – onto the floor, and sat.

'Mr Holmes is not with you?'

'As you see.' Was that a sigh I heard? He sat down.

'You two haven't any news of Robert Goodman, have you?'

'Is that why you asked me here, Chief Inspector? To follow up on the last case?'

'No, no. I just thought I'd ask, since the man has vanished into thin air, and whenever something like that takes place, it's extraordinary how often Sherlock Holmes happens to have been in the vicinity.'

'No, we have not heard news of Mr Goodman.' The literal, if not actual, truth.

'Why do I get the feeling that you know more than you're telling?'

'I know a great number of things, Chief Inspector, few of which are your concern. Now, you wrote asking for assistance.'

'From your husband.'

'Why?' Lestrade had always complained, loud and clear, that there was no place for amateurs in the investigation of crimes.

'Because the only police officers I had with the necessary skills have become unavailable.'

'Those skills being . . . ?'

'The ability to make educated small-talk, and mastery of a type-writing machine. It is remarkable how few gentlemen are capable of producing type-written documents with their own ten fingers. Your husband, as I recall, is one who can.'

'And yet the city's employment rosters are positively crawling with educated *women* typists.'

'I had one of those. A fine and talented young PC. Who is now home with a baby.'

'Oh. Well, now you have me.'

'Yes.' Definitely a sigh, this time. 'Oh, it might as well be you.'

My eyes narrowed. 'Chief Inspector, one might almost think you had no interest in this matter. Is it important enough to concern Holmes and me, or is it not?'

'Yes. I mean to say, I don't know. That is—' He ran a hand over his face. 'I dislike having outside pressures turned on the Yard.'

'Ah. Politics.'

'In a manner of speaking. It has to do with the British moving picture industry.'

'Do we have a moving picture industry?' I asked in surprise.

'Exactly. While the Americans turn out vast sagas that sell tickets by the bushel, this country makes small pictures about bunnies and

Scottish hillsides that are shown as the audience is taking its seats for the feature. I'm told it's because of the War – all our boys went to the Front, but the American cameras just kept rolling. And now, when we're beginning to catch up, we no sooner produce a possible rival to the likes of Griffith and DeMille when a rumour – a faint rumour, mind – comes to the ears of Certain Individuals that the man they're backing may be bent.'

I put the clues together. 'Some members of the House of Lords are worried about the money they put up to fund a picture; they mentioned it to the Chancellor of the Exchequer over sherry, and Winston sent someone to talk to you?'

'Worse than that – the Palace themselves have invested in the company, if you can believe that. And the trouble is, I can't say for certain that there's nothing to it. The studio has been linked to . . . problems.'

'I should imagine that picture studios generate all sorts of problems.'

'Not generally of the criminal variety. There are some odd coincidences that follow this one around. Three years ago, they made a movie about guns, and—'

'An entire moving picture about guns?'

'More or less. This was shortly after the Firearms Act, and the picture was about a returned soldier who used his military revolver in a Bolshevik act, accidentally killing a child.'

'The Bolshevist terror being why the Firearms Act was introduced in the first place.' The 1920 Firearms Act meant that every three years, Holmes and I were forced to go before our local sheriff for weapons permits, demonstrating that we were neither drunks, lunatics, nor children.

'That and the sheer number of revolvers knocking around after the War waiting to go off. Which more or less concealed the fact that someone sold quite a few of said firearms in this country, unpermitted, shortly after the picture came out.'

'What does that—'

'Wait. The following year, Fflytte did a story about a young woman whose life was taken over by drugs – *Coke Express*, it was called. The month following its release in the cinema houses, we had an unusual number of drugs parties along the south coast.'

'Yes, but—'

'And last year, one of their pirate movies was about rum-running into America. It came out in November.'

'I was busy in November. What happened?'

'McCoy's arrest. "The Real McCoy"? The man's made a small fortune smuggling hard liquor into the United States.'

'Hmm. Is this perhaps the same studio that was making a film about Hannibal?'

'Fflytte Films, that's them.'

'Odd, I don't recall hearing about a sudden influx of elephants racing down the streets of—'

'I knew this was a mistake. Never mind, Miss Russell, I'll—'

'No no, Chief Inspector, sit down, I apologise. Surely there must have been something more concrete to interest you in the case, even in a peripheral manner?'

He paused, then subsided into his chair. 'Yes. Although even that I can't be at all certain about. We were beginning to ask some questions – in a hush-hush fashion, so as not to set the gossip magazines on fire – when the studio's secretary went missing. Lonnie Johns is her name.'

'When was that?'

'Well, there's the thing – it was only four or five days ago. And there's nothing to say that the Johns girl didn't just quit her job and go on holiday. The girl she shares a room with said it wouldn't surprise her, that Lonnie's job would shred the nerves of a saint.'

'But Miss Johns didn't say anything to her, about going away?'

'The room-mate didn't see her go – she'd just got back herself from a week in Bognor Regis.'

'Any signs of foul play at the flat?'

'Neither disturbance nor a note, although some of her things did seem to be missing, tooth-brush and the like.'

'If the girl had run off to the Riviera with a movie star, she'd probably have told everyone she knew,' I reflected.

'Normally, we'd barely even be opening an enquiry into a disappearance of a girl missing a few days, but time is against us. The entire crew is about to set sail out of England, and if we don't get someone planted in their midst, we'll lose the chance. And when my likely officers were unavailable, I thought, just maybe Mr Holmes would have a few days free to act as a sort of place-holder, until I could get one of my own in line for it. But never mind, it was only a—'

'And in addition, if it does blow up in the face of a gaggle of blue-bloods and splatter them all with scandal, it would be nice if Scotland Yard were nowhere in sight.'

'Miss Russell, I deeply resent the im—'

'Chief Inspector, I have nothing in particular on at the moment. I'll be happy to devote myself to the Mysterious Affair of the Coincidental Film-crew.'

He looked shocked. 'You mean you'll *do* it?'

'I just said I would.'

'I thought you'd laugh in my face.' He gave me a suspicious scowl. 'You aren't a "fan" of the cinema world, are you?'

'By no means.'

'And yet you seem almost eager to take this on.'

Motion pictures, or Mycroft? I reached out to snatch the folder from his hand. 'My dear Chief Inspector, you have no idea.'

Chapter Three

Pirate King: Away to the cheating world go you,
Where pirates all are well-to-do.

From Lestrade's office, I went directly to that of Fflytte Films. It overlooked the friendly confusion of the Covent Gardens flower mart, where I dodged sweepers, buckets, carts, heaps of pulped blossoms, and a dark and winsome young lady aiming a heather sprig at my lapel.

At the top of a flight of stairs, I found a door standing open, a ring of keys protruding from its lock. Inside, the chaos was nowhere near as colourful as that on the street outside, and the cries of vendors had been replaced with a raised telephonic voice from an inner office. I followed it to its source.

'—don't care what he says, the alcohol is to go into the hold, not in his quarters. Yes, I know it's not your job to search him, I'll take care of that, you just – That's right, into the hold, and we'll worry about his rooms on the day. Great, thanks.'

The telephone clattered onto its stand, and I rapped my knuckles against the half-open door, then repeated it when I realised that the man's muttered epithet had hidden my first attempt.

Geoffrey Hale, the general manager of Fflytte Films, raised his head from his hands, presenting me with a pair of cornflower-blue eyes in a face too young for the white of his hair – or, what I had thought was white hair, but with a closer look became merely very pale blonde. He was in his late thirties, and would have been quite attractive but for his haunted expression. 'Yes?' he said, a syllable that tried for irritable but came out more than a little fearful.

'I've come about the position,' I replied. 'Sir Malcolm—'

For Hale's benefit, I began to trundle out Lestrade's manufactured story, which in point of fact was a reasonably efficient means of inserting a person (male or female) into Fflytte Films. In the manner of all things English (particularly things in any way connected to the House of Lords) it had drawn its particulars from the old boys' network: a luncheon conversation at a club; Hale bemoaning the abrupt loss of his secretary-assistant and going frantic over the number of hours required to grease the machinery of a moving picture company; the old boy/luncheon-mate saying that he might know someone, if Hale didn't require a person who knew the industry; Hale answering that he'd hire a myopic orang-utan if the chimp could take dictation and manipulate a telephone.

And here I was, with three of those four characteristics.

(That, in any event, was how Hale remembered it. According to Lestrade, it had begun the other way around, with Lestrade actively hunting for a man with links to Fflytte or Hale; on finding one, he had arranged for the old boy to invite Hale to lunch, drawing the scent of a potential assistant before his nose.)

(That, at any rate, was how Lestrade remembered it. However, knowing the House of Lords and its fondness for meddling in the lives of those who actually worked for a living, I thought it equally possible that Lestrade had been handed the plan ready made: *Here's our suspicions*, the peers had told him; *here's what your man is to do; here's the path we've paved for him to get there.*

It had been a set-up from the beginning, although there was no knowing at this point how many layers of deception there were: Hale definitely was being manipulated, Lestrade possibly, me almost certainly. Even that conveniently missing secretary had the faint odour of red herring, a ploy designed expressly to attract the attentions of the police. And if Lonnie Johns was safely tucked up for a quiet holiday in the south of France, it was more likely that the House of Lords was paying her bills than Scotland Yard.

Apart from which, Lestrade was not a good enough liar to manufacture a false concern for a missing girl.)

(Only some days later, as I leant miserably over the storm-tossed railing, desperately searching for something to bring my mind up from my stomach, did it occur to me that Mycroft's threatened trip to Sussex had been an oddly convenient piece of timing. And once that idea had swum to the surface, a great cloud of morbid thoughts boiled up in its wake: Since the notion of Mycroft Holmes doing the bidding of any number of Lords was laughable, it suggested that the House of Lords were not the instigators of this investigation, but the puppets of Mycroft Holmes. Mycroft had moved them: They had moved Lestrade: Lestrade had moved—

Which in turn suggested that Mycroft had wanted me to do this, but knew that if he were to ask me directly, I would refuse.

Later, when I was not in quite such a vulnerable position, I decided that it was a ridiculously convoluted, Heath Robinsonian piece of machinery, a bit much even for Mycroft. My brother-in-law was sly, but he was practised enough to know that setting a fox before Lords might take the hunt in any direction.

One thing I was certain: If plot there was, Holmes had not been in on it.

But all the doubt and suspicion came later, when it was too late. Had I put the pieces together earlier, I would not have found myself standing before Geoffrey Hale's chaotic desk in his Covent Garden office that November afternoon, laying out the story Chief Inspector Lestrade had provided for me.)

'—so I don't actually know anything about the picture industry, but a friend mentioned this and I'm between projects just at the moment and I thought it sounded like a lark. I'm a whiz at typewriting,' I added with a bright smile.

I was none too certain how Hale would feel about the person being thrust towards his manly breast – one Mary Russell, who, although well dressed and reasonably energetic, was far too young for the sort of placid, maternal, secretarial authority that his typhoon-struck offices cried out for, who moreover admitted that she knew exactly nothing about co-ordinating a film-crew. But before I could finish my prepared explanation, dawn came up across his unshaven features and he rose as if to fling himself at my feet.

I hastened to stick out my hand, forestalling any greater demonstration; he clasped it hard and pumped away with hearty exclamations.

'Oh how utterly jolly, a life-saver in sensible shoes, you are so very welcome, Miss – what was it? Russell, of course, like the philosopher, although I'd guess looking at you that you're a dashed sight more practical than him. Oh, Miss Russell, you can't believe what a mess things have got into here – I had a perfectly adequate assistant who seems to have upped and left, just as we're about to set sail. Both literally and figuratively.'

'Er,' I said, retrieving my squashed hand and glancing down at my shoes, which were the most fashionable (and hence impractical)

I owned. 'Do you want to see some letters of recommendation or something?'

'You speak English and you're dead sober at two in the afternoon, what else could I ask for? You know your alphabet?'

'I know several alphabets. And shorthand.' Holmes, when going undercover, could disguise himself as anything from garage mechanic to priest; I was forced into the more womanly rôles of secretary or maid. (Although after one stint in the kitchen of a manor house, I tried to avoid being hired as cook; still, the fire had been quickly doused.)

'And you have a passport, and no small children or aged grannies needing you at home? If you spoke with Malcolm, you'll know that we will be away from London for some weeks? Although we'll try our best to be home by Christmas.'

That was either a gross and self-delusional underestimate, or a blatant lie designed to soothe a nervous would-be employee. But I did not blink. 'I am aware that the job entails travel, yes.'

'Perfection. Can you start with these?'

He stabbed the air with a desk spike impaled with more than four inches of paper. Avoiding the wicked point, I extracted the object from his hand. 'You want me to begin immediately?'

'Absolutely. That is, could you?' he asked, recalling his manners with an effort.

'I could, although it might be good if I had some idea what you'd like me to do.'

When he flung himself out of the office six minutes later, late for a meeting with a last-minute addition to the cast on the other side of town, I had not much more of an idea. However, I soon discovered that by identifying myself as '—with Fflytte Films', the voice in the earpiece would instantly break in with the urgent business at hand, much of which had to do with unpaid bills. At 6.40 that evening, I reached the bottom of the spike, having taken care of roughly half its problems and transferred the remainder onto a single sheet of lined paper for consultation with Hale. With that in hand, along with another page holding a list of cheques needing to be sent, I locked the door with the abandoned keys, and set off for Hale's home.

At 7.00 that morning, Mrs Hudson's coffee in hand, I'd neither heard of nor cared about Geoffrey Hale, Randolph Fflytte, or the business of putting a moving picture before the great British public. Twelve hours later, I felt I had been intimately involved for weeks.

Geoffrey Hale was the lifelong friend, long-time business partner, and (another inevitability in English business arrangements) second cousin of Randolph Fflytte himself. Hale was the man who enabled the director's vision to inhabit screens around the world. Hale was the one to assemble cast and crew, negotiate with the owners of cinema houses and would-be filming sites, and in general see to the practical minutiae of taking a film from initial discussion to opening night. Hale was the one to ensure that the actors were sober enough to work, that the actresses had enough flowers and bonbons to soothe their delicate egos, the one to make certain that the country house where filming was to take place actually possessed four walls and a roof.

Hale, and now me.

CHAPTER FOUR

PIRATES: A rollicking band of pirates we.

GEOFFREY HALE LIVED in St John's Wood. A rotund and shiny-headed person on the far side of middle age opened the door, his chins gathered above the sort of collar that labelled him a butler of the old school.

'Mary Russell, for Mr Hale,' I told him. His manner made me regret keenly that I did not have a card at hand for him to carry upon a polished salver.

He bore up under the disappointment, parked me in the room designated for the parking of intruders, and glided away, returning a precise four and a half minutes later to convey me to the presence of the master of the house, up a set of magnificent mahogany stairs that looked as if someone had recently dragged a piece of light artillery down them. I avoided the worst of the splinters, wondering if Hale's cousin and partner was experimenting with a scene from a forthcoming war movie.

Despite what I had said to Lestrade, I had in fact heard of Fflytte Films. ('Fflyttes of Fun!') I believe even Holmes would have known the name. Over the course of a decade of film-making, the trademark element of Fflytte Films had become Realism. In an industry with papier-mâché Alps and Babylonian temples made of composition board and gilt; where Valentino's *Sheik* pitched his tents a quick drive from Los Angeles (rumour even had it in Queens), and *Blood and Sand* showed not Spain, but a Hollywood back lot; where even *Robin Hood* had been born in Fort Lee, New Jersey, Fflytte Films made it known that when *this* company made a movie about the open seas, to the open seas the crew went; and when Fflytte Films produced a story about an aeronaut, by God the cameraman and his instrument were strapped in and set to turning. In *Quarterdeck*, half a ton of equipment had gone down in a storm; in *Jolly Roger*, men had been washed overboard – and if no lives had actually been lost, the great movie-going, gossip-magazine-reading public stoutly believed to the contrary.

One might have expected this rigid commitment to authenticity to require that any version of *Pirates of Penzance* be filmed in Penzance. However, during the course of that long day, I had come to suspect we were not bound for that sleepy watering-place on England's south coast.

Hale had shaved since flying out of the office that afternoon, although the smears of tiredness under his blue eyes were no lighter. He crossed the opulent library with his hand out, a ready apology on his lips.

'Miss Russell, can you ever forgive me for my state this afternoon? You must have thought you were in the company of a raving maniac – Thank you, Pullman, that will be all – or, no, ask Mrs Corder to send up a tray of – coffee, Miss Russell? Or tea? To go with these sandwiches and what-not? Coffee, then. Do sit down, Miss Russell, honestly, I'm not always in that sort of state.'

The first three minutes were spent with my mouth full as Hale delivered honeyed apologies while simultaneously performing the sort of dance upper-class males do when faced with a woman both of a lesser rank and in their employ: a polite, brotherly flirtation that lacks the faintest element of sex. It is amusing, particularly when based on invalid assumptions, but it must be even more exhausting to generate than it is to receive. Once I had relieved a meal's worth of dainty snacks from the platter, I used my linen napkin, then cut the dance short.

'Mr Hale, I have a degree from Oxford, I am on the boards of several companies, I speak four languages fluently, five haltingly, and can read several more. As I said, this is a lark for me, since I'm at loose ends at the moment and I'm always up for a new experience. This is not a job I need to pay the rent. Why don't you tell me what you are looking for, and I'll tell you if I can do it?'

He sat back, startled as much by my blunt attitude as by what I had told him. 'Er, yes. Very well. Perhaps you'd care for a drink instead of coffee?'

And so over glasses of brandy, he told me what I was in for: actors, crew, sets and costumes, local negotiations, food and housing, the lot. 'We're scheduled to spend ten days in Lisbon doing rehearsals – which, since you have little experience with the picture industry, I should note is not always the case, that many companies have neither rehearsals nor scripts. Fflytte Films uses both. We've found that if we don't prepare the choreography, as it were, of the fight scenes, we waste a lot of time and miles of film.'

'And you have a number of fight scenes?'

'We do.'

'Sorry, but I'd understood that you were filming *The Pirates of Penzance*?' Which I remembered as a distillation of saccharine songs, much tip-toeing about, topsy-turvy logic, and slapstick chases. My attempt to keep any dubious feelings out of my voice was only partly successful: Hale's quick glance at me glimmered with understanding and humour.

'Nothing so simple as that, Miss Russell, although making a silent film about a musical performance would be just the sort of thing Randolph would love to try. This is *Pirate King*: a film about a film about *The Pirates of Penzance*.'

'Very well,' I said slowly.

This time he laughed outright, and his face lost its pinched look, becoming both younger and more nearly handsome. 'What do you know about Fflytte Films?'

'Not a whole lot. Randolph Fflytte is in the papers from time to time, of course, but I have to admit, I only go to the cinema a handful of times a year.'

'Don't let Randolph hear you say that. Not unless you want to be sat down for a marathon screening of his work. You might say that Fflytte Films began in 1902, when Randolph got his first camera. He was seventeen at the time. For some years it was a summer-holiday toy, recording the antics of friends, playing around with effects. Randolph's first serious attempt at telling a story on the screen came in '07, when he bought up a lorry-load of Boer War uniforms and had every working man on his estate dress up to re-enact the Siege of Mafeking.'

'I don't know that I've seen that one.'

'You won't, either. There were only three prints made, and nine years ago, he threw them on the fire. Nearly burnt the house down – cellulose nitrate is remarkably flammable. He was unhappy with *Mafeking* even as he was editing it, since a battle across Berkshire countryside looks nothing like a battle across open veldt. Every time he looked at it, he regretted that he hadn't just piled his workers on a boat and taken them to South Africa.

'Two years after *Mafeking*, he took some friends to Paris to make a film, as a joke more than anything. This time, once he'd done the editing, he sold it. And decided that was what he wanted to do with his life. Before we knew it, we were making films commercially – most of them so dreadful they've blessedly disappeared from the scene, although *Hester's Grandmum* wasn't too bad, and *She Begs to Differ* had its moments.

'Then came the War, and while the Americans happily went on building studios and hiring actors, Randolph was reduced to filming the local evacuees and German prisoners on pig farms. But in 1915, he talked his way into France, where he shot *The Aeronaut*, about a spotter balloon. Two and a half years later, in the winter of 1917, he managed to return, and was thrilled to come under live fire. Or within a mile or so of live fire, at any rate.

'It was a revelation. Randolph came home and burnt those copies of *Mafeking* as a sort of vow, that utter realism would be the guiding light of Fflytte Films. And so it's been to this day: We make the audience feel "the wind in your face and the lash on your back".'

'I do remember that – the Roman galley film!'

'The first time Fflytte Films hit the headlines.'

'But wasn't the case dismissed?'

'Not dismissed: settled out of court. Randolph paid the actor off, although, truth to tell, the chap hadn't actually been beaten. It was camera tricks. Occasionally, we are reduced to mere verisimilitude.'

'I'm glad to hear you don't sacrifice your actors for the battle scenes. Or bury them under volcano ash. But why on earth pay the man off?'

'One cannot buy that kind of publicity, Miss Russell. Fflytte Films pummelling its actors bloody for the sake of realism? Priceless word-

of-mouth. Almost as good as burning down the village in *Krakatoa* –
although the ash there was flour, and the volcano was only waist high.'

'Good to know. And now you're doing *The Pirates of Penzance* –
or at any rate, a picture about a picture about it.'

'The plot is, a film-crew is making a picture about the pirates
who come to Penzance in the Gilbert & Sullivan operetta. And
as they film, the crew gets involved with real-life Barbary pirates.'

'Er, you do know that there aren't any more Barbary pirates?' An
American film-maker might not have picked up on this little fact,
but a man with Hale's accent would surely have had a modicum of
history thrust down his throat.

'Of course. On the other hand, there will always be pirates of
one stripe or another in the world.'

'And this film-within-a-film is about real pirates wrapped around
fictional pirates?'

'You're catching on.'

'It's a farce, then?'

'No, actually, it's more along the lines of an adventure. Do you
remember the story in *The Pirates of Penzance?*'

'Dimly.' I had probably fallen asleep halfway through the first
act: Music has that effect on me. A source of continual outrage
from my musical husband.

'The young pirate Frederic, on the eve of his twenty-first birthday,
announces to his fellows that he has never been able to stomach
piracy, and that even though this particular band to which he has
been apprenticed is soft-hearted, he intends to leave them and devote
himself to fighting piracy. He falls in love with the daughter of a major-
general, but through a piece of trickery, the pirates take him back into
their ranks, capturing the girl and her sisters to take as their wives.
There follows a great deal of Gilbertian shenanigans before the pirates
are revealed to be not only Englishmen, and loyal to the Queen, but of

noble birth as well, which makes them appropriate husbands for the Major-General's many daughters. Happy endings all around.'

To such had the wit of Chaucer and Shakespeare descended.

'How many daughters?' I asked.

'Productions of the opera have varied in the numbers of both daughters and pirates – there are four named sisters and simply a "chorus" of pirates. In addition to Mabel and Frederic, Randolph has decided on twelve of each.'

'*Thirteen* daughters? Wouldn't that make some of them a bit young to marry?' Or old.

'We're classifying them as four sets of triplets. And Mabel, of course.'

'Mustn't forget Mabel. And a dozen constables as well?'

'For symmetry, one might imagine, but no, only six of those. Plus the sergeant.'

'Twelve and twelve and two and seven – thirty-three actors?'

'We won't have pirates at first, but you have also to add Ruth, Frederic's piratical nursemaid, and Major-General Stanley, Mabel's father.'

'And you want me to help keep that lot happy, healthy, and in some kind of order?'

'Plus the crew – cameraman and assistant, make-up woman, seamstress, three or four others. No servants; Randolph banned the actors from bringing their servants along after *Anna Karenina* – two illegitimate pregnancies, one divorce, and a bullet wound between them. Because of the cold,' he explained.

'Of course.'

'So no personal maids or valets. However,' Hale added, his voice innocent but his eyes taking on a wicked gleam in their depths, 'the four youngest sisters – youngest in fact, not youngest on film – will bring their mothers.'

'Oh, Lord,' I said. I had encountered the mothers of young prima donnas before.

He laughed aloud. 'You begin to see why I greeted you with such enthusiasm this afternoon.'

'You all but wept in joy. Well, if that's the case, I'd best—' I started, but he cut me off.

'There's something else.'

What on earth could surpass what he had already described? 'Yes?'

He reached for the decanter, replenishing our glasses. The level in the glass rose; I braced myself. 'You seem a sensible kind of person, Miss Russell. The kind of person who pays attention to details.'

'I try.'

'And the kind of person who dislikes . . . wrongdoing.'

The very model of an unwilling apprentice pirate, one might say. 'Yes,' I ventured.

'And quite, well, sensible.'

Like my shoes? I wondered.

'Plucky, even.'

Plucky?

'Because I was thinking, perhaps you would be willing to . . . extend your assignment. Just a little.'

Please, please don't ask me to dress up as one of the daughters. 'Er,' I said.

'So that in the course of your job, if you come across something – how to say this? Something out of the ordinary – you will bring it to my attention.'

I kept my face still, although my heart gave a little thump. Was the man aware of the same activities that had attracted Lestrade's attention? Or had one of his blue-blooded chums dropped a hint about the investigation, and he wished me to share any findings with him? Or – further concern – could he be laying a false trail for me by claiming concern for illicit behaviour?

Pirates within pirates, crime within crime . . .

'Perhaps you'd best explain what you mean by "out of the ordinary".'

He picked up his glass, to swirl the contents into an amber whirlpool.

'Three years ago, Fflytte Films made *The Moonstone*. Do you remember it?'

'I did see that one, yes. Very realistic, as I remember, the scenes in India.'

'As I said, our hallmark. The actor playing Ablewhite – who you may remember dies in the story – was killed a few days after his final scenes were filmed.'

'How unfortunate.'

'He was drunk playing the Dame in a Christmas panto and fell into the orchestra pit, breaking his neck on the kettledrum, but yes, it was a tragedy. Later that year, we went to Finland for *Anna Karenina*, Finland being the closest we could come to Russia without getting involved with the Reds. But as I said, it was cold, and our Anna got frostbite when the filming was only halfway through and went home (quit the profession entirely, I heard the other day; she now runs a boarding house in Leeds), so we had to turn the story into a short about the frozen North instead. And even then, the polar bear rather chewed up its handler.'

'Oh dear. Perhaps a crew as accident-prone as yours ought to go into a less hazardous business.'

'And then in *Jolly Roger*, we almost lost two men in a freak wave.'

'Yes, so you mentioned.'

'With *Krakatoa*, two of the cinema houses where it was running burnt down. In *Coke Express*, one of our actors decided to drive through town in the altogether – that one took a *lot* of work to hush up. I had to prove that he was just drunk, not coked.'

I said nothing: True, the coincidences were piling rather high, but clumsiness in stunts did have a way of bringing its own punishment, and Hale himself had pointed out how inflammable film could be. And actors had been known to drink.

'*Hannibal* was cancelled, but one of the men we'd used as a consultant for *Rum Runner* was arrested, for rum-running. *The Writer*, about a failed writer, well, failed.' He knocked back a hefty swallow from his glass, and continued bleakly, 'We're cursed. Whatever the movie's about, it *happens*. There: Now you'll probably quit on me, too.'

I blinked. Lestrade wanted me to look into chronic lawbreaking; Hale was suggesting I investigate—

'You want me to help you with a curse?'

Hale went on with an air of determination. 'Miss Russell, this current picture is about piracy. And yes, I will admit it sounds mad, but I've got the wind up about it. Getting fined for mistreating an actor is one thing, but I don't have time for a court case involving some dastardly deed on the open seas.'

I opened my mouth to say something along the lines of *If a beaten galley slave sells movies, wouldn't a pirates' curse make for a sure-fire hit?* but caught myself. If someone in Fflytte Films had come up with *that* brilliant publicity scheme, it would either be Hale, or Fflytte himself.

Still, looking into a fantasy threat would give me the ideal excuse to snoop, if Hale happened to catch me at it. And he would be so grateful I stayed with the company – at any rate, stayed long enough to find who was responsible for the crimes that concerned Lestrade: say, fourteen days, 336 hours – that he would overlook any oddities in my behaviour.

'It would appear that building a reputation for realism has its drawbacks,' I remarked.

'It's a major pain in the backside,' Hale replied. 'But it is what we do. When we're filming *The Moonstone*, we send a camera to India. If we're making a film about the Punic Wars, we take some elephants to the Alps. Even if it nearly kills us all and leaves us bankrupt.'

'And when the script says pirates, you go to sea.'

'Lisbon first.'

'"*On, on, the vessel flies, the land is gone.*"'

He cocked his head, and replied, '"*What beauties doth Lisboa first unfold!*"'

'"*But whoso entereth within this town / That, sheening far, celestial seems to be / Disconsolate will wander up and down.*"'

'Yes, Byron was not fond of Portugal, even before he had an unhappy *affaire* there.'

Long, long ago, as an unschooled orphan preparing for university examinations, I had a tutoress with a marked, even startling, affection for Lord Byron. There were lines of *Childe Harold* that the Byron-besotted Miss Sim had taken care to skip lightly over – thus guaranteeing that her adolescent student should commit them indelibly to memory. Triggered by mention of the Portuguese capital, some of those phrases began to rise now to the surface of my mind: *memorials frail of murderous wrath, and the shrieking victim hath / Pour'd forth his blood beneath the assassin's knife, and Throughout this purple land, where Law secures not life* . . . I could see from the way Hale fiddled uneasily with his cigarette case that those phrases were pressing at his memory as well.

'No doubt much has changed in the past eleven decades,' I observed.

'So I have been reassured.'

'Very well: We set off on Monday for some weeks in Lisbon.'

'And Morocco.'

'Africa?'

'The town of Salé, on the coast north of Casablanca. In the seventeenth century, it was a pirate kingdom.'

"'Sun-burnt his cheek, his forehead high and pale,"' I blurted out. "'The sable curls in wild profusion veil."'

"'There was a laughing Devil in his sneer / that raised emotions both of rage and fear,"' Hale agreed. Before any more of Miss Sim's Byronic *Corsair* images could trail before my eyes, I pushed the glass of brandy away from me. 'Mr Hale, you're making a film *about a film* about pirates. Unsuccessful Victorian pirates from fifty years ago, not blood-thirsty African pirates three hundred years in the past. And from Penzance, not Salé. Why on earth don't you just film the thing in Penzance?'

'Because at some point real pirates enter the scene, and they are based in Morocco.'

'But if you are telling a story about some people telling a story, why not just construct a fake-Africa studio? Which, since you're after realism, is what your fictional film company would have done, in any event.' Real realism about realistic verisimilitude . . .

'As I said, *Pirate King* is about a film-crew that is making a picture – which is also called *Pirate King* – about *The Pirates of Penzance*. The picture's director – the fictional director, not Randolph Fflytte – is dissatisfied with the looks of the men in England, so he takes the production to Lisbon to hire some swarthy types, only to have their boat captured by actual pirates, who take them to Salé. The fictional director and the apprentice pirate Frederic are both played by Daniel Marks. The fictional director's fictional fiancée is an actress. That is to say, she is an actress working on the fictional film, playing the part of Frederic's girlfriend, Mabel, both parts being played, I'm afraid, by Bibi, who is an actual actress. Or so she claims. You don't know Bibi? Oh, blessed innocence!

'But lest you think there's a further stratum of reality, Daniel Marks and Bibi are not, in turn, romantically connected. Daniel is, shall we say, otherwise inclined. Then there's Major-General Stanley, who is not only Mabel's father but the fiancée's father, and also a financial backer of the film. The fictional film, that is – the actor himself, Harold Scott; you've heard of *him*, I expect? – is unrelated to Bibi, and doesn't have a sou. Spent it all on drink and horses.'

I made a small noise rather like a whimper.

'I know, it gives one a headache. Still, that's Randolph's plan. Ours not to reason why.'

Ours but to do and die? God, I hoped he wasn't thinking of blending in 'The Charge of the Light Brigade': *Cannon to the port of them, cannon to the starboard of them; some major-general had blundered . . .*

Where were we? 'So, you load everyone on a boat for Africa?'

'Lisbon first.'

'Don't tell me: Mr Fflytte also wants to hire swarthy actors?'

'In part – and it's true, English actors just don't look very piratical. Plus, Will the cameraman threatened mutiny at what an extended period of sand would do to his delicate machines, even though I don't believe Salé is very sandy, and Bibi – the female lead – put her tiny foot down at the idea of what sand would do to her delicate complexion, so compromise was reached. We'll cast the parts in Lisbon, then start rehearsals and work out the choreography of the fight scenes. After ten days, we'll load the entire circus onto a boat – everything but the horses, thank heavens: I managed to convince Randolph that horses were one thing Morocco had plenty of – and sail to Salé. Or actually Rabat across the river, which I am told is friendlier to infidels.'

'And you're filming there so as to capture the essence of a seventeenth-century pirate kingdom within a nineteenth-century comic opera for the edification and amusement of twentieth-century house-maids, factory workers, and garage mechanics.'

He grinned. 'You've got the idea now.'

Even in the early stages, it turned out, the script would make for a two-hour picture, and Hale admitted that it was likely to grow by at least half. Apparently, embedding an operetta into a film, then making a film of the process, requires time.

And although the *The Pirates of Penzance* is all about the songs and the silliness, *Pirate King* would be dead earnest and without the songs.

In addition, to put the cap on the enterprise, certain portions of the film were due to be tinted, in an as-yet secret (and, I suspected, as-yet unperfected) technique similar to the DeMille-Wyckoff process, which Fflytte intended to patent under his own name.

Pirate King would either set the standard for movie-making for a generation to come, or it would set a match under the Fflytte fortune, incinerating a boat-load of careers along the way. And displeasing the Chancellor of the Exchequer, the current resident of Buckingham Palace, and a number of Peers of the Realm.

Actual peers, one assumed, not fictional and piratic peers.

CHAPTER FIVE

FREDERIC [*looking off*]: By all that's marvellous, a bevy of beautiful maidens!
RUTH [*aside*]: Lost! lost! lost!

T HAT FIRST EVENING, Hale and I worked until nearly midnight. At 7.00 the next morning I turned the key to the Covent Garden office, and the telephone rang: The shipping agency was concerned that a trunk labelled with the name of Scott appeared to be leaking something that smelt of whisky. I made a note for Hale, reached to take off my hat, and the instrument rang again. I laid the hat on the desk and took up the receiver: An irritable voice demanded Hale, asked who I was, said never mind that I'd do, and issued a command that the offices were under no circumstances to be left unattended for so much as ten seconds that day since a delivery was to be made that would have disastrous consequences if someone were not there to receive it. Or so I guessed was the message, it was a bit garbled and before I could get a single word in, the man rang off. I set the earpiece into its hooks, reached for the buttons of my coat, and it rang again.

It did not stop ringing until the evening, alternating with the arrival of telegrams. (The new actress whom Geoffrey Hale had offered a part the previous afternoon agreed to his terms: I found the blank forms in a filing cabinet while the telephone balanced atop the files, its cord stretched to its full length; typed in the relevant information as I fielded three more telephone calls; handed the forms to Hale for signature as he dashed past an hour later; he handed them back to me as he went out for lunch; I folded them into an envelope, addressed the thing – in between two more telephone conversations – and thrust it into the hands of the building's mail-boy just in time for the mid-morning post.)

When Hale returned, he carried a grease-stained parcel by way of peace offering and, more to the point, swore a blood oath not to step foot from the offices for five minutes lest the urgent parcel arrive in my absence. When I returned, much comforted by my wash-room outing, he was just ringing off the telephone and three more telegrams had arrived.

'I have to go out again, Miss Russell,' he announced, picking up his hat.

'Very well,' I said, ripping open the flimsies. 'Would you bring some milk when you come? The bottle's gone sour. Oh, wait. Do you know anything about a Mr . . . Can this be right? Pessoa?' Surely not Pessary?

'Who? Oh, Pessoa?' He pronounced it *Pess-wah*. 'He's the translator chap, in Lisbon. A friend said he was good. Why, what's wrong?'

'Nothing, just a request for confirmation – I did see something about him, somewhere . . .'

Hale left; the phone rang. I spoke to a mother of one of the actresses, one-handed, while lifting various elements of the previous day's avalanche of papers that I had tidied into piles but not yet filed away. Eventually, I unearthed an inch-thick pile of letters and telegrams that Hale had exchanged with a Portuguese translator. The voice continuing to stream into my ear – something about her daughter's delicate digestion – good luck with that on a steamer crossing the Channel, I thought – I soon had them in chronological order, and read through them, frowning. It was possible that their infelicitous style reflected the inherently brutal prose of the telegraph. However, if the choppiness was a sign of inadequacy on the part of our would-be translator, I should have to do something immediately, since we were going to be heavily dependent on the fellow from the instant we landed.

I put the earpiece on its stand, wondered vaguely what I had agreed to with the mother, and immediately picked it up before it could sound again. Once I had phoned around to the translator chap's references, I felt somewhat better: Senhor Pessoa (Pess-*oh*-ah) had a good enough grasp of English to have published verse in the language, but more to the point, he had attended an English-language public school and worked for a number of English companies in the translation of actual documents. There were going to be enough flights of fancy from my new charges without adding a poet's nonsense into the mix, and I did not intend to stay long enough to add Portuguese to my store of languages.

I set that stack of papers aside, wrote a brief telegram confirming the date of our steamer's arrival in Lisbon and a letter reviewing our needs on arrival, then went on to the next pressing task.

Clearly, I would not be given more than thirty seconds at a time to question mail-boy, tea-lady, charwoman, or inhabitants of neighbouring offices concerning Fflytte Films' missing secretary.

However, by giving up on a second night's sleep, I could go through Hale's files during the night – and I'm sure I would have learnt a great deal, except that at five that afternoon, a team of large men arrived and carted the files off, cabinets and all.

The advantage of being immersed in a mad flurry of preparation was that I could push to the back of my mind the voyage itself. The disadvantage was that I could push the voyage to the back of my mind.

My own list of Urgent Tasks was necessarily short to begin with, and of the twelve items on it (*dress footwear, dinner frock, ammunition, hair-cut,* and so on) I only managed to check off half, most of which had to do with clothing.

Hale and I went down to Southampton on the train, he dictating letters to the last possible instant. Which meant that my actual arrival on the docks, standing and looking up at my home for the next few days, came as a dreadful shock.

I loathe ocean travel. After what felt like a lifetime of Atlantic crossings, I had only to glimpse a smoke-stack to be hit by nausea. I pulled the bottle of paregoric from my pocket and took my first swig of many. Not that the drug lessened the sea-sickness, but it did put it at a distance.

Moments after Hale and I set foot on the ship, a tornado of blonde heads descended on us to pelt our ears with questions, complaints, and helpful suggestions. Hale, cowardly male that he was, pointed to me and said, 'This is Miss Russell. She's my new assistant. Introduce yourselves to her. If you have any problems, she's your woman.' And walked away.

There on the deck, valise in one hand and portable type-writer in the other, still wearing hat and coat, I was verbally assaulted by what sounded like a girls'-school luncheon hall. I surveyed the expanse of young females, decided that these were the Major-General's thirteen daughters (with maternal chaperones looming in the background), and decided further that I did not need to submit to the assault then and there. I chose one, based on the ill fit of her dress and the impatient arrangement of her hair, and held out the slip of paper with my cabin number on it.

'Can you find that for me?' I asked her.

And bless the child, she turned instantly on the heels of her new, too-large shoes and led the way, the others trailing behind.

At the door to my cabin, I handed my possessions to the attendant and took up a position in the door, to keep the girls from following me inside. I held up a hand. The voices died away.

'If anyone is in need of medical attention, talk to your cabin's attendant. If your baggage hasn't shown up, talk to your cabin's attendant. If you need anything else, I will be on the foredeck in ten minutes. I suggest you wear your coat.'

And I shut the door in their faces.

'Actresses,' I told the wide-eyed young man, and pressed a coin in his hand.

'Yes, Madam. Will your maid—'

'Didn't bring one, don't need one.'

'Very well, I shall make certain your cabin is included in the ship's service.'

'I won't need that, either. I shan't be spending very much time down here.'

Hard experience had taught me that the best way to cope with sea-sickness was fresh air, copious and uninterrupted. I planned on establishing a well-wrapped beach-head on the foredeck, out in front of the smoke, and staying there until we docked in Lisbon. If things went well, I could celebrate with a riotous cup of tea and a water biscuit. If not, well, it was the open air, after all.

And, it now occurred to me, although being trapped on the deck might make it more difficult to carry out my investigatory duties, it might have the advantage of discouraging all those yellow-haired young beauties from seeking me out too often. The wind on deck could be chill, and hard on permanent waves.

The initial novelty of Hale's assistant holding court, as it were, among the deck-chairs meant that when I got to the specified location, my arms laden with fur coat, fur hat, two woollen travelling rugs, three books, a writing pad, mechanical pencil, small tin bowl, and flask of weak tea, almost every one of Hale's actresses was waiting for me. The questions (and their Greek chorus of echoes) began as soon as I appeared.

'What happened to Miss Johns?'

('Who?' 'Mr Hale's secretary.' 'But isn't this—?')

'I don't know, I was just hired three days ago.' Although I was beginning to suspect why the woman might have run off.

'Will there be a decent band for dancing tonight?'

('There was a socko band the other night at—' '—oh I saw them coming on—')

'I don't know.'

'When will the sun come out?'

'I don't know.'

'Is there going to be a script for the picture?'

'I don't know, that's Mr Fflytte's decision.'

'Is it true that last spring Mr Hale went to the cinema with Agnes Ayres?'

('Ooh, can you imagine being her?' 'I can imagine being her in *The Sheik*, cuddling Valentino!' 'More than cuddling, I'd like—' 'Shh, darling, the children!' 'Who are you calling—?')

'I really don't know.'

'Did he meet Valentino?'

(Instant silence, as all ears awaited the answer.)

'I don't know.'

('I'll bet he did.' 'I heard Valentino was supposed to be our Frederic until Daniel got it.' 'Can you *imagine*? On a ship with Valentino?' 'Did you see *The Young Rajah*?' 'Wasn't he the *dreamiest*?' 'No! Mama wouldn't let me!')

'How long before we get to Spain?'

At last, something I could answer. 'I think we put in at Coruña the evening before we arrive in Lisbon.'

'Where's Coruña?'

'In Spain.'

'But Lisbon's in Spain.'

'No, Lisbon's in Portugal.'

'Isn't Portugal part of Spain?'

'No, it's a separate country.'

'Have *you* ever met Valentino?'

'Have I— Heavens no.'

'Would you like a table for that?'

'I don't— What? Oh, yes, that's very thoughtful of you.' The child in the too-short frock and too-large shoes settled a small table at the head of my deck-chair. I arranged my books, bowl and flask on it, and thanked her. She appeared to be chewing cud, or some similarly tough substance. 'What are you eating?' I asked her.

'Bibi gave me some chewing gum. It's Doublemint. She gets it from America. Want one?' She held out a packet.

'No, thanks. And I'd appreciate it if you wouldn't chew around me.' *Not unless you want to encourage me to use that small bowl on the table.*

'OK,' she said cheerfully, and spat it onto the deck. I closed my eyes, and asked her to take it with her and find a waste bin for it.

'When weel we be given a place to rehairse?' I opened my eyes. Neither the questioner's accent nor her appearance fit our crew

55

– would not fit many places, come to that. She was as tall as I, but dark, her lithe form dressed in what appeared to be stitched-together scarves. She wore a turban-like hat of multiple colours of scarf. Her feet were bare. And blue.

'I'm sorry, who are you?' I asked.

'Graziella Mazzo.' She stretched out an artistic hand. 'I teach the girls to dance.'

'Very well. I'll find out where you can practise, and when.'

The ship's horn blasted away the next question, and the girls jumped and squealed and rushed off to the rail to watch the lines fall and the land recede. The wind would soon pick up – the rain, too, by the looks of the sky, although the bit of overhang above me should keep the worst of it off. I put on my fur coat, stretched my legs onto the chair, and picked up a book.

'The porter said I'd find you here,' Hale said. He looked curiously at my little encampment.

'As you shall until we dock in Lisbon. I get sea-sick, down below. And people tend to be rather put off by holding a conversation with someone who is retching over a basin the whole time.'

'"*Thou, luxurious slave! Whose soul would sicken o'er the heaving wave.*"'

'Please!' My upheld hand stopped him from further *Corsair* lines.

'Er, well, will you be able to . . . ?'

'Oh, I'm fine, so long as I'm in the fresh air,' I lied. 'But it does mean you'll need to come up here if you need me.'

He gave a mental shrug and pulled up a stool, to go over some of the last-minute business, including La Graziella's temporary dance studio. We finished about the time the girls grew bored with the process of leaving England behind, and they returned, to fling questions at him for a while.

He stood up and interrupted the rapid-fire attack. 'Could you girls line up by height for me? Left to right, shortest to tallest. No, you're not taller than she is. That's right. Is Bibi here? No, of course not. She *is* on board, isn't she?' he asked me in alarm.

'I'm told all our members are here,' I confirmed.

'Well, I suppose she doesn't matter, since she's the M,' he said, confusingly. 'Now, girls, we need a way of telling you apart. It's such a bother to learn two complete sets of names, I'm going to ask you all to answer to your rôle name. Makes life much simpler all around. You,' he said, aiming his forefinger at the tallest actress, a classic English-rose beauty with crimson Clara Bow lips. 'You'll be Annie. Next is Bonnie. Celeste – Celeste, you didn't wear spectacles before. Can you see without them?'

'Oh yes sir!' She whipped them off and gave him a myopic simper. He shook his head, but soldiered on, to Doris, Edith (she of the ill-fitting clothes), Fannie, Ginger, Harriet, Isabel, June, Kate, ending with the shortest (if by no means the youngest), Linda.

Arranged like that, a dozen girlish stair-steps, one began to see differences: Their hair ranged from June's pale, wispy curls to Fannie's rich (suspiciously so) brassy yellow; their eyes ran the gamut, too, from icy translucence to near-violet; their ages went from knock-kneed adolescence to full womanliness. The personalities they had already begun to reveal could now be attached to names: Annie was the one with the air of beatific innocence; Doris the one whose hands were constantly fiddling with her hair; Edith was my gawky and eager assistant; little Linda had the sour face.

Hale stood back and beamed with satisfaction at his newly named girls, so perfectly spaced in their heights that a straight-edge rested on their crowns would have touched each one (until one noticed that Edith had bent knees and Annie was stretching

– no doubt they'd worn different footwear when Hale hired them). 'For the duration of this project, you'll answer to the name of your character, not your own, do you understand?'

None of the girls seemed very happy about that, but those familiar with the company looked resigned. I had to say, it was going to make my job that much easier.

The rain began then, and the girls ducked for cover, leaving me to my deck-chair, my tea, my books – and my paregoric.

Before the day was over, my singular method of travel had ceased to rouse comment. When anyone needed me, they could find me. I made a point of responding to their gossip with eagerness, since that appeared to be the only kind of criminal investigation I would be permitted until we reached Lisbon: I laughed at Bonnie's description of our Major-General passed out into his blancmange, exclaimed at Harriet's news of Bibi's tantrum over the seating chart, and made disapproving noises when Edith described the wrestling match between Clarence and Donald, two of our fictional police constables (most of whom were odd-looking, if not frankly ugly – which did simplify the job of chaperoning the girls, a bit). The constables had also received fictional names, although theirs had been based on a sequence of age rather than height.

When I was not required to perform the duties of an audience, I sat on the deck and read in peace.

Read my way through the three too-slim volumes I had managed to bring, in fact, which was most distressing.

Before the dinner hour, Hale came to dictate a couple of letters and to review what we should need when we arrived in Lisbon. When he had finished, he stood there for a moment before asking, 'Can I have some dinner brought up?'

'No,' I said quickly. 'No, I'm just fine.'

'After dinner, we'll be using the dining room to screen a couple of Fflytte Films, if you'd be interested?'

'Attractive as that may sound, I think it is not a good idea.'

'But you're not planning to stay here all night, are you?'

'I'm quite comfortable.'

'Really? Well, if there's nothing I can do—'

'Actually, there is. I didn't have much time to shop in London, and only brought a few books. If anyone has any reading material, I'd appreciate it.'

'Certainly. And I'll send the ship's librarian along, too.'

'Very good of you.'

Beginning that night, I had a constant stream of women bringing me their bound treasures. One title was brought by no fewer than three of the girls' mothers, each of whom presented it in an identical, surreptitious manner. The first two I thanked and handed it back, but after the third such indication of prize and respect, I thought I might as well give it a try: E.M. Hull's *The Sheik*.

The novel, made into a moving picture that put Valentino onto the world's lips (in more ways than one), had been written during the War by a woman whose husband was at the Front. Whose husband had clearly been at the Front for a long, long time.

It was appalling. Not so much the writing itself (which was merely the lower end of mediocrity) nor the raw pornography (which it was), but its blatant message that an independent and high-spirited young woman would be far happier if she were just slapped around a bit by a caring sadist. I read every word about fiery young Diana Mayo and her encounter with, abduction by, and ultimate submission to Sheik Ahmed ben Hassen. Then I went to wash my hands, and took the novel back to Mrs Hatley, with a fervent plea that she not let any of the girls read it. She turned pink and said of course not. But had I enjoyed it?

I closed her cabin door and went back to my wind-swept perch to examine by lamp-light my further literary options. Which to read first: *Desert Healer, Desert Love, The Hawk of Egypt,* or *Zareh the Cruel?*

CHAPTER SIX

MAJOR-GENERAL: This is a picturesque uniform, but I'm not familiar with it. What are you?

THE NEXT DAY, the sky grudgingly cleared. My solitary roost was invaded, with Signorina Mazzo leading the girls in swaying dances meant to evoke trees or trailing smoke, with Edith, my admirer of the ill-fitting footwear, offering to fetch things for me, with regular passengers taking exercise on the deck. In the evening, after the dining room was refused for a second night's transformation into cinema-palace, Randolph Fflytte managed to inveigle the First Officer into stringing a bed-sheet out-of-doors on the deck – *my* deck – and opened the showing to anyone possessing a First Class ticket and sufficient warm clothing.

The impromptu cinema-house nearly closed on its opening night when Will Currie, our laconic Welsh cameraman and general machinery-operator, was nowhere to be found. His assistant, Artie, proved so fumble-fingered under the pressure of threading film through a constantly-moving projector that his hands more or less ceased to function. Randolph Fflytte and Geoffrey Hale admitted incomprehension.

Hope stirred that I might be permitted a solitary evening after all, but then one of the actors – our 'Bert-the-Constable' – stepped forward to see what he could do. Bert was a fit, swarthy-looking young actor whom I was sure the camera would appreciate as much as a couple of the girls did (although thus far, he had maintained a degree of aloofness towards them that I, for one, was grateful for). He had a brilliant white grin, a Cockney accent, and fingers as clever as Will's when it came to machines. In a moment, the projector was turning, and the outside lights were switched down.

Roman Galley began to sail across the bed-sheet (although I thought the topic of ship-wrecks might have been avoided) followed by the first reel of *Moonstone*. At that point, some of the older girls (the younger having been dispatched to their beds) began to murmur a rebellious desire for something other than a Fflytte offering. Hale was prepared, and handed a film can over to Bert.

I took another swallow from my bottle, nestled into my furs in a haze of drug and moving picture, and was startled out of my wits when my husband's name appeared on the flickering screen.

Buster Keaton in 'Sherlock Jr'

I jammed the cap onto the small bottle and launched it overboard: too late.

Sherlock Jr was, bizarrely, a similar film-within-a-film, the embedded adventure of a young fantasist whose nap-time clamber onto a cinema screen translates into a picture by the 'Veronal Film Company'. The audience around me laughed uproariously, but it made me quite dizzy to watch Keaton's phlegmatic battering by a rapid change of scenery. It was no less disorientating when he became a Crime-Crushing Criminologist with an assistant named Gillette faced by a pretty girl, a dastardly foe, a criminal butler, and the most astonishing sleight of hand and stunt-work that I had ever seen. I blinked, decided that I was plastered to the gills, and waited for the next film to be as hallucinatory.

But that one was called *The Perfect Flapper*, and although many of the characters projected onto the sheet were drunk, I was clearly not.

I went the rest of the voyage without benefit of opiates. Sobriety did not help: I remained ensnared in a make-believe world.

Eventually, on a dreary, sleet-spattered November morning a thousand storm-swelled miles from that untidy Covent Garden office, I wove down the Lisboan gangway in search of a poetical individual. It being 1924, and the weedy, artistic look being all the fashion even in this distant enclave, there were several melancholics who fitted the description. I eliminated those bearing expensive accoutrements – two wrapped in thick overcoats and one sheltered under an elaborate silken umbrella – since any man taking stray translator jobs was unlikely to have generous resources. When I had also dismissed those men already in groups, I was left with three persons. One looked far too eager: He had to be waiting for a loved one. Another looked as if he should be in bed: If that was my man, his pallid languor suggested it would be less work to learn the language myself. When my boot touched down on the solid dock, I elbowed my way through the crowd to the undernourished, bespectacled figure that remained.

'Senhor Pessoa?' I asked.

He dashed the stub of a hand-rolled cigarette to the ground and snatched off his hat. 'Miss Johns?'

'Her replacement, Miss Russell,' I said. 'Is all ready?'

'I booked cars for the day, as you requested,' he replied, 'although as foreigners, you should have been safe enough . . .' A disturbance behind my back made his voice trail away and his jaw ease open.

I did not need to turn around to know what he was seeing, although I did. There is an undeniable fascination with oncoming catastrophes, a basic human inability to tear one's eyes away from runaway lorries, banana peels on crowded pavements, and overbalancing waiters with over-laden trays. Such was what stood now at the top of the gangway.

Between the built-up shoes and the oversized hat, the man now taking his place in the miraculously vacant passageway barely cleared five feet, but by his attitude, he towered over all he surveyed. The sun seemed briefly to emerge from the gloom, although that could have been the effect of the newcomer's brilliant white fur coat, his equally brilliant teeth, and the enormous diamond on his right pinkie finger, which had been expertly mounted so as to adorn a finger considerably narrower than the stone itself.

Randolph St John Warminster-Fflytte, founder and sole director of Fflytte Films, the man on whose boyish shoulders the future of the British film industry sat, Hollywood's coming rival, whose five generations of family fortune were riding on the surviving heir's keen understanding of the taste of the common man.

From all I had seen of him on the voyage from England, which was rather a lot, the wager was close to being a sure thing. Fflytte had spent his youth embracing the taste of the masses; now he had more in common with his young would-be actors than with the likes of Barrymore and the generation trained by stage.

Fflytte had made his name ('Fflyttes of Freshness!') with three pictures that cumulatively did for pirates what Valentino had done for rajahs and desert sheiks. As the girls had said, Valentino had even been mooted for the current project, when it was being thought of as a modern version of *The Pirates of Penzance* but without the songs (this being cinema and therefore, in 1924, blessedly without sound – although I had no doubt technology would catch up with us before long, inflicting audiences with a flood of opera-movies and driving tin-ears like me out of cinema houses for ever). However, when Fflytte managed to smuggle Valentino into an elaborately negotiated secret meeting (secret due to the draconian contracts tying actors to their studios) the two men ended up staring at each other in mutual incomprehension, Valentino not understanding Fflytte's English accent and the Englishman unable to decipher whatever language it was that Valentino spoke. The meeting was not a success.

Instead, Fflytte would make his own star. His eye had lit upon a rather stupid young man with symmetrical features and luscious hair whose chief ability was an imitation Valentino intensity, a gaze that struck me as dyspeptic although the average film-goer reacted with the breathlessness of a blow to the solar plexus. Daniel Marks ('Making his Marks!' 'Hitting the Marks!' et cetera) had a more important knack: He never, ever, made Fflytte feel short.

Even now, the actor automatically took up a position well behind his director at the gangway's head, so that any photographs from below would place them on an equal plane: famous director, dashing young man in fashionable soft cap, beautiful girl in flapper clothes and drooping spit-curls furiously chewing her chronic wad of Doublemint. One would have thought them Americans, although all three were British; but for the weather, the trio might have been getting off a train in Los Angeles.

However, there were no photographers, to the irritation of the man in the white coat. And far from the sun coming out, the rain gathered its petulance and threw itself at the fur and the hat.

Fflytte, Marks, and Bibi, the leading lady – just Bibi, no surname – slid down the boards and dove into the first of the waiting motor cars.

Marks might be Fflytte's invention, but Bibi was the most prominent of several near-stars stolen outright from Valentino's own Famous Players-Lasky company earlier that year. It was a coup that had shaken the California studios and dubbed Fflytte with his current (and appropriate) *nom de cinéma*: The Pirate.

I watched the car take away my blue-blood piratical employer and his two prized possessions, and turned to Mr Pessoa. Both of us reached up to wipe the rain from our spectacles. He, and his coat, looked sodden through.

'I'll introduce you when we meet them at the hotel,' I told him. 'First, we have to see to the rest of the lunatic asylum.'

Mr Pessoa looked startled, clearly wondering if his English had failed him, but I just waved him at the motley crew gathered on the decks before committing themselves to foreign territory, and we got to work.

CHAPTER SEVEN

PIRATE KING: And honorary members of our band we do
elect you!

THE FIRST ORDER of our Lisbon business was to hire actors to
play the pirates – although we might have been hiring actors
to play actors who played pirates, who were actually pirates who . . .

As Hale had suggested, it was better not to think about it too
closely.

As I understood matters, Fflytte's initial impulse had been to
use actors from Morocco itself – I was already sick of the word
Realism – but Hale had convinced the director that finding people
both decorative and capable of acting in front of a camera, in a
country so backward it had no motor cars until ten years previously,
threatened to consume a dangerous amount of time and hence
money. They had compromised on collecting actors along the way.

The English cast was already with us: Daniel Marks, playing
the director and the apprentice pirate Frederic; Bibi, the fictional

director/apprentice pirate's romantic interest, Mabel (Bibi presented herself as a Parisian-born American, although she was in fact a product of the East End, named Eleanor Murphy). The dual part of Bibi's fathers – the investor/chaperone and Major-General Stanley – was filled by a red-faced and invariably tipsy Yorkshireman named Scott, a stage actor of Holmes' era. His twelve other daughters were played by the twelve yellow-haired girls, the symmetry of whom was threatened by the growth spurt of Daughter Five, Edith – it had not been her shoes that made her seem taller, and by the start of filming she would have to bend her knees to fit between Doris and Fannie. The youngest four girls were accompanied at every moment by their mothers, who (as Hale had warned me back in London) constantly jostled for primacy.

I had the impression that Holmes' original idea – and perhaps Lestrade's, although he hadn't the courage to suggest it to my face – had been that I try out for the part of Ruth, the forty-seven-year-old Piratical Maid of All Work who fancies herself as a future wife for her young charge, Frederic. Fortunately for us all, Lestrade had come up with an alternative. My job was to make note of the commands issued by Hale, Fflytte, and Will, the chief cameraman; delete any of Fflytte's that contradicted one of the other men; delete any of Will's that went against Hale's; then see to the implementation of said commands.

Beginning with the hiring of pirates.

I'd only had time for a single exchange of telegrams with Mr Pessoa before we set off from London, although I'd read his previous cables and letters closely. The film industry would be as new a venture for the translator-poet as it was for me; however, on the taxi over, he seemed sanguine that one industry would be much like another in its need for skilled labourers, nourishment for the overfed egos of its principals, and grease on the wheels of communication.

But then, he hadn't met Bibi or her dozen 'sisters'. So instead of checking into my room, I abandoned my luggage and took Mr Pessoa to one side for a review of wants and needs, finding a chair close to a radiator. He took off his hat, but before I could unfold my list, he had a concern.

'I was not given guidelines as to bodyguards.'

'Bodyguards? Good heavens, Mr Pessoa, we're not working with Rudolph Valentino and Mary Pickford, here. I shouldn't think the masses of fans are going to make us need bodyguards.'

'These are troubled times, in my country. Your ladies and gentlemen may require—'

'If anyone needs guarding, it's the populace, not my girls. No, our first order of business is to hire actors.'

He shrugged, and took out a tobacco pouch to roll a cigarette. 'I have hired a theatre, posted notices, and taken out advertisements announcing the casting sessions this afternoon.'

'We don't need a theatre, just a large room,' I protested.

'It was inexpensive, so long as you end each day before their evening performances.'

'How inexpensive?'

He took a sheaf of papers from his inner pocket and showed me various figures, comparing an actual theatre (having both lights and heat) with a bare, cold warehouse. I nodded.

'Very good, thanks. Next, as you may have been told, we'll need the various accoutrements of pirates.'

He looked puzzled.

'Things like costumes and make-up – you'll need to help Sally and Maude, two of our crew, find what they need.'

'For pirates?'

'Yes. Didn't Miss Johns tell you what this picture is about?'

'Not in detail, no.'

'Oh, Lord. Say, I don't suppose she mentioned to *you* where she was going?'

'Your telegram was the first I knew that she was no longer with Fflytte Films.'

'Odd. Well, do you know the comic opera *The Pirates of Penzance*?'

'I have heard of it, but not seen it.'

Lisbon began to sound appealing. 'This picture is about a moving picture company that is making the film version of *The Pirates of Penzance*. In the process, they encounter actual pirates, based on—'

He sat forward, frowning. 'Pirates, both fantasy and authentic?'

'I don't know how authentic—'

'A picture with two layers of dream. A picture which is itself a dream? Artifice upon artifice . . .'

The conceit of the film-within-a-film appeared to be exciting some poetical instinct behind that melancholic face: Pessoa's dark eyes went darker, his cigarette drooped alarmingly close to his knee. He smiled, a dreamy and faraway smile. Before he could either catch fire or reach for his pencil to write down whatever literary inspiration had seized him, I cleared my throat loudly and said, 'One of the girls asked me to find a shop in Lisbon where she might buy chewing gum.'

The spell was broken, and we went back to my list, not pausing over a hasty lunch – the steamer having been delayed by the weather, tryouts began a mere three hours after we'd docked. Near the end of the list, if not the meal, Hale and Fflytte came in, both of them tidy and, no doubt, well fed. I looked down at my clothes, the same I had worn off the ship that morning, and at the half-eaten meal, then stood to introduce my employers to their translator.

Pessoa led us under threatening skies along pavements of

attractive black-and-white mosaics to the hired theatre, a large, handsome, and surprisingly new building called the Teatro Maria Vitória. I was handed a list of Portuguese names, the men trying out for the parts, and we took our places in the comfortable seats, Fflytte and Hale third row dead centre, with Pessoa and me behind them. The actors had been given a badly roneographed copy of the Major-General's song for their reading, which would have been a peculiar choice even for native English speakers. After the third man attempted to decipher the blotched printing and the unfamiliar words, Fflytte's hand came up (lifted high enough to clear the seat-back in front of him) and his voice cut into the stumbling, heavily accented attempt.

'No no no, that'll never do. Give me anything.'

Pessoa hesitated, then asked, 'What does this mean, "give me anything"?'

'It means, these are supposed to be actors; have them give me any speech or bit of dialogue they've used for a rôle. Any rôle. So I can see what they look like.'

Pessoa addressed the stage with a flood of Portuguese, guttural and sibilant. The actor lowered his sheet and asked something; Pessoa responded. After several exchanges, another face popped around the curtains to make a remark, then several more short, dark men came out until the stage was filled with enough argument to establish a riot scene.

'Enough!' Instant silence, as every face turned towards the astonishingly loud command from the tiny director. Fflytte said to Pessoa, 'We want pirates. Tell them to act like a pirate.'

The Portuguese command was terse and to the point. Fflytte settled back into his seat. Pessoa sat down, fishing out his tobacco pouch. I sat back. The man on the stage contemplated the piece of paper he held, folded it neatly into his pocket, then stared at his empty hand as if a sword might appear there. He cleared his throat, raised his head, and lowered his eyebrows into a terrible scowl. '*Eu sou um pirata!*' he stated, although it came across less of an exclamation than a question.

Hale rested an aristocratic forefinger on his furrowed brow.

I drew a line through the first name on my page.

One man after another would wander onto the stage, feebly pat at his pockets, take off his hat and search for a place to lay it, put it back on, and then turn to the audience of four, assume a fierce scowl, and declare himself a pirate. After the third such declamation, Pessoa ceased to bother with a translation.

Four hours later, Hale had filled three of the eighteen parts, two of whom would only be adequate for the dim recesses of a pirate horde. Sounds from backstage made it clear that the afternoon's performance was about to get under way. Hale told Pessoa to inform the would-be pirates that the process would resume the following morning, and two sets of irritated theatre-folk grumbled past each other, one onto the stage, one off.

Fflytte decided to stay for a time to watch the performance, on the chance that he could steal a few of its players, but five minutes was enough: There is not sufficient make-up in the world to turn a Portuguese comic actor into a Barbary pirate.

Out on the street, the director stormed away, talking furiously to his friend and assistant, Hale. They made an odd pair, since Hale did not bother himself with the foot of height he had over Fflytte, but walked straight-backed at the small man's side, one slow pace for every two of the director's. Pessoa trailed behind, unsure if his services would be required. I followed after, examining the city around me.

In the fifteenth century, Portugal had become the world's first truly global empire, planting its flag on four continents, beginning with Ceuta, just across the Mediterranean, and stretching to Macao in one direction and São Paulo in the other. *Lusitania* to the Romans, *Portucale* to the Moors, and troublesome to all, at its peak the pugnacious little country had possessed sea-borne chutes that filled royal coffers to overflowing with gold and spices and power, its Navy making full use of the enormous harbour at Lisbon's door. Now, its heyday well past, Portugal was a small country with a robust sense of importance, giving one the impression that its walls hid untold riches.

Most of which description would also apply to Randolph St John Warminster-Fflytte, come to think of it.

Craning my neck at an ornate façade overhead, I promptly walked into a man crouched on the pavement tapping stones into place. Reeling away from him, I collided with our translator's outstretched hand, pointing in the direction of the water.

'An interesting idea,' Hale was saying. He sounded dubious.

'A great idea,' Fflytte corrected him. 'We should've thought of it ourselves.' Meaning: *You* should have.

'They'd be rank amateurs,' Hale countered.

'Sorry,' I cut in. 'What is this idea?'

'This chap said – well, you tell her.'

Pessoa inclined his head. 'I merely suggested that if Senhor Fflytte requires men who look like pirates, he might wish to search among the sea-folk rather than among those who make their living in the theatre.'

'It's a great idea,' Fflytte repeated.

'An interesting possibility,' Hale mused.

I could not imagine that this would end well.

CHAPTER EIGHT

ALL [*kneeling*]: Hail, Poetry, thou heaven-born maid!
Thou gildest e'en the pirate's trade.

13 November
Lisbon

My dear Holmes,

The ides of November have come. And are (I fear) far from over. The next time you see Lestrade, you can tell him he owes me three weeks on a warm beach somewhere, by way of repayment for this.

It's a madhouse. I knew before ever I left Sussex that the situation would be a lunatic one, but who would have suspected that every person I have met since my London interview with Geoffrey Hale ought to be lodged in Bedlam?

Beginning with Fflytte himself. His Christian name might as well be Napoleon for all his megalomania, with the stature to match. *His films are, to his mind, the defining markers of the modern age, and require from each and every one of his small army of experts the scrupulous attentions of a Fabergé enamellist.*

I discovered him on the ship – in one of its calmer moments, when I was not stretching my torso over the railings – deep in a discussion with the third-mate concerning the proper hand position to be used in a knife fight. I'll grant that all signs testified to the sailor's experience *with knife fights; however, his missing ear, notched eyebrow and scar-striped forearms did not have much to say for his* expertise. *I was tempted to correct the man's lecture, but decided that knife fights were not included in my job description, and made do with a gentle remonstration, pointing out that shedding First Class blood would be a sure guarantee of never working on a passenger ship again.*

Had I followed my initial impulse and stepped forward to demonstrate, Fflytte would no doubt have contrived to write a female pirate into the script.

That demented attention to detail pervades the enterprise. Evenings on board the steamer began well enough, but as soon as the weather permitted use of the deck, Fflytte had a projector set up there, and my quiet evenings were taken over by screenings of at least three moving pictures a night, each of which had portions replayed at the demands of one or another member of the company: Our 'Isabel's' mother wished to repeat a scene in which her young daughter appeared – three times over; Mabel had many remarks concerning the actress in The Flapper; *and in – why have I not seen this picture before? –* Sherlock Jr, *Buster Keaton climbs into a cinema screen and becomes a detective. Several of its scenes are now etched indelibly onto my mind's eye, as our cameraman wished to re-examine the (admittedly clever) effects.*

Did I say that attention to detail pervades every aspect of the enterprise? That is not strictly true: rather, every aspect of it except those that might actually be of benefit.

For example, might not someone have noticed early on that Portugal is on the brink of some kind of revolution? That its capital city might not be the ideal place to drop a film-crew? That a movie about pirates does not require convenient access to bread riots and clashes between the Army and the National Guard? (Although should we be so fortunate as to experience an uprising as we go our way in the streets of Lisbon, you can be certain that the cameras of Fflytte Films will capture every moment of it.)

Similarly, the cast. We have brought with us all the English characters, from Frederic to the Major-General, managing successfully to keep the daughters (thirteen *of the creatures – even W.S. Gilbert would have quailed) from falling overboard, or falling into bed with one of the sailors. Having hastily read Gilbert's libretto before we left, I protested to Fflytte that since all the opera's pirates turn out to be English noblemen fallen on hard times, we needed only hire Englishmen – and could even avoid sailing to Morocco altogether (yes, we are headed there next) by sticking to the original story, which takes place entirely in Penzance. I might have convinced him, had he not remembered that he was not making a movie about* The Pirates of Penzance, *but a movie about a movie about* The Pirates of Penzance, *and because his fictional movie crew goes to Lisbon to hire its pirates, so must we. (Is your head spinning yet, Holmes?) The logical next question being, if the fictional movie crew is, in point of fact, fictional, could not we adjust chosen elements of the fiction?*

No.

(Did I say three weeks on a warm beach? A solid month, I think, will be required.)

In my brief hours between being hired by Hale and leaping

with my valise onto the departing steamer, I had no spare minute to hie me to a bookseller, and thus my choice was limited to the three books I had brought from Sussex, supplemented by offerings from some of the film company and some well-thumbed novels from the ship's library. As one can only bear so much Ethel M. Dell, and even I cease to discover new revelations in the Holy Writ after an unrelieved diet of it, I seized on a Defoe title that I had last read as a child.

And regretted having done so. I'd forgotten that the book starts out with Robinson Crusoe taken prisoner by the pirates of – yes – Salé. However, Crusoe managed to escape. Eventually. Perhaps I shall be as lucky.

In any event. This morning we docked in Lisbon, half a day late, and scurried off to a borrowed theatre with Hale's translator, to hire us some pirates.

Our translator is a singular gent by the name of Pessoa, neat of dress and polished of shoes. He carries about him an air of distraction, as if his mind is on Greater Things than translating for a moving picture crew. (He is a poet, which you might have guessed.) Still, he appears to know his business and seems intelligent enough to be of assistance, with the occasional faint betrayal of a sense of humour. He seemed much taken with Fflytte's peculiar vision of what Pirate King *is to be, although whether that is the humour speaking or the intelligence, I have yet to discover.*

Perhaps I shall soon know. The day draws to an end, a cup of some liquid purported to be tea has been drunk, but as yet, piratic actors have we none. In a quarter of an hour, Senhor Pessoa will return to guide us to an alternative source for these creatures (no doubt a drinking establishment of the lower sort) where a friend of his may be found. Pray with me that the would-be pirate is not also a poet.

Still, if the den in which the fellow hides out sells local wine, it shouldn't be too bad.

In haste, R.

Postscript: It may not have escaped your notice that this missive contains a dearth of data concerning the true reason for my presence, namely, a missing secretary and the illicit selling of cocaine and firearms. Perhaps that is due to the circumstances of my employment, which is rather that of a person attempting delicate surgery whilst standing in a hurricane.

I shall persist.

— R

CHAPTER NINE

PIRATE KING: And it is, it is a glorious thing
To be a pirate king!

Pessoa stood in the hotel lobby, hat on head and cigarette in hand – a commercial cigarette, this time, not hand-rolled. He was gazing out the window at a group of unloading passengers, his thoughts far away. Perhaps he was composing an ode to the taxi. The poet-translator was a thin figure in an elderly black overcoat, about five foot eight and in his middle thirties. One could see a slight fray to the collar beneath his hairline.

He started when I said his name, causing a length of ash to drop at his feet, and hastened to press the stub out in a receptacle. He took off his hat, revealing black hair, lightly oiled and neatly divided down the centre.

'I'm sorry,' I said. 'I didn't mean to surprise you.'

'Life is a surprise, is it not?' he said. His accent was neither British nor purely Portuguese, but shaped by the British school that his curriculum vitae said he had attended during his formative years in South Africa. His owl-like spectacles could not hide the attentive gaze or the gleam of humour, no more than the brief triangle of moustache could hide the slightly drawn-in purse of his lips. Everything about him was watchful rather than outgoing, although the previous day's pristine but slightly out-of-date neck-tie had been replaced by a tidy if well-worn bow tie, suggesting a minute relaxation of standards. His overcoat, hat, suit and shoes were those he had worn the previous day, brushed and polished.

This was a man with pride, if little money.

'If we're fortunate, life will not inflict on us too many more surprises,' I replied. 'You haven't seen either of the others?'

'Not yet. I have only been here a few minutes.'

Long enough to burn down one cigarette. 'Well, we could be waiting some time. Shall we sit down and have a drink?'

Pessoa seemed to know the hotel as well as he knew the rest of the city, and led me to a small table with a view of the lobby. He waited until I was seated before he placed his hat on a chair and prepared to sit, then paused to remove a folded magazine from his overcoat pocket. This he put with rather elaborate casualness on the table before gathering his overcoat tails and lowering himself to the chair.

The gesture was too off-hand to be anything but self-deprecation, like a man accidentally letting drop the photograph of a first-born son. I stretched out a hand, asking, 'May I?'

'Oh, it is nothing,' he said, predictably. 'A small publication some of us started up recently.'

Athena, it was called, a literary journal, handsomely produced. Although it seemed to be in Portuguese, I opened it with respectful hands. To my surprise, it did not appear that any of the poems had been written by Pessoa, merely an essay.

'You're the editor?' I asked. 'I was told you wrote poetry yourself.'

'I am. And yes, in a manner of speaking, I have several poems.' He laid a nicotine-stained finger beside a name, then another, and another. And a fourth.

'Pseudonyms,' I commented. It was one way to add literary credibility to what would otherwise look like a single man's collected verse.

But he corrected me. 'Heteronyms, rather. Reis and de Campos are not Pessoa, but their own men, with their own history, style, opinions. About Caeiro I am sometimes not so certain,' he mused.

I did not permit my gaze to come up from the page; only Holmes would have detected the minuscule raise of an eyebrow. However, silence encourages elucidation.

'To lie is to know one's self. I see in Pessoa a living drama, but divided into people rather than acts,' he told me. 'To some extent, all men are thus: The modern belief in the individual is an illusion.'

To hear that Pessoa's alternative personas had their roots in Modernist philosophy rather than psychological aberration came as something of a relief. Still, I couldn't help suggesting, 'I shouldn't mention that to Mr Fflytte, if I were you. He's pretty dedicated to individual statement.'

'Ah, but if you *were* me, perhaps you would.'

I flipped the journal shut, my taste for sophomoric debate having been worn thin before I turned seventeen; he tucked it with care into an inner pocket.

'Miss Russell, you seem to me a young lady with both imagination and common sense. Tell me more about the structure of this project. How the stories are envisioned to combine.'

I had heard the film-in-a-film speech often enough to repeat portions of it backwards, but a recitation was not what Pessoa wanted. He nodded a few times in politeness, then interrupted.

'Yes, I understand the conceit, and the manner in which the two worlds will wrap around each other. I will admit that I hesitated before accepting employment from a picture crew, live translation not being my usual pastime. However, I find myself intrigued by the possibilities in Mr Fflytte's story. Shakespeare betrayed his talent when he stooped to writing plays. One can but imagine the results had he freed himself from dramatic conventions and turned Hamlet loose to *be* his character.'

I opened my mouth to object, or perhaps to enquire, but in the end could come up with no graspable point. He did not notice, but went on, speaking (so it appeared) to the burning end of his cigarette. 'The dimensions of a single life, the many levels of artifice within a reality, can only excite the mind of a person tuned to that chord. Thus the philosophy behind Mr Fflytte's moving picture, the men and women who are simultaneously artifices and real-artifices, as well as being real-real outside of the realm of the camera. But what I wish to know is, why pirates? Is piracy a thing that speaks to the English soul as well as my own Portuguese one?'

'Er,' I said.

'That is to say, the multiple natures of "pirate" within the bounds of this single piece of art is akin to a room filled with mirrors, is it not? Here on this wall, one sees the image of pirates as buffoons, silly and easily outwitted and ultimately proven to be empty of any piratic essence. On the next wall, one sees the piratic image of the interior director, the handsome boy who pretends to be a pirate, as well as the image held in the mind of the overall director, Mr Fflytte, the invisible God-figure in this story. And just when one thinks to grasp the duality of piracy, another set of mirrors comes up and the play-pirates become true pirates, doing battle with their own natures in the person of Frederic, who is at one and the same time an outsider and a true pirate.'

All this talk about pirates had made Mr Pessoa's gaze go far away. Two lengths of ash had dropped unnoticed as his monologue unfurled. Then he looked at me, as if in expectation of an answer, to a question I could not begin to recall. I felt an absurd urge to lay my head down on the table and go to sleep. Or to weep.

'Mr Pessoa, I do not know. Could you tell me, what are the plans for this evening?'

He was greatly disappointed, that I had not leapt to my feet and declared my undying love for buccaneers and corsairs – perhaps I ought to have brought Miss Sim along, they could have recited Byron at each other. He brushed off his coat, emptied his glass, and assembled his thoughts. 'As I mentioned, Mr Fflytte's desire for actors who look like pirates drew to mind a local . . . *character*, I suppose one would call him.' As opposed to Senhor Pessoa, an everyday Lisboan with multiple personas? 'A . . . colourful man I met some years ago. It may take a little time to locate him precisely; however, the evening shall not be wasted. I shall be your . . . *cicerone* to one of the most picturesque sections of Lisbon, where we are sure to find him.'

The optimism of my note to Holmes began to shrink.

I asked Pessoa about Lisbon's literary community, which diverted him until Fflytte bounced into the lobby, followed by his tall shadow, some twenty minutes late. Pessoa eyed the director's dramatic hat and white fur coat, but merely tamped out his third cigarette and led us to the door.

The evening air smelt of coming rain. We made to step from the hotel's forecourt onto the pavement proper, then Pessoa's arm shot out, a barricade to progress. Three armed police trotted by, intent on something up the road, and I became aware of a crowd noise from the Rossio, the wide rectangular plaza that formed the centre of the town.

Pessoa seemed unconcerned, once the intent constables had passed, and set off in the direction from which they had come. I glanced over my shoulder, and decided that if a riot erupted, we were as well off in the town's outskirts as in the central hotel.

Our path took us along gently sloping cobbled pavements through a district of expensive shops and white-linened restaurants discreetly scattered with banks – not for nothing was the street named *Rua do Ouro*, or Gold Street. Fflytte's head turned continuously, scanning alleys and the buildings' heights for potentially scenic shots, paying no attention to Pessoa's scrupulous narration. At the bottom of the street ('This triumphal arch displays Glory crowning Genius and Valour') another vast plaza spread out, this one perfectly square and lined on three sides by what could only be municipal buildings. A tall bronze equestrian statue stood in the centre. As he led us across the space, Pessoa's running commentary told us that this was the *Praça do Comércio*, known as Black Horse Square to Englishmen; that the gent on the horse was King José; and that the statue had been put up to mark the rebuilding of Lisbon after it was more or less levelled by an earthquake in 1755 (an earthquake that was felt throughout Europe and caused a major tidal wave along the English coastline).

Which served to remind me that we were not only in a city where police-attended riots were commonplace, it was also liable at any minute to be reduced to rubble.

Across the square, we followed the river east for a few minutes before veering uphill, into a dark jumble of buildings. Pessoa's narration never faltered, although the pace he set kept Fflytte at a near-jog, and even Hale and I had to move briskly. This, Pessoa's trailing voice informed us, was the most ancient part of Lisbon, the Alfama, which oddly enough was spared much of the 1755 destruction. Oddly because it had been long abandoned by the wealthy, left to the fishing community – who must have been amused at the irony. It was a place with ancient roots, felt in the labyrinth of narrow streets and featureless buildings: the architecture of the Moors – the district's name was from the Arabic for *springs* – with its life and beauty turned inward, away from public view.

Not, I imagined, that there remained much beauty here, not after centuries of working class practicality, but life there most certainly was, even if one only judged by a constant sequence of cooking odours. Most of them seemed to involve fish.

We travelled in Pessoa's wake, Fflytte's head rotating left, right and upwards until it threatened to come loose from his shoulders. After a while, Pessoa turned into an alley that had been invisible an instant before we entered it. A door came open.

The interior of the building was little lighter than the alleyway had been; as we patted our way inside, Fflytte's coat was the brightest thing in the room. Pessoa gestured us to a table, held out a chair for me, and asked what we would drink.

I said I would try a glass of white wine; Fflytte wanted a cocktail; and Hale, a glass of brandy. Pessoa went to the bar – a journey of five steps – and described our request in lengthy detail. From the time it took, he might have been talking about the weather and the state of the nation's politics, but the regular gestures at the bottles behind the bar suggested a debate about the nature of the requested cocktail.

He came back and lit a cigarette. After a great deal of activity, the man behind the bar brought us our libations: *vinho verde* for me, something called *ginjinha* for Hale, and a cloudy glass for the director. Fflytte looked dubiously at his drink, which contained an object that might have been an olive or a maraschino cherry, or a smooth stone. He took one sip, and put the glass down with an air of finality. My wine was not too bad, although Hale's startled expression suggested that his palate had never encountered a drink quite like that *ginjinha*.

Pessoa, on the other hand, took a hefty swallow from what appeared to be a light port, and looked satisfied.

'So, is he here, your man?' Fflytte asked.

'I haven't asked. It is always best to blend in a little before asking questions.'

I blinked: How long would it take before a young blonde woman nearly six feet tall, an Englishman wearing an Eton tie and a vicuña overcoat, and a midget in white sealskin would blend in here?

'Er, perhaps we shouldn't wait for that,' I suggested. 'Could you just ask him now?'

Pessoa finished his drink and carried his empty glass back to the bar. My eyes having adjusted somewhat to the gloom, I noticed that two customers stood there, slack-jawed.

I couldn't blame them a bit.

Fflytte gingerly lifted the object out of his drink, examined it, then allowed it to slip back under the murky liquid. Pessoa launched into conversation with the barkeep while the man refilled his glass. The customers soon chimed in. A tiny, wizened woman with a scarf around her hair poked out from a set of curtains at the back. The Portuguese conversation, as always, sounded furious to the edge of violence, but I had already learnt to suppress the urge to draw my knife, and indeed, the shaken fingers seemed mostly to be pointed at the walls rather than into the face of an opponent. Still, agreement seemed either to be unreachable, or not to the point. Eventually I stood up and approached the bar with my note-case in my hand.

Nodding and commenting all the while, yet another cigarette dangling from his mouth, Pessoa plucked the money-purse from my hand and pawed through the dirty bills, dropping a remarkably small amount of money on the bar. He handed me back the case and drained the glass (his third?) as the consultation wended its way to a close. I blew a gobbet of ash from the remaining bills, and we went out into the night.

'They have not seen him today,' Pessoa informed us, and walked off down the street.

We repeated the ritual at four more establishments, each smaller and dimmer than the last. Fflytte abandoned any thought of a cocktail after the second version, one sip of which had him coughing and pale. Hale and I, too, gave up on our initial choices and settled for port, which seemed harder to ruin by maltreatment. Pessoa was the only one who polished off his drink each time; the man had a heartier constitution than first appeared.

The fifth bar was so small, even Fflytte looked oversized, and the rest of us ducked our heads like Alice after the growing cake. It was getting on to eleven o'clock; I had not slept a full night since leaving London; I had not eaten a full meal in that same time. I was exhausted and cold and so hungry that the plate of fly-specked objects on a shelf (pies? boiled eggs? bundled stockings, perhaps?) made my mouth water. Hale looked far from hearty. Fflytte's air of determination had gone a touch grim. Only Pessoa remained undaunted. He looked no more fatigued than he had when I met him on the quay-side half a day earlier.

We ordered the requisite drinks. Pessoa took a swallow and reached for his packet of cigarettes, then addressed the saloonkeep with the question that, following repetition, I could understand. 'Have you seen La Rocha?'

Each time before, the query had set off a lengthy back-and-forth of identification: Which La Rocha? The old man with the scar (Pessoa inevitably drew his finger down the left side of his face at this point). The barman (or in one case, -woman) would narrow his (or her) eyes in concentration, at which point a customer (there were never more than three) would speak up from where the bar was supporting him (always a him) and suggest some further characteristic – a quick swipe at the chin to ask if it was the La Rocha with a beard, a pass of the hand over the hat to indicate baldness, once a thumb shoving the nose to indicate a distortion of that protuberance – and Pessoa would generally shake his head and go on with further verbal description of his man.

This time, however, the barman pursed his mouth to indicate understanding, then jerked his chin up to point at a spot behind Pessoa. All four of us swivelled to look: The wall had a hole in it, concealed behind a hanging heap of garments so large and so permanent in appearance, I would not have been surprised to find a Moorish burnous at its base. When we turned back to thank the man, he was standing with his hand around the neck of a bottle. It was unlike any bottle I had seen that evening – indeed, unlike any I had seen for a very long time.

Dark rum, from Cuba, very old. The vessel had the air of a king before peasants. The way the barman's hand clasped its shoulders made a clear statement: The rum was the price of being permitted through that door.

I retrieved my note-case. This time Pessoa by-passed the small denominations (the *escudo* was worth so little, coins had all but disappeared from use) and thumbed a 100 *escudo* note into view. The bottle retreated a quarter of an inch on the sticky wood; a second such note came up behind the other. A third note edged up before the man's hand slid the bottle forward and accepted the 300 *escudos*.

Pessoa reached for the expensive tipple, but my hand intercepted the glass neck first. I thrust the bottle at Fflytte. 'I think we're seeing our man now,' I told the movie mogul. 'This appears to be your gift to him for the honour of an audience.'

On the one hand, Randolph Fflytte was not a man to beg an audience, especially in a place like this. However, I was betting that the whole rigmarole would appeal to his dramatic sensibility, and so it proved. He studied the petrified cobwebs for a moment, then hefted the rum and lifted his eyes to Pessoa. 'Lead on,' he commanded.

It was something of a relief to see that Fflytte wasn't idiotic enough to go first through a dark passageway with a pirate at the end of it – even a would-be, fictional pirate. Pessoa did not look quite so phlegmatic. For the first time, it occurred to me that our *cicerone* perhaps might not know this La Rocha as well as he had given out.

We went through single-file: Pessoa, Fflytte and me, with Hale bringing up the rear. Only Fflytte could walk straight-spined, and as we approached the end of the brief passageway, the upturned nape of my neck tingled with vulnerability.

However, we stepped into the open room without a scimitar removing any heads from shoulders, then fanned out to examine our surroundings – but in truth, it was only later that the details of the room itself were recalled to mind, its generous proportions in relation to the outer room, the ancient wood and rich colours, three age-dark paintings, and an ornate carved door in the back, glimpsed through a pair of heavy curtains. The room faded into unimportance, compared to the two men it contained.

One stood, although there was an empty chair – an impressive figure, well over six feet tall and hard with muscle despite his grey hair, a man with watchful eyes, weathered skin, and an air of private pleasures. Still, it was the seated man in front of him who instantly caught, and held, our attention.

The old chair in which this man sat became a throne, his royal hands cupping the arm-ends, his enormous, once-red boots planted like trees on the rich carpeting. Seated, his head was below our eye level – even Fflytte's – but it felt as if he were towering above us on a raised dais.

His eyes were black, his skin was leather, and the grey in his hair was iron rather than age. A gold ring glinted from the shadows beneath his ear. The man had to be in his sixties, although he could as easily have been ten, even twenty years older. He occupied the chair like an ageless crag of rock on which countless ships had gone to their doom.

Fflytte recovered first.

He stepped forward, to set the expensive bottle on the table before the fire. 'My name is Randolph Fflytte,' he said. 'I'm here to make a movie about piracy.'

He stopped: concise, dignified, and with a sure grasp of the dramatic. Pessoa cleared his throat. '*O Senhor disse—*' he began, head inclined as if he were addressing the Pope. Only to be cut short by a dismissive twitch from La Rocha's fingers.

'I unnerstan' English,' the man said – or rather, squeaked.

At least three of us felt an urge to giggle at the unlikely sound coming from such an impressive figure, but the urge fled before it entered the room, killed instantly by the shocking sight of the scar that came into view as he shifted. It had been a terrible wound, beginning just in front of his left ear and following his jaw-line to the larynx. It looked as if his head had been detached; the blade must have come within a hair's breadth of severing any number of vital vessels. That he could speak at all was a miracle.

Even Fflytte gulped in reaction, but again, he recovered first. He walked across to the empty chair, hesitating briefly with his buttocks hovering, a silent request for permission. La Rocha's eyes gave a slow blink; Fflytte gathered his ridiculous coat around him and sat. Hale took up a position behind the director, forming a mirror image with the pair on the other side of the table. Pessoa and I stayed on either side of the entrance like two eunuchs guarding a harem, the translator clasping his hat in both hands, intent on the seated man.

La Rocha lifted one hand, palm up. The man at his shoulder placed two small glasses in it. He set them down on the table, wrenched the cork from the ancient neck with his brown teeth, and filled both glasses to the brim.

Fflytte picked up his glass, took a swallow, set it down again, and leant forward to gaze into the other man's face. 'I need a pirate,' he stated. 'A pirate king. I think you're my man.'

CHAPTER TEN

SERGEANT: . . . we should have thought of that before we
joined the Force.

It was near two in the morning before we left the pirates' den
and stepped into a rain-drenched alleyway slick with grime.
When we entered the door of the Avenida-Palace, Pessoa might as
well have been dropped into the Rio Tejo, Hale's vicuña coat would
never be the same, and Fflytte resembled a drowned white puppy.
My shoulders were clammy beneath my normally efficient rain-
coat; my shoes squelched. Wordlessly, the two Englishmen slithered
across the lobby towards the lift. I turned to Pessoa.

'I shall see you in the morning. Perhaps Mr La Rocha will come
up with some more likely pirates.'

'One can but hope,' he agreed. With some effort, he retrieved
his near-flat packet of cigarettes, looked mournfully at their state
of damp collapse, and inserted them back into the pocket. With a
brief tug at his hat-brim (sending a dribble of water to the floor)

he took his leave and went back out into the night.

I enjoyed a deep, hot bath, then crawled into a bed that neither tossed nor rolled beneath me, and slept for many hours.

Rested, warm and clean, I descended the next morning with a bounce in my step, buoyed by the anticipation of a breakfast that would remain *in situ*. My benevolent mood lasted until the first sip of coffee.

My hand jerked at the shriek that tore through the hotel restaurant; coffee shot over my table and my person, the gentleman at the next table contributed a juicy expression to my Portuguese vocabulary, and one of the waiters dropped his tray. Simultaneously mopping my clothes and searching the vicinity for the source of the harpy's scream, I soon found it, and the day disintegrated around my feet.

The thirteen daughters of the Major-General formed, as I said, a stepping-stair of curly blonde heads. Their height-determined names had been assigned that first hour on the steamer: 'Annie', 'Bonnie' and 'Celeste' were the picture's nineteen-year-olds; 'Doris', 'Edith' and 'Fannie' played seventeen-year-olds; 'Ginger', 'Harriet' and 'Isabel' sixteen; and 'June', 'Kate' and 'Linda' assigned the age of fifteen. 'Mabel', the eighteen-year-old lead, was out of place in the arrangement, being a middle daughter in the opera.

In truth, half of the girls were in their twenties – even 'Mabel' (Bibi) admitted to twenty-six, and I suspected the woman playing 'Annie' was nearing thirty – where the others' heights did not match their ages: middle sister 'Fannie' looked the youngest of all, although as I got to know her better I decided that her wide-eyed simplicity was acute stupidity; sister number five, 'Edith', had a tom-boy personality that made her seem less than the fourteen years her mother claimed for her, and a world younger than the seventeen her height had automatically assigned her; 'Linda', on the other hand, was eighteen, but so tiny she had no problem playing the youngest sister (although her growing bitterness at being treated like a child – by attractive young men, most of all – was already threatening to incise frownlines on her diminutive features).

(Oddly, considering his passion for realism, Randolph Fflytte did not bother to explain a family with four sets of triplets. And it goes without saying that The *Pirates of Penzance*, even with its lesser chorus of daughters, has no rôle for the heroic mother responsible for producing them. Neither did our own *Pirate King*.)

It was tom-boy 'Edith' who had proved a problem from the beginning, first because she had shown up on the docks at Southampton half an inch taller than when Hale had hired her three weeks earlier, and second because she was such a handful. If Isabel or June (ages 'sixteen' and 'fifteen'; actually fifteen and fourteen) discovered a fish head between the sheets of her bed one night, it was sure to be Edith who had been spotted sneaking away from the galley with a bundled newspaper. If Doris's hair-comb was mysteriously coated with honey, Edith would be discovered with sticky fingers. She was one of the actresses who had come with mother in tow (or in the case of 'fifteen'- [fourteen] year-old 'Kate', an elder sister) but the maternal person could do little to keep Edith under control.

For some reason, on board the steamer from England, Edith had forged something of a tie with me, despite my spending most of the time in solitary contemplation of the waves. Unlike the other girls, who came looking for me when they had a complaint and otherwise regarded me as beyond the pale (my sensible shoes, no doubt), Edith seemed actively to seek my company. Why the child should regard me as a kindred spirit, I could not think. Certainly any vague affection for me did not stand in the way of her troublemaking.

All of which meant that when a youthful shriek split the peaceful coffee-and-toast-scented air of the hotel, one's immediate thoughts went to Edith.

I stood, pressing the linen to my damp thigh as I went in search of the catastrophe. Sitting on the floor before the closed lift door was June (who, although fourteen, at the moment looked more like eleven) with one hand clapped to the side of her head. I hurried to kneel next to her, examining her fingers for signs of seeping blood.

'June, what happened?'

She shook her head vigorously, letting her hand slip a little – still no gore.

'June, let me see. What's wrong?'

She bent over, shaking her head so quickly that some hair ripped free – but no, that was unlikely. I reached down to peel her fingers away. With them came an alarming quantity of hair. She began to weep.

With her hand off, I could see a shilling-sized patch where someone had taken a pair of scissors to her pretty head. 'June, who did this to you?' I demanded.

She squeezed her lips together to keep any revelation from escaping. Good Lord, I thought: extortion among the adolescents.

'Was it Edith?' I asked.

At that, the child scrambled to her feet and confronted me, her face pink with fury. 'My name is *not* June! *I'm* Annie, not Annie!'

Oh, heavens. 'I know that, dear, but we have another Annie because silly Mr Hale wanted to give you all nick-names. Surely it wasn't Annie who did that to your hair?'

Annie – that is, 'Annie', the 'oldest' and I thought probably oldest – did have a butter-wouldn't-melt look that rode on her peaches-and-cream English features and made one overlook her nosey-parker habits until she turned up in one's state-room. Still, she'd never demonstrated open aggression towards the younger girls.

June turned and fled for the stairs. I looked down at the sad drift of pale curls, and got to my feet. If I wasn't quick, the day would be upon me before I had a chance to snag any breakfast at all.

June's mother found me at the same moment my egg did. Manners might have demanded that I put aside the meal, but I had a suspicion that if I were to pause for every interruption, I would starve. Instead I hunched over my plate to shovel in fuel while the woman stormed and fumed and demanded that I assemble all the sisters this instant.

'Did June tell you who did it?' I mumbled around a full mouth.

'It could be any of them. They're all jealous of my Annie's hair – she's a real blonde, I hope you know, unlike some of the others.'

And unlike Annie/June's mother herself. 'Yes, your daughter has lovely hair, and I'm sure we can comb it so the cut patch doesn't show on camera. Maybe she could wear a hat.'

'Why would she wear a hat? It would hide her pretty hair!'

'Or maybe pin on some kind of ornament? Honestly, Mrs, er—' What was this woman's name, anyway? She was there both as chaperone and to play the part of our nursemaid, Ruth, and acted as if she ruled not only the crew but the principals, judging by her conversation with Hale that I'd half-overheard on the steamer that day, just before the wind blew off her – ah: '—Hatley, it will be easy to conceal, I'm quite certain. I'll talk to Mr Fflytte about it.'

The director's name served generally as an anodyne to affront, and I had come to make shameless use of it to reduce various irate actresses, mothers or sisters to cooing females. Mrs Hatley was of harder stuff, being a veteran in the world of films and having known the director for years, but even she melted a degree under the warmth of his name. 'Would you? I hate to bother him with this, but truly, my baby is quite upset. If Mr Fflytte has a word with the others, to tell them how tender her sensibilities are . . .'

If Mr Fflytte did, I thought, every one of them would instantly turn on June and peck her to shreds. 'I'm sure he'll make it right,' I promised, holding her eyes in all earnestness while my hand surreptitiously snaked out to claim another triangle of toast. 'Perhaps you should go make sure your daughter is all right?'

It took several repetitions of the suggestion before the woman grudgingly withdrew, and I was free to press shavings of hard butter into the cold toast and glue them down with a very tasty marmalade. I scraped the side of my fork on the plate to get the last of the egg yolk, and felt the next interruption standing at my elbow.

'Hello, Bibi,' I said – no need to look up for purposes of identification, not for a person accompanied by smacking lips and the odour of mint.

'Hello, darling, have you seen Daniel?' she demanded.

Where is Daniel?

'Mr Marks? No, I've only been down here for—'

'He *swore* he'd be down here, he *insisted* that we had to work on a scene, although *really* it's a *rotten* hour, I must look absolutely hell.' She paused for me to deliver a stout rebuttal of the devastation of her looks, but I merely chewed my toast and turned on her a pair of bovine eyes. Bibi glared. 'I mean, it's all very well for people like you to be dragged out of bed at an ungodly hour, but it's just not a part of my *régime*, don't you know? Daniel *said* to be here so here I am, only he's done a bunk, and I can't *think* where he's got to.'

I stopped chewing. "'People like me."'

'Oh, I don't mean . . .' she said, although clearly she did mean. She waved her manicured fingers to indicate my appearance, but had just enough sense to grasp that she stood on the edge of danger. Instead, she stamped her little foot and half turned away, looking, if not for Daniel Marks, at least for someone with the authority to produce him. Without further word, she wandered off.

My appetite seemed to have wandered away, too. I dropped the remains on my plate, swallowed the last of my coffee, and went to see what other disaster awaited me.

I got twenty feet when it dropped on me. Rather, *he* dropped on me.

Major-General Stanley (or Harold Scott, the actor playing the Major-General – Hale's habit of calling the actor by the rôle was contagious) came across the lobby on the shoulders of a pair of uniformed hotel employees. I exclaimed and stepped forward, but again, there was a singular absence of blood. Except in the whites of the good gentleman's eyes – and then the smell hit me, and I halted.

The Major-General, however, shook off his supporters to stagger in my direction, weaving from side to side as if he'd just come off the ship. 'My dear Miss Russell!' he exclaimed. 'How superb to see you. Come and have a drink with me.'

I dodged his grasp, saw him begin to overbalance, and stepped back inside his stinking embrace to keep him from falling. He beamed happily into my face for a moment, then frowned. His eyes took on a faraway look, and I wrenched myself out from under – there are things the job of film assistant most emphatically does not cover. Fortunately for the Major-General, the two young men reached him before he hit the floor. Unfortunately for them, they were not as quick in the techniques of avoidance as I.

I left them exclaiming in disgust as they more or less carried the now-reeking Yorkshireman towards his room, while a platoon of mop-wielders took up formation behind them.

I cast a despairing glance at my wrist-watch: It was not yet nine o'clock in the morning. We had been in Lisbon just under twenty-four hours.

Chapter Eleven

SAMUEL: Permit me, I'll explain in two words: we propose
to marry your daughters.
MAJOR-GENERAL: Dear me!

THE PAVEMENTS OF Lisbon were a sea of cream-coloured stones
with patterns picked out in black. The streets of Lisbon
range from mildly sloping to positively vertiginous. The stones are
invariably worn smooth. That morning, I wore shoes I'd purchased
in London after Hale's unwitting snub to my fashion sense – the
sturdy pair I had worn the night before were steaming on the
radiator.

Two steps outside the hotel door, my feet went out from under
me. I was saved by the ready hand of a doorman, who was probably
stationed there for that express purpose. After that I went more
cautiously until I discovered that a sort of ice-skating gait best
kept me upright. Other pedestrians seemed not to have a problem.
Perhaps it was these shoes?

I skated along the rain-slick Avenida da Liberdade for a while, barely glancing at the fine boulevard with its statues, fountains, plantings, and black-and-cream mosaic pavement. Electric trams clattered past, Lisboans skipped merrily up the glassy footways, and I reached the remembered kink in the road before my foot came down on a sodden leaf and I went down again, this time catching myself on a lamppost. After that, I tottered. A tiny, hunchbacked ninety-year-old woman with a walking stick tapped briskly past. Two chattering women bustled past balancing baskets of fish on their heads; one of them was barefoot.

The Maria Vitória theatre evicting us in the afternoons required that we get an early start in the morning. I expected that I would be the first one there, since I'd already got the clear impression that Lisbon's clock was two or three hours canted from that of London: Here, 10.00 p.m. made for an early dinner.

To my surprise, the outer doors were unlocked and I could hear voices. I shook the rain from my coat and hat, following the sound.

Three hats occupied the centre of the second row of seats, looking like the set-up for some Vaudeville jest: The one on the left barely cleared the seat-back; that in the middle was exaggeratedly wide and battered even in outline; the one sticking up on the right bore the perfect shape of the best in British haberdashery.

Fflytte on the left, Hale on the right, and between them La Rocha. All three were intent on the man occupying the stage.

In the seat behind La Rocha, straight-backed and hatless, sat Fernando Pessoa.

I draped my outer garments on the seat at the beginning of the row and sidled along to sit next to our translator. He gave me an uncertain smile before returning his attention to the conversation in front of him which, although it was in English, gave indications that it might require his services at any moment.

'No,' Hale was saying, 'we only need twelve pirates.'

'Have more,' La Rocha's incongruous high-pitched voice urged. 'I have many.'

Fflytte, his eyes on the stage, said in a distracted manner, 'We only have thirteen daughters.'

La Rocha stared down at the small man. Then he turned to his lieutenant from the previous evening, whose big figure was planted on the edge of the stage. '*Treze filhas! É mais homen que parece.*'

Pessoa's back went straighter and his mouth came open as he prepared to spring into action, but he paused at the pressure of my hand on his sleeve.

'There may be a slight misunderstanding,' I suggested: La Rocha's meaning had been clear in his tone of voice, if not his words, and I did not think relations would be improved by a translation of 'He's more of a man than he looks.' I leant forward to explain. '*Mr Fflytte* does not have thirteen daughters. There are thirteen girls in the *story.*'

The pirate king craned back to look at me, then again at Fflytte. '*Entendo.* Thirteen girls. And they need 'usbands, yes? Then thirteen *piratas.*'

'Just twelve,' Fflytte insisted. 'Mabel is already taken by Frederic.'

Hale spoke up. 'Frederic is the apprentice pirate.'

''Prentice? What is this? 'Prentice?'

'*O aprendiz de pirata,*' Pessoa contributed.

The black eyes swept each of us in turn, silently, before La Rocha showed me his back and returned his gaze to the stage. '*Aprendiz,*' I heard him mutter. '*De pirata.*'

The current would-be pirate on the stage resumed the monologue from his printed sheet, but I found it hard to pay him any attention, distracted as I was by the man ahead of me.

I rather wished I had come in by the other door, which would have put me on Pessoa's right: At this angle, my view was entirely dominated by La Rocha's terrible scar. Temple to larynx, the thing must have spanned ten inches. The heavy red-gold earring winking above it made for an eccentric contrast. Why didn't the man grow a beard to conceal the injury? One's own throat went taut, seeing that shiny raised track.

'No,' Fflytte said, sounding as if he had been contemplating some profundity. 'The colour's wrong.'

'Clothes can be changed,' La Rocha declared.

'Not the clothing, the skin.'

'This, too, can be changed.'

'No, he's just too light. These are Barbary pirates. This man looks Swedish.'

It was an exaggeration, but not by much. The other men trying out for the parts of pirates were swarthy, hard-looking men with nicely photogenic moustaches or beards, but the person currently at stage centre would have looked more at home in a European counting-house than as a high-seas privateer. He wore elderly but well-polished shoes, his shoulders were stooped, and his hair was not only thinning, but a most unthreatening light brown colour. His facial hair consisted of an apologetic line above his lip.

'He's just not . . . swashbuckling enough,' Fflytte said. La Rocha cocked his ear back, and Pessoa struggled for synonyms.

'Er, *romântico. Exôtico*? Swashbuckling.'

'Ah. *Swashbuckling*. He can swashbuckle.'

'I really don't think so,' Fflytte said. 'He looks like my book-keeper, Bertram, who's the least exotic person I know.'

'Next,' Hale called.

'No!' The syllable echoed through the empty theatre like a crack in glass; the entire theatre stopped dead. The balding Swedish accountant looked near to fainting. I fought an impulse to leap for the aisle. Hale, veteran of the trenches, appeared to be wrestling the same urge.

Fflytte, on the other hand, turned to peer up at the source of the countermand, frowning in disbelief. 'Mr La Rocha, are you making this picture, or am I?'

I had thought the silence profound before; now one could have heard a hair settle on the floor. The cracked pane trembled, preparing to shatter in an explosion of deadly shards – until La Rocha looked back at the stage.

'Go,' he squeaked. The accountant fled. Fflytte sat back in his seat. The rest of us drew breath. Hale settled more slowly, but within a few minutes he, too, was wrapped up again in the casting process. Pessoa's shoulders gave a motion that was halfway between a shrug and a shiver, as if to shake off an idea he could neither justify nor account for.

It took somewhat longer for the hair on the nape of my neck to go down. Something large and dangerous had flitted through the theatre. I did not know who or what La Rocha was, but the man's potential for violence had snarled at us, just for a moment. That he had so easily shut it away again was perhaps the most unsettling part of all: Having this man play the pirate king was like hiring a lion to play a tabby.

I studied his scar, and was struck by the image of the man standing before his looking-glass each morning holding a razor to his face, deftly manoeuvring its keen blade around that obstacle, touching weapon to scar . . .

That was why he went clean-shaven – and why he wore a loop of gold that attracted the eye: He wanted people to notice the scar. Wanted them to see it, and to consider the man who had survived that injury, and to be afraid.

* * *

Well short of mid-day, Fflytte and Hale had eliminated three men too ancient (even in this post-War era) to marry a major-general's young daughters, a couple of others too ugly, one with a disconcerting facial spasm, and another with a mouth that refused to shut. In the end, they settled on fourteen men, allowing for two extras. These were all friends or associates of La Rocha. None had any experience with the stage. Two were mere boys, one of them so young he carried a pet mouse in his pocket. Some were willing, others sullen, a few treated the enterprise as a huge joke, but they would all make believable pirates, and they all obeyed La Rocha. Of course, if Fflytte's pirate king decided to quit, the picture would go up in smoke, but that was hardly my problem.

Today there would be no matinée, so the theatre belonged to Fflytte Films until six o'clock. Hale dismissed the unwanted actor-pirates, handing them each a day's pay to make up for their rejection, while Pessoa translated Hale's words and I began to fetch chairs from backstage. Fflytte wanted them set in a circle, although I did not get the chance to carry even one since the pirates instantly seized it from me. By dint of dragging my insistent helpers across the stage and using emphatic hand gestures, I got the chairs assembled in only twice the time it would have taken me to shift them myself.

When Pessoa and Hale had finished with the others and the doors were closed behind them, Fflytte pulled a break into the circle and told Pessoa, 'Have them sit down.'

The instructions were passed on, and the men and boys (after a glance at La Rocha for permission) drifted into the circle, each taking up position before a chair. Hale sat. La Rocha and his right-hand man sat. The others looked at me; they remained standing.

Fflytte took no notice. 'Miss Russell, we'll be working here for the rest of the afternoon. See what you can do about bringing in some sandwiches or something, would you?'

'Right away?'

'One o'clock would be fine. Now, sit, you men.'

Fourteen large rough figures hovered over their chairs as if waiting for the gramophone needle to drop. I snorted as I turned away, but the image of piratical musical chairs kept a smile on my face until the pavement nearly had me on my backside. After that I concentrated on my feet.

I made it to the hotel without mishap and told the maître d' what I required. He stared at me blankly, although that morning, he had spoken a quite serviceable English.

'Sandwiches,' I repeated. 'For twenty.'

'These are English men?'

'What does it matter? They're men, they need to eat.'

'This is lunch?'

'That's right. In an hour, if you please.'

'Sandwiches.'

What was wrong with the fellow? 'Yes. Sandwiches. For twenty. In an hour. And some drinks – I suppose most of them would like a beer. I'll also need someone to help me carry everything,' I added, just imagining myself trying to negotiate the paving stones with a load of glass bottles.

'Very well,' he said dubiously, pulling a small tablet out of his pocket and writing a few words. He went away, frowning at the message, but I had no interest in pursuing the minor mystery.

I only had an hour in which to burgle my employer's rooms.

CHAPTER TWELVE

PIRATES: Let's vary piracee
　　　　 With a little burglaree!

ON THE STEAMER out from London, in the calmer intervals when my head and stomach were not spinning, I had tried to get a sense of which members of the cast and crew were permanent fixtures, and thus conceivably linked to any criminality that Fflytte Films might be trailing behind it. Fflytte and Hale, of course, were omnipresent, but I had been surprised at just how many of the others were long-time employees.

From cameraman to costumer, at least a dozen members of Fflytte Films had consistently worked together for five years or more. Another twenty individuals had come and gone in various projects. Sister two, 'Bonnie', had acted in half a dozen Fflytte films over the years – although one would never know it by the way Fflytte and Hale treated her, which was with the same mild lack of interest that they used to address any of the girls. Mrs Hatley, whose daughter 'June' was the victim of an involuntary hair-cut, had herself acted in four or five Fflytte productions, including one so early, it was before Fflytte Films actually existed. Daniel Marks' first Fflytte production was the 1919 *Quarterdeck*, and since then he had appeared in five others, in various hair colours and styles, with facial hair or clean-shaven, peering through spectacles or not.

The only people I had eliminated for certain were Bibi, who had worked in America for the past few years, and the six of her 'sisters' who were under eighteen: Surely I could omit children from my list of suspects?

I had compiled a rough list of those whose careers spanned the years that troubled Lestrade, but before I investigated the shell-shocked camera assistant and the petite redheaded Irish lass whose needle produced costumes ranging from Elizabethan collars to beggars' weeds, I wanted to eliminate the two men in the best position to manipulate the company. By breaking into their rooms.

In my experience, hotels generally count on the presence of doormen and desk personnel to repel potential burglars. All one need do is become a guest of the hotel, and defences are breached.

My choice of targets was a toss of the coin: Hale, or Fflytte? Granted, I could not envision Fflytte wasting any energy on an enterprise not directly connected with the making of films; on the other hand, I could well imagine our director simply not taking into account that the laws of nations applied to him, so why not dispose of the drugs or guns that one had assembled for the purpose of a *realistic* (damn the word!) film by selling them? I might imagine Hale involved in a surreptitious criminal second career, but he must surely be aware of the consequences were it to be uncovered – and in any event, why then encourage a newly hired assistant to watch for untoward activities?

It might help to know if Lonnie Johns, the missing secretary, had been located yet. Back in Lestrade's office, the woman's unexplained absence had a sinister flavour, but the longer I lived in her shoes, as it were, the more sensible a tear-soaked flight to a Mediterranean beach or the Scottish highlands sounded.

My choice was made by the hotel's cleaning staff: As I came out of the lift, they were coming out of Hale's room. I walked around the corner, waiting for them to disappear into Fflytte's room next door.

They went in – and they came out rapidly, moving backwards, blushing and apologising and making haste to get the door shut between them and whatever had startled them. Or rather, whomever. Three middle-aged Catholic ladies stood in the hallway, given over to a shared gale of stifled laughter, then scuttled down the corridor to the next room. Where they knocked loudly before letting themselves in.

When no-one popped instantly from the director's room, I sidled down the corridor and applied myself to the latch. Less than thirty seconds' work put me inside Hale's suite. I took off my shoes to pad silently through the four rooms, checking for a sleeping guest or a particularly diligent cleaner, but all I found were the sitting room, a bedroom, a second bedroom from which the furniture had been stripped, and a bath-room with fittings considerably more elaborate than those in my room on the floor below. No missing secretary stuffed into a travelling-trunk; no packets of unsold cocaine in the sock drawer. Yes, there was a small hand-gun in the bed-side table, but I had no way of knowing where it had come from.

In the suite's second bedroom, the bed and dressing table had been replaced with a desk, a laden drinks cabinet, four comfortable chairs – and a small mountain of wooden file cabinets, which I had last seen going out the door of the Covent Garden office. They were held shut with locks. I laid my shoes on the desk, and got to work.

Because Fflytte Films spent so much of the year in locations around the globe, Hale was in the habit of carrying his office with him. The file cabinets bore labels, 1 through 12, and as I'd expected, the last two bristled with details concerning *Pirate King*, while the files in the first were concerned with early films. I started with 3, looking for the year of Lestrade's earliest suspicions.

I quickly realised two things. First of all, these files were not complete – which made sense, because trailing every scrap of paper around the world would make for cumbersome travel indeed. And second, that even with the condensed files of the earlier drawers, my search would take me a lot more than the hour at hand.

Take *Small Arms*. The picture was three years old and Hale still carried around a dozen folders concerning its making; several were about the personnel (mostly actors, type-written pages annotated by Hale and Fflytte); four covered technical matters. (Film used; problems encountered; letters from cinema-house managers; carbon copies of letters to cinema-house managers – most of these were complaints over the speed at which they had run the film; and one long, furious, epithet-dotted complaint from Will-the-Camera over the impossibility of working with small children who are supposed to lie dead but keep smirking and giggling and peer into raw film canisters and ruin a day's shooting and burst into tears whenever an adult shouts at them, with a strongly worded postscript asking that he be given a budget for laudanum. It did not specify whether the drug was for himself or for the young actors.) One file contained distribution records; another held details on the sites used; and the slimmest of all had chaotic notes on the history of *Small Arms*, in Fflytte's hand, which looked to have been made with an eye to an eventual autobiography.

No receipt for the illicit sale of a large number of revolvers.

I put the last *Small Arms* folder into place and reached for

Hannibal, but before I could get tucked into a lamentation on working with elephants, the sound of a key hitting the door had me slapping the drawer shut and leaping for the desk.

Hale walked in to find me with a shoe in one hand and a corkscrew in the other. I jumped, nicking the ball of my thumb and dropping the implement.

'Ow!' I gasped, and stuck the wound into my mouth. 'Heavens, you startled me!'

'What are you doing in my rooms?' he demanded.

'Fixing my shoes.' I pulled out the thumb, looked at it, and shook it in a demonstration of pain.

'No, I mean—' He looked down at my oozing wound, then at the shoe. 'What's wrong with your shoes?'

'Their soles. Haven't you noticed how deadly those pavements are?'

I directed his gaze to the sprinkling of tiny black divots lying on his blotter. He frowned. 'But why are you here?'

I checked the scratch, which had already stopped bleeding, and retrieved the tool to bend over the sole again. 'I know, you didn't give me a key, but I didn't know the Portuguese words for *knife* or *wood rasp* or *corkscrew*, and I knew you'd at least have one of those, so I came up to see if maybe you'd followed me back and I found the cleaning crew just leaving—' I looked up, feigning alarm. 'Please don't tell on them. They'd lose their jobs and they're such nice ladies, and they'd seen us talking downstairs so they knew I worked for you.'

One advantage of not really wishing to do a job is that it becomes easier to risk losing it. If Hale fired me, I should be free to take the next steamer home, where with any luck I would find Mycroft gone. Better, I could set off on a nice, terrestrial train, and spend a few days in Paris. However, Hale responded more to my attitude than my words – not that he liked having his rooms broken into, but he could see the shoes and had no particular reason to accuse me of criminal trespass. His ruffled feathers subsided.

'You hurt your hand.'

'Just a scratch,' I said. 'Better than a broken leg.'

'Those pavements are a bit hazardous, aren't they?'

I looked up from my task. 'I've ordered a pile of sandwiches. Was there something you forgot?'

Hale cast a last glance at the proclaimed reason for my invasion of his rooms, and dismissed it from his mind. 'Yes, I didn't bring the sketches and I thought they might help those imbecile pirates understand what we're doing.'

'They're not much as actors, are they?'

'They're not much as human beings. But there's no denying, they have the look of the sea about them, and that's what Randolph wants.'

He went over to the second *Pirate King* cabinet, opened it with the key, and drew out a file so thick its string tie barely held it shut. He shoved the drawer closed with his foot, pocketed the key, then straightened, looking dubiously at me.

'I'll leave,' I offered, 'but may I borrow your corkscrew?'

'That's all right, just lock the door when you go.'

And he left me there with his secrets – any of his secrets that might lie in the cabinets.

However, I merely finished gouging some holes in the shoes, locked the cabinet I had broken into, and left.

I didn't really expect to find him standing outside the door, but I didn't think I should take the chance.

In the dining room, the picnic meal and a young man to carry it were awaiting me. On the pavement, the tread I had carved into the soles of my shoes improved my traction. In the theatre, the actors were still in their circle, the colour sketches spread at their feet. At the interruption, Pessoa looked grateful for the respite in translating six simultaneous conversations. After instructions, the hotel employee handed around the sandwiches and beer. Upon finishing, the pirates looked content. And at the stroke of 1.30, all sixteen pirates got to their feet and paraded out, to the consternation of the two Englishmen.

'Wait!' Fflytte exclaimed. 'Where are they going?'

'To lunch, of course,' Pessoa answered.

'But that's what the sandwiches were for!'

The poet looked up from buttoning his coat, his eyebrows raised in disapproval. 'For a Portuguese man, a sandwich is not a lunch,' he said with dignity, and walked down the theatre aisle after his countrymen.

CHAPTER THIRTEEN

MABEL: IT's true that he has gone astray.

THE AFTERNOON WAS somewhat truncated, since our pirates did not reappear until 3.00 and we had to be out of the Maria Vitória at 6.00. In addition, they'd had a somewhat liquid luncheon – and moreover, had brought the alcoholic portion of the meal back with them, since at least four of them paused every so often to swallow from small bottles.

By five their boisterous shouts were rattling the lights, and Fflytte hastily cancelled the scheduled swordfight rehearsal. While I went through the cast with a box of sticking plasters, he threw up his hands and stormed out. La Rocha watched him go, looking amused, and one of the younger pirates took half a dozen steps in the director's wake, mocking Fflytte's pace. Which I had to admit was rather funny, the gait of an outraged child.

I glanced at Hale, who stood motionless, his eyes drilling into La

Rocha. When the door banged shut behind Fflytte, the pirate king turned, still smiling, and saw the Englishman. The two locked gazes for a long minute before La Rocha's fell, and he spoke a word that caused the hubbub to die.

'Be here at nine in the morning,' Hale said through clenched teeth. Pessoa automatically translated, causing a couple of the men to protest. La Rocha cut their complaints off with a sharp twitch of the hand.

Hale picked up his hat. As he went past my seat, midway down the aisle, he paused. 'Have a word with Mr Pessoa,' he told me. 'See that his friend understands that Fflytte Films is making a moving picture, not providing entertainment for amateur actors. We can find others willing to show up and work.'

'Why me?' I protested.

'Would you rather have the job of convincing Randolph that he shouldn't pack up and go home?'

'Er, no.'

However, Pessoa had himself not stinted at lunch-time, and was distracted by the antics of the pirates, who had spilt over into the ropes and gangways above the stage and were trying to inflict concussions on their mates with the dangling sandbags.

'Mr Pessoa,' I began, making my voice sharp as a schoolmaster. He snapped to attention, as any public schoolboy would. 'I need you to come to the hotel tonight at eight o'clock. I need you to be sober. And I need you to clear these men out before they damage something that Fflytte Films has to pay for.'

I watched them go, a few minutes later, herded by Samuel, following La Rocha. Pessoa made to stay, but I sent him off, too, hoping he had a long walk home to get rid of the wine in his veins. Then I hunted down a broom and did what I could to corral the spilt sand, happily turning the cleaning over to the man who came to open the theatre at six. He stared at the dangling ropes. They looked as if a herd of monkeys had got at them.

I made a mental note to learn the Portuguese for *I'm sorry*. It looked to be a phrase Hale's assistant was going to use a lot in days to come.

I was waiting in the hotel lobby at eight that evening, my official Assistant's Notebook in my lap. I was still waiting at 8.15. At 8.30, I gave up and went into the restaurant. At 8.40, Pessoa came in, although it took me a moment to recognise him.

He wore a monocle in place of the black owl spectacles. His hair was parted on the side and his maroon-coloured bow tie was dashing rather than snug, but beyond the details, it was his overall air that was so very different. Coming to the table, he gave a little click of the heels and a brief inclination of the head, the humorous gesture of a friend, not an employee, before dropping into the chair across from me. There he sat sprawled, an expansive set to his shoulders, with not the slightest sign of his normal prim attitude.

I leant forward to study the man's features: Yes, there was the fleck in the right iris, the mild disturbance in the hair over his left brow, the nick from that morning's razor. I sat back, breathing a sigh of relief: For a moment, I feared I'd strayed into the clichés of an unlikely detective story. As if William S. Gilbert were collaborating with Edgar A. Poe.

CHAPTER FOURTEEN

I need truth, and some aspirin.

Friday, 14 November, 11.30 p.m.
Avenida-Palace, Lisbon

Dear Holmes,

I have spent any number of odd evenings (generally in your company, come to think of it) but I've just had one of the oddest. Even after having it explained to me, I'm not at all certain I understand it.

This afternoon, our hired pirates turned up drunk from their lunch, and it was given to me to explain to the translator that it simply wouldn't do. Since he, too, had of drink taken, I commanded him to dinner. When he showed up, I would initially have sworn that he and I had become characters in 'The Case of the Substitute Twin'.

Now, it is true that I occasionally feel myself going translucent and fictional (again, often in your company). However, the stories I occupy are not generally so lowbrow as to depend on the mechanism of twins. This being a new experience for me – what next, I could only wonder: white slavery? opium dens? – I pursued the anomaly with interest. What had caused our translator's transformation from a quiet, unhealthy-looking, marginally shabby and humorously self-deprecating melancholic into an intense, ardent, witty gentleman-about-town? He wore the exact clothes he had earlier, but with panache rather than apology.

And although I'm not at all certain I grasp the details, it would appear that I have spent the evening within a poetical conceit.

I believe I mentioned previously that our translator, Mr Pessoa, is a poet – and according to him, not simply any poet, but the poet who will define his country to the world. It matters not that he is well into his fourth decade and few have heard of him. No: In his mind, Portugal is due to become the world's leader in the modern era – in artistic and literary matters, if not political and economic – and Fernando Pessoa is due to take his place at its head. A Fifth Empire, less the apocalypse, ushered in by this narrow country on the edge of Europe – just as soon as he obtains government funding for his journal. And finds a publisher for his poetry. And finishes his detective story, and finds acceptance for his Arts Council, and . . . And he did not show any indication of being under the influence of drugs.

Holmes, I am awash in a sea of megalomaniacs.

In any event, I settled to dinner with this fellow who was both familiar and unknown: hair parting different, monocle in place of spectacles, wide gestures instead of controlled, a flamboyant vocabulary, a shift in accent. He even looked taller.

After some minutes of increasingly disorientating conversation, I had to ask. It turned out the man across from me was both Mr Pessoa, and another.

Modern poetry, in Pessoa's eyes, is required to be outrageous and exaggerated. The modern poet, he believes, must do more than sit and write verse: He must become his poem, he must transform himself into a living stage. Only through lies is the truth known; only through pretence does one achieve revelation. The dramatis personae of Pessoa's life are the embodiment of theatre, a solemn game, a celebration of the counterfeit. He calls them (apparently there are quite a few) his heteronyms.

And lest one assume that Pessoa thus makes an ideal partner for a moving picture company, he has a theatrical scorn for the theatrical. He holds in polite contempt the contrivance of stage trickery, regarding the theatre as 'low' because it limits a playwright – even a great playwright such as Shakespeare, whom he otherwise admires – to the dull formality of a script. At best, theatre or film itself provides the stage on which the actor can make a new thing. 'A true play is one not intended as a performance, but as its own reality.'

Which is why, although he looks down his nose at scripted stage-craft, this one picture has thrilled his imagination (someone's imagination – Pessoa? de Campos? Ricardo Reis perhaps?) because it counteracts the formal script with a 'boundless unreality' of free association. (That, and the pirates – he is completely besotted with pirates, and went on and on about freedom and masculine imagery and the sea-going heritage of Portugal, and cannon. I'm sure there was something about cannon.)

If you are a touch confused, I will pause while you fetch yourself strong drink: I found that alcohol helps considerably.

All of this came spilling out of this new and excitable version of Mr Pessoa (whose surname, I should point out, translates as 'Person') after I had made the mild remark that he looked . . . different.

With our soup, we drank in philosophical reflection, which settled our palates for the main course of revelation: that his changed appearance reflected this true theatre, this true-faking, this poet's grasp of play. That Fernando Pessoa does not, in fact, exist, that he is a vácuo-pessoa, *a vacuum-person.*

Before taking up his knife and fork, this non-person fished into a pocket, then extended his card across the table linen. 'Álvaro de Campos, at your service.'

Senhor Álvaro de Campos is not a translator, but a naval engineer. He is from the south of Portugal, born Jewish (although he seems not entirely certain what this entails) though raised Roman Catholic, studied in Scotland, and travelled widely before settling in Lisbon. He is a Sensationist and admirer of Walt Whitman, and his tendency to flamboyance and lusty flirtations with decadence are reflected in his writing. A thick packet of which he then handed me.

Oh, indeed: Senhor de Campos is a poet, too.

It took us until coffee to reach this dramatic revelation, having spent the interim in a monologue: the great history of Portugal; the greater future of Portugal; piracy as an allegory for the Portuguese identity; his experiments with automatic writing; Pessoa's schooling (to which he referred in the third person) in Durban (where – he gave a disbelieving laugh – the students were woefully ignorant that Vasco da Gama, a gentleman of Portugal, had not only discovered their land, but named it); the publication of two volumes of English verse; his belief that the greatest artist is the one who writes with the most contradictions, the clearest writer is he who writes the most baffling prose. . . .

Or I may have got some of that wrong, because by this time I was near cross-eyed with tiredness and my only lusty flirtation was for my own quiet rooms. He had been telling me about a 900-verse ode he had written to pirates, or perhaps about pirates, some years before, when I broke in to inform Pessoa — or de Campos — that I was tired, that we both were needed at the theatre by nine o'clock, and that if he did not have a word with his friend the pirate king about keeping his retainers under control, Fflytte would fire the lot of them and take his company off to Morocco, seeking his piratical actors there.

And I left the poet with his multiple personas at the table, and shall now stagger off to bed.

Saturday, 6:30 a.m.

I finish this seven hours later, in what will no doubt be my only quiet moment of the day, before setting off for my theatre of the mad.

You might, by the way, enjoy the antics of our pirates, and especially our designated Pirate King, a man who would have the air of a brigand even were it not for his gold earring and the considerable scar down the side of his face (which must have come near to taking out an eye, if not the throat itself). La Rocha lacks only a peg-leg and parrot to complete the storybook image. He impresses Randolph Fflytte mightily, as well as the men hired as his pirate band. Which is good: If he can keep that rabble in line, this film may actually get made.

Yours, R.

Postscript: Again, I fear I have given the impression of having greater concern with the demands of my façade employment than with the darker matter that may be at its core. I confess, I keep hoping that word will reach me of Miss Johns' safe reappearance at her flat. Still, lest you (and Lestrade) imagine me taking my ease here, I assure you that I am pressing forward, albeit on an indirect path. If there is wrongdoing on the set of Pirate King *along the lines of the guns of* Small Arms *and the drugs of* The Coke Express, *it may be possible to anticipate the new crime and solve the old at one and the same time. I merely have to figure out what it may be. If, as I say, crime exists.*

– R

CHAPTER FIFTEEN

ALL: How pitiful his tale! How rare his beauty!

SATURDAY MORNING BEGAN at the specified ungodly hour of nine o'clock, when a cohort of unkempt and ill-shaven pirates came face to face with a flock of scrubbed and radiant young ladies. It would be hard to say which side had the greater shock. The girls put their curly yellow heads together and giggled; the men turned (according to their age) surly or scarlet beneath their stubble, kicking their dusty boots against the boards.

Fflytte mounted the stage steps and took up a position between the two groups, rubbing his hands in anticipation. 'Now,' he said with the air of a schoolmaster calling together his unruly class, that they might be inculcated into the amusements of the Latin deponent. 'Here we are! We'll be working together for several weeks, and although some of us know each other, many of us are strangers. Let me do a quick run-through on the story we'll be working on, just to remind you, and then I'd like to introduce each of you before we split up to begin our rehearsals.

'Once upon a time,' he began (thus proving himself a quick judge of an audience), 'there was a musical stage-play about a young pirate named Frederic.' He lit into the worn tale as if he'd just invented it that instant: Frederic repudiates the pirate band to which he has mistakenly been apprenticed all these years; repudiates, too, the affections of his middle-aged nursemaid; encounters a group of pretty sisters, bathing on the shore; falls instantly in love with Mabel.

Hale and I stood looking on, Hale with amusement, me with amazement: The little director might have been a storyteller around a camp-fire, flitting between the interests of the girls (romance!) and those of the men (sex!) and weaving together apprehension (the police!) and tension (can Frederic and Mabel ever be together?) with humour (the sisters speak pointedly of the weather, to permit the flirtation of the young lovers) and satisfaction (a good fight scene!). The girls gasped when Fflytte revealed that the pirates were taking them captive; the pirates looked uneasy when they heard that the Major-General was bringing in the troops. And when Fflytte revealed that the pirates were, in fact, noblemen in disguise, and thus acceptable husbands –

> *I pray you pardon me, ex-Pirate King!*
> *Peers will be peers, and youth will have its fling.*
> *Resume your seat, and legislative duties,*
> *And take my daughters, all of whom are beauties.*

– they applauded, one and all. Personally, I'd found the story both thin and somewhat distasteful, a sort of nineteenth-century precursor of *The Sheik*, concluding that, because the pirates were peers (and marriageable), the abduction of a group of young girls would be forgiven. Still, both girls and pirates seemed to find the story satisfactory, and Fflytte bowed.

When the huzzahs and buzz of conversation died down, Fflytte went on. 'However, we are not making a movie about *The Pirates of Penzance*. The subject of our tale is the movie crew who is making a movie about *The Pirates of Penzance*, and whose lives come to intertwine with the lives of their stage counterparts. For example – Daniel, stand up, if you would – Mr Marks here plays Frederic, and he also plays the man directing the film about Frederic. And – Bibi? – this lovely lady is at one and the same time Frederic's Mabel, and the director's fiancée. And our Ruth – Mrs Hatley, please? – is also the fiancée's aunt. Major-General Stanley, the father of all those girls – Harry? – is also William Stanley, the director's fiancée's father and financial backer of the film.

'And now for the daughters themselves.'

Fflytte's voice paused for the translator to catch him up, yet Pessoa went on, and on. The pirates were all gawping at him with expressions ranging from confusion to outrage, and he went on, with increasing volume and insistence, until his gestures began to look more like those of Álvaro de Campos than those of Fernando Pessoa. Eventually he ran out of breath, and in the pause, questions shot across the stage at him. In an instant, we were back in the same wrangle we'd had before. The voices climbed in volume until, at a crescendo, La Rocha's squeaky voice cut in with a sharp question. To which Pessoa responded, in a state of considerable frustration, with a brief phrase, half of which I'd heard the previous morning from the startled man in the breakfast-room. The phrase was accompanied by a hand flung in Fflytte's direction, and its meaning was crystal clear: 'Because he's a [blithering] madman.'

It must have been a strong adjective, because as one, the pirates blinked, looked at each other, looked at the waiting Fflytte, and burst into laughter.

This time, La Rocha got them back into order before Fflytte could blow up. The pirates rearranged their faces and pasted a look of expectancy over their mirth. Fflytte glared, but the techniques of working with actors could be applied to Portuguese non-actors as well: He stretched his arm towards the girls, to regain the men's attention, and began to introduce them.

Fflytte's variation on the original plot – that there be thirteen girls, all of marriageable age – caused the pirates less concern than it had me. I could not fit my mind around the ghastly gynaecological and logistical nightmare of four sets of triplets (and one single birth, Mabel); they merely nodded. Perhaps they assumed that the Major-General had several wives.

In any event, the actresses had been hired first by their looks (blonde) and then for their variations in height. Fflytte had not yet noticed the creeping imperfections of their precisely regulated heights. He might not notice until he turned his camera on them, since only Linda was shorter than he. I made a note on my pad to consult a shoe-maker, to have lifts made for the laggers. Edith – and one or two others – would have to slump.

He ran through their names, from 'Annie' to 'Linda', blind to the moues of dissatisfaction that passed over several rosebud mouths at these substitute identities. 'June' turned her back in protest.

Then he had the pirates remove their hats and line up by height, to give them identities as well: 'Adam', 'Benjamin', 'Charles', and so on. (In the play, the only named pirate is the king's lieutenant, Samuel – naturally, Fflytte had assigned that name to La Rocha's man, who invariably lingered nearby, as bodyguard or enforcer. As if La Rocha needed either.) It was my job to follow behind the director with a prepared set of cards on which those names were written, pinning each to its pirate's chest.

Had I not been a woman, 'Adam' would have knocked me to the boards. As it was, I permitted him to seize and hold my wrist. I then spoke over my shoulder to the translator, 'Mr Pessoa, would you kindly explain to the gentleman that this is merely a way of simplifying matters. We all need to be able to remember what rôle he is playing. And the girls may not have Mr Fflytte's instantaneous memory for faces.'

Pessoa began to explain, but was cut short by a phrase from Samuel. Adam's dark eyes did not leave mine, but after a moment, he let go of my wrist, grabbed the card and the pin, and applied the name to his lapel. Wordlessly, I went down the line, handing to each man his card and pin. Some of the names I thought oddly inappropriate – a pirate named Irving? – but their only purpose was to permit Hale and Fflytte to keep track of them.

I had no cards for the two extras, since they were only there in case something happened to one of the others, but as I drew back from Lawrence, the youngest pirate in both height and fact, the spare pirate standing beside him gave a twitch.

The man's face was half-hidden by the brim of the hat he still wore; if he hadn't made that sharp and instantly stifled motion, I might have taken no notice. But the movement caught my attention, and my eyes, once drawn to the tension in his clasped hands, could not help noticing that they were different from the hands of the others. His were clean, to begin with, free of callous, the nails trimmed. I bent to look up under his hat-brim; half the stage went still.

It was the Swedish accountant, in black hair-dye and no glasses.

His eyes pleaded. I looked at the fear, heard the heavy silence in the row of men. Then I straightened and spoke to the young boy beside him. 'Pin your card on, there's a good lad, so we know you're Lawrence.'

As I turned away, I looked over to where La Rocha and Samuel stood, as tense as the others. I gave them a smile, just a small one. La Rocha's eyebrows rose in surprise. Samuel just studied me; I could not read his expression.

Fflytte noticed none of this. Once the last card was pinned on, he spread out his arms and cried, 'Let's make a picture!'

The actors divided forces, Fflytte taking the girls away to some backstage room while Hale drew the men (less Frederic and the Major-General, they being too grand for rehearsals) into a circle. The cameraman's assistant carried out a tea-chest, setting it with a flourish before Hale. Hale squatted, working the latch with enough drama to make the overhead ropes draw a bit closer, and eased back the lid. He reached inside, coming up with a wicked-looking knife nearly two feet long, its blade sparkling in the light. The pirates leant forward, interested at last. Hale held it high – then whirled to plunge the fearsome weapon into 'Gerald's' chest.

In the blink of an eye, twelve marginally smaller but equally wicked knives were also sparkling in the lights. Hale exclaimed and stumbled back from the steel ring, permitting the great knife to spring away from Gerald's person and tumble to the boards with a dull thud.

Only half the pirates noticed. The others were in motion, and Hale would have been left haemorrhaging onto the stage if Samuel hadn't been faster yet. I didn't even see the man move before Benjamin's hand was slapped into that of Irving, who in turn bumped into Jack. An instant later, La Rocha's voice reached the others; they stopped dead.

Hale looked down: A knifepoint rested against his waistcoat.

A button dropped, the sound of the bone disk rolling along worn boards clear in the stillness.

Then Gerald gave a cough of nervous laughter and bent to pick up the fake weapon. Knives vanished, manly exclamations were exchanged. Hale fingered the tiny slit in his clothing and slowly regained colour. I took a shaky breath, and fetched the first-aid kit to repair the slice Irving's blade had left in Jack's hand.

We'd been at the theatre less than an hour, and had our day's first bloodshed, our first narrowly averted fatality.

Following that little demonstration of stimulus and response, Hale took care to explain the stage props. The cutlass he took from Gerald's hand might collapse into its handle, but the blade was steel. Even dull, it could inflict damage if used for anything but a flat stab. For slicing motions, there was another tea-chest of weapons with similar looks but made of painted wood, wide and blunt enough to be aimed at clothed portions of the body. For faces, there was a third set made from rubber, although their appearance was not entirely satisfactory.

In the matter of luncheon, compromise had been reached, on the days when a matinée was scheduled, anyway: We would work straight through, fortified in the late morning by a brief respite with the despised sandwiches, then end at three o'clock.

So the pirates merrily slashed away at each other for a few hours, and we broke for our not-a-luncheon, after which Fflytte returned with Mabel and her sisters.

And I had my first inkling of the true problems of a film-crew.

By this time, the men – who, as I said, had not begun the day in the most pristine condition – had been leaping vigorously about for a couple of hours, and were not only tired and aromatic but had relaxed into the novelty of being paid to play games.

Then the girls came in.

I should explain that the way Fflytte and Hale intended to compensate for the lack of sound in what is basically a musical event was to design a chorus of motion instead of voices. For example, in the opera, the girls' initial appearance is cause for a song – *Climbing over rocky mountain, / Skipping rivulet and fountain*' and so on – but in a moving picture, there would be little point in showing thirteen mouths going open and shut. Instead, they would skip gaily, a chorus of motion along a flower-strewn stream, pantomiming the incipient removal of shoes and stockings for the purpose of a paddle whilst the increasingly shocked (and stimulated) Frederic looks on from his hiding place.

On the ship from England, I had been dimly aware that Graziella Mazzo (the tall, voluptuous and generally barefoot Italian who had trained under Isadora Duncan [and with whom (despite a comical eleven-inch difference in height) Randolph Fflytte seemed to be much taken (which, come to think of it, suggested what, or who, had so startled the hotel cleaners)]) would occasionally assemble the girls on a free patch of open deck, or below decks when the weather was unfriendly, humming while they progressed in unison with exaggerated gestures of coquetry, alarm or humour. They looked insane, but then, a group of girls often does.

By now, the thirteen sisters were well practised in coordinated movements. Shortly before mid-day, the girls came back onstage, name cards pinned to their frocks, hair freshly combed, eager to return to their alphabetical counterparts amongst the pirate crew.

Who were instantly struck dumb. Even the older men looked down at themselves, abashed, and ran their hands over their heads. They watched the girls trip merrily over to the trays of sandwiches, commenting on the choices, exchanging wide-eyed exclamations, laughing at each other's jests, utterly ignoring the males.

The tension between the two groups grew like a taut-strung wire: the silent men on one side, the girls with their increasingly self-conscious laughter on the other, until I thought I should have to do something. It was Benjamin who broke it, one of the younger pirates. His clothing was a shade more modern than some of the others', and if his hair was rather long and tousled, he had at least shaved that morning. Girding himself for battle, he swaggered across the boards to the luncheon spread, took possession of a plate, laid a sandwich on it, and raised his deep brown eyes to the girl opposite him – shy, myopic Celeste.

''Allo,' he said, and with a lift of the eyebrow, added, 'I am Benyamin.'

Titters broke out anew, but with the first venture made, the others surged forward. I watched with an almost parental pride as two cultures met, and achieved flirtation.

Some minutes later, I became aware of a presence at my side, and looked up at Hale, then down at his de-buttoned waistcoat. 'I'm glad our Samuel is fast on his feet.'

'Not half as glad as I am. I should've known better.'

'I take it one doesn't expect a group of actors to have knives?'

'In England, a pocket-knife might be used for opening adoring letters. Those blades were the real thing.'

'Perhaps for safety's sake, we ought to collect their armament each day. It would be unfortunate if one of them grabbed a real weapon by mistake.'

'That's an idea.'

'Interesting, how many of them speak some English. I haven't found that among the populace in general.'

'Yes, I was just noticing that. I wonder if La Rocha specified English speakers when he put out his casting call?'

'Whatever, it'll make things easier for you and Mr Fflytte.'

'In some ways,' Hale said. 'Perhaps not in others.'

I followed his gaze to the far end of the luncheon table. There stood Annie and Adam, the two tallest among their respective choruses and thus our designated eldest. He was holding out a plate to her. Her peaches-and-cream complexion had taken on a becoming degree of pink, her eyes were downcast; his dark stubble looked romantic rather than unkempt. He was all but crowing with manliness.

'Oh, dear,' I said.

Chapter Sixteen

SERGEANT: When the enterprising burglar's not a-burgling,
When the cut-throat isn't occupied in crime,
He loves to hear the little brook a-gurgling
And listen to the merry village chime.

THE NEXT DAY was Sunday. This being an emphatically Catholic nation, an odd assortment of things were shut. Which included our theatre, whose management was not about to provide the keys and electricity for a group of Protestant (or Jewish) heathens to risk their immortal souls by committing labour.

Instead, the cast was set adrift to see the sights. The weather was not inviting; on the other hand, it was not pouring, and we were, after all, Englishmen, to whom a drizzle is a summer's day. Over breakfast tables, train schedules were consulted, cars were hired, and a giddy sense of holiday prevailed.

Fflytte and Hale observed the spirit with looks of gloom, since the cost of a workless day remained on the company's books. I watched with an equal lack of enthusiasm, since I suspected that a number of the girls had arranged rendezvous with their piratical counterparts. I told myself that I had not been hired as a governess, and drank my coffee in peace. As I passed through the dining room afterwards, Hale waved me over, to ask how I intended to spend my day.

'I thought I'd see something of the city, and do a bit of reading.' And with luck, find the two men (and their guests) gone from their rooms and resume my Scotland Yard-sanctioned burglary.

'What about coming with us?' he said. 'That Pessoa chap is showing us around the city, in case there are places we might want to use. It would be helpful if you were there to take notes. If,' he added, 'you don't mind working on a day off.'

Damn. 'Of course not. When are you going?'

'Twenty minutes?'

'I'll go change my shoes.'

The shoes I'd worn the first night were still damp, but they were less likely to result in a broken neck than the pair that had been my attempt at fashion. I retrieved my overcoat from its place across the radiator, and put my notebook in my pocket.

Ten minutes after I went down, Pessoa came in – Pessoa this time, I was relieved to see, not the flighty and enthusiastic Senhor de Campos. He removed his gloves and shook my hand, immediately taking out his pouch of tobacco (cheaper, and less vulnerable to the elements, than the packaged variety of cigarettes).

'I trust my . . . demeanour last night was not disconcerting?' he asked, sifting leaves onto paper.

'Disconcerting? No.' Of course not; I often dine with heteronyms.

'Even my friends occasionally find him so,' he remarked. 'Senhor de Campos can be . . . fervent.'

He licked the paper to seal the tobacco in, lit the end, and raised an innocent gaze. So I made a remark about the weather.

We chatted about the relative miserableness of London and Lisbon in November and whether such climates drove countries to become world powers, that they might gain a foothold in the tropics, until Fflytte and Hale appeared. They greeted me, greeted Pessoa, held back that I might go out the door first, then put their heads together and ignored me completely. Pessoa led the way, followed by the two Englishmen, with me on their heels, straining to hear as they discussed the theatre, the mechanics of filming, and how best to weave together the fight scenes and the girls' chorus. I was soon hoping that I would not be called upon actually to write anything down, since the frigid damp that radiated off the pavements and walls found its way into the bones in no time: I was not certain that my fingers would be able to manipulate the pencil.

Up and down the two men went while on their heels I trod, hands in pockets and making the occasional memorandum on my mental note-pad: Find silver paint to touch up the rubber knives. Ask Sally (the seamstress/costumier) whether we need any traditional Portuguese clothing. Find out what traditional Portuguese clothing might entail. Cable to America to find out if Howard Pyle is still alive; if so, contract with him to illustrate the one-sheet poster. Tell James-the-Composer (whom I hadn't met) that the sheet music needs a lot of minor chords. Check with Will-the-Camera to see if the girls will need darker make-up under the bright African sun; if so, check supplies; if needed, help Maude-the-Make-up find some before leaving Lisbon.

Occupied with the two English voices, I was but dimly aware of our guide's occasional contribution, until he pointed to a church and said that the convent was where the *autos da fé* took place beginning in 1540.

Fflytte's ears perked up. 'The Inquisition, eh? I don't suppose it was still active fifty years ago?'

Hale hastened to squelch any idea of incorporating a nice stake-burning into the tale, and we went on, my mind trying to reassemble my mental list, which had been rather shaken by the knowledge of what these stones had witnessed.

The list was running to eleven items when I found that we were boarding a tramcar, and that I was expected to come up with the fare.

I fumbled my small purse out of my pocket without dropping it, turning it over to Pessoa so as not to further irritate the driver and the other passengers. When he had paid, we claimed seats, separated from the other two. I took out my actual note-pad to laboriously transfer memory onto page. Between the jolts of the little car and the state of my digits, the result was hardly legible, but I thought I should be able to make out a few key words to jog my mind onto the correct path.

I hoped I wasn't missing some essential secretarial function: Whenever I glanced at my employers, the two men seemed fascinated by the houses built along the ever-climbing tramline. Fflytte would point at one tile façade; Hale would scrunch up his face in thought, then point at another; Fflytte would respond with his own lack of enthusiasm. Every so often the two would agree. I wondered if I was supposed to come up with an address *en passant*, then decided it would be simpler to put Will on the tram and just tell him to film the buildings with the most startling colours, since that seemed to be the criterion on which they were choosing.

At the top of the considerable hill, the poet and all non-Lisboans disembarked – that is to say, the three of us and one elderly Scotsman, who had perhaps come to Lisbon for the balmy November weather. I looked around to see what attraction had caused the city fathers to run the tram up here, and found we were at the castle that brooded over the city, a run-down but impressive pile with a spectacular view.

I think Fflytte had some vague idea of filming a scene or two within the walls, although I'm not sure how he would fit it into the story. It was a barracks now, with a gaol that had to be the most miserable place in the city. While Fflytte and Hale argued amiably and my nose began to drip, our guide went in search of the day officer to request permission for a visit – taking with him my note-purse.

When he returned, he was accompanied by a round man in uniform, unarmed, who shook our hands, welcomed us in what he believed to be English, and ushered us inside the castle of St George, former site of a Moorish citadel, before that the centre of Roman *Felicitas Julia*, the second largest city in *Lusitania*.

Eighty generations of soldiers had nursed their chilblains on this very spot.

Inside the castle walls, we circled around to the right, and although our military escort clearly did not approve, nothing would do for Fflytte but that we climb one or two very hazardous-looking walls. Pessoa took one look and stayed resolutely on the ground. I decided that if the men went up, I might have to – although I let them go first, and farther. Teetering atop one such precipitous barrier, peering over into a lot of nothingness, Hale remarked that anyone who tried to get reflective screens and camera up here would be guilty either of suicide or homicide. Fflytte, much smitten by the scenic possibilities, vehemently disagreed until his foot hit a loose stone and he nearly disappeared over the edge himself. We picked our way down to a dank and dreary courtyard, to the relief of Pessoa and the escort. Hale pointed out various pieces of wall and ancient stone stairways that would film well; Fflytte found something wrong with all of them. Finally, we emerged from the more hazardous portions of the castle onto a sort of esplanade that overlooked the city and most of the harbour. Hale and I followed

Pessoa to the low wall, and let him proudly point out the sights: the Rossio below (its wavy black-and-white pavements covering the ashes of the Inquisition), the train station beyond it, the long stretch of the Avenida da Liberdade, its trees going bare.

The director listened with half an ear, busy framing with gloved hands an olive tree that looked like the play-thing of a petulant elephant. Eventually rejecting the tree as insufficiently picturesque for his purposes, he drifted over to join us. There we stood, hunched into our coats while Pessoa valiantly lectured on the glories that were Lisbon, a brisk wind out of Antarctica making it difficult to admire the view through watering eyes. Fflytte seemed the most impervious, and the most appreciative, visually devouring the red tile, the white walls, the noble dimensions of the plaza far below, the ruler-sharp line of the Avenida. On the rising hillside across from us, a patch of green among the red tiles indicated a garden at the back of the Teatro Maria Vitória.

Pessoa, dressed in the thinnest coat of us all, methodically worked his way down the central valley of Lisbon: here the skeletal remains of a famous convent, there the lines of the shopping district and the roof of our hotel, across from us the odd construction of an outside lift used to raise pedestrians up yet another of the city's cliff-like hills. I muttered that the city must have been originally settled by mountain goats, a jest that either Pessoa did not understand or did not appreciate, because after a glance at me, he led us down the esplanade towards the waterfront, where the buildings at our feet grew smaller, their right angles grew skewed, and the streets, to all appearances, disappeared completely.

And there the director froze. He stood with his toes against the stones of the wall, bending his waist forward, his attitude so fervent one expected a vision of the risen Jesú to glisten against the faraway southern shore. A hand shot out, forefinger extended – then, as if leather made an intolerable barrier between himself and the object of his attentions, Fflyte tore off his glove and extended the bare finger, trembling gently with passion, or cold.

'Look!' he breathed.

We looked. At a harbour, a nice large harbour with the ocean off to the right somewhere. We studied the hills across the water, and boats of all sizes and descriptions, sailing or (more often, it being Sunday for fishing-folk as well) resting at anchor. From Fflytte's attitude, I expected a cavorting whale or mermaid, or someone strolling on the surface of the grey water. I took a closer look at the angle of his pointed digit, then tried again.

'The boat?' Hale asked, after a similar reconsideration of the forefinger. Which words didn't help me much, since there were perhaps a hundred boats out there, but Fflytte looked up at his cousin with a face lit with the joy and yearning of a young girl cajoling for a Christmas pony.

'Oh, it would be perfect.'

As my eyes continued to examine and reject one floating object after another, my memory dug out and brushed off for my consideration a topic that had been touched upon during our meandering walk to the tram: Fflytte saying that we should need a boat in Morocco for one or two shipboard scenes. However, since this was still Lisbon, and since I knew the director well enough to suspect that his needs changed by the hour, much less the week, I had not inscribed his remark onto my mental to-do list.

However, it had concerned a boat, and there were a lot of boats before me. I cleared my throat. 'Er, which . . . ?'

Fflytte whirled on me with an outraged look, as if I had failed to pick out which in a group of otherwise unremarkable girls was his own adorable, beautiful, and in all ways unique fiancée. '*That* one!'

'Two masts,' Hale murmured, rather more helpfully.

Having had it both confirmed and narrowed down, I looked along the waterfront until I indeed came to a two-masted sailing boat.

Or what had once been a two-masted sailing boat. At a distance, I could not be certain, but it did not appear to me as if the masts stood quite parallel to each other. And as a non-sailor, I could not be certain, but drunken masts did not strike me as a promising start.

Fflytte whirled, his eyes burning with need. 'How do we get down there?' he demanded of Pessoa, who for once seemed prepared for the strange impulses of his temporary employer. He pointed so readily at the exit that he might have been expecting the director's demand. Fflytte seized the translator's arm and hurried him towards the exit. I glanced at Hale, whose expression was, as I'd feared, somewhere between irritation and amusement.

'Tell me he's not serious,' I pleaded.

He looked after the back of his fast-retreating cousin, and the complicated visage settled into a sort of sad affection. 'Of course he's serious, Miss Russell. That's how Randolph looks when he falls in love.'

CHAPTER SEVENTEEN

PIRATE KING: I sink a few more ships, it's true,
Than a well-bred monarch ought to do.

SHE'D BEEN A brigantine, once upon a time – from the Italian for *brigand* – and if this was love at first sight, love truly was blind. She was a wreck.

No, she was worse than a wreck: A wreck would at least carry a faint trace of romance from the by-gone days and the glory that was sail.

Her name was *Harlequin*, and she was every bit the hotchpotch that name suggested. Granted, her lines had once been clean, but that was before she'd been converted into a fishing boat and given an engine and strewn about with lines and props and cabins and God-knows-what-all. An Arab mare with bobbed tail and denuded mane, daubed with spots and hitched to a rag-and-bone cart, wouldn't have had her beauty more thoroughly hidden than this boat.

But Randolph Fflytte saw it. He saw instantly through twenty years of cart-horse behaviour, two decades of make-shift make-do, thousands of nautical miles of heavy-handed adaptations to her original lines, to the sleek, quick beauty she'd been when she danced down the rollers from her birth dock to slip demurely into the sea.

He stood on the dock and gazed across the intervening water at her, his face transformed. He looked inches taller. I would not have been too surprised if he had stepped off the chewed-up boards and trotted across the oily, debris-clogged water, just to touch her scaly hull.

'But we leave for Morocco in six days!' I protested. Geoffrey Hale and I were standing back, keeping an eye on Fflytte and Pessoa, two unlikely outlines side by side at the edge of the dock nearest the *Harlequin*. 'We'd have to write whatever scenes he wants and rehearse them and then film them – assuming that boat doesn't founder as soon as three people board it.'

'With any luck, it'll go down before morning.' Hale sounded no more pleased at the prospect of arranging to film on this floating anachronism than I was. I opened my mouth to offer my services as amateur incendiarist, then reminded myself that revealing unlikely skills was not compatible to an undercover investigation. I changed what I had been about to say.

'Maybe he can shoot whatever scenes he has in mind while it's at anchor? Draping sheets where the sails are supposed to be?'

My only answer was Hale's slow sideways glance and raised eyebrow. I had to agree: With a reputation for realism (God, that word!) to protect, bed-sheets would not meet Fflytte's standards.

With a sigh, I took out my note-pad. 'What are we going to need?'

'Pessoa can find out,' Hale answered. 'He's the one who drew Randolph's attention to the boat; he's the one who can wade through fish guts to find the owner. By the time he's finished, he'll regret not hurrying us past that view-point.'

Hale looked sourly at the two men: Mr Pessoa looked remarkably pleased with himself, smug as any match-maker. It had not yet occurred to him that the racket he heard in the background was the sound of a spanner clanging against the finely tuned machinery of a film-crew.

I gave a brief laugh. 'Will-the-Camera may murder him.'

'I'd hold the camera while he did so.' A veil of rain moved towards us across the water, the dock, and then our hats. Hale sighed. 'I need a drink.'

Fflytte shook his head, scattering rain in a wide circle, when Hale told him it was time to go, and insisted on accompanying Pessoa on his search for the *Harlequin's* owners. Only when Hale pointed out that having a wealthy foreigner along, openly mooning over the ship, would drive the hire price through the roof did the director allow himself to be pulled away.

At the dock's end, Pessoa pulled together his lapels and walked off towards what I assumed were the harbour offices. Fflytte watched him go, then turned and give a last soulful look at the once-proud ship. From this angle, one could see that even her name was not original, that beneath the fading letters some previous incarnation strove to peep through.

Even slapping on a rough coat of paint was going to cost Fflytte Films a fortune.

We returned to the Avenida-Palace just before three o'clock, and although Hale pulled Fflytte towards the bar, I was very glad to see that tea was being served. I peeled away my damp overcoat and wrapped my hands around my cup, welcoming the obscuring steam on my spectacles.

I could write Holmes another letter, bringing him up to date on the entrance of a sailing vessel into our lives, but I had to admit, the investigation I'd been sent to carry out had been rather pushed onto a back burner. And Fflytte and Hale would be in and out of their rooms for the rest of the day, making trespass hazardous. Perhaps there was some stray member of the crew, abandoned here in the hotel, ready to spill the beans about Fflytte Films.

As if my thoughts had been a wish and my personal genie was sitting bored at my side, a familiar figure appeared at the door, a wizened, bow-legged man in rumpled tweeds and a soft cap. Will retained the looks of the Welsh farm labourer he had been when he first wandered onto the Fflytte estate some forty years before, a sixteen-year-old orphan seeking work that didn't involve a mine-shaft. Now, he was clearly looking for someone, but I stuck my hand in the air and waved in a gesture too energetic for him to ignore. With reluctance, he came in.

'Will-the-Camera,' I said. 'We were just talking about you.'

Will was not one of your garrulous Welshmen. He merely glanced his question at the empty chairs.

'I've been out with Mr Fflytte and Mr Hale. Here, sit down. Like some tea? Waiter, another cup,' I called, ignoring the cameraman's protestations that no, he really— 'We just got back from a sight-seeing trip around the town with Mr Pessoa, and you'll never guess what we found?'

'A rhinoceros?'

I paused, taken aback by this unexpected note of levity from a man who looked not in the least like he was making a joke. 'Er, no. A ship. A very old and beat-up brigantine that Mr Fflytte decided is just the thing for a couple of scenes.'

Will dropped his head into his hand with a mutter that sounded like, 'Jaizus.'

'I imagine you've been involved with any number of, well, challenging situations. Haven't you worked with Fflytte Films for a long time?'

'Since before it was Fflytte Films,' he agreed. He scowled down at the cup I'd poured for him, doubtless wishing it might turn into something translucent and more fortified.

'Really? What was it then?'

'It was young Master Fflytte with a camera. Which he didn't know how to work, so he hunted me down on the estate and shoved it at me, told me to learn how to run it.'

'Well, you certainly did that. You've filmed almost all of his movies, haven't you?'

'A fair number.'

'What a lot of stories your camera could tell! Were you there when the equipment went overboard?'

'I went overboard after it,' he replied.

'Good . . . heavens. The wave took you, too?'

'Nah, I jumped. Thought I might be able to save it, but it went down too fast. Left me with nothing but a tape-measure. Granted, my favourite tape-measure.'

Again, I couldn't tell if this was laconic humour or mere fact. His expression gave no hint. He reminded me of a friend of my father's, an older man who'd spent years around cowboy camp-fires in the West, mastering the art of the tall tale in a way my childhood self could only dimly appreciate, or even recognise.

'Well, that's good, then,' I prattled cheerfully. 'Have a biscuit? What about that short Mr Fflytte made during the War, filmed from an observation balloon? Was that you?'

'It was. Two years later we filmed in the trenches. Under fire. That one was never released.'

'Oh, for a peaceful life,' I commented. 'But even after the War it doesn't sound peaceable – wasn't there one film where a polar bear went berserk?'

'Started as *Anna Karenina*. Shifted to *The North*. That got scrapped, too. I couldn't look at the rug they made out of him for years. After that, I told Mr Fflytte I did not care to work with dangerous animals.'

'So when they made *Moonstone*, someone else worked the camera?'

'For the cobras, you mean? No, *Moonstone* was before the polar bear. But when I saw the script for *Hannibal*, in '22, I said no thanks.'

'And yet here you are, working with thirteen girls.' He shot me a glance, decided I was joking, thought about that for a moment, and then sat back in his chair with a chuckle.

'You're right. I must be mad.'

The point of my questions had not been the perils of making a Fflytte film, but to find out if the man had held a camera for Fflytte during the War years. *The Aeronaut* was made in 1915, and I knew that his proposed film *The Front* took place two and a half years later.

'It sounds as if you've handled Mr Fflytte's cameras pretty much his entire career.'

'There've been two or three he had other operators for – I broke my hand just before *Krakatoa*. And there was a year when my wife was dying. Other than those, yes, it's all Will Currie.'

I expressed condolences about his wife, and asked a question about the cameras, and film, and what problems he might anticipate shooting on board the *Harlequin*. My curiosity about the technical side of his profession disarmed him, loosing his tongue a shade. I went on in that vein, sliding in the occasional investigatory question about the crew and cast, but taking care to keep the emphasis light, even when I asked about my predecessor, Lonnie Johns.

'What about her?' he asked.

'What was she like?'

'She's what Daniel Marks might call a "good kid". Nice. Hard working. Not terribly quick in the wits. Why do you ask?'

'I just wondered why she'd left. Wondered maybe if she didn't get along with someone.'

'Like who?'

'I don't know. Mrs Hatley, perhaps?'

Will snorted. I raised my eyebrows. When he did not explain his wordless comment, I probed a little. 'Well, Mrs Hatley seems a bit on the formidable side. And she doesn't appear always to get along with Mr Hale and Mr Fflytte.'

But that took things just a bit too far. He smiled, and said, 'Yes, they've known each other a fair time now,' and reached for the watch on his chain.

I slipped in a last question. 'I'm a little surprised Mr Fflytte hasn't made a War movie, other than the balloon one. I mean The Great War – I know about the Boer film.'

He popped open his watch, giving an expression of mild alarm that suggested he'd forgotten he was looking for someone when I waylaid him. 'Hale won't have it,' he said, getting to his feet. 'Made it clear when he was de-mobbed that any movie about the Front would be made without him. And Fflytte won't work without Hale, so that's it. Thanks for the tea, Miss Russell. And for the warning about the boat.'

He hurried out. I gathered my damp coat and, more slowly, my thoughts; and finally my instruments of writing.

CHAPTER EIGHTEEN

PIRATES [*springing up*]: Yes, we're the pirates, so despair!

Sunday afternoon
Avenida-Palace

Dear Holmes,

I have just come from an informative conversation with William Currie, Fflytte's long-time cameraman, a Welshman in his fifties who worked on the Fflytte estate as a young man, keeping its various engines running. A man who walks with a slight hitch to his step, who has carried a camera for Fflytte since 1902, including during the War years (which suggests that his limp predated 1914, and would explain why he was free to carry a camera instead of a rifle). In the course of our tête-à-tête, he filled in some missing pieces of information that I thought of interest.

I shall not trouble you with the minutiae of gossip, merely convey to you the following points:

1. *Our 'Ruth', the woman known as Mrs Myrna Hatley, is also the mother, and hence chaperone, of the film's daughter 'June'. Mrs Hatley was herself in several Fflytte films, from 1907 to 1909, then did not act again until 1919. I mention her because there is a certain degree of delicacy when the others refer to her matrimonial state, and Will openly snorted: One suspects the lady did not submit to legal bonds. Her daughter (unlike two of the other 'sisters') has naturally blonde hair and bright blue eyes, and looks to be 14 or 15.*

2. *The first commercial film of Fflytte enterprises to star 'Mrs Hatley' was* Gay Paris, *in 1909. Mrs Hatley would have been in her late twenties. Fflytte was 24, Hale 22 or 23.*

3. *Randolph Fflytte has dark hair and eyes and, as I may have mentioned, is remarkably short. His right-hand man and second cousin, Geoffrey Hale, is tall, with tow hair and cornflower eyes.*

4. *On the ship here, while otherwise occupied, I overheard a small piece of tight-voiced conversation between Mr Hale and Mrs Hatley on the deck above me – rather, I heard her voice, while she was in conversation with him. The gist of her monologue was that although she appreciated the opportunity for employment, she could not but feel some resentment at being given the rôle of a middle-aged and unattractive harpy who is not only responsible for young Frederic's mistaken apprenticeship to a band of brigands but, on his reaching the age of twenty-one, attempts to trick the boy into marrying her. I did not hear*

*Hale's response, but the slap she dealt him as a consequence
nearly sent him over the side. I thought at the time that he
was making advances upon her, although why her, of all
the women to hand. . .*

*Regarding the other members of this travelling circus, our director
has fallen in love with a sailboat, which I am led to understand
will delay everything, drive his crew to distraction, and cost a
small fortune. If no-one else murders the man, his cousin may,
since Hale is responsible for keeping the company financially
sound.*

*(Have I told you about Geoffrey Hale, Holmes? Hale is a
veteran of the Front, retaining the reactions which saved his life
[why does my hand feel driven to add, 'once so far'?] following
a misunderstanding during rehearsals. Hale is somewhat aloof
from the others, although manifestly fond of Fflytte [their mothers
are cousins (Hale's father descends from the Hale of the Hale
Commission [Wasn't that Hale also involved in witchcraft trials?
(I ask because I've been making notes for a monograph linking
the repression of witches with that of modern suffragists.)])] –
Where was I going with this? Oh yes: Hale's lack of personal
involvement with the others may be a combination of shyness
and discomfort with his authority over them. It is not unknown,
with officers who served on the Front, that they are unwilling to
assert authority over any person, ever again.)*

*Our translator, Mr Pessoa, seemed mightily pleased with
his rôle in introducing Fflytte to this decrepit ship,* Harlequin.
*He does not yet grasp the amount of turmoil this introduction
will entail, and I have no doubt that it will come as a surprise
and a great disappointment to Pessoa (not only financially but
personally, since the translator clearly relishes his involvement*

with piracy, even fictional piracy) when Hale invents good cause to fire him.

The necessary work of my position has made it difficult to move the investigation along at the speed I might wish – and then today's potential snooping-time was given over to sight-seeing and mooning over a glorified fishing boat. It will not be possible to break into rooms until tomorrow, when rehearsals recommence, but I can see what little knots of actors are gathered here in the hotel, and see what golden titbits of gossip they can contribute to my hoard.

More later,

– R.

Chapter Nineteen

FREDERIC: How quaint the ways of Paradox!
At common sense she gaily mocks!

IT WAS STILL too early for dinner, but I found three of the younger girls and their mothers settled in before a substantial afternoon tea. Our interactions up to now had largely been professional rather than social, since the crew tended to sit at tables apart from the actors (a pattern of segregation for which I had been grateful). When I joined them now, the mothers exchanged looks of puzzlement verging on shock, as if the maid had helped herself to a breakfast buffet and sat down among the guests. Still, short of being ill-mannered before their girls, they couldn't very well drive me off.

Adolescent girls are a race apart. When I was June's age, a motor accident had injured and orphaned me: Other than my friendship with Holmes, my early teen years were solitary, leaving me ill equipped for light conversation about . . . well, whatever it is girls that age talk about.

In any event, I was the wrong age for both sets of females here. I spent several increasingly uncomfortable minutes manufacturing painful topics of conversation (clothing? memorisation of lines? the weather, for pity's sake?) before a moment of desperation had me hauling out a remark about the pirates Fflytte had hired, and waiting for that to flounder around and die.

Except it didn't. All three mothers smiled fondly, one of the girls giggled and turned pink, the other two spoke simultaneously.

'I'm *so* glad—'

'I never expected—'

They stopped, and leant into each other with shrieks of laughter that rattled the chandelier.

'Sorry?' I said when my ears had stopped ringing.

'I was going to say,' said Isabel, 'that I'm *so* glad Mr Fflytte didn't bring a bunch of spotty boys from England to play our pirates.'

'Yes,' Kate agreed. 'Who'd have thought Portuguese boys could be so good-looking?'

'Um.' I cast a sideways look at their mothers. 'You do realise they're not exactly boys, don't you?' Apart from Lawrence, scarcely pubescent, and Jack, who seemed about fourteen, the pirates were in their twenties and thirties, and these girls were . . . well, they claimed to be at least fourteen, even Fannie, although I had serious doubts about her.

'Oh, pooh,' said Isabel. 'At least it'll give us something interesting to do on the way to Morocco. I always wanted to go to Arabia!'

'Morocco isn't in Arabia.'

'It isn't?'

'It's on the north-west coast of Africa.'

'Are you sure?' She seemed disappointed.

'Unless they've moved it.'

'Well, I s'pose Africa's all right.'

'Jungles and tigers,' popped up Fannie.

'You won't find too many jungles in Morocco,' I told her. 'More likely desert.'

'Ooh, a desert – so there *will* be sheiks?' Isabel wanted to know.

The mothers looked interested. I sighed, and gave up.

It was not raining at the moment, so I wrapped up against the chill and went for a walk before dinner. The streets were quiet, with restaurants not yet open and shops closed tight, although I thought I saw one of the taller girls – probably Annie, who seemed to be everywhere – dart into a side-street. When I reached that corner, I looked, but saw no-one. In any event, I reminded myself that I was not responsible for every crew member at every moment.

My feet took me down to the waterfront where, although there was more activity than the rest of the city, the loudest sounds were still the gulls and the slap of water. I wandered east, along the road that kept the tight-knit, almost medieval Alfama district from spilling its piled boxes out across the modern docklands like a tipped toy-box. Pristine tiles abutted flaking plaster; ornate façades grew out of unhewn stone; a sleek modern window stood next to one installed when Columbus was venturing into the Atlantic; a stone lion's head set into a wall dripped water into a faded tin that had once held olive oil. It was nearly dark, and I was entering an area without street-lamps, so I turned to retrace my steps, intending to follow the next lighted thoroughfare.

Then I saw a pair of men, some distance down the waterfront, coming in my direction. They were too far away to identify with any confidence, but something about their shapes made the back of my mind prickle, and I retreated into the deep shadow of a boarded-up entrance-way. In a couple of minutes, I peered out again. Sure enough: our translator and finder of pirate ships, with our pirate king.

I faded into the stinking darkness. The men went past, speaking in Portuguese.

I followed. Of course I followed.

They took the next entrance into the Alfama, not far from where we had begun our Thursday night search for La Rocha. At the time, Pessoa had known neither the saloon nor La Rocha – it takes a good actor to craft an air of assurance-atop-uncertainty, and I did not think Pessoa a good actor – but it would appear that had changed. And I was not surprised when their goal was that same grubby hole in the wall.

I was too far behind to hear any exchange of words when they entered the place, but I pulled my scarf up and my hat down, and risked a quick glance through the bottle-thick, salt-scummed window as I passed. Enough to see that in the thirty seconds after they had gone in, they had also gone out.

Which could only mean that they had gone through the bar proper and into the same back room.

A room with, as I recalled, a back door – narrow and half-concealed by heavy curtains, but there.

It took me some time to find the right door amongst the warren of tiny lopsided dwellings jostling shoulder to shoulder beneath the castle walls. None of the streets – streets! one could stretch an arm across some of them – connected at right angles. Half of them came to an end in courtyards; many were enclosed overhead; most were unlit. The houses were occupied – I could hear voices and smell cooking, but it was late (and cold) enough that the children were inside, and the adults, too, were mostly invisible behind shutters. Feeling my way in and out of various brief passages, at last my eye was caught by a narrow line of light at the far end of a tunnel-like lane.

The thin strip was the only thing I could see, and although I had a torch in my overcoat pocket, I was loath to use it. Instead, I found that if I blocked the actual light with an outstretched hand, its reflection along the stone walk and walls would permit me to creep forward. I crept forward, and heard a voice. A voice I knew.

Not that I could understand what he was saying, but Fernando Pessoa was talking. And talking. I pressed my ear to the crack, hearing nothing but his voice, going on and on. It sounded like a recitation.

So I went down on my knees to put my eye near the half-inch gap between door and stone.

The horizontal slice of room that came into view contained three chairs and a merry fire. There were men in the chairs, and although I could only see their legs, I knew who the room held. La Rocha's scuffed and elephantine red boots were stretched out to the coals, ankles propped, his right toe pulsing slightly as if keeping the beat of private music. His lieutenant – 'Samuel' – sat on the other side of the fire, his own shiny black boots flat on the floorboards; a glass of some brown liquid hung from his fingertips, the arm itself resting out of sight on the chair. The third legs belonged to Pessoa: their knees were crossed with the right toe tucked behind the left calf, an uncomfortable position suggesting intense concentration. I could just see a corner of paper, drooping from his knee. As I watched, he lifted it, rearranged it out of my sight, then laid it back down. He continued reading.

This was not some report he was conveying to La Rocha and his man, not unless he had set his report in verse (although this being Pessoa, anything was likely). His words had a rhythm that drove La

Rocha's toe, and caused Samuel's glass to swirl gently.

Then the rhythm broke off. Pessoa said something in a more normal voice – rather, in the voice he had used the other evening when he wore the monocle, not the deferential intonations of Fernando Pessoa, translator. He seemed to be asking a question, because La Rocha's squeak answered, then Samuel contributed something. It went on that way for a few minutes, before Pessoa cleared his throat, paused for a swallow from his glass, and set to again.

I peeled my cheek off the grubby stone and sat upright, thinking, *Good heavens, they're holding a piratical poetry reading!*

This literary salon continued for another quarter-hour before Pessoa came to what was clearly, even through a closed door, some kind of conclusion. The other two men did not applaud, but they did make encouraging noises. I placed my eye back to the slit, thinking that they would pour the poet a drink and talk it over, but instead all three of them stood. I positioned my hands for instant flight in the event they decided to use the back entrance, but they did not – and to my surprise, it was not Pessoa who left, but the other two.

Instead, Pessoa made a circuit of the chairs, stood before the fire for a minute – I could only see to his bagged knees, but I pictured him rolling a cigarette. Then a spent match sailed into the coals, and Pessoa returned to his chair, and his pages.

Only this time, he read his words in English.

It was – inevitably – a poem about piracy, beginning with hard, romantic, masculine images of a man's life at sea:

> *To the sea!*
> *Salt with windblown foam*
> *My taste for great voyages!*
> *Thrash with whipping water the flesh of my adventure,*
> *Douse with the cold depths the bones of my existence,*

But then the harshness slipped sideways, into imagery even a pirate might have found unnerving:

> *Make shrouds out of my veins!*
> *Hawsers out of my muscles!*
> *Flay my skin and nail it to the keels!*

Was this what he'd been reading to La Rocha and his friend? It was hard to picture those two men receiving these images with such calm attentiveness. No, I decided: The poet must have read them a less inflammatory portion, and set these verses free into the room only after they had left.

It went on in this vein for some time, the poet asking that his eyes be torn out, bones smashed, blood spilt. I listened in fascination as the pale, thin landsman dreamt into existence a tropical sun that made his taut veins seethe, Patagonian winds that tattooed his imagination. There was a bizarre fascination in overhearing the man's inner vision, of himself and his people; my cheek went numb against the frigid stone as his maritime ode unfolded. His voice became increasingly caught up in the recitation, gaining in fervency at the erotically charged violence, the fire and the blood, until from deep within booms the savage and insatiable Song of the Great Pirate, sending a chill down the spine of his men:

> *Fifteen men on a dead man's chest*
> *Yo-ho-ho and a bottle of rum!*

The abrupt shift from bloody rapine into children's adventure story startled a noise out of me, and I slapped a hand over my mouth. The dramatic recitation cut sharply off. I staggered upright and forced my stiff limbs to shamble down the tunnelled lane, clearing the corner only an instant before the bolt rattled and the door spilt light down the stones.

I was waiting at the front of the tavern when he left a short time later, and followed him long enough to confirm that it was the flamboyant, monocled Álvaro de Campos striding along the deserted streets, not meek, bespectacled Pessoa. I trailed behind him long enough to decide that he was headed to his home, on the city's other set of hills, and then I turned off towards the hotel, and dinner.

I will admit, my dreams that night were a touch . . . confused.

CHAPTER TWENTY

SCENE: A ruined chapel by moonlight.

THEN CAME MONDAY morning, and everything changed.

The cast – most of it – was at breakfast when Fflytte swept in, dressed in the most remarkable suit I'd yet seen, a canary yellow twill with a bright orange cravat spotted with green fleurs-de-lis. He stood in the doorway and clapped his hands to gain our attention, gaining that of all the civilians and waiters as well.

'Good morning, everyone!' He paused, as if expecting a classroom of dutiful replies. Hale loomed behind him in the doorway, looking as if he had not slept well. He might have simply remained where he was, but behind him came Will Currie, who shouldered the yellow twill aside and gestured to a waiter carrying a jug of coffee. Hale took advantage of the opening, as did a couple whose departure had been blocked by the director. Fflytte disregarded them all.

'Fresh day, fresh week, fresh ideas!' he boomed. 'Now, as some of you may have heard, I found a ship yesterday that's going to transform what we do with this picture. It will take a bit of attention to get it in condition for the cameras, so, rather than delay the rest of the production while we're doing that, I'm going to divide us up. Now, we've done this before,' he cajoled, although I had heard no protests, 'and we're all professionals here. Well, most of us. And the newcomers to the trade are fast learners. Here's what we'll do. Team One is composed of me and Mr La Rocha: He and I will get the ship ready to film.' *And to limp into the harbour and back without going down*, I added by way of silent prayer. 'The second team, with Mr Hale, will rehearse the pirates and their fight scenes with the constables. Mr Hale will be in charge of that, assisted by Mr La Rocha's, er . . . well, we know him in the part of Samuel. And our translator, Mr Pessoa, will remain with them.' I drew a relieved breath: I could not let the man who'd composed what I overheard the previous evening remain near young girls, but I was not looking forward to telling Hale why. 'Team Three will be the girls, with Mr Currie and Miss Russell. Oh, and you, Daniel. Girls, I'm sending you on a little working holiday just near the coast, to film the scenes where Frederic first sees Mabel. I'm told it's a lovely place, we've made arrangements for you to spend the night, the charabanc will be here in an hour. And—'

Whatever he'd planned on saying next was drowned in a gale of shrieks and exclamations, as a score of females threw down their table napkins and stormed for the door. Amused – he'd done it deliberately, I could tell – Fflytte stood aside to let them race past, then turned to the depleted audience, consisting of the crew, Daniel Marks, and the police constables. Harold Scott – our Major-General – was not there. One rarely saw him before noon.

'Maude,' Fflytte said to the woman in charge of make-up, 'you'll go with the girls, of course. And, Miss Russell? Will's assistant,

Artie, is a touch, er, under the weather. You don't mind helping Will with the equipment, do you?'

I looked at Will, who was grimly stirring sugar into his coffee. He'd known about the plan beforehand – going by his lack of bounce, he'd spent a large part of the night protesting. 'Happy to,' I replied.

Then Fflytte turned to the woman in charge of costuming. 'Sally, you'll stay with me and Mr La Rocha. He tells me there's going to be a lot of repairs needed to the sails, and—'

'No!' she and I objected, at the same instant. She didn't wait for me to cede the floor. 'I'll not ruin my hands on canvas.'

'You've sewn canvas before.'

'Yes, when you needed a shroud for a burial at sea,' she retorted. 'But there's a world of difference between wrapping a mannequin and producing an acre of canvas sail.'

'Oh, hardly an acre,' Fflytte cajoled.

'I'm not doing it!'

'Mr Fflytte,' I interrupted, 'I have to agree. Because if Sally's not there, any decisions and repairs to the girls' costumes will be up to me and the girls.'

He opened his mouth to ask what was wrong with that, then looked at what I was wearing; considered, too, what his actresses would wear if given free choice; and closed his mouth – rather more rapidly than manners would require, I thought: My dirt-coloured woollen trousers and tweed hacking jacket were a lot more practical than his garments. Certainly warmer.

'Very well, I'm sure La Rocha will know a sail-maker down near the harbour.'

No doubt La Rocha was well acquainted with all sorts of men willing to garnish their bills and pass him the difference. But I did have one question.

'Have you consulted La Rocha and Samuel about this division of labour?' Samuel was La Rocha's shadow; I had never seen the two men apart.

'They're fine with the idea,' the director said.

But when I looked at Hale, I could see that *he* was not. I had to agree: Fflytte and La Rocha out in the world, unchaperoned, would be a terrifying picture for the man in charge of the chequebook.

The charabanc might have been arriving at the hotel in an hour, but I did not expect that it would leave soon after that. And indeed, two hours later, Will Currie was still in argument with Sally the seamstress as to which set of equipment was the more vulnerable to weather. In the end, I bodily hoisted her sewing trunk to the man whose feet were dangling from the roof of the 'bus, told Will he could prop his camera in the seat beside me, and we were away.

Cintra was, or so I had been told, a picturesque little hilltop town nearer the Atlantic coast, fifteen miles or so from Lisbon. Normally, one would take the train that left from beside the hotel, but Fflytte and Hale had decided that a charabanc would put the equipment at less risk, and (I realised this only later) would make it more difficult for one of the actresses to slip away.

As soon as we had left the centre of town, I regretted the decision. The road was in the same condition as the charabanc – bad – which would mean that what would have been a forty-minute train ride was going to take us two or three hours. We jostled and rattled, raising a cloud of dust through which could be glimpsed olive trees and windmills, cork oaks and a very Roman-looking aqueduct, boulders and an occasional figure – young boy, old man, or mummified scarecrow? – seated on a boulder, watching over a flock of dirty sheep or goats.

An hour out, the murmur of complaint and discomfort had

swollen to a tide. I told the driver to halt at the next likely place. He answered in Portuguese. I tried Spanish, then French, and in that tongue he told me that the next likely place would be Cintra. I replied that he could in that case stop anywhere the girls might stretch their legs without falling off a cliff or being attacked by a pack of dogs.

Twenty minutes later, I tapped the driver on the shoulder and told him that here would be fine.

When the worst of our accompanying dust cloud had drifted past, a bevy of females staggered from the charabanc, coughing in chorus, groaning at their bruises (the older ones) and exclaiming at the dust in their clothing (mostly the younger). They dispersed along the roadside. Will Currie clambered to the roof to check the tight shrouds on his equipment. Daniel Marks stepped down, grimacing at the surface underfoot. We stood listening to the engine tick and the dust settle, alone on a rural road a short mule ride from the capital city, when, like magic, local residents drew into existence, to all appearances materialising from out of the dust, bearing cups of water and baskets of oranges, bowls of raisins and tubs of oil-washed olives. Trades were made, combs and hair ribbons, cheap bracelets and money offered, first through facial expressions, then gestures and, when those proved popular, full-blown charades. The natives sat in awe-struck appreciation when Annie, June and little Linda dragged Daniel Marks into their wordless play, enacting something that was either the 1910 Portuguese revolt or *Love's Labours Lost* – my attention was occupied with counting our heads, lest we lose one of our alphabet of girls. When I herded my charges back onto the charabanc, leaving behind a carpet of orange peel and olive seeds, I discovered that the locals had been selling other things as well.

'Wait! What's that noise?'

In the back, six scrubbed and innocent faces turned to me. If one of them had possessed the wits to claim that she was merely whining at the thought of getting back onto the 'bus, they might have got away with it, but instead they blinked their lashes and asked, 'What noise?'

I heard it again, and traced its source: of course.

'Turn out your pockets, Edith. The other pockets. No, Mrs Nunnally, I'll handle this. Edith, give the boy back his puppy. In any event, it's far too young to be away from its mother – its eyes aren't even open. How much did you pay him? Really, for that scrawny – never mind, give it back. No, let him keep your money, it can be a lesson to you.'

I tried to get the driver to chide the enterprising local that a puppy that small would only sicken and die if taken from its mother; judging from the amused reaction of the people lined up at the charabanc door, either the Portuguese were disturbingly heartless, or the exhortation changed somewhat in translation.

I climbed on, counted heads for the twentieth time, and off we drove.

Someone from the Avenida-Palace, it seemed, had made the arrangements not only for our transportation, but for our welcome at the other end. We were greeted, gathered up, refreshed with luncheon at a nearby café, then loaded upon a fleet of decorative if rickety wooden carts and aimed at the hill under whose side Cintra sheltered.

Most of us took pity on the animals after half a mile or so and climbed down to walk. (Daniel Marks, after due consideration, decided that *noblesse* – or perhaps *virtus* – *oblige*, and joined us; Bibi did not.) The exertion helped to dispel the effects of the faint drizzle that had begun to fall, or at least take our minds off it. A few of the girls tried to rouse community feeling with song, but that soon petered out when the pedestrians lacked sufficient breath to participate other than in brief gasps, while those huddled beneath their travelling rugs felt an uneasy suspicion that singing might be taken for lightness of heart.

It was a long hill.

I wondered if I was drifting towards the hallucinations of hypoxia when, on raising my head to appraise the next unforgiving rise, a garden party appeared. There was a taut canvas marquee. A queue of what could only be servants stood just beneath the cloth roofline; three uniformed grooms trotted out to take our horses' reins.

A small fortune in hot-house flowers stood, incongruously, in three enormous tin buckets. I could even smell them. But then, I thought I smelt bacon as well, which was every bit as unlikely as the flowers.

Our party, stunned respectively either by breathlessness or by cold, stumbled towards the oasis. To my astonishment, it did not shiver and fade away as we drew near. Cups of piping tea were thrust into our hands, platters of fresh, buttered rolls laid with crisp bacon were set before us, scones with – well, no, not clotted cream, but with butter and jam were shovelled onto the plates of famished adolescents.

Cheeks that had been variously hectic pink or blue with cold took on a more uniform glow. Blue eyes began to sparkle.

After my third cup, I worked my way over to Will Currie to ask, 'Have you any idea how this came to be?'

'Ah,' he said. 'It's all very well for a country to stage a revolution, but after fourteen years, buildings do want keeping up. Windows don't wash themselves. Seems the staff of the Royal Palace, just up the road, were happy to take on some pounds sterling in exchange for a day or two of alternate service.'

'Let that be a lesson to us all.'

'When the Revolution comes to Britain, it'll be no time at all before we set the toppled statues upright and beg the King to come back and pay his own bills. You finished with your tea, Miss Russell? Let's take a look at where we're meant to film.'

Our impromptu garden party was at the edge of the road near the ruins of *Castello dos Mouros*, the Castle of the Moors, overlooking a wide plain of rich farmland with the Rio Tejo to the south and the Atlantic to the west. The castle (which had, in fact, once been Moorish) had guarded the vitals of Portugal for centuries. In the twelfth century, the place was sacked by passing Norwegians on their way to the Holy Land. They must have recalled with fondness this frigid, wind-shoved, rain-whipped place as they plunged into their Crusader hell. (Had they decided to stay, I reflected, it would have made for an interesting shift in Iberian history.) By the fifteenth century, the hilltop fortress had been more or less abandoned, when finally even the Jews decided that Cintra in the lee of the mountain had to be more comfortable.

'They say it's quite pleasant in the summer,' Will said sourly. 'We have to make do with the flowers.'

'Flowers? Ah, I see: to give the impression of spring-time in Penzance.'

'Three hundred of the bloo—of the dratted things. We stick them in the earth so they look natural.'

'Whatever happened to realism?' I murmured.

'Pardon?'

'Where does Mr Fflytte want you to film?' I said.

Will set off to explore the walls – which, upon closer examination, looked more like an elaborate Victorian folly than an actual working castle. I followed him for a while, since I was supposed to be his assistant, but as he clambered and dangled and risked his neck on walls designed more for decoration than for invasion-repulsion, I went back to where we had begun, huddling into my coat until he returned.

'We'll shoot here. No need for lights. Pain in the neck, lights. Maybe a reflector.' He was thinking aloud, frowning at the sort of glade or small amphitheatre in which we stood. It had a pool at its centre. I stood beside him and looked, imagining it transformed into black-and-white images on a screen, and had to admit, the setting would bring an unexpected degree of drama to what was a rather fatuous scene.

'I have to admit,' I told him, 'the setting will help that scene.'

'The girls can dance in from the left, there. Gather in front of that section of wall, wondering if they dare remove their shoes and stockings to wade. Then pantomime the beginning of doing so. Fflytte and Hale may think it's too risqué to show, but they're the editors. Marks goes behind that tree; the camera will see him but the girls won't.'

'And the flowers?' Fortunately, the rains had brought a faint stubble of growth, so blossoms wouldn't be springing out of bare rock.

'Put them where the girls sit. Give them something to do while they're taking their shoes off.'

I had to wonder if the laconic Welshman had ever made a more, as he called it, risqué film. I wasn't sure I wanted to know.

We returned to the tent, hearing music as we came along the hillside path, and found that someone had set up a gramophone. The girls were kicking up their heels and were nicely dry and pink-cheeked. When I pulled the needle from the record, their complaints were short-lived.

We led them through the mossy boulders to the proposed site, told the girls and Frederic what we planned, allowed Graziella Mazzo (wearing a coat today over her scarf-frock, and sandals) to flutter around her assigned dance-stage, and then sent them all back to town. By the time Will and I got the daffodils in the ground, it would be too late to begin filming: Plant now, and shoot in the morning.

I received my bucket and my hand-trowel, and we got to planting.

A hundred or so stems later, my hand was numb, my back was on fire, my garments were soaked from labour and mist. Will finished his last dozen, and we stood back to look at our handiwork.

'I have to say, that's going to look fabulous,' I told him.

'Cost a fortune. I thought Mr Fflytte was mad – but then, I usually do. I've stopped arguing with him, he's always right.'

We retrieved our empty buckets and walked in friendly accord back towards the tent. As we left the castle proper, we passed through a pair of oddly placed stone structures that I had seen earlier. This time, I stopped to look at them – then looked more closely, climbing up on the right-hand structure to rip away some fingers of obscuring ivy.

A skull and crossbones, carved into the stone.

The marquee remained, but the staff had gone. One of the carts was there, the driver stretched out on a bare table, snoring. We roused him and let the horse trot us down the hill to the town.

The hotel was adequate, the evening meal a step better than adequate, and the wine the best I'd had yet in this country. A holiday spirit took hold of the girls, aided no doubt by other spirits, and Marks and our Bonnie were moved to offer a series of duets, spoken and in song, from other ventures they had shared. We took to our beds well pleased with our side of *Pirate King*, and ready for the initial filming on the morrow.

In the absence of handsome pirates, I did not even feel it necessary to patrol the hotel corridors that night.

Will and I finished our breakfast before the others had come down, heading up the hill in a cart laden with his tools of the trade – cameras and reflective screens, cases and bundles, even an arc lamp he did not intend to use. The equipment was bulky, but lighter than half a dozen girls had been, which meant that this morning, the horse was positively frisky in its ascent. We found the marquee unoccupied, other than a small mountain of provisions that had been delivered during the night. The cart-man helped us unload our equipment, then Will set his tarpaulin-wrapped camera on his shoulder, I picked up the aluminium screens, and we went back along the path.

Past the pirate-stones, into the fort's main gate, down to the clearing with its pond.

And face to face with a goat. A chewing goat, with an expensive, hot-house daffodil bobbing from its lips.

It was the last flower in sight.

I dropped the satchel and caught the camera being ejected from Will Currie's shoulder as he launched himself at the devil's spawn, a roar in his throat and murder in his eyes. The goat took one look and shot through the picturesque ruined gate to skip light-footedly away on the tumbled stones towards the valley below.

Telegrams were exchanged, the phone lines having proved erratic. Hale assured us replacement flowers would be there by afternoon. The girls introduced themselves to the residents of the decidedly bizarre royal palace uphill from the ruined fort, where most of the marquee employees normally worked, and desported themselves through the once-royal hallways (bereft of tourists, what with the weather, the economy and the political turmoil) of the former convent (which had borne the cheering name *Nossa Senhora da Pena*: Our Lady of Punishment) while Will and I planted a second set of flowers.

I hired a guard for the night, a fit young man who understood that a return of goats would mean his instant death, and we arrived on Wednesday morning to find the daffodils intact, the sun out, the walls still standing.

But no pond. Had the goats consumed that, too?

'I thought this was a pond,' Will screamed at the hapless young man.

'Pond?' said the man.

I knew he spoke some English, so I contributed a few synonyms. 'Lake? Pool? You know – a body of water.'

'Water? Yes, puddle.'

'Well no, not exactly—' Will started, but I laid a hand on his arm.

'I think it may be, exactly.' And so it turned out: What we had thought to be a conveniently located pond was merely a puddle; in the absence of rain the day before, it was now more of a wallow.

'Well, perhaps we could still . . .' I started, but Will was already shaking his head.

'A dozen nice English girls are not going to be stripping down for a frolic in mud. Without water, there's no reason for them to be here. Fflytte will toss it all out.'

'So,' I persisted, 'let's bring in some water. Don't look at me like that. If we can bring in flowers, we can bring in water.'

'I'm not carrying buckets up that hill.'

'I hadn't thought of doing it personally, no.'

Thus it was that on Thursday, four days after we'd come to Cintra, the camera finally started turning. Before us lay a pond of very expensive water, trucked and carried in before dawn that morning by a small army of hirelings, local farmers and servants from the palace – and if it was mere inches deep and more mud-choked than

178

sparkling, on film it would be fine. Around the pseudo-lake, the surviving flowers stood – and if they looked moth-eaten and wilted up close, despite several sprinklings of water, again, they would look just fine on film. As we came off the carts at the garden tent, the sun even came out – and if it was cold enough to put a rime of frost on the blossoms and set the girls to shivering, well, we had a brazier going behind the camera to warm up between takes, and adding a blush to cheeks was the reason we'd brought Maude, the make-up woman.

Of course, some of the girls had tried to insulate themselves by wearing jumpers and woollen hose under the spring frocks the scene required, making Sally complain at the ill fit of her laboriously constructed costumes. However, once I had mused loudly about how fat this Portuguese food was making the girls, there was a flurry of activity around the impromptu dressing-room, and the problem went away.

The girls took their places. Graziella flitted about (tripping over a pair of shoes I'd ordered her to put on). I consulted my heavily annotated copy of the *Pirate King* script, printing the scene's details in big, clear letters on the slate. Will, soft cap reversed, put his face to the camera and had Frederic stand against the tree, then shift an inch or two at a time, while I adjusted the reflective screen. When he was happy with how the light hit the actor's face, Will told Signorina Mazzo to stop breathing in his ear, asked Mabel to move her head left a fraction, and finally said, 'Miss Russell, hold up the slate in front of the girls for a few seconds, then say "Camera!" and get away fast.'

'Me?'

'Just say it.'

So I pronounced the word, and thus began my career as a moving picture director.

The scene went beautifully, even a rank amateur like me could see that. Bibi had a natural bent for placing herself at the forefront of any scene, with the other girls forming a visual chorus around her. Daniel Marks set his shoulders to indicate a degree of intense fascination, wrapping his torso around the tree to watch the girls without being seen. Will's arm worked the crank with a smooth and unvarying speed, until he stopped cranking and stood up, saying, 'Cut.'

The scene disintegrated with Mabel jumping up to exclaim that she'd been sitting on something sharp and Bonnie complaining that Celeste had been blocking her light, and Frederic objecting that we weren't filming his good side. He became quite upset when I made the mistake of saying I couldn't see any difference, but Will smoothed things over by saying that he would be doing a number of close-ups from the desired side, since Fflytte would be sure to want them.

Then he pulled the girls together to do the scene again. It took a couple of hours to finish the group shots, some of which required me to act as his assistant, turning the handle as he panned the camera. He had to correct me a couple of times, telling me I was slowing my turning speed, but the takes seemed to satisfy him. Later, he shifted the camera to Daniel Marks, then to Bibi, first in their rôles as Frederic and Mabel, then in modern dress as the director of *Pirates* and his actress-fiancée. Afterwards, he had Bibi change back into her *Pirates* garb, to shoot three takes of Mabel's expression on seeing Frederic, then an assortment of different poses – looking down in contemplation, raising a startled hand to her mouth, casting a look of mischief at a sister. He also filmed several versions of Bibi slowly drawing one stocking down a shapely ankle: with flowers in the background; dangling over the pond; with flowers and pond; with a flower floating in the pond . . .

'I think the sun is going,' I finally said, drawing an end to this fascination. The rest of the girls and Marks had long since retreated to the refreshments of the tent, and the wind was growing chilly. Bibi jerked up her stocking and stepped into her shoe, wrapped herself in her warm furs, and flounced away down the hill, leaving us to carry the film and equipment.

'How was that, do you think?' I asked the cameraman.

'Some of it looked very nice, although I won't know for sure until I see it later.'

'What, tonight?'

'Have to be – can't leave until I'm sure we got everything Mr Fflytte needs. I can give it a squint, just to see there aren't any major boobs.'

'Do you want some help?'

'You don't need to.'

'What can I do?'

'Come to my room tonight and give me a hand with the developing.'

It did cross my mind that Will might intend something other than film to develop within his room. However, I knocked on his door just after dinner, and although he answered in a state of relative dishabille, the stink that wafted out was in no way suggestive of romance.

Some of the odour was the film itself. But when he crossed the room again to the inner door, I could see why he had demanded the luxury of a large bath-room when we checked in: This was his developing room. I eyed the carboys of various noxious liquids, and rolled up my sleeves.

We finished shortly after midnight. My back ached, my hands were raw, my head spun from the unrelenting stench of the

181

developing fluids. But when at last Will switched off the dim red lamp under which we had been working and held the strips of negative up to the strong light, he pronounced the film usable. He told me he would polish and pack it away in its tins after it had dried. We could return to Lisbon, triumphant.

'Want a drink?' Will offered.

'I think I'll take myself to bed,' I told him. I said good-night, let myself out into the hallway, and came face to face with Annie and Celeste.

'What are you doing out here?' I demanded.

They looked at each other, and giggled.

It would seem the girls had discovered that Cintra did, after all, possess young males.

I sent these two to their rooms and patrolled the hallways for a couple of hours, just in case.

No catastrophes spoilt the film during the night. The hotel was not struck by lightning, earthquake or pestilence. None of the girls disappeared from their rooms (or if they did, they had found their way back by morning). The charabanc came soon after breakfast, and we loaded ourselves and our precious film inside. We were back in Lisbon in time for a late lunch.

To be greeted by the information that the *Harlequin* would up anchor at eleven o'clock the following morning.

With everyone on board.

Sailing for Morocco.

CHAPTER TWENTY-ONE

PIRATE KING: When your process of extermination begins,
let our deaths be as swift and painless as you can
conveniently make them.

'MOROCCO? BUT – but I thought we were going to film on
the boat for a day or two and then get on the steamer!'

'She's a *ship*, by the way, in case you'd rather avoid a lecture
from Randolph – "boat" from a new hand suggests derision.
Randolph decided that using her as transport would be a way to
recoup some of the money we'd put out for repairs.' Fflytte hadn't
the courage to tell us himself, I thought: He'd sent Hale to do the
job.

'We'll all drown.'

'Actually, I was surprised. She's more sea-worthy than she looks.'

'A bath-tub without a plug would be more sea-worthy than that
boat looks.'

'Believe me, my reaction was the same as yours. I went down
yesterday and poked around in all the corners. Beneath the surface

untidiness, she's been maintained – the bilge is even dry. I had to have them add water to test the pumps.'

I put a hand to my forehead: The very word *bilge* made me queasy. 'But, the sails?'

'There's enough to fill the camera lens,' he answered, adding, 'It does have an engine.'

Oh, this was getting better every moment: stinking fumes to add to the heave of the boat.

'Although it only goes forward, for some reason,' he added. 'But we have the sweeps, as back-up.'

'Sweeps?'

'Long oars.'

'I know what sweeps are. But who do you envision pulling them? Bibi and Mrs Hatley? The girls? Oh God – has Fflytte got it into his head that the pirates would use the girls as galley slaves?' I really would shoot the man. Or brain him with one of his oars. Sweeps.

'The crew will pull them. And as I said, it's only as back-up.'

'How many days . . . ?'

'To Morocco? Three or four.'

Meaning five, on a small and leaky tub, shoulder to shoulder with three dozen members of Fflytte Films and sixteen pirates – plus the ship's crew, however many that was. I may have groaned.

Hale laughed, and gave my shoulder a comradely slap. 'Don't worry, it'll be over in no time.'

I could always go home. I was not proving very successful in my assignment in any event, which in all probability meant not that I was failing, but that there was no case here to investigate. Secretaries flee, drugs and guns are sold: The reasons for suspecting criminality among Fflytte's crew were so ephemeral as to be nonexistent.

But I knew I wouldn't.

Instead, I retrieved my increasingly splayed note-pad from my pocket, unclipped the pencil, and asked, 'What do you need?'

He handed me a list, a daunting list, filling a sheet to the bottom, and then some. 'Oh, and I meant to add, Mr Pessoa promised to find us some traditional Portuguese clothing.'

'I suppose he's coming with us?' My heart sank at the prospect of explaining that our translator wrote enthusiastic poems about lascivious violence – and worse, explaining *how* I knew. But to my surprise, Hale was shaking his head.

'No. When I told him that we were going to leave on Saturday, he suggested that enough of the pirates spoke a rudimentary English for us to get by without him.'

'So you didn't fire him?'

'I didn't have to, no. In fact, I got the impression that he was quite relieved when I didn't beg him to stay on. However, there were one or two things left undone, and although he said he'd come by first thing tomorrow, it's probably better not to depend on him. If he has the clothing, you could give him his final cheque.'

I agreed, somewhat distracted by Hale's list, and by his information. If there was any villain in this piece (indeed, if there was any villainy) I had thought that Pessoa would be in some way involved. For him willingly to retire suggested either that his part was done, or there had been no part to begin with, other than acting as translator.

As for the rest, it was a very long list.

I ran Mr Pessoa to earth in an office in the Baixa district, a remarkably unremarkable setting for the would-be poet laureate of Portugal. He was one of a number of men sitting at type-writing machines, cigarettes in mouths, oblivious of the clamour of clacks and dings. I waited for a surge of distaste when I spotted him, but somehow I could not feel it.

He was a poet; he wore many personalities; one of those personalities took joy in repugnant images. But I could no more dislike the man himself than I could a young boy who played at shooting Red Indians.

As I wound my way between the desks, trying not to choke on the palpable grey mist oozing into my lungs, he came to the end of his document, jerked it from the machine, tucked it into an envelope, and dropped the result into an out-tray on his desk. He looked up and saw me swim out from the smoke.

'Miss Russell! I did not expect to see you again.'

'Mr Hale asked—' He waited politely for my paroxysm of coughing to clear. After a minute, he took his cigarette and crushed it into the overflowing tray, as if that would help. Finally, I managed to get out, 'Can we speak outside?'

The shock of clean air made matters worse for a time; when I finally drew an uninterrupted breath, Mr Pessoa was looking quite alarmed. He suggested that we get something to drink.

I waved away his concerns, but accepted the offer of refreshment. Which – no surprise – was only a brief walk away, a narrow room fragrant with coffee and sprinkled with student types. Pessoa was so well known there, his cup was handed to him without enquiry. I told the waiter I'd have one of the same, which turned out to be the dribble of powerful coffee essence called *bica*, similar to the Italian espresso, and just the thing for clearing the lungs. When we were settled and he had begun to roll a cigarette, I said, 'Mr Hale wanted me to ask you about Portuguese fancy dress?'

'Er, do you mean the traditional clothing?'

'Precisely.'

'That should be delivered to the wharf before evening. Do you wish me to check on it?'

'It might be a good idea, thank you. Which reminds me – *your* cheque.'

He received the slip of paper and tucked it away in his wallet. 'It has been an interesting experience, Miss Russell.'

Interesting. Yes. 'I understand you won't be coming on the *Harlequin* with us.'

'I find I have neither desire nor need to leave my city. Although I will admit, were I to do so, your enterprise might be the one to prise me away.'

I took a cautious sip from my cup, and reached for the sugar. 'I don't think I ever heard how you came to be involved in the first place.'

'A connexion through that office you just saw. They arrange for translations of business documents. I have skills in English and French, and I can work the hours I like. Poetry feeds the soul, but does little to nourish the body or keep out the rain.'

'So Mr Hale contacted you through the translation service?'

Pessoa struck a match, squinted at me through the resulting smoke cloud. 'Indirectly, I believe. He has a friend in London, a solicitor for whom I have translated any number of documents. The friend gave him my name and, when I received his enquiry, I decided that I could as easily do vocal translation as written.'

'Was it Mr Hale himself who wrote to you, or his secretary, Miss Johns?'

'I should imagine it was she, although I don't remember precisely. I have exchanged letters and telegrams with both.'

'Would you have the letters?'

'Undoubtedly. Although they may have a poem or notes for a story on their reverse side by now. I tend to make full use of all the scraps of paper that come into my possession,' he explained. 'Why do you ask?'

'Well, my predecessor in the job quit rather unexpectedly, leaving one or two tasks unfinished. I'd like to ask her about them, if I could only find her.'

'Yes, I did wonder at the abrupt stylistic changes in the last communications I had from Mr Hale. That would explain it. But if you're asking, no, she gave no indication that she was leaving, much less where.'

'Ah well, we'll make do. Perhaps I shall see you on our return to Lisbon, Mr Pessoa.'

'I should enjoy another of our discussions, Miss Russell. Although I don't imagine I shall be accepting a position as live translator again. Once was an experience; twice would be somewhat . . . disruptive.'

'Well, I shouldn't think most translating positions would be as innately disruptive as working for a film-crew.'

'You certainly have your work cut out for you, Miss Russell,' he agreed, with a definite twinkle coming from behind those spectacles.

The twinkle nearly loosed my tongue: I was hit by a powerful urge to tell the man who I was. Knowing that he was sitting knee to knee with the real-life wife of the storybook Sherlock Holmes would send Fernando Pessoa/Álvaro de Campos/Ricardo Reis/etc. into throes of intellectual and poetic ecstasy, and give him a lifetime of material for his theories of deliberate pretence and personal identity. But however much I liked the fellow, I did not know that I could trust him.

And so we ended, with Fernando Pessoa taking out his pouch to fashion another cigarette, every bit as enigmatic as he'd been when I'd first met him, eight days before.

I did not get to bed that night, and as a result, drew a line through the final item on Hale's list – 'check hotel rooms for items left behind' – at ten minutes after nine on Saturday morning. I'd even managed to scribble a brief letter to Holmes, telling him of the change in plans and reminding him that if the *Harlequin* went down at sea, my most recent will was at the solicitor's.

Of course, absolute chaos seethed at the wharf. Edith's mother was frantic because her diabolical child had contrived to leave their passports in a drawer: I handed her the documents (which had, rather, been thrust into the farthest reaches of the bed). Bibi was in a fury because someone had stolen her pearl hair-clasp that the Duke of Edinburgh had given her: I assured her it had merely worked its way into a chair's cushions, and held out the bag in which I had placed it, along with three frilly undergarments, an ivory-handled hair-brush, a pair of belts left on a hook in the bath-room, one red patent-leather shoe, five silk stockings, and a number of objects from the drawer of the bed-side table, which I took care not to examine too closely. Hale spoke in my ear – shouted, near enough – that he'd forgot to tell me that Major-General Stanley had drunk himself into a near-coma the other night and was in no shape to go anywhere, so he'd hired a replacement; that Will-the-Camera was going to need to take over one of the cabins to develop any film shot on board; that Will's assistant, Artie, had had another nervous collapse and was currently in a Lisboan sanatorium; and that he'd brought on board two sail-makers, who would also be available for sewing costumes if Sally needed them.

A dozen similar near-catastrophes and pieces of news assaulted me. Most of the problems I could deal with then and there, sending the complainants up the gangway onto the boat.

Unfortunately, the crowd soon thinned, a feather bed was successfully folded and inserted into the companionway with only a minor eruption of down, the last parcels were brought aboard (including, yes, Mr Pessoa's traditional Portuguese dresses), and I was left with no distraction from what lay before me.

A very small boat, wasn't it? And despite being in rather better condition than I'd anticipated, and showing signs of very recent and highly aggressive cleaning, it was still an old boat, *and* laden with a distressing number of chronically excitable people. My gaze travelled unwillingly down the twin masts (they did look more nearly parallel, didn't they?) seizing on the occasional encouraging sign of a new rope and a gleam of varnish. The masts and beams showed no obvious sign of rot, the fore mast appeared to have a full complement of sails, and the aft mast, although naked of canvas, seemed to have the rest of its rigging in place. There were even a few scraps of fresh paint, one of which was her name.

'Ready to come aboard, Miss Russell?'

The high voice brought my eyes down to my next immediate challenge: the deck itself. La Rocha stood at the far end of the gangway, his meaty hands gripping the top of the bulwarks. His teeth were bared in a grin, and he exuded a most proprietary air. A pirate king, in all his particulars.

'Mr La Rocha—' I began.

'Captain.'

I sighed: another actor who had fallen in love with his character. 'Won't that rather confuse matters? I mean to say, the *Harlequin*'s captain may object.'

'I am *Harlequin* captain, Miss Russell.'

My jaw fell open. I felt it drop, and could only stare, but he just grinned all the wider. 'Mr Fflytte buy *Harlequin*, I sail it for him. What, you think I was schoolteacher, maybe?'

'But, I thought . . . a fisherman?'

'Yes! On ship. Ship just like this, once. Come, Miss Russell. Everyone else on board.'

Yes, that was the rub, wasn't it? *Everyone else*: all the people for whom I was responsible. I stood gaping up at him, wondering why I felt as if a spider had just invited me to see his nice web.

I took a deep breath, and set my foot on the worn gangway.

CHAPTER TWENTY-TWO

MAJOR-GENERAL: As I lay in bed awake, I thought I heard a noise.

EVEN WITH THE tide sucking us towards the open sea, it took us forever to reach it.

La Rocha's crew was – I should have guessed it – our pirates.

Except that most of the men clearly hadn't worked under sail for years, if ever, yet La Rocha absolutely insisted that we use the sails. The rest of us shifted around in front of the crew like herded sheep, trying to find a square foot of deck that might not be required by a man pulling on a rope – and continually failing to anticipate the antics of the racing, sweating figures. Eventually we were driven into four or five tight knots, and there we stayed, gazing at the antics.

Except that the antics of unpractised men made La Rocha roar, then sent him rigid and silent with fury while Samuel took over the roaring. The girls tittered when our captain's voice climbed shrilly and commented at every slip of the hand and foot. Then the sailors' tongues started as well, the meaning of their words plain despite the foreign languages, and the mothers hastily escorted their charges below, joined by most of the other girls.

Which left the rest of us – the men, six women, and me – shifting from amusement to discomfort to growing alarm. Finally, when we had spun lazily less than a mile from the port and twice nearly collided with other ships, Fflytte decided to take charge of operations. Hale tried to stop him, but the director shook off his cousin's hand and marched down to the quarterdeck, where La Rocha's hands gripped the wheel so hard one imagined the wood creaking while Samuel cursed one of the younger men dangling overhead – Irving or Jack, I wasn't sure – for pulling on the wrong rope and sending everything into a tangle.

'I say,' Fflytte called as he went up the two small steps, 'wouldn't it be easier to just set the engine going and try out the sails when we have a little more elbow room? That last fellow seemed a bit—'

Only Samuel's lightning reactions saved the director from a hospital bed. The belaying pin left La Rocha's grip just as Samuel's fist made impact, deflecting the heavy wood three inches shy of its target: Instead of smashing into Fflytte's face, it took a chunk out of the rail, spun in the air, and splashed into the water. La Rocha turned on his lieutenant with his own clenched fist, but Samuel stood his ground. The two men stared at each other for an unnerving length of time before La Rocha's shoulders subsided a fraction and Samuel raised his chin to yell at the boy in the rigging. Neither man acknowledged Fflytte's presence, ten feet away.

White-faced, Fflytte crept back to where Hale and I stood. I removed my hand from the knife in my boot, and made myself sit. Fflytte mopped his forehead with a handkerchief, and said in a shaking voice, 'Best not to interrupt the fellow when he's upset. He'll sort them out in a minute.'

Indeed, in a minute Adam (who seemed to know what he was doing) directed Jack (or Irving) to the correct rope, and the dead canvas overhead began to stir, as if dimly calling to mind its purpose in life.

And then, magic: The canvas awoke.

With a startling crack and a jolt of the ship, the canvas filled, proud and taut. *Harlequin* gave a little sigh of relief and settled into place behind her square-rigged foremast, creaking all over as ten thousand planks, long accustomed to the ignominious drive of an engine's screw, made their infinitesimal adjustments to the draw from above. The men cheered, Fflytte leapt up and clapped his hands, and I tipped my head back to watch the wind carrying us to sea.

Harlequin was, now that the accretions of the fishing trade had been hacked away, a brigantine, a two-masted ship (as Randolph Fflytte, instantaneous expert on all things maritime, had informed anyone who came within earshot the day before) designed expressly for nimbleness and flexibility. The fore mast had square sails, the kind that fly at right angles – square – to the line of the hull. These had beams along their tops – called yards – and a great deal of the shouting had been in encouraging the men to inch along the looped ropes strung beneath the yards, clinging for their lives as they prepared to loose the ties and drop the canvas. Not a job I would care for, myself, even in the softest wind.

The other mast, rising up just in front of the quarterdeck, held a different kind of sail. Fflytte had called them fore-and-aft sails and, as one might expect, they were arranged along the front-to-back line of the ship, rather than across it. Where the fore mast was fitted with four yards that sails dropped down from, the aft mast possessed a long yard at the bottom from which the big mainsail would be lifted. This yard, which was low enough to require the occupants of the quarterdeck to duck under it, looked a bit naked, since it had no canvas – no doubt the reason we'd brought two sail-makers on board at the last minute. Studying it, I decided its current nudity was probably a good thing: That massive beam would surely swing around when the wind hit its canvas, and in the confusion of getting out of the harbour, it would have bashed in the skull of anyone but Randolph Fflytte or the diminutive Linda.

As I traced the myriad of ropes and canvas and bits of machinery over my head, I saw that there was a third variety of sails on the guy-wires – stays – that ran between the two masts and from deck to masts, locking everything in place. These staysails were long triangles, and like the mainsails, they rose from below instead of dropping from yards.

Once the men were safely down from the yards, orders came to haul on various ropes. By close concentration, I could follow the lines from men through tackle and up into the heights – and I saw the yard lift from its locked position to swivel on the mast, reaching for the wind.

What a remarkably complicated piece of technology this was.

Harlequin did have an engine (at any rate, she had a mass of metal connected to a propeller – I tried not to think what it might do if someone tried to start it up) but she was old enough that it had to be an addition. Originally, in the absence of wind (or, for tight manoeuvres in the days of the *brigantino*), she would have depended on the sweeps – long oars – for propulsion. There was still a handful of the brackets to fit them into.

Of course, were she an actual pirate ship, *Harlequin* would also have carried up to a dozen cannon; I counted among my blessings that she was not fitted for them now. If she had been, surely Fflytte and La Rocha would have goaded each other into capturing a passing American passenger steamer. For the sake of realism.

With our captain's squall of rage safely past and the little ship on the move, the girls drifted back on deck. To my surprise, they voiced no outraged complaints, no-one stormed across the deck to demand that we instantly put back to land. I was braced for the reaction of civilised English girls faced with the filthy, cramped and stinking conditions of a fishing boat below decks, and it did not come.

Looking around, it dawned on me that a minor miracle had taken place: *Harlequin* was clean, scrubbed down to raw wood in places. The air smelt not of fish, but of Jeyes Fluid. The change extended to the deck fittings themselves: Without the various bins, nets and tackles that it had worn on first sight, the vessel looked almost bare. A tall deckhouse rose behind the fore mast, with a raised sky-light under the main mast and the quarterdeck at the back: Apart from those interruptions, the deck (its surface currently pocked with bolt-holes and fresh splinters) was clear.

Our crew, keenly aware of that chorus of blue eyes upon them, gained in confidence; a few of them even demonstrated a bit of piratical swagger. There came another dangerous moment when we reached the sea, and either the wind changed or it was just that we turned southward. The deck took on an alarming tilt; the wind began to whistle around our ears. Activity erupted, involving a lot of complicated adjustments and running about, with enraged cursing in several languages – this time the girls found their own reasons to retreat hastily below decks, to change for dinner. Eventually, we settled into the new course, having neither keeled over nor witnessed murder.

Without a mainsail, we could not move very rapidly despite the brisk wind. So I was not surprised, as cooking smells rose from below, to see the sail-makers go to a small hatch in the bow and begin to haul out an incredible quantity of canvas. When they'd completed this magician's scarf trick and covered the deck in canvas, they set to work.

As I watched the two men tug and measure, I became aware of the steady tick of the camera, recording the activity despite the setting sun and an absence of sail-makers in Fflytte's script. Will had told me that he always came away from a movie with hundreds of feet of excess film, some of which was never intended for the subject at hand. And lest I imagine those hours were of stockings being eased down ankles, he revealed a secret passion for nature photography. 'Most amazing shots I got one time of porpoises playing. Like ballroom dancing, it was.'

Tonight, the light was too dim for much, so he folded away his equipment and said to me, 'We've got Maurice cooking, at last.'

'Who's Maurice?'

'Ah, that's right, you're new, and he's just got in from Paris. Maurice was Mr Hale's idea. He figures that if you're asking actors to spend weeks locked at sea or in the desert or what have you, the least you can do is see they're well fed. Which is a fine theory until you go looking for a cook who doesn't mind being locked at sea or in the desert. But he finally found Maurice, who's mad enough to love every minute of it. Swears he hates it, does Maurice. Crashes his pans and curses up a storm – not much in English when there's girls around – and acts like it's a personal victory to come up with lovely food under the most appalling conditions. Wait 'til you see.'

This was a long speech from Will, suggesting great affection for the cook and his labours. I hated to disappoint him; however:

'I, er, tend not to eat much on board a ship.'

'I remember. You don't look too bad at the moment.'

I considered the statement, and said in surprise, 'No, I'm feeling all right, so far.'

'How's the food smell?'

'Delicious, actually.'

'Then you might try it. Maybe you've got used to sailing.'

It seemed unlikely, as I'd been ill on every voyage I could remember, but he was right, the odours trickling up onto the deck had my stomach rumbling rather than clenching, which was an entirely new experience. Gingerly, I followed him down the narrow steps, ready to retreat into fresh air at every moment. But the air smelt of nothing but good, and all remained calm as I washed my hands and changed from the trousers I had put on in Cintra the previous morning, then ventured into the galley.

It was set with linen and crystal. The air smelt of honey, from a small forest of beeswax candles that brought with them the odour of home. Laden bowls and platters were carried in, and I found that still, the food smelt gorgeous. It tasted better. I had a glass of wine, and ate everything.

Gazing down at the fruit compote that was dessert, I laughed aloud.

Annie, sitting across from me, looked over with a question. I explained, 'It would appear that sail travel agrees with me.'

She smiled, uncertainly, and poured a dollop of thick cream over her plate.

Later that night, the girls, worn out by fresh air and excitement compounded by a rich meal, turned early to the singular experience of making one's bed inside a hammock (except for Bibi, who was ensconced into a private cabin so small, her feather bed ran up the walls on three sides). They giggled and wrestled their way into the strange objects, shrieking in merry alarm as the taut canvas cradles flipped them out the other side. Then Annie either analysed the problem or recalled past experience, and loosened the ropes through her hammock's overhead hooks. Sagging, the object proved less impossible to mount, and the others followed her example. Although a couple of the mothers absolutely refused to submit to the indignity, settling instead onto the hard bunks around the edges, the others were soon bundled triumphantly inside their soft wrappings. Talk and restless adjustments of extremities and blankets quickly gave way before the rocking motion, and soon the hold was nothing but a collection of silent cocoons, swaying in gentle unison.

And me.

After a while, I cautiously descended from my hammock and made my way above decks. I was well accustomed to spending most of a voyage braced in the fresh air, but that night I came up to escape nothing more troubling than the faint odour of fish and the snores of my cabin mates. In fact, I came up because I wanted to enjoy the sensation of a boat that did not make me ill.

The sail-makers had long since bundled their project out of the way. The only persons I could see were a pair of shadowy outlines on the quarterdeck. Adam – who, although by no means the eldest of the crew, was clearly deemed one of the more responsible – was at the wheel; with him was young Jack. I gave them a small wave, but wandered in the other direction towards the bow. There, as far as I could see in the faint lamp-light, I was alone beneath the sails.

I paused halfway up the side, watching the delicate coruscations of the aft lamp dance across the sea, listening to the constant motion of the sails and ropes and all the complex, sophisticated, and nearly anachronistic mechanism of this form of travel. For the first time, I understood why people referred to a hull and its means of propulsion as 'she'. *Harlequin* was alive, our partner in this enterprise. I would have sworn that she was grateful for Randolph

Fflytte's mad, romantic vision, which restored her, even temporarily, to her true self.

I could almost sympathise with his wish for active cannon.

I smiled, and leant over the rail, hoping for a ballet of porpoises, for a—

A hand came down on my shoulder, and I screamed. Like any mindless female who had permitted herself to become oblivious of a world of danger, I squeaked and punched hard at the large, silent, threatening figure who had taken advantage of my idiotic preoccupation with beauty to corner me on the deck.

My arm is strong. Had there been three steps of distance to the bulwarks, my assailant might have recovered. There were but two. The man staggered away, arms outstretched, and the back of his legs hit the side. One hand clawed at the worn wood but his centre of balance was compromised, and over he went. Calling my surname as he fell.

I leapt forward and grabbed the ropes, staring back helplessly at the splashing figure who dropped farther and farther behind us in the featureless sea.

Holmes.

BOOK TWO

The Harlequin

November 17-27, 1924

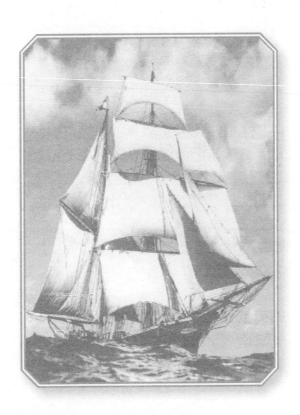

CHAPTER TWENTY-THREE

KATE: Far away from toil and care,
Revelling in fresh sea-air.

Meanwhile, the
previous Monday . . .

ABOUT THE TIME the charabanc full of Major-General Stanley's thirteen blonde daughters was crawling out of Lisbon's last hill on Monday, its War-era engine gasping for air much in the way its passengers would do on the hill above Cintra later that day, Teams One and Two arrived at their respective destinations. Within minutes, anger flared.

Team One, composed of Randolph St John Warminster-Fflytte

and his piratical highness, La Rocha the First, disembarked from the taxi that Fflytte had judged necessary for the sake of face (even if, as he had to admit, they might have walked there and back in half the time) and presented themselves to the offices of the harbour master.

Which were shut, it having been judged time for morning coffee.

When the harbour master and his secretary returned, fifteen minutes later, Fflytte had worked himself into a state of high dudgeon and was ready to turn his aristocratic fury on someone, whereas La Rocha was . . . well, he was La Rocha. Anything might happen.

The harbour master was young, educated and new to Lisbon (a beneficiary of the country's current impoverishment and general dissatisfaction with The Way Things Were, young newcomers being both cheap and unaffiliated with the status quo). His secretary was a Lisboan, born and raised, who had lived within gull-cry of the water his entire life, and who had worked as a stevedore until an accident had cost him a few essential body parts. His wits, his modicum of literacy, and his ability to hold a pen landed him in the office instead of on the street, and here he remained, a valuable resource for three decades of harbour masters.

And this man knew La Rocha, oh yes. His hand came out as if to seize his employer's coat, then faltered as his initial philanthropy was countered by craven self-interest: the impulse to turn heel and run. But the urge got no further than a brief step backwards before his nobler instincts regained control.

He caught his employer's shoulder and murmured in that young man's ear. The fresh face went from an expression of curiosity at the pair of men waiting to mild irritation at being manhandled by his inferior, followed by a frown of concentration at his secretary's words, until his eyes went wide and his throat convulsed in a nervous swallow. The grey-haired assistant let go his grip. The boss settled his narrow shoulders inside the jacket, and came slowly forward.

'Good morning, gentlemen, I apologise for my absence. Are

you waiting for me?' He spoke flawless English, and would have presented a face of complete assurance but for the tight wobble that was the final word. He made haste to get inside his office and around the back of the polished counter, as if personal territory combined with solid wood might offer a defence.

'Yes,' Fflytte answered. 'There's a ship in your harbour called *Harlequin*. I need to talk with the owner.'

'The—'

One word was all he managed before La Rocha began to speak. Everyone listened, even Fflytte, who did not understand a word of it but could appreciate authority when he heard it: incongruous voice, looming presence, and the texture of promised violence at the back of La Rocha's torrent of words. The scar helped, too: The harbour master's gaze wove in fascination between the compelling eyes and the terrible scar.

Within a couple of sentences, the young man was making a hurry-up gesture to his assistant, who ducked under the counter and began to pull out files. Less than a minute after La Rocha opened his mouth, the secretary stood up with a piece of paper in his good hand, and made to proffer it to La Rocha. The harbour master snatched it, then laid the page cautiously on the wood between the two strangers. La Rocha picked it up.

'*Obrigado*,' he said, like a pat on the head. He handed the page to Fflytte, who repeated the thanks in a surprised voice.

As the two men left the office, the sweating employees of the Lisboan harbour authority heard the tiny Englishman's comment: 'I say, they're certainly more efficient than one might expect. They didn't even have to look it up!'

The name and address were for a ship's chandler near the harbour. This man, too, seemed almost to be expecting an enquiry concerning the *Harlequin*, although he was clearly not interested in a temporary arrangement. He flatly turned down Fflytte's offer to hire the vessel for the week. When Fflytte pointed out that he would be returning the ship in considerably better shape than it was currently, the man's eyes flicked briefly sideways in the direction of La Rocha before they locked back on Fflytte. No: It was for sale, to the right customer, but only for sale. And no: He could not introduce Fflytte to the owner, whose instructions had been clear, and who was in any event out of the area. The entire country, in fact. Perhaps for ever. But to be absolutely honest (he said, earnestly holding Fflytte's eyes, as if another glance at La Rocha would mean being reduced to smoking bones) the *Harlequin* was a bargain. Yes, she was not pretty, but the owner was getting out of the fishing business and wanted only to sell. To the right customer, as he had already indicated. And if he could be so bold to suggest, if the good gentleman did not wish to take the *Harlequin* back to England with him, once the ship was restored to beauty, she could be sold again, perhaps by sailing her around Spain to the coast of France where the wealthy gathered with little to—

La Rocha cleared his throat, and the man went a touch pale, dropping his gaze to his papers and scrabbling them about for a moment. Then he returned to his suggestion: Perhaps if Mr Fflytte would look at the proposal, he would see that purchasing *Harlequin* would be a far more beneficial arrangement.

So Mr Fflytte sat down with the papers, and to his surprise, what the man had said looked to be true. The purchase price was so reasonable it made him wonder what was keeping the vessel afloat.

Love might be blind, but it was not completely witless.

'I'll have to have someone survey it for me,' he said firmly, expecting the man to quibble, but far from it, the fellow seemed quite relieved.

Fflytte took away a sheaf of papers, which he studied with the attitude of an unlovely octogenarian handed a marriage proposal by a charming young beauty: What am I not seeing here?

'I must speak with Geoffrey.'

CHAPTER TWENTY-FOUR

PIRATE KING: Although we live by strife,
　　　　　　　We're always sorry to begin it.
　　　　　　　For what, we ask, is life
　　　　　　　Without a touch of Poetry in it?

Also the previous Monday . . .

IN THE MEANTIME, Team Two had gathered in the Maria Vitória to continue the arrangement of the pirates' scenes. Without La Rocha to keep the men in line, Geoffrey Hale was anticipating problems, and his heart sank when his first instruction to gather round was completely ignored by the merrily chattering men.

Then Samuel's single word crackled through the theatre, bringing instantaneous silence. He fixed the others, one by one, with a baleful eye, then turned to Hale and waved a hand of invitation.

Hale had no subsequent problems with discipline.

Not that there weren't problems aplenty without discipline entering in.

Hale began by introducing the stand-in cameraman, William Currie's assistant. This was a nervous and spotty Liverpudlian named Artie, who wore a soft cap that he never removed and prefaced each speech with a series of tugs at the beard he was attempting to grow. The pirates looked him over as if he were a puppy, or dinner.

'Artie is here to see that the fight scenes we plan out will work on the screen. Remember, the camera lens stands at one place, so if, for example, Adam – come here, Adam – goes to stab Charles – yes, you stand there – and in the meantime Earnest is in the way, the audience will make no sense of it when Charles falls with his hands to his stomach. You see?'

Charles said something, and Pessoa said, 'He wants to know if he is going to die in the picture.'

'I don't know, that's up to Mr Fflytte.'

Pessoa translated that, then Earnest spoke, and Pessoa said, 'He says, who is he fighting with while the other two are stabbing each other?'

'Again, I don't know.'

Translation, then Kermit spoke up, followed by Pessoa: 'He wants to know if he can fight Irving. I think the two boys both have eyes for one of the girls. That is my comment, not what the boy says.'

'Tell him— Oh hell, this is going to make me crazy. Mr Pessoa, your English is really quite good. Do you think you might just try to keep up a running translation rather than pausing to say "He says" and "He wants to know"?'

'I will try,' Pessoa said, and after that he did. At first he was slow and scrupulous, but within the hour he was caught up in the rhythm of it and even took to duplicating the inflections of the speaker.

It made things much easier.

The first scene took place in the pirate stronghold. Fflytte had marked the script with 'pirates clown about', which suited Hale as a starting place, since clowning was a good way both to break the ice and see what his amateur actors could do in the way of physical emoting.

'Now,' he told them, 'I want you to remember that your audience won't be able to hear your words. You have to tell them everything by your gestures, the expressions on your face, how you stand and move. Imagine that your audience on this stage is made up of deaf people. You—'

'Do you want us to shout louder?' Lawrence, the smallest and youngest, asked.

'No, they don't hear at all. Surely you've all seen a moving picture?' All the heads nodded. 'The only thing you hear is the music, isn't it? Now, imagine that the cinema is filled with all those pretty girls, the sisters. They won't be able to hear your words, will they? You have to impress them by how you act. You have to tell them your story without using words.'

The heads nodded again. Encouraged, Hale went on.

'Your first scene takes place in the pirate stronghold. You're gathered there to celebrate the end of Frederic's apprenticeship, since he has turned twenty-one.' The plot had been laboriously explained to them already, but reviews, Hale had found, were essential when amateurs were involved. 'It's a party, there's drinking – although no, we're not breaking out the rum today for the rehearsal—' (Hale was pleased when this brought groans and jokes from his pirates.) '— and there's a lot of clowning around and . . . sorry, Mr Pessoa? Oh, clowning around is jokes, merry-making, games. It's a celebration.

209

So let's pretend for a minute that you're all at this party. I'll play the part of Frederic, since he's off with the sisters filming in Cintra. Raise your glasses – yes, just pretend – and . . . what would you do? Dancing? How about some dancing?'

He began to clap loudly, and Adam followed by Francis gave themselves over to the spirit of it and jumped about. Some of the others joined in, singing and leaping, and then two of them started a wrestling match and in moments the birthday party had disintegrated into a free-for-all of arms and legs and happy shouts. Hale waded in to separate the nearest pair of combatants, and a fist came out of the melee, sending him reeling.

For the second time, the pirate lieutenant's voice sliced through the air, freezing a stageful of men in their places. Samuel moved fast, sending one lad flying and hauling another upright and off the boards in a single jerk.

'Stop!' Hale managed to wheeze. Samuel paused, looking over his shoulder. Hale coughed and said, 'I'm Frederic, remember?'

The lieutenant studied him, then lowered the lad he had been holding – Earnest, looking very frightened indeed – gently to the floor. He brushed the boy off, bent to pick up a couple of hats and restore them to their respective heads, and stepped back to the side of the stage.

So much for clowning. Still, it suggested some additions to the scene, and when Hale had his breath back, he began to run through them: Several of the lads could perform cart-wheels (Lawrence took care to button his pet white mouse into its pocket first); middle-aged Gerald had a quite impressive squatting dance move, almost like a Russian folk-dance; Irving had a face like rubber; Benjamin had a dark intensity that would play well next to fair-headed Frederic.

And so it went.

Still, before long they ran up against the limitations of using a stage to practise scenes that took place out of doors. And other than the initial party, that included all of the scenes. Time and again, Hale would have to exhort a man to imagine that there was a tree there, or water behind him, or a boulder behind which he could hide. Each time he did so, a string of questions came trailing across the stage: How big a tree? (It doesn't matter.) What kind of water? (Salt, with small waves.) Why is there a solitary boulder there? (Because I put it there.)

It did not take too many of these diversions before Hale felt like beating one of the less-imaginative pirates over the head with an invisible chair. He looked at his watch and put out one hand, calling a halt and sending them all to lunch.

'And I want you sober when you come back!' he shouted at their backs. He sighed, gingerly prodded his bruised stomach, and retrieved the jacket he had shed in the heat of frustration. Pessoa, halfway down the aisle, paused to look back at the stage.

'Would it make a difference if you were to practise in the out of doors?' the translator asked with diffidence.

'Not in the manicured little parks you have around here, they'd be no better than the stage.'

'I was thinking, perhaps, the botanical gardens?'

Hale considered the suggestion, and told himself that not all of the translator's suggestions would be as fraught as the *Harlequin*. He finished straightening his neck-tie. 'Show me?'

The gardens, right adjacent to the theatre grounds, proved ideal. Particularly as it wasn't actively raining when the men – more or less sober – came back from their luncheon. And Pessoa knew the man in charge, who let them in at a special rate for the group. There were trees and a little water and even a few diminutive boulders, and Samuel's crew responded to the setting with the relief of men coming home after a confusing time abroad.

Originally, Hale had intended to bring the police constables in for the scenes, but after seeing the enthusiasm with which the pirates had thrown themselves into the party melee, he was glad he had decided to wait a day. Or two.

He explained that the scene he needed them to think about was when the police came – 'The police are coming? Here?' 'Only in the picture, Charles.' – when the *pretend* police came, because the pirates had taken the Major-General's daughters captive – 'I'll take them captive, yes!' 'I can have two?' 'Harriet is mine!' 'No, she is mine!' at which point Pessoa's translation bogged down. Since there was little need for translation Hale merely raised his voice and went on. '—taken the girls captive, but freed them to return to their father. The Major-General then sends the police – yes, the pretend police – and that is when you fight them.'

As he talked, he had taken off his jacket and worked his way into a special, heavily padded waistcoat he'd asked Sally to fashion after the knives came out on Saturday. She'd had to cannibalise other garments – none of the costume corsets had whalebone now – but it ended up a garment that might protect his more vital organs from any stray non-collapsing blades.

'All right, first thing is to give your own knives to Samuel, here.' When none of them moved, Hale said, 'You'll get them back at the end of the day, and it saves you from worrying about pulling the wrong blade.' When still none of them moved, he added, 'If I end up in hospital, it's going to slow the production down considerably.'

Samuel's hand went out, and one by one, the pirates filed past and divested themselves of their arms. Fourteen men: Hale stopped counting at twenty-three weapons.

He felt somewhat more confident when they began lining up to practise stabbing him.

* * *

That night, while Hale was attempting to dress for dinner, his cousin let himself in. Fflytte stopped dead.

'Christ, Geoffrey, what happened to you?'

'Impressive, isn't it?'

'Looks like the time just before the War when that bloody mare tossed you into the stream. What was the creature's name?'

'Thumper.' Hale prodded a small patch of his torso that was not black or blue, and winced: even that hurt. 'So long as you're here, help me with the plasters? I don't want to bleed all over another shirt.'

Fflytte took the packet of plasters and began to cover the open wounds Hale had trouble reaching – all minor, although an alarming number of them. As he worked, he asked, 'Have you decided how we should pair up the constables?'

Unlike the girls and the pirates, who would be matched up by their respective heights, the smaller number of constables required a more deliberate pairing to get the full effect of the fight scenes. And where the girls were for beauty and the pirates for masculinity, the constables (with their tall, thin Sergeant) had been chosen for humour. Short, bald-headed 'Clarence' in his brass-buttoned uniform would be perfect battling Samuel, as sixty-year-old Frank with his protruding ears and missing teeth was going to look absurd facing handsome young Benjamin. Trying to ignore his cousin's none-too-gentle ministrations, Hale ran over his pairings. '—and the Sergeant with Lawrence, who comes up to his belt-buckle. The only one I'm none too sure about – ow, watch it! – is Bert.'

'Which one's Bert?'

'The dark Cockney.'

'The pretty one. Yes, I meant to ask about that: I thought we were going for odd with the constables?'

'I wouldn't say he's pretty. Not exactly. Though I'll admit, he's prettier than I remembered.'

Fflytte made no comment, which was comment enough. Hale opened his mouth to defend himself against the unspoken charge of a personal interest, but decided there wasn't much he could say. He didn't recall hiring an actor with good looks – indeed, if anything, he vaguely remembered a runt with a twisted nose. But he had been rushed at the time, and then the problem with Lonnie came up, and in any event, here was Bert, with nothing particularly odd about him. And if he wasn't pretty, exactly, his looks were interesting enough that his attentions to Annie were reassuring.

Hale was abruptly called back to himself by a prod in a tender zone. 'Was there something you wanted, Randolph?'

'Oh yes – it's about the ship.'

Hale stood, watching in the big cheval glass as Fflytte slapped on plasters while waxing lyrical about *Harlequin*. However, he'd known two things the moment his cousin came in the door. First, that whatever the director had in mind, Hale wasn't going to like it (and Fflytte knew that Hale wasn't going to like it). And second, Randolph had already made up his mind.

Eventually, Fflytte ran out of wounds and Hale retrieved the sticking plasters before he ended up bound head to toe. 'Let me look at the papers before you sign anything,' he said sternly.

With a look of pleased surprise, that the job of convincing Hale had not been harder, Fflytte dropped a distressingly thin envelope onto the table.

Hale stifled a sigh. 'I'll read it, and be down for dinner shortly.'

Fflytte bounced out. Hale finished his drink, painfully threaded his arms into a formal shirt, and picked up the day's suit-jacket, intending to hang it in the wardrobe. However, when he held it to the light, the lovely wool had a lace-like quality that would have given its tailor the vapours. He quietly dropped it into the dust-bin, and poured himself another drink.

Tuesday they spent at the Botanical Gardens, learning how to stab, pummel, bash and impale a man for the camera.

On Wednesday, cursing as he extricated himself from his bed, Hale decided that his pirates could now be trusted to avoid committing manslaughter. That morning, he brought in his six police constables and their sergeant, a Paris-born, Irish-accented Englishman named Vincent Paul. The previous day's ease went instantly stiff-legged, with both sides bristling at each other far too convincingly. After separating one pair – Edward-the-Constable and Earnest-the-Pirate – for the third time, Hale ran his hand through his hair and contemplated cancelling the entire project: Fflytte Films really did not need a homicide on its hands. *That* headline might not be so easy to shake.

'They need to eat together.'

Hale was startled, not having noticed the cat-like Samuel at his side. 'Oh, a great idea – let them sink the cutlery into each other's throats.'

'They are boys. Boys wrestle, then become friends.'

'They're grown men.'

'Not in their hearts.'

'You can't guarantee me that your . . . boys wouldn't lose control.'

'I can.'

Hale looked at the big man, and after a moment admitted, 'You probably could. Well, if you want to try, I'll have a talk with my men. Maybe I can convince them that if they get into a serious fight, they'll never work for Fflytte Films again.'

So they broke for lunch and trooped in two separate groups to a nearby restaurant. The men sat at opposite sides. Once they were seated, Samuel went around and lifted every other man up by his collar, pirates and constables alike, rearranging them until the tables were mixed. While the diners glared at each other with hackles raised, he went to the back of the restaurant, and returned with a waiter carrying a large tray covered with bottles of beer.

'Hey,' protested Hale, but Samuel just held up a hand and went through the tables, placing a bottle before each man.

One bottle, each.

They ate, in silence. The cutlery remained in the vicinity of the plates.

When they left, they resumed their separate groups. Hale, following behind, could not decide if the additional degree of relaxation was a good thing.

Apparently, neither could Samuel, because when they got back to the grove where they had been practising, he lined up the men and walked along, hand held out to every third or fourth one – and not just the pirates. The first few turned innocent faces on him, but when his great forefinger pointed to a pocket, an ankle, or in one case the back of a collar, the man would sheepishly retrieve the weapon he had kept back and hand it over.

Nine more knives.

Then he turned them loose.

Ten minutes later, Hale was sure it was a severe miscalculation. Five minutes after that, his heart climbed into his throat, and he pulled two flailing men off of each other. Three minutes more, and a dogfight erupted. A tangle of enraged males threw themselves body and soul into the struggle, roaring and cursing in many languages – only to break apart when tall, handsome Adam, contorted into such a furious knot with the gargoyle-faced Donald that it was impossible to tell which leg was linked to which arm, gave a shout of laughter. In seconds, a dozen separate struggles-to-the-death broke apart, leaving the men filthy and dotted with scrapes, bruises and future black eyes, but also leaning back on their hands, laughing until the tears came.

Samuel looked sideways at Hale. 'Boys.'

Not one of them needed to be carted off to the morgue, or even the hospital. And after that, they were indeed like lads who had tried each other's muscles and found friendship.

On Thursday, with Will stuck in Cintra because of a flower-loving goat, Fflytte tore himself away from his ship long enough to help Hale and Artie film the pirate-constable battle scenes. The pirates and the police had no need for Maude-the-Make-up, although their groans may have been due more to the drinking they'd done together during the night than from the previous day's brawl. Fflytte sat in his folding chair. Artie, bursting with pride, turned his hat-brim back and cranked the second-best camera. Hale did everything else: checking the costumes and adjusting the reflectors and reminding the director of what the men had rehearsed.

The practised motions of the fighters intertwined perfectly. La Rocha and Samuel stood and scowled and gestured photogenically. Pessoa translated excitedly. And at the end of the day, no actual blood had been spilt – or, so little it hardly mattered.

Once the scenes were finished, Fflytte and La Rocha hurried away to check on the day's progress down at the docks, leaving behind a sense of anticlimax after this, the first day of actual filming. Hale watched the mismatched pair scurry off, and muttered to Pessoa, '*Fflytte's Folly*'.

'Sorry?' the poet asked.

'Oh, nothing. Just, the ship.'

'I begin to regret my part in introducing Mr Fflytte to the vessel.'

Little late for that, Hale thought. 'Call the men together, would you?'

He watched Pessoa move over to the tired actors. Over the past week, the translator had become his shadow. Standing at his side and effortlessly mouthing his words in Portuguese, then the pirates' responses in English, Pessoa was gratifyingly invisible. Despite his earlier irritation, Hale was sorry the fellow had chosen not to come to Morocco with them.

When the men were gathered around, Hale climbed onto a stump and gave them the most paternal smile he could muster.

'I have to say, what you've done is remarkable. You men work together marvellously. If you can do half as well before the cameras in Morocco as you've done here, you'll all be film stars, and Hollywood will be fighting over you.'

As always, the response came in two pulses – one among those who understood his English, the other a beat later when Pessoa had finished. Hale started to say that their week's pay would be distributed early, in the event they wanted to spend some of it here before they left, but broke off to let Pessoa finish his translation of a remark from young Jack.

'—doesn't matter if we're not going to be actually ma—'

Out of nowhere, Samuel's fist smashed Jack to the ground. Pessoa stuttered to a halt; Artie gave a girlish squeal; Adam took one angry step forward and then stopped; all the other men, pirates and police alike, reared back, looking as stunned as the lad in the dirt.

'What the hell did you do that for?' Hale demanded.

Samuel watched the boy climb to his feet, rubbing the back of his head and shooting Adam a quick glance before turning his gaze to the ground. 'Do not interrupt Mr Hale,' the big man growled.

'Jesus Christ, you didn't have to hit the boy,' Hale protested.

Samuel's gaze drilled into Jack until the lad's eyes came up. The two looked at each other for a long minute, and when Jack dropped his eyes again, Hale was left with the impression that a whole lot had been said, of which he'd understood not a word.

Samuel turned an unreadable face to Hale – who, when no further explanation was forthcoming, tried to recall what he'd been about to say.

The news that their pay would be available at the hotel the following morning cheered the men, but they left the gardens with more haste than they would have had that final incident not taken place. The last one away was Samuel. Hale stood and watched the big man go.

'What do you suppose Jack was about to say?' he asked Pessoa.

He hadn't really expected an answer, which was a good thing, since Pessoa had no suggestions.

This man, Samuel. He was an exceedingly odd bird, for the friend of an unemployed fisherman.

CHAPTER TWENTY-FIVE

FREDERIC: The Major-General comes, so quickly hide!

FRIDAY DEGENERATED INTO chaos, as Hale stood, alone and assistant-less, to receive the barrage of last-minute necessities, undone tasks, and everyday emergencies. He went out to Randolph's damned boat every few hours, holding firm to his threat that if every surface was not spotless and fragrant, no actress would set foot on *Harlequin*. He dragooned Artie, whose hands had begun to shake again, to distribute the pay envelopes, trying to sound soothing as he ordered the young man to give each envelope to its destined owner and to him alone, then to write down when he had done so. And he made a list for Miss Russell, praying that she would be back from Cintra in time to take over a few of the tasks.

He managed neither lunch nor dinner – but then, at this stage of a production, he was well accustomed to surviving on cold coffee and stale rolls.

The sail-makers weren't going to finish in time: Hale arranged to have two and all their equipment go along and finish the job while at sea.

Maurice, the kitchen's prima donna (and that was definitely the correct gender) came wringing his hands, having seen the conditions under which he would be forced to labour. Since every kitchen Maurice encountered was inadequate for his purposes, beginning with that borrowed from a famous Parisian restaurant for *Gay Paris* fifteen years ago, Hale had anticipated the visit. He handed Maurice a note to the city's top restaurant supplier in the Bairro Alta, instructing them to bill Fflytte Films for anything the chef might require. Maurice seized Hale's face and kissed both his cheeks, as he always did, and went away singing '*Va, pensiero*' in an eerie falsetto.

Then one of the hotel's staff – Harold Scott's unofficial valet – came in with a piece of paper in one hand, and Hale's heart sank. The actor playing the Major-General had spent the last week with his foot on a cushion, partly due to the gout but also because he required little rehearsing with the others. But it had been a mistake to leave him alone, and here was the result. 'In hospital? For God's sake, it's only gout!' The cowering non-valet tried to reassure Hale that Scott would be fine in a few days. 'I don't need him in a few days, I need him *now*!'

'Mr Scott feels terrible about it, but truly, he is in miserable condition. And he's found you a replacement, a most adequate replacement.'

'Oh yes, some scruffy drinking companion who doesn't speak any English. I can't believe—'

'No, honestly, the gentleman is a very presentable Englishman. He lacks the, er, physical attributes of Mr Scott, but he's worn padding before, and is an accomplished actor. He even knows the lines, although I realise that won't be nec—'

'Hell. Where is this paragon? I should at least see him before I go out to the hospital and skin Mr Scott alive.'

'He's just downstairs, shall I—?'

'God, can anything else go wrong? Yes, bring him along and we'll see how deep the hole is.'

But in the event, the hole proved a shallow one, and although the substitute Major-General was entirely the wrong build, being very tall and thin and about a decade older than Hale would have wished, there was a certain air about him, and he clearly knew the part.

Hale listened to the man's precise, if spoken, rendition of the words, grudgingly admiring the combination of speed and clarity: He might be saying '*IamtheverymodelofthemodernMajor-General*,' but one heard each word clearly. He even shaped a decent cadence around the impossible bits, and when he produced '*I quote in elegiacs all the crimes of Heliogabulus / In conics I can floor peculiarities parabolous*' without pausing for breath, Hale waved him to a halt.

'I don't know if you're running from the law or selling cocaine to the convent girls, but I'd appreciate it if you try not to get yourself arrested before we leave tomorrow. If you do, I'll have to play the damn Major-General myself.'

As he shook the thin hand of this newly minted father-of-thirteen, Hale reflected uneasily that the fellow looked far too intelligent and sensible for an actor. But that was all the time he had for reflection: At that moment Artie appeared in the doorway, tears running down his face while two irate pirates glared over his narrow shoulders.

The new Major-General excused himself, saying that he would see if he could locate portions of a uniform suitable for his frame.

Artie sidled into the room. 'Mr Hale, I'm so sorry, but these two fellows tell me they didn't get their pay, although I could have sworn—'

And after Artie, Fflytte came with news of how the swarms of workmen they'd hired had done wonders on the *Harlequin*, rendering it not only sea-worthy, but actress-worthy. And then the charabanc-load of girls made it back at last and he had to hear how that went, and somehow fit in a review of the film Will Currie had shot. After which Bibi came to demand that her feather bed be installed on the ship, if she wasn't to look haggard from lack of sleep when the camera was on her. Then Graziella Mazzo slithered in, batting her dark eyelashes at him and saying that surely she had misunderstood the arrangements, that she could not possibly be expected to sleep with all the girls in one room, and when Hale patiently explained that there were few actual cabins available on the ship, and that it was only for two or three nights, she pouted; when that did not soften his heart, she looked daggers at him; and when he still would not give way, she flounced out in her Isadora-inspired draperies to find Fflytte. Then Maurice came back and needed Hale to approve of the menus he had devised. And Randolph put his head in to say Graziella had decided to go visit her family in Naples. And . . . And . . . And . . .

And eventually, they had the last boxes, last actors, last crew crammed on board – except for Artie, who (Hale was not surprised to hear) had arranged to place himself in a sanatorium rather than risk the *Harlequin*. There was another unsettling incident shortly after they'd cast off, this time with La Rocha rather than Samuel, but the belaying pin missed, and the temper-tantrums of actors was a thing Hale was used to. He made a mental note not to push La Rocha too far, then let Fflytte's near-concussion slide into the category of Life's Lessons for Randolph Fflytte.

And so Mr Geoffrey Hale took to his bunk at last, exhausted to the edge of collapse, but content: He had done as much as any man could to bring *Pirate King* closer to completion.

He slept peacefully, until the screams began.

CHAPTER TWENTY-SIX

Enter the MAJOR-GENERAL's daughters led by MABEL, all in white peignoirs and night-caps, and carrying lighted candles.

A T LEAST I had the sense not to scream out my husband's name as I saw him floundering behind us in the dark waters. 'Hol—' turned into 'Help! Man overboard!' as I ran down the deck, flinging into the night anything that might function as a life-ring.

Sailing ships have no brakes. Thus the rescue of a man overboard becomes a somewhat leisurely event (unless, of course, a shark happens by) that degenerates into a cinematic farce, as if scenes of a man falling out of an aeroplane were interspersed with the calm arrangement of his means of rescue by those on the ground: discussion; the fetching of mattresses; further discussion; many lookers-on; the arrangement of pillows; the substitution of one pillow for another; and all the while the individual is tumbling closer and closer towards solid ground. Or in this case, farther and farther away from solid ship.

Adam immediately began to shout and crank the wheel around, while Jack ran forward along the rapidly tilting deck to throw himself at various bits of rigging. I clung to the rails to keep from following Holmes overboard; before I regained my balance, sailors were pouring onto the deck in a fury of activity, directed first by Adam (who seemed to have tied off the wheel before joining the others) and then by Samuel. Men hauled at ropes; sails beat angrily on their beams; other sails made an abrupt collapse down their lines. In less than two minutes, I could feel our forward drive die away.

In the sudden silence, the first of *Harlequin*'s passengers ventured out, tugging at dressing gown belts, patting at rumpled hair, picking their way through the unbelievable quantities of rope that now littered the decks. Soon, the ship's entire population was at the rails, all of them with suggestions as to engines, reversing, coming about, and diving in to get our lost Major-General. Edith suggested that we could shoot an arrow with a rope upon it; fortunately for Holmes, no-one had a bow.

The experts – that is, Samuel and La Rocha – were in agreement that were we to circle back for him (at least, I believe that is what they were saying) we would do little more than move farther out of his range.

'What about the motor?' Mrs Hatley asked.

'I heard one of them say that they'd broken it altogether,' Annie said. Inevitably, it was Underfoot-Annie who had overheard a conversation.

'What about the oars?' I suggested. They might slow our drift, if not actually reverse it.

Samuel had the same idea, and began shouting orders at the men, who leapt to do his bidding, tripping over the girls, puzzling over how to fit the lengths of wood into the brackets, dropping them overboard, cracking each other's skulls . . .

I hauled Annie down the deck to where one of the ship's boats hung in its davits. I jerked loose the front tie, thrust the rope into her hand, then jumped to loose the other end. 'Let it out at the same speed I do,' I ordered.

The men were too occupied to notice what we were doing. In a minute, the boat's hull kissed the water, and I – knowing enough about small vessels to have a clear image of what would happen if my weight hit in off-centre – scrambled out over the tackles above it. I paused a moment, to be certain the thing had not immediately sunk, then dropped gently into it.

Samuel's voice rang out, commanding me to stop. But I had the tackles and painter free and managed to shove away from the hull before he could interfere. 'I won the school rowing championship when I was fifteen,' I called. 'It'll only take me a few minutes to reach him, you'll just weigh us down.' I lit the small lamp that dangled from the skiff's prow, then dropped myself onto the seat and the oars into their rowlocks.

There was a pang I cannot deny as the lights of the only firm place in many miles grew farther and farther away. On the other hand, the man I had nearly killed grew ever closer, letting fly with the occasional splash to keep me on the right path.

Nine minutes later, I shipped the oars and looked over the side at Holmes. 'You look like a drowned rat,' I said, and put down a hand to help haul him up.

'I'm grateful that your aim was off, or I'd have gone over the side unconscious.'

'My aim wasn't off, I changed my mind at the last moment. Here, this blanket should be warmer than the coat.' We peeled away some layers of sodden wool, and I wrapped him in the thick blanket that I had been keeping warm with my backside.

I looked over my shoulder at *Harlequin*. She was alarmingly small and indistinct. I grabbed the oars and got to work.

'All right, Holmes, what the *hell* are you doing here?'

'I'm your new Major-General. I thought it best to stay out of sight until we'd had a chance to talk.'

'Good Lord. Hale said that Mr Scott was taken ill, but – why?'

'Mr Scott was taken ill because I paid him – generously – to exchange a sailing ship for a sleeper train bound for the south of France.'

'You know damned well that is not what I was asking. Talk, and be quick about it – once we reach the ship, we may not have a moment to ourselves until we get to Morocco.'

'The letter you wrote on Saturday very fortunately reached me on Wednesday. It was a test of my brother's machinery to get me to Lisbon in twenty-four hours.'

'But, why?'

'Because I was beginning in Sussex, and as you will recall—'

'Holmes, I'll tip you back over the side!' I hissed. 'Why. Are. You. *Here?*'

'Because of the scar on your pirate king.'

'La Rocha?'

'A man can have many names, but few men could have that wound.'

'Who is he?'

'A pirate. Among other things.'

I looked over my shoulder at the ship. It was close enough now to see by the swinging lamp-light that most of the others had gone back to their bunks – once they knew who had gone over, and saw the skiff beat the dorsal fins to the swimmer, they'd grown bored and returned to their warm cocoons. Still, we only had a few minutes before our voices would be heard by those remaining.

'Don't be ridiculous, Holmes. Piracy was squashed two hundred years ago.'

'So long as men sail the seas, there will be pirates. La Rocha comes from a Moroccan family with a history of piracy – the accent is not as strong in his cousin.'

'Cousin? You mean Samuel?'

'His name is Selim, and they may be half-brothers instead of cousins, but yes. Although not all of the men share their linguistic history.'

My hands faltered as the Arabic name trickled down and stirred a memory: Selim. Selim the Grim. Who in 1512 became the Ottoman emperor and promptly set about slaughtering his brothers and nephews, lest they become a threat. . . .

I bent over the oars again: best to think of something else.

'I thought the men were Portuguese.'

'Oh, Russell, surely you—'

'*Holmes!*' This was no time to scold me for a mistake in accent identification.

'La Rocha took that scar in the second year of the War, when a small boat laden with gold and valuables escaped Turkey ahead of the Allied Forces. Nothing could be proved, no evidence was found. No doubt he is aware that the eyes of many agencies have been upon him for all this time, but to all appearances, he lives in peaceful retirement in his new home.'

'By "agencies", you mean Mycroft?' Damn: I *knew* this had something to do with the man.

'Keep rowing,' he ordered. 'We don't want them to wonder what topic two apparent strangers find so engrossing. Bad enough that it was you who came after me.'

'You'd have drowned, waiting for the others to make up their minds. Mycroft?'

'I'd have made it eventually. Yes, no doubt La Rocha is on Mycroft's long-term list of interests.'

I thought that Mycroft's interest was more immediate than 'long-term', but prising an admission out of Holmes – since that admission would also mean that Mycroft was ultimately behind my own presence here – might necessitate rowing in circles around *Harlequin* until the new day dawned, and I wanted my bed. Hammock. I went on as if Holmes had readily confessed an active focus from his brother's shadowy agency.

'Is this to do with the missing secretary, Lonnie Johns? Has she been found?'

'A shoe very like hers was found at the top of a cliff near Portsmouth. The other was retrieved from a Jack Russell terrier, well chewed. Police theory being that the woman committed suicide, but that her note had been held down by the shoe the dog removed.'

The shadowy boat before me was replaced by images from a screen: pretty young girl; flowered frock that the wind presses against her lithe form; made-up eyes stretched with sadness; a note, tucked under her shoe; with a last woebegone look around her, her figure is replaced by:

> **I can live no longer,
> please forgive me!**

And then: empty cliff-top; the approach of a small and business-like dog, applying its button nose to the shoe atop the fluttering note . . . I shook the images from my head. 'So what is La Rocha up to?'

'I have no idea.'

'Right.'

'On my honour, Russell, I do not.'

'Then why risk life and limb to race down here? A telegram would have sufficed. Oh, don't tell me you're going all protective on me, Holmes?' Granted, our last case had been rather trying, scattering us across half of Europe as we strained to communicate, but still.

'I thought you might be glad of reinforcements.'

We had come into the edges of the light from the ship, just enough that, by leaning forward, I could make out his features. I stared at his expression, then resumed my rowing before he could scold me. '*You* wanted to get away from Mycroft, too!'

'Shh,' he urged. Pulling the edge of the blanket forward so his face was in shadow, he murmured, 'Is there any language you are certain is not spoken by any of those on board?'

'I haven't tried them all, but I'd guess Hindustani.' And before he could scold me about that as well, I added, 'Yes, guessing is deplorable, I know.'

The shadowed face seemed to fold into a brief smile, and then he sat upright into the lamp-light and said in normal tones and a Midlands accent, 'I have to thank you again, Miss Russell. Quite ridiculous of me to tumble over like that, ought to make the railings tall enough to hold a man instead of tipping him overboard. What if you hadn't been there to see me go?'

'There was a man on watch,' I loudly reassured our Major-General Stanley. 'He tossed you a life-ring, too.'

'Well, I hope you haven't spoilt your lady-like hands on the oars, you really should have let me take them.'

'I didn't want to risk having you over again. Catch that line, would you?'

He caught at it, missed it, nearly fell in again, dropped his blanket in the water, and finally got his fist around the line. By dint of my pushing him from below – a tricky manoeuvre, when braced in a skiff – and others pulling from above, we got the Major-General back on deck.

'Take him to galley,' La Rocha ordered Adam, then to his damp passenger, 'Warm there, you be dry in no time.'

The young pirate led him away; I did not think Holmes' shivers were entirely an act.

The boat was made fast, and La Rocha ordered the sails raised. I wished him a good night and headed below, but his voice stopped me.

'Why you on deck?'

'When he fell, you mean? I was enjoying the quiet – I'm not used to sleeping in a room full of people – and he came up and . . . Well, I thought he was assaulting me, so I . . . I'm afraid I shoved him, and he went overboard. That's why I sort of felt I had to go after him. My fault.'

The pirate king stared at me, then stared at me all over. And he laughed. As if a man making advances on Mary Russell was quite the biggest joke he'd heard in years.

Which was more or less what I'd intended. Still, he didn't have to agree with quite so much gusto. Feeling very cross, I went down the stairs and, instead of going directly to my bunk, went to the galley instead. I thrust my head inside, to find my husband and partner arranging his wet garments over various chair backs. Adam was with him; both men looked up.

'From now on, you keep your hands to yourself!' I stormed. 'Next time I'll use a belaying pin, and let you drown!'

The young man looked startled, but Holmes' face ran a quick gamut of surprise, disapproval and distaste, before he pasted on an expression of sheepishness for the benefit of La Rocha's man.

I'd had to let him know what explanation I'd given for our little adventure. I dimly recognised that saddling him with a reputation for lechery – a reputation he would find repugnant every time he was forced to uphold it – was a displaced revenge on his brother. However, I will admit that the thought of it was a small warm satisfaction, nestled to me as I drifted off in my canvas sling.

Where I slept peacefully, until the screams started.

CHAPTER TWENTY-SEVEN

MAJOR-GENERAL: In fact, when I know what is meant by
'mamelon' and 'ravelin',
When I can tell at sight a Mauser rifle
from a javelin . . .

I SHOT UPRIGHT in my hammock, instantly flipped over, and by
dint of hanging on hard to the canvas, managed to describe
a complete circuit before crashing dramatically to the floor. The
hold seemed to be populated by dangling pupae with startled
faces, but everyone else managed to remain in their canvas, and
no-one appeared to be writhing in agony or fighting off an attack.
I snatched my glasses from the nearby shelf and looked again. No:
The noise was coming from above.

Grabbing my dressing-gown from the laden row of hooks, I tied
the belt while hurrying up the companionway towards the thin
dawn light. When I stepped out on the deck, I knew I was still
dreaming.

The last time I'd seen Captain La Rocha, near midnight, he'd
been dressed in a pair of striped pyjamas and a dark dressing-gown

– extraordinary in their unexpected ordinariness. Now . . .

Either our captain had decided to immerse himself wholeheartedly in his assigned rôle, or I had knocked myself cold falling from the hammock.

His hat was scarlet. From it danced an emerald ostrich plume the length of my arm. His jacket was brocade, orange and red, over a gold waistcoat, burgundy trousers, and knee-high boots a musketeer would have killed for, also scarlet. His small earring had doubled in size overnight, and half a dozen fingers bore rings – gold rings, with faceted gems. The henna in his beard gleamed red in the sunlight.

The only missing details were an eye patch, a peg-leg, and a parrot.

'Good-morning, Miss Russell,' his incongruous voice piped. 'Meet Rosie.'

He tipped his face upwards. I, too, lifted my eyes to the rigging, then lifted them some more, wondering what female on board the ship would dare to clamber the lines. Surely Edith wouldn't have – then the scream came again, and I saw its source.

A parrot.

I felt someone beside me and looked over, then down. Randolph Fflytte, who for the first time looked almost nondescript in a violet dressing gown, was rubbing his eyes.

'This is your fault,' I said bitterly.

His eyes caught on La Rocha and went wide. His jaw made a few fish-like motions; at Rosie's next shriek, it dropped entirely. He stood gaping at the bird, who screamed its challenge at the rising sun, then turned to me. 'I never,' he declared.

'You wanted a pirate,' I told him. 'You got one.'

'Jaizus' came Will's voice in my ear, 'he's even put up a pirate flag!'

He was right. A skull and crossbones taller than a man rippled in the bow breeze, flashing its grin at the pirate, the parrot and those of us along for the ride. The Jolly Roger, a declaration that no quarter would be given. The voice of the Byron-loving Miss Sim seemed to thrill in my ear: *These are our realms, no limits to their sway – / Our flag the scepter all who meet obey.*

'Is that legal?' It was a woman's voice – Mrs Hatley, sounding disapproving. I had to agree: Surely maritime laws frowned on such frivolities as pirate flags?

The rising sun touched the top of the mast, exciting our avian alarm. It flapped its brilliant wings and shouted something in response.

'What did it say?' someone asked.

'Probably Portuguese,' came an answer.

'Not Portuguese,' said a man – our pirate crew was now awake, too, and clearly as astonished by La Rocha's antics as the English passengers.

The bird screamed again, and I blinked as the sign-board appeared before my mind's eye:

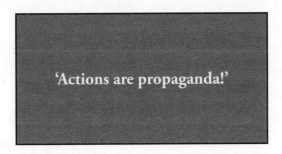

'Actions are propaganda!'

I repeated it aloud.

Fflytte said, 'What the devil does that mean?'

'I don't know, but that's what it said.'

'She's right,' said Will.

Three dozen people in various stages of undress, and one

pirate in extraordinary dress, stood agog, awaiting the next pronouncement. The bird gazed down at its audience.

'Destroy the state!' it shouted.

'Those are Anarchist slogans!' I said. 'It must have belonged to Anarchists.'

Our necks were growing stiff, but we listened, wrapt, for the next pronouncement. What came was a long garble of apparent nonsense. We looked at each other. 'Did you catch that?'

It was Annie who ventured a translation. '"I think that I shall never see a poem as lovely as a tree"?'

Followed the sound of forty-some people puzzling.

Clearly, I had knocked myself unconscious.

I waited in vain for an awakening hand on my shoulder, but with reluctance decided that I was not lying stunned. I went below with the others, some of whom attempted a return to sleep, but I had smelt the coffee and got dressed instead, to join the first seating at Maurice's breakfast, questions at the ready. Annie was there, looking remarkably chipper after a night dangling above the floor, and was already grilling Adam about the newest member of our crew.

The parrot – a scarlet macaw – had been a last-minute addition: La Rocha's idea, Mr Pessoa's find. Its cage had been brought on board under heavy shrouds, that the creature might wake to a new day in a new home, undistracted by the call of the land.

Its original owner had been a lady much taken by lyric poetry in the English language – Longfellow proved an avian favourite. When she died, the bird took up residence with her grandson, who had flirted with the attractions of Anarchist doctrine from the comfort of his twenty-room estate on the outskirts of Lisbon until his arrest a few months before, followed by the sale of his house, lands, and possessions. The bird had several Portuguese phrases, and a handful in French, German and Spanish, but he – and it was a he, despite the name given him by the old lady, who'd thought it inappropriate for a maiden lady to have a male companion – seemed to prefer English.

A few of his Portuguese utterances, to judge by the reactions of the crew, would have condemned him to his cage – if not to Maurice's pot – had they been in English. When Kate and Linda began to, well, parrot those phrases, I had a word with their mothers.

The political and poetic exhortations would soon become a part of the background noise of the ship, punctuating the sounds of sail and rigging, hull and voice. At least while the bird was talking, it did not emit those blood-curdling screams.

Piecing together this narrative took our allotted breakfast time, was continued on the deck, and was still under way when the second seating began to emerge into open air: Annie's questions were occasionally pertinent but often most roundabout, and her dual flirtations with Adam and Bert did not speed the flow of information.

The girls came up, dressed now and exclaiming at the prettiness of the morning. The pirates followed, exchanging glances at the prettiness of the girls. Rosie grumbled and recited from her perch at the captain's left hand, taking the occasional snap at anyone else who ventured within range.

By the time Fflytte came on deck, the bird was taking a nap, the sail-makers were hard at work, the girls were lounging in the sunny spots, and the pirate crew were busy at various tasks (and shooting the girls looks both admiring and disapproving, as the girls shed clothing and lit cigarettes).

Our diminutive leader rubbed his hands together, then frowned at the vast canvas drapes on all surfaces.

'We need this cleared,' Fflytte declared. When the sail-makers continued their needlework, he turned to the quarterdeck and repeated his demand.

'I'd planned on filming some scenes this morning. We need the decks cleared,' he insisted.

'When sail is up, decks will be clear,' La Rocha countered.

'*"Sail on, O Ship of State!"*' Rosie urged.

Samuel said nothing.

'When will that be?'

'*Braak!*' Rosie answered.

La Rocha and Samuel studied the horizon.

'What are we to do in the meantime?' Even Rosie said nothing. 'Captain La Rocha, we had an agreement. We need to do our filming on the way to Morocco.'

'Point camera here,' our pirate chief said, waving a ham-like hand at the quarterdeck. 'No canvas.'

Fflytte squinted at the area in question, and turned to Will. 'Would this be a good time?'

'We'd only use a few feet of film, if we can't shoot the deck as well,' the cameraman replied.

'Captain—' Fflytte began, when La Rocha took pity on him.

'Two hours, maybe little more. Go, look around ship, find places to point camera.'

'I really—'

'Mr Fflytte,' I broke in. 'That might not be a bad idea. If you haven't seen all the nooks and crannies, a tour might give you some interesting angles.'

He thought for a moment, then nodded. 'Very well, we will take a tour of the ship. Will you lead us?' he asked La Rocha.

Samuel had been frowning at a point among the forest of ropes where Adam and Jack were smearing some disgusting-looking grease into the wooden pulleys and all over themselves. Inadvertently, his elbow ventured into Rosie's territory. La Rocha's feathered familiar lunged, but quicker than the eye could follow, the quarterdeck erupted into a flurry of brilliant plumage as Rosie fought the hand wrapped around its throat. La Rocha stepped forward; Samuel let go; Rosie took off. A trail of scarlet and blue feathers traced the outraged bird's path into the heights.

The two men looked at each other; the wind held its breath; the sail-makers' needles held the air; waves held back from lapping our wooden sides. Then La Rocha turned on one shiny red heel, and said to Randolph Fflytte, 'Your "Samuel" will guide you through ship.'

Samuel's normally dead-pan face registered a slight flush. He started to speak, but La Rocha cut him off, in Arabic. '*The* whole *ship, Selim.*'

Personally, I would not have turned my back on a man with that expression on his face (*Selim the Grim*) but La Rocha was made of sterner stuff than I. Either that or he knew just how far he could push his second in command.

Samuel's gaze left the captain's hat, played across the passengers standing motionless about the deck, rested on the two grease-spattered lads (who hastily bent to their work), and then flicked briefly towards the presence that perched above us in the rigging.

He gave a brief nod, as if confirming some private idea, and descended from the quarterdeck, saying 'Come' as he walked past Fflytte and Hale, leading the way to the bow. They followed Samuel; after a moment, I followed them; Annie and Edith came, too; soon half the ship's population was gathered to hear Samuel's voice.

Samuel waited for us to go still – or as still as one can go on a moving deck. Then, with a final dark glance at the quarterdeck, he faced the open sea and pointed. 'Bowsprit,' he said. His forefinger went up. 'Outer jib.' The finger dropped a few degrees. 'Inner jib. Fore stays'l.'

And so he went. We learnt what the lashings around the anchors were called (in English, to my surprise and relief) and which neat coil of rope was connected to which sail, and whether it was a halyard or a sheet; where the upper topsail ended and the topgallant began; the various staysails as opposed to the jibs. Or rather, we heard the labels recited. It was as if Samuel had been assigned the job of naming every minute portion of the ship – but naming alone. He would occasionally answer a direct question, if it reached him in a pause between recitations, but for the most part, he was a dictionary rather than an encyclopaedia. When Bibi asked why the sail was called 'square' when it was a rectangle (in fact, they were trapezoidal), he simply looked through her and went on.

Most of the others went back to their sunbathing and cigarettes before we progressed twenty feet down the port side. Fflytte and Hale were looking stunned, Will ignored the lecture entirely, Edith developed a dangerous fascination for the knots holding the various lines in place, and Annie most helpfully kept pulling the child's exploring fingers away from the belaying pins. Daniel Marks and Bibi seemed transfixed by the reflections in Samuel's black boots.

Halfway down the side, only two of the audience were paying attention. Jack was one, the young pirate focussed on every label, every brief explanation, his lips in constant motion as he either tried to guess the name before Samuel could say it, or repeated the name under his breath once it was given.

The other attentive one was me.

I can't say that it mattered in the least whether the bundle of rope before me was a sheet or a clewline, or if pulling on it raised the third sail of the fore mast (the fore-upper-topsail-halyard) or adjusted the angle of its yard (the fore-upper-topsail-brace), since I had no intention of running the ship myself. However, it was a mental challenge, along the lines of mastering basic Arabic in a month or committing to memory the by-ways of London. And Samuel's whole attitude was that of a gauntlet thrown: *None of you landsmen will be able to follow this, but I've been ordered to give it to you, and by God I will.*

So I paid attention.

I admit that at first I cheated, writing down key words to reinforce their place in my mind. But once I had the patterns (clewlines and buntlines, halyards and braces, each going higher up the mast as we went aft) it became easier. Of course, my brain felt as if it were about to explode long before we went down the steps (companionway) and past the kitchen (galley) to the orlop deck, but it was all there, neatly catalogued and waiting for the next time I found myself on a brigantine.

Finally, at the nethermost reaches of the ship, Samuel came to a halt. Some ninety minutes had gone by. Jack was not far from tears, Fflytte looked bored out of his skull, Hale and Will had slipped away somewhere around the middle of the second level below decks, and Annie acted as if she had weights attached to both ankles. God only knew where Edith had got to.

Our sadistic guide held up the oil lamp with which he had ill-lit our way, and announced, 'Is all.'

Fflytte seized his hand, thanked him vigorously, and fled. Jack thumbed his forelock and trudged back to his grease pot. The big man looked at the two young women he'd been left with, and for the first time, permitted a grimace to cross his face.

'I waste my time,' he said.

Annie protested, so weakly she might have been agreeing, but I decided there was no harm in letting him know that his efforts had not been entirely in vain.

'Not at all,' I assured him. 'It's extremely helpful to have a clearer idea of how all those bits tie together.'

'Yes?' he said, disbelief clear in his voice and stance. 'Then what you call this?'

He kicked his boot (for the first time, not so shiny) against a piece of wood that I probably could have guessed had I never set foot on a sailing ship.

'That's the mast – the mainmast,' I told him.

'That?' he said, indicating a lump of wood and metal.

'A knee.'

After the third such easily named object, it occurred to him that these would be fresh in my mind. Without a word, he pushed past and clumped up the ladder, restoring the lamp to its hook.

Without a word, he pointed to a triangular scrap of canvas overhead.

'That's the main topmast stays'l,' I told him. 'That's the mains'l throat halyard. Fore t'gallant brace. Port deadeyes. Catharpins. Snatch block.' This went on for two or three minutes, attracting rather more attention than I had intended. I was considering allowing a few mistakes to creep in, just to take the eyes off us, when Samuel made a noise I would not have thought possible from him. He laughed. Then his hand slammed down on my back, nearly shooting me off the deck and causing my spine to tingle from toes to jaw-line.

He turned to the quarterdeck, where Rosie had resumed his perch and La Rocha, unable to hear our voices, was watching intently.

'I have parrot, too!' Samuel shouted at La Rocha, then asked me, 'You maybe want to learn how they work?' A jab of the thumb upwards indicated that the lessons would not be given on deck. My heart instantly climbed up my throat.

'Er, perhaps tomorrow?' I said. There was no way in which my brain would accept further information, especially over the internal screams of terror.

His hard palm came down on the top of my head and rumpled my hair as if I were a small child. '*My* parrot,' Samuel repeated, and strode back to the quarterdeck, humour restored.

Chapter Twenty-Eight

[GIRLS and MAJOR-GENERAL go up rocks, while PIRATES indulge in a wild dance of delight on stage.]

ONE OF THE bits of actual information Samuel had let drop was that a brigantine this size would originally have held up to a hundred crew members – numbers necessary less for running the ship, I thought, than for manning the cannon and adding heft to boarding parties. Currently, we had something over half that original number, but even that was proving a trial. When it had rained our first afternoon out and the girls retreated below, the ship rang with spats and squabbles. With the main portion of deck off-limits under canvas, our choices were below decks, or on each other's toes.

Finally, at mid-day, the sail-makers reached the end of their labours, and began to arrange huge armfuls of canvas at the foot of the aft mast. One of them reached into the apparently featureless expanse of cotton and pulled out a tie, dragging it to the upper spar (which, I knew now, was called the 'gaff') and attaching it, followed by a string of like attachments, to the length of the gaff. Once the sail's upper-most side was firmly linked, the gaff was raised a bit, and the forward edge of the sail was tied to a series of wooden hoops that circled the mast like a giant's game of ring-toss. The gaff was occasionally raised a little more, freeing the next hoops. Eventually, the lower edge of the sail was uncovered enough to fasten to the big lower spar, the boom (named, perhaps, for the final sensation of the incautious sailor whose skull it hits). When it was tightly fitted, and the upper corner of the gaff portion had been made taut, the crew went below. They came up with hands clean, hair-combed, and dressed for the first time in piratical attire – Will's pleas to film the event having nicely coincided with La Rocha's own sense of the dramatic.

We mere passengers stood back, out of the way of sailors and cameras. Samuel's voice rang out, and the crew jumped to seize the big halyards on both sides of the ship. They hauled, and hauled, and *Harlequin*'s mainsail began to rise, transmuting from a puddle of canvas to a living thing. Up it went, deck to masthead, lashings tight, lines passing through blocks in a bewildering zigzag of rigging. When it was stretched to its fullest height, the crew gave a few almighty heaves to tighten the gaff, and made haste to tie off the halyards and loop the ends across their pins.

The sail above us luffed lazily in the slight breeze, then found its angle and began to fill.

Cheers rang out. The parrot took to the air, circling the masts before coming back to its perch near the wheel, to flap its wings energetically and declare, "*Wandered lonely as a cloud!*" Samuel scowled at it; Will filmed it; La Rocha fed it a piece of biscuit. The ship gave a small shiver, and bent more fully into the wind. I do not know if *Harlequin* felt happier, but I know the rest of us did.

Particularly the two sail-makers, whose hands were worn raw with their efforts.

The crew tied off the lines in neat array, looking a touch self-conscious in their raggedy costumes. Will folded away his camera. La Rocha stroked his reddened beard and ordered a tot of rum all around. I smeared salve on the sail-makers' hands and told them thank you in Portuguese and English. Maurice appeared with a cake. And when Frederic then conjured up a gramophone, a dance commenced.

Since I had returned the Major-General to safety, some eighteen hours earlier, Holmes and I had taken pains to avoid each other, limiting our communication to the occasional courteous remark. Now, with music going and thirty people bouncing about, he contrived to be standing beside me.

He tipped his hat with his free hand and feigned a sip of the poisonous rum that he had been nursing for the past ten minutes. He wasted no time getting to the point.

'Who do you make for the villain of the piece?' he said, to all appearances making a comment on the weather.

With the same polite expression on my own features, I replied, '*Is* there a villain in the piece?'

'Sure to be, with those two in charge.'

'Which two – La Rocha and Samuel, or Fflytte and Hale?'

'The Englishmen are paying the bills, but do you honestly imagine they're in charge?'

My response was delayed by our police sergeant, Vincent Paul (an Englishman with a French name and an Irish accent) who stood before me and asked if I would care to dance. A response was obviated by Holmes setting down his glass and saying, 'A major-general outranks a sergeant, my good sir,' as he seized me in his arms.

Fortunately, the tune to which the others were gyrating and leaping, although it seemed to have no tempo at all, could be interpreted as 3/4 time, making a waltz possible: A waltz permits conversation; Charleston and fox-trot do not. And due to the layout of the deck, with raised housing that forced a rotation of couples along the rails (other than those dancing atop the sky-light, who risked being swept off by the boom if we had to tack), few of the couples were in a position to overhear more than a few words at any given time.

'Tell me about this Pessoa chap,' Holmes demanded.

Distilling the character of Fernando Pessoa into the duration of one recording disk was no simple matter, but I fed him a brief synopsis, from Pessoa's translation skills to the poetry journal; his appealing humour and dubious grasp on reality; his erotic fascination for pirates and the multiple personas he had crafted; how he had led us to La Rocha and to *Harlequin*. 'And as you heard, he knew where La Rocha could buy a parrot, one that had been owned by an Anarchist.'

'You suggest Pessoa is himself an Anarchist?'

'He's definitely anarchic, but his politics could be anything, depending on which "heteronym" is in supremacy at the moment. I'd say his "Ricardo Reis" persona lacks the drive and dissatisfaction for Anarchy, although "Álvaro de Campos" might perform an anarchic act if he felt it emotionally justified. I don't know about—'

But the music ended, and before the next recording could be wound up, the police sergeant was there, awaiting his turn. And I had little choice but to permit him the closeness of the waltz, since to all intents he was less of a stranger than the Major-General was. However, I took care to tread on his toes several times, which left him more than willing to relinquish me to Holmes.

When the music started up, my husband-cum-suitor swung me onto the impromptu dance floor and continued where we had left off. 'Do you know how long Pessoa has used the name "Ricardo Reis"?'

'Some years, I should say. Why?'

'There's a Lisboan embezzler named Artur Reis who's clever enough to be planning a crime that's visible only in bits, such as transferring guns from prop cabinets into private hands, or finding a use for a bit of extra cocaine. I wondered perhaps if the name might be a poet's homage to a criminal.'

'Reis is a common enough name in Portugal.'

'True.'

'It means "captain" in Arabic.'

'And several of the Barbary pirates were called that – Murad Reis, one of the most vicious of the Salé Rovers. He started out as a Dutch merchant marine, named . . . Jan Jansen, that's it. He was the one who sailed into St Michael's Mount and seized a ship-load of captives, then later did the same on the west of Ireland. And Dragul Reis, who served with the Barbarossa brothers towards the end of the Barbary kingdoms – he died in fifteen fifty-something.' Holmes, clearly, had taken the opportunity to raid a book-store before boarding his own steamer. But the mention of Barbarossa reminded me—

'Do you think La Rocha's new red beard is a bow to the Barbarossa brothers?'

'More likely that than an homage to the Holy Roman Emperor,' he replied. 'But to suggest that Pessoa is to Reis as La Rocha is to Barbarossa seems to invite unnecessary convolutions into the matter.'

Since my mind was still struggling to untangle itself from the morning's terminological convolutions, and since the record would only last another minute or so, I hastened to get him up to date on what I knew about the others as well.

It's remarkable how much a person can say in two minutes, particularly when speaking to an ear as familiar with nuance as the one that lay inches from my lips. I took care to maintain an expression of courteous disinterest on my face, but by the song's end, I had managed to convey to Holmes the central points of my past two weeks.

When the music ceased its bawling from the metal trumpet, my husband stood away and, as the Major-General, gave me a slight bow. One of the police constables came to me next, but I claimed fatigue and stood to one side for the next few numbers, looking with care at my companions.

Bibi made a brazen approach to the quarterdeck to venture a flirtatious overture to, of all people, Samuel. The big man cast a sideways and clearly amused glance at La Rocha, then looked back at her and slowly gave a single shake of his head. The young woman voiced an unconcerned laugh, as if to say she had only been playing with him (How long was it since Bibi had been turned down, I wondered?) and flounced down the steps, chewing her gum all the while, to seize Adam away from Annie. Annie glowered as she watched them start the next dance.

Hmm: Annie and Adam.

Mrs Hatley, Edith's mother and our Ruth-the-incompetent-piratical-nursemaid, was dancing with the police sergeant, although neither seemed particularly taken with the procedure, spending most of their time watching those around them. Daniel Marks was ignoring the glances of the girls currently unclaimed, preferring to stand beside the pirates Benjamin and Jack. Marks and Benjamin were opposite sides of the coin of masculine beauty, one fair and tall, the other dark and lithe. Marks laughed at something Jack said – here was one pirate with enough English to communicate a joke.

Edith had shaken off her mother's urging towards the younger pirates to form a trio of the younger girls, elbows and heels flapping the air in time to the music. Will Currie had stashed his equipment and film below, since the lack of cohesive costuming here made film pointless. Now he tapped the second-smallest girl, Kate, on the shoulder, and when she turned to see, he bowed and held out a hand. She glanced uncertainly at her chaperone sister (on the sidelines talking to June's mother) for permission. When it was given, Kate turned her back on Edith and June and began to dance with Will, tentatively at first, then with more confidence as he encouraged her with avuncular dignity.

Then the music changed, to a true waltz. Some of the couples drifted apart, but Bibi dug her fingers into Adam, Will adopted a formal posture with Kate (who came up to his shoulder), and Edith, after a glance towards the waiting pirates, stepped forward and set her hands on June's waist and shoulder. Why not?

Holmes had been trapped by Isabel's mother. She was a woman of forty whose stays were well exercised by a figure best described as 'lush'. From her coy attitude towards my husband, I saw that she had caught word of the Major-General's purported lechery and intended to make the most of it.

Holmes' face was priceless, keen with interest on the surface, alive with apprehension underneath. The crowded shipboard conditions proved a distinct advantage for those desirous of chaperones, but the crowding brought disadvantages as well, making it impossible to get away from a determined female. As they circled about, I took pity on Holmes and made a quick jerk of the chin. His eyes registered a flash of relief, but he continued the dance without interruption.

Moving around the edges of the merry-makers, I glanced upward, and with a cold sensation realised that Samuel was watching me. Had he seen my gesture to Holmes? Would it have betrayed us as being too familiar for the communication between strangers?

I could not risk giving myself away: This was one tight place Holmes would have to get out of on his own.

Before the Major-General could shed his admirer and work himself around to me, I shifted past some bouncing couples to boost myself onto the railings beside the one pirate who seemed perennially shy and retiring, the one who rarely took off his hat even below decks, the one who looked out of place in that crew.

The one who resembled a Swedish accountant.

I swung my legs and nodded to the music and said without looking at him, 'Don't pretend that you don't speak English.'

It took him a while to decide what to do. Then he said, 'Very well.'

'What is your name?'

'Gröhe.'

'Why did you come back, after Mr Fflytte had said he didn't want you?'

'I . . . Mr . . . *Captain* La Rocha needed me to come to Morocco with them. This was the most easy way.' His English was adequate, the accent beneath it Turkish with a hint of his German heritage below that.

'Why does La Rocha need you?'

'Odd to say, I am his book-keeper.'

I looked at him, eyebrows raised. 'So Mr Fflytte wasn't far off, at that.'

Gröhe smiled wanly. 'No.'

'I don't understand why Mr La Rocha needs a book-keeper in

Morocco,' I said, taking care not to come across as an interrogator, merely a curious if sharp-eyed assistant.

But it was a question he clearly did not care to answer, saying weakly, 'He often requires a book-keeper.'

'But I thought he was a semi-retired fisherman?'

The pasty face turned even paler; the narrow throat swallowed; the eyes darted around in search of rescue. 'I'm . . . it's a family matter. I, that is, I couldn't afford to get to Morocco on my own, but I have family there, and Captain La Rocha said, he thought if I took this job . . .'

I'd known we would soon be interrupted, but Gröhe didn't feel Samuel's approach until a big hand clapped onto his shoulder, at which time he gave a shrill cry remarkably like mine the night before.

Samuel left his hand where it was and leant past the small man, baring his teeth in a grin that contained none of his earlier affection towards his human parrot. 'What you asking my friend, here, Miss Russell?'

I raised a face of good-natured innocence. 'I recognised this gentleman from the day Mr Fflytte asked him to leave. I wondered why he hadn't gone.'

I kept the expression raised like a mask, kept my feet casually swinging, although I could feel the rapid beat of my heart and wanted nothing more than to flee from those black eyes. They bore into me, and after a minute, I permitted myself – permitted my character, Miss Russell the assistant – to frown a little. 'Is there something wrong?'

'You can tell me that, I think.'

'Well, if you mean am I going to report it to Mr Hale, no, I hadn't intended to. I mean, what could he do, throw the poor fellow overboard? As far as I can see, there's little harm done. However, perhaps he shouldn't collect any more pay packets from Fflytte Films.' I pronounced the last sentence like a chiding schoolteacher. Then I waited, hoping his ears wouldn't pick up the pounding of my heart over the music.

Samuel's eyes slid shut in a slow blink, then he was looking at the book-keeper and I was breathing again. He spoke, and Mr Gröhe tugged at his hat and scurried away, below decks. Then Samuel turned back to me.

'You will not tell Mr Fflytte and Mr Hale about this.'

I decided that Miss Russell had taken enough. I tipped my head to the side, frowning. 'You know, that sounded suspiciously like a command. I'm going to assume it is a problem with your English and not that you imagine me to be one of your employees. I told you I did not intend to expose your Mr Gröhe. But I'll admit that if you try to bully me about it, I'll be tempted.'

His eyes went even darker; the fingers of my left hand crept towards the blade in my boot-top.

And then he smiled. In amusement and appreciation, as if I'd done something just adorable. He stretched out the hand that had dug into Gröhe's shoulder and patted my cheek, then turned on his heel and passed through the revolving couples to the quarterdeck.

Furious and perplexed, I realised that we'd had an audience for the tail end of our meeting. Annie stood nearby, watching Samuel's retreat. Behind her I spotted Holmes, alert to the tension and oblivious of the demands of the dance.

'Did you want something?' I snapped at the girl. (Silly, really, to call Annie a girl – she was older than I was, no matter what she claimed.)

'Oh! Sorry. It's just, well, some of us were just wondering how long we're going to be at sea, but there's something rather intimidating about the quarterdeck, isn't there, even though it's only a couple of steps above the rest. And when I saw Mr Samuel come down I thought I might ask, only he seemed somewhat . . . preoccupied.'

I pulled myself together and shot Holmes a glance while summoning a rueful laugh for Annie's benefit. 'He's a strange one, isn't he? Touchy.'

'Oh, isn't he just? At first one thinks Mr La Rocha the more terrifying of the two, but then Samuel will snap at one of the men over something and one feels oneself sneaking off like a scolded kitten.'

Annie had more intelligence in her than those wide blue eyes and ripe-cherry mouth suggested. I turned the talk to the approximate length of journey ahead of us, and from there to supplies, and then to Maurice's cooking.

But my mind was holding up Samuel's words to Gröhe, examining them, considering.

Samuel had spoken in Arabic, a language I understood well enough: *If you don't want me to feed you to the fish*, he had said, *you will disappear until we hit land.*

The party showed all signs of continuing until luncheon, and no doubt after that, Fflytte would claim the deck and all actors for his purposes. If Holmes and I were to finish our conversation, we had to be out of earshot for longer than three minutes at a time.

The only way I could think of required steeling my nerves and donning an additional layer of clothing. And if I found the below-decks deserted, as I expected I would, I could take the opportunity for a bit of snooping.

But as I made my way to the common cabin, I was surprised to hear voices from below – surely everyone was on deck except Mr Gröhe? And Maurice, of course, at work transforming inadequacy into magnificence. But this was a woman's voice, answered by a child: Aha, Edith and her mother, Mrs Nunnally.

I pressed my ear against the cabin door. What was the woman doing? Edith's whines of complaint were punctuated by sharp exclamations of discomfort: 'Ow! I wasn't doing anything, I was just dancing like Mrs Grimley taught—Ouch!'

'I *told* you to take care, that we didn't have a chance to do this yesterday and that if anyone came too close – stand still!'

Edith's voice kept whining, until I could not stand it. Yes, the child had made my life a trial, but there was no cause to mistreat her. I lifted the iron latch and stepped inside. I am not sure what I expected to see, but it was not what lay before me.

Mrs Nunnally was bent over Edith's face, the customary below-decks gloom brightened by the light from a small lamp. She whirled, and I looked in confusion at the object in her hands. A pair of tweezers. What . . . ?

She dropped the implement into a pocket and presented me with a wide and utterly artificial smile. 'We were just finishing up here, I noticed that my Edith had neglected to keep her eyebrows neat, and there's nothing Mr Fflytte dislikes more than—'

I looked around her at the child, whose cheeks gave clear evidence that the tweezers-work had not been above the eyes. Many things about my tom-boyish admirer fell into place.

'Perhaps I should call you Eddie?' I asked.

CHAPTER TWENTY-NINE

SERGEANT: With stealthy step the pirates are approaching.

'Oh please, miss,
have mercy on us!'

THE WOMAN BURST into tears and threw herself on my mercy and at my feet, but as she pleaded and tried to explain, all I could think was, why had it taken me so long to recognise a child of changed gender? Heaven knows I'd dressed in boys' clothing often enough myself.

I pushed the dreary female to one side and dropped to my heels before Edith. 'Do you want to continue on this picture?' I asked her – or, him.

He nodded. I could see a couple of dark hairs Mrs Nunnally had missed, where this adolescent chick was beginning to fledge. It explained the sudden height gain as well.

'If I let you stay on, you have to promise me: no more pranks. No more cutting June's hair or gluing together the pages of Celeste's romantic novels or putting push-pins through the soles of Linda's shoes. No more torturing the others, or me. Absolutely none. Or I tell Mr Hale, who will send you home instantly. Agreed?'

The pretty blonde head jerked vigorously up and down. I held the child's eyes long enough to be sure he meant it – and long enough for him to know that I did, too.

God knew where Fflytte Films would find another blonde child at this late date. And Edith was going to have a tough enough time concealing all that sprouting pubescence by the time filming ended next month.

It was not really my problem.

I fetched my jumper and went back up on deck.

Holmes was dancing – still, or again – with his buxom admirer, and I thought it would not be long before his desperation began to show to the others. I pulled on the woollen garment and set my fingers into the rope ladder – no, call it by name: the ratlines of the fore shrouds.

I had seen the men climbing often enough to know it was not only possible, but possible to do it with equanimity. The first few hemp rungs were easy; then the ship rolled to the side I was occupying, and I knew instantly, without a doubt, that the entire vessel – deck, rigging, French cook, and parrot – was about to tip over and come down on top of me, smashing me into the surface of the sea.

I clung, whimpered, and waited to die.

And after a minor eternity, the ship's roll slowed, and paused, then returned the way it had come. The angle of the shrouds returned to the oblique, the mast ceased to loom above me, the rope ladder I clung to stopped sagging and went firm again. I could not move, but I could breathe. When the ship rolled back again, I was ready for it; I ignored the looming mast, the sag of the shrouds, waiting for *Harlequin's* pause. When her mast swung back away from me, I managed to climb three whole hempen rungs before feeling her collapse again onto me.

It was inelegant, and a sailor would have been laughed off the ship, but I climbed.

At the lower yard – the top of the lowest sail – I made the mistake of looking down. I probably whimpered again, although I could not hear myself over the wind. My insouciant air became a great deal more difficult to maintain after that, even though I had seen Holmes' head near the base of the mast and knew it would not be long before he found excuse to join me in the heights. I resolutely turned my gaze upwards, to where the mast tapered into nothingness. And, more encouragingly, to where a simulacrum of solidity awaited me.

Just above my head was the tops, what I would previously have called a crow's nest – or parrot's nest – with a bit of a hole in the bottom next to the mast that had lines passing through it. I wriggled in beside the lines, knowing full well that using this 'lubber's hole' was scorned as cowardly. Inside the tops, I let go a deep breath, profoundly grateful for the faint sense of protection imparted by the shrouds around me and the wood beneath me. This was quite far enough, to escape inquisitive ears. The protection was spurious, the deck's mild sway giving way to a sense that I was about to be violently flung through the air. I wrapped both hands around nearby ropes, hoping with some small part of my mind that from below, my appearance would preserve some vague attitude of nonchalance rather than appear what it was: a landlubber clinging for dear life.

Rosie came to see what I was up to. I was grateful that she – he – took up a position ten feet down the yard, rather than directly overhead.

A cough came from below. Without loosing my fists, I leant a fraction forward, far enough to see the crown of Holmes' head. I tried to move clear of the hole, but my hands would not obey.

However, to my surprise, he appeared, not from the hole at my feet, but among the lines at the outer edges of the platform, clambering the shrouds with the ease of a monkey.

'Show-off,' I muttered.

'If you shift a bit to the right, I can get past you,' he suggested.

'I don't think I can move,' I informed him. The wind, non-existent fifty feet below, snatched the words from my mouth and threw them towards the African coastline.

'Try.' He waited, to all appearances oblivious to the wind's attempts to slap him from his perch, for the several minutes it took me to commit my weight a few inches to the right. Then he swung a long leg around the shrouds and dropped in beside me with nothing but the fingers of his right hand to hold him in place.

There were times when I came near to hating the man I had married. 'Don't tell me: You spent two years before the mast when you were a lad.'

'Only eight months. When I was twenty.'

'I think I'd prefer sea-sickness.'

'Yes, I'd noticed you seem remarkably free of the affliction here.'

I groaned.

'What did our Mr Samuel have to say?'

With an effort, I recalled that earlier sense of threat, and told Holmes about the conversation.

'Interesting,' he remarked. At some point while I'd been talking, he had looped his arm through a rope and was picking at a frayed place on his shoe. I shuddered, and squinted at the distant horizon. 'You've told me about your Mr Pessoa, and I have a basic picture of Fflytte and Hale. Perhaps you'd give me your opinion of any others who have made an impression upon your mind.'

'You probably did not receive my third letter?' I said. 'Then I shall start with William Currie, the cameraman. He's been with Fflytte since the very beginning, including the War years. An intelligent man and a likeable rogue. Although I'd say that, despite his popularity, he keeps himself to himself. Unlike his bosses.' I reviewed for him my points of interest from the missing letter: June's mother working for Fflytte Films in 1909; June's birth in 1910; June's sharing of Hale's colouration; Hale and Mrs Hatley's ship-board conversation that ended with a slap.

'Unlikely to be blackmail,' he said.

'I agree, plus they act like old . . . well, perhaps not friends. Acquaintances. Although I can't decide if Hale doesn't realise June may be his, or if he knows and they're all just very casual about it.'

'With stage people – or in this case, cinema folk – it could easily be the latter. Have you uncovered the process by which this production came into being?'

'What do you mean?' A question I always disliked having to ask Holmes.

'Oh, surely—'

'Let's leave out the rebukes, Holmes. Just tell me what you're getting at.'

'If we are to solve the disappearance of Lonnie Johns, and prevent some hypothetical further crime, it might help to know what the end point of this elaborate project is to be. Other than a cinema adventure.'

I clung and I pondered, then shook my head. 'I still would not wager that there is any further crime in the offing here, Holmes.'

'With La Rocha and Selim involved?' he scoffed.

'Oh, I agree those two have something in the works, I meant on the part of Fflytte Films – which is where I was brought in, if you remember. The criminality of our pirate crew could be nothing more than two men following the scent of money: Randolph Fflytte walks into Lisbon and starts littering the streets with pounds sterling; he's practically begging to be taken advantage of.' What was the Portuguese for *to fleece*? Or the Arabic?

'So the ship, the men, the smooth arrangement under the nose of the Englishmen,' he said. 'You suggest that all that is mere opportunism?'

'Look at the sequence: Geoffrey Hale hires Pessoa; Pessoa introduces Fflytte to La Rocha; La Rocha sees a man with far more money than sense; he uses his authority on the Lisbon waterfront to bully the *Harlequin*'s owner to sell it cheap to Fflytte, arranging that all the paperwork is ready to go when Fflytte walks up. No doubt La Rocha also received a slice of the takings from the ship chandlers, the sail-makers, and everyone else along the line. Just as he'll have claimed a percentage from the pay packets of the crew we hired – and got free passage for any of his men headed for Morocco.

'In fact, even if the men have different accents, it wouldn't surprise me if all of them were headed home. What would you wager that if we told them in Arabic to see the bird, every pirate on the ship would look up?

'And,' I added as I mentally sorted through our large collection of troubling details, 'Hale told me about something odd that

262

happened the other day. After the first filming, one of the pirate crew – Jack, the second youngest – started to say something about practice not mattering because they weren't going to – but before he could complete the sentence, Samuel smacked him down. Although that might only mean that the crew don't intend to bother finishing the picture because they're just here for a ride to Morocco.'

Holmes was shaking his head before I finished. He protested, 'Never have I known those begging a free ride to be so industrious.'

I added, 'When they are accumulating generous pay packets in the meantime?'

It was Holmes' turn to ponder, a juncture at which, had we not been in a young gale and surrounded by tar-soaked rope and dry canvas, he might have brought out his pipe. I shifted, to keep my backside from going numb against the wood, and allowed my gaze to go down. The sails beneath me were pregnant with wind, a vista of living cloth. It would have been quite beautiful, had I been able to see past the terror. Holmes finally said, 'It is a poor fit. Sixteen pay packets is petty crime, for those two.'

'Portugal doesn't have a lot of ready cash lying around, just at the moment. And – wait.' A thought was tapping at the back of my mind, a faint thought, pressing to get through. What . . .

He was still talking. 'However, if this is but the tip of an iceberg, if what we are seeing is the Moroccan equivalent of the Italian criminal syndicate currently taking such a firm hold in America, thanks to their Prohibition – the Brotherhood of the *Jolie Rouge*, shall we say, along the lines of the Red Circle—'

And then I had it. I broke into his monologue, smiling for the first time since laying my hand on the ratline. 'The paint! Holmes, when I first saw her, I noticed that Harlequin's name was the only relatively intact paint in sight. One could even see the ghost of a former name. Which I think was "*Henry Morgan*".'

'The privateer.'

'What if this ship actually belonged to La Rocha all along? What if it's a nice simple swindle: La Rocha finds a rich victim, sells him a ship under another name so it doesn't look suspicious when La Rocha takes charge of fixing the old tub up, tricking his mark into spending money right and left to refit her? I was impressed by how fast they laid their hands on sails that fit, used riggings that were precisely what was needed. Even the oars.'

'Sweeps,' he corrected me absently, chewing on his lip.

I leant forward, an angle that would have been impossible five minutes earlier. 'I know you'd prefer to find that La Rocha has woven an elaborate tapestry of crime, but isn't it more likely he's just grabbing at passing opportunities? Nine years ago, with the Turkish gold: Did he actually plan the theft? Or did he simply catch its scent and reach for it?'

'Your theory being that there is nothing to the sale of guns and drugs? That Lestrade has a bee in his bonnet? That the death of Lonnie Johns – the apparent death – was the suicide it appears?'

'Not necessarily. I'm merely suggesting that the one has nothing to do with the other.'

'Coincidence?' He pronounced the word with distaste.

'Co-existence, say. A man with a history of felonies would readily seize the chance to commit another.'

'Which brings us back around to the question: Which man?'

'I do not know. But I believe we will have at least a couple of weeks to figure it out: Hale doesn't distribute the final pay cheques until the picture is in the can.'

He said nothing, thoughtfully, just looked downwards. 'Perhaps we ought to descend and continue our investigations.'

'I'm not sure I can.'

He ignored me, and instead wondered aloud, 'How are we to explain our prolonged conversation up here, before they come to see?'

I put my head beside his, looking down the long stretch of mast to the deck below. Annie and Edith were peering up the mast in curiosity; any moment now, one or both would scramble up like a monkey. I peeled a hand recklessly from its iron grip and waved to the pair of faces, letting them know I was coming down. Then I forced my feet to inch towards the access hole.

'I came up for the curiosity,' I told Holmes. 'You followed to flirt with me. However, from this height, I think I should not risk another hard slap.'

'I would appreciate that,' he answered.

CHAPTER THIRTY

KATE: Let us compromise
    (Our hearts are not of leather):
    Let us shut our eyes,
    And talk about the weather.

AFTER THE MORNING'S larking about, the afternoon was all work. Lunch was a brisk affair, although tasty. Once the plates were cleared, the pirates were all carried off by Fflytte and set before the critical eye and deft brush of Maude, the make-up woman.

One might have imagined she wanted to dress them in lace and silk stockings.

They would not have it – or rather, those who initially had no objection to paint were brought to task by those who ridiculed and refused. Had Maude, a no-nonsense Yorkshirewoman, been a man, our pirates might well have broken her fingers.

She protested. Fflytte protested. Will pointed at the sun and protested. Samuel and La Rocha had a long and inaudible argument on the quarterdeck, at the end of which Samuel descended to deck level and planted his reshined boots in front of Maude. She had to clamber on top of the sky-light to reach, but – brave woman – she applied her brushes to his stormy face without hesitation. The pirate crew looked on in appalled silence.

Kohl and rouge installed on that fierce countenance, Samuel stood back, and raised one eyebrow at his men, daring them to smirk.

They dared not.

After that, one by one, the pirates submitted to Maude's attentions, gathering self-consciously to chuckle at each other's outlined eyes and rouged lips. When she was finished, Maude looked up at La Rocha – and packed away her paints.

The Pirates of Penzance takes place entirely on land. Initially, Fflytte's *Pirate King* had been designed with minor variations on that theme, with a few ship-board scenes to link together those in Portugal (which appeared to be standing in for the original's Penzance) and in Morocco (which had no place whatsoever in the minds of Gilbert or Sullivan).

However, that plan went out the port-hole the instant Randolph Fflytte fell under *Harlequin*'s spell. Instead, Lisbon and Rabat would act as book-ends for the substance of the tale in the middle – which would draw heavily on Fflytte Films' reputation ('Fflyttes of the Faraway!') for sea-going authenticity. Will had already shot two reels of shipboard life, from the meaty hands of the sail-makers to Rosie on the yard-arm. Now we had three hours of strong daylight left in which to record some of the actual story.

Hale had put me in charge of ensuring that the clothing and appearance of the girls and Daniel Marks matched how they had looked at the Moorish Castle's 'pond', since this ship-board portion would follow immediately on the heels of that bucolic and flower-bedecked scene, and the Major-General's thirteen daughters would have had no chance to return home and pack their bags before being gently abducted by the appreciative bachelor (and, being orphans, lonely) pirates.

I went through the girls with my notes, confiscating various brooches and hair-pins, exchanging two pairs of shoes to their correct feet, plucking one feather out of Ruth's hat (which only had five in Cintra) and collecting seven bracelets, three necklaces, five colourful sashes, and one pair of spectacles. Ten of the girls I had scrub kohl from their eyes; six of them I ordered to spit wads of chewing gum over the side.

When the pirates were painted and the girls restored, Fflytte clambered onto the sky-light with his megaphone.

And the first hitch came up.

La Rocha was an essential part of the story, and hence of the filming process. But he stuck fast to his position: Unless we were to furl all the sails and reduce the rigging to bare yards and empty lines (which would leave us insufficiently photogenic) we required a person of authority on the quarterdeck.

Samuel went to talk to him, and another ten minutes went by. The previous bonhomie between captain and lieutenant seemed to be wearing thin, although Samuel made no overt sign of rebellion or even disrespect. I caught Holmes' eye, and knew that he, too, was wishing their conversation could be overheard by someone more sensible than the parrot. Eventually, it was decided that our spare pirate (no sign of Gröhe) with Maurice and the two sail-makers to back him up (heaven forbid we should make use of the seven surplus women on board) might be installed at the wheel, the four men between them being judged capable of keeping us from sinking or sailing off the edge of the world. Fflytte put the megaphone to his lips. Will bent to the camera. Rosie dove out of the rigging to attack the plumage on Ruth's hat.

Mrs Hatley screamed, Will cursed, Fflytte shouted, and eventually La Rocha ordered his bird away. To everyone's astonishment, the creature obeyed. Rosie took up a position on the port-side ratlines, there to mutter a Greek chorus of imprecations and Anarchist phrases.

Megaphone up; slate poised; Will's eye to the camera; Harriet shrieked and leapt atop the sky-light, sending the megaphone flying and nearly the man holding it. Harriet's twin admirers, Irving and Kermit, leapt to her rescue, although it took a good minute for her words to become comprehensible: She had seen a rat.

I shouted her down, before panic could seize our little project and all the girls leap for the life-boats. 'It was a mouse, only a mouse! Haven't you seen Lawrence's pet mouse? It was only Lawrence's pet.'

It had, in fact, been a rat. The accused pirate reached into his pocket to prove the innocence of his small passenger, but Samuel proved himself as quick mentally as he was physically. He growled to the lad, in Portuguese.

Lawrence stared up at the big first-mate, yanked his hand out free (fortunately, *sans* mouse), and nodded his head vigorously. 'Yes yes, Miss Mouse gone for a walk, so sorry, she very nice, no scare.'

Samuel bent to retrieve the megaphone, handed it to Fflytte, and fixed Harriet with a gaze of utter authority. 'Mouse small, very clean. You play with her later, yes?'

Harriet swallowed, herself as mesmerised as a mouse facing a snake. She nodded, and Samuel held up a hand to assist her descent to the deck.

The other girls patted her. With a shiver, she returned to her assigned place, keeping one keen eye on the aft hatch where she'd seen the dread creature. The megaphone went up again.

And this time: 'Camera!'

The scene played out nicely, the girls and the pirates acting together on film for the first time. I held my breath at the moment where Frederic had to lunge out from the centre of the pirate mob, since, according to Hale, most of the rehearsals here had ended either in a fall or a fist fight. But it went beautifully, with Adam and Francis shifting at precisely the right moment, and Fflytte's amplified prompts more by way of encouragement than command.

Will's arm turned the crank with its mechanical precision; Rosie kept to the heights; the pirates even remembered not to stare at the camera and nudge each other with their elbows; and after the requisite performances, Fflytte called, 'And, cut! That was mostly fine, but let's see if we can get a little more swagger into your walk, men.'

Protest, at which Hale reminded them that sometimes (usually) a scene had to be repeated (several times) and that a ninety-minute picture took rather more than ninety minutes to make. Then he had to explain what *swagger* meant. After which the next take was cut thirty seconds into it when the men's exaggerated sway of the hip and shoulders made them look like male courtesans, or perhaps victims of St Vitus' Dance. Four tries later, Fflytte called 'Cut' and decided that he would go on to the next scene, which had been transplanted from the original's sea-side setting, with the girls plus Frederic, to the ship's deck and the entire cast.

Now, girls and pirates alike were required to make innocent and blatantly oblivious conversation about the weather while permitting Frederic and Mabel to bill and coo. The difficulty of ship-board privacy having been forcefully brought home to me, I watched this scene with fascination.

Various gazes wandered in the direction of the young lovers, but then, they did in the opera as well. Bibi as a shy and virginal Mabel was only slightly more believable than Daniel Marks' manly wooing, but they were actors, and got the job done.

Fflytte decided he wanted a second version with more specific interaction in the background: Ginger and Gerald admiring a particularly fine knot; Adam and Annie together at the rail (Bert didn't even scowl – he was a more experienced actor than I'd realised); Henry and Harriet ('*I* go with her,' Irving declared; '*Me*,' claimed Kermit; 'Henry!' bellowed Fflytte through his megaphone, setting every ear to ringing) would stand and point back at the stern.

I hoped no skilled lip-readers would be seeing this picture in the theatres, because some of the conversation was wildly inappropriate to the setting, but it looked good, and the assigned couples balanced nicely – until suddenly La Rocha stood away from the shrouds where he'd been told to lean ('Like a proud parent,' Fflytte had instructed, with the retort, 'Proud, of these?') and barked out a phrase.

Instantly, the scene flew to pieces. Girls dropped from supporting arms, girls fluttered their eyelashes at nothing, and in two cases, girls were knocked to the boards by sailors leaping to obey their captain.

The entire enterprise nearly came to an abrupt end then and there, saved by Samuel – who noticed that, although Will had hastened to grab his camera to safety, Randolph Fflytte was still standing on the sky-light, thus for once of a height to be endangered by the swinging mainsail boom. Samuel's solution was once again startlingly direct and effective: He knocked Fflytte's feet out from under him. The megaphone flew overboard. When Fflytte had his breath back, he began to shout at La Rocha, who – fortunately – did not have a belaying pin or marlinspike to hand.

I had not noticed the shift of wind that required a tack, but La Rocha had. When the manoeuvre was finished and the lines stowed again, when the pirates were back and the loops of rope restored to their exact positions, when Jack's lost hat was replaced by a reasonable facsimile, we set up camera and director, fashioned a substitute megaphone out of one of Maurice's baking tins, and continued.

Finally, Will called matters to a halt, saying that the light was going. Fflytte protested, but Will was firm that any more film through the camera would be film wasted.

The entire ship gave a great stretch of the limbs and drew a breath of relief.

And then looked around for entertainment.

In a flash, Bibi, Bonnie and Ginger vanished and reappeared in swimming costumes, dancing about on the foredeck for a moment to tuck their hair into caps, then over the side they went. The wind had already died down considerably, but Samuel ordered the sails furled, sent David into the shrouds as watchman, and had one of the skiffs put out, just in case. There were volunteers aplenty for manning the oars: Adam won the honour. He was soon surrounded by half a dozen water nymphs cavorting in the calm ocean. The other pirates found tasks that kept them in the front half of the ship, and cast envious glances at Rosie, who sidled out on the bowsprit to crane his head at the girls.

Maurice appeared with a pair of fishing rods, thrusting one of them at Hale and attempting to give the other to Bert-the-Constable. However, Bert had other ideas, and passed it to Vincent-Paul-the-Sergeant before stripping down to his trousers and diving over the side, surfacing midway between Annie and Jack. Annie was treading water to talk to Adam-at-the-oars, while Jack was attempting to talk Edith into fetching 'her' swimming costume and coming in. Edith looked enviously at Lawrence – dangling upside-down from the martingale stays, his head plunging in and out of the water with each swell – but had enough sense not to risk the inevitable exposure of a skimpy and waterlogged costume. Jack splashed Bert, in an effort to tempt Edith in; Bert swam circles around Jack; Daniel Marks dove expertly in and came up to swim circles around Jack in the opposite direction; Mrs Hatley appeared in a startlingly revealing costume and stuck close to Daniel Marks; handsome dark Benjamin arranged to fall in from his task at the bow and, when there was no furious protest from the quarterdeck (where Samuel watched closely, but did not move to intervene), he urged shy Celeste to venture down the ladder, daringly leaving her spectacles above.

Randolph Fflytte and Will Currie stood with their heads together, debating whether or not to film the activity.

Geoffrey Hale, meanwhile, settled atop the bulwarks with his pole. Collar open, face going pink with the day's sun, mind far away, the man looked at ease for the first time since I'd met him. I simply could not envision him as a seller of illicit firearms and cocaine. Nor could I see him carrying out the cold-blooded murder of a young female assistant. Still, he had seen long years of active and bloody duty on the Front. And I have been wrong before.

The water around our bow boiled with activity, as if a school of small fish were being driven to the surface by deep and unseen hungers below.

Jack was the first to emerge, clambering up the rope ladder, blind to the disappointment he brought to an apprentice pirate and a constable. Edith was pleased to see him, however, and the two were soon immersed in the intricacies of knot-tying, as the young pirate showed the Major-General's daughter how to construct a perfect monkey's paw.

Dusk drew near, giving Adam an excuse to row after Annie and Bert, who had contrived to fall behind the slowly moving *Harlequin*. Annie's shrieks of laughter at being hauled aboard the little boat rang across the intervening water, and although she was shivering when she came on deck, her eyes shone with the pleasure of having admirers.

Appetites were hearty for Maurice's dinner. Afterwards, the gramophone was brought out again, and lamps were lit, and we danced beneath the stars.

It is, as one can see, impossible to keep much hidden in a universe 150 feet long and 23 feet wide. One need only keep one's ears and eyes open, to overt behaviour and to nuance, for much to be revealed.

The problem being, it works both ways, making it necessary to construct a believable reason for such questions as: Why did Miss Russell climb a mast for a lengthy conversation with a gent she barely knew – and whom she had nearly drowned at first meeting?

Yet another story-within-a-story, with the only possible script being: A haughty young woman encounters, rejects, and ultimately is won over by a most unlikely man. *The Taming of the Shrew*, with pirates. And considering that with my trousers, hair-cut, and spectacles I might at first glance be taken for a man, and that Holmes was nearly thrice my age and already established on board as a lecher, the only way to construct the play was as a comedy.

Which placed us in the awkward position of being two married people engaged in a prolonged and very public flirtation, while three score of onlookers sniggered behind their hands at the unlikely pairing. At least our audience cooperated – egged us on, as they thought – by granting us a few square feet of privacy during our tête-à-têtes.

I had to be grateful this voyage was only 350 miles; had we been crossing the Atlantic, we'd have either had to stand before La Rocha while he performed an on-board marriage, or beside him while he performed at-sea burial services for a series of shroud-wrapped fellow passengers. Probably both.

Setting aside the burden of this exquisitely uncomfortable wooing performance, and its unfortunate effect on Holmes' blood-pressure, the round-the-clock ship-board intimacy provided wide opportunity for a reverse espionage: While Holmes and I enacted a stage comedy at our end, we could also watch a series of other performances unfold among those who considered themselves our audience.

For example, I should never have come to realise Geoffrey Hale's simmering resentments and irritations with Fflytte were it not for this continuous close surveillance. As it was, the entire ship heard him shout, 'Oh for God's sake, can you talk of nothing but this damnable film!' one night from the tiny cabin the partners shared. And I feel certain that the reaction of my fellow passengers was the same as mine: *Of course he cannot; why would you even ask?*

The next day, Hale's usual long-suffering amiability was back in place, but once the slip had been given voice, it was difficult for him to disguise further small ventings of frustration as the good-humoured grumbles they had seemed before.

Further reasons to appreciate the brevity of our voyage cropped up almost hourly. I noticed that wherever Annie was, Adam-the-Pirate and Bert-the-Constable would often drift over to stand, listening casually. Although I'd caught the occasional flash of wit sullying Annie's big blue eyes, and although she seemed to treat Bert with a sister's dismissal, Adam's attentions made her go all fluttery and girlish. Even though she had to be five years older than he.

Taking this to an extreme, Mrs Hatley seemed to be rehearsing her part of Ruth-the-Nursemaid even during her hours of rest, making much of Daniel Marks, our Frederic, patting his hair, adjusting his coat, laughing at his jokes.

Frederic seemed oblivious, because his eyes were usually on the beautiful young pirate Benjamin.

Benjamin's beautiful eyes, however, followed Celeste.

And Celeste often looked back at him.

The older girls alternated their flirtations between the pirates and the constables, stirring the antagonism between the picture's enemies. Two of the pirates were old enough to interest the mothers, who took to powder and paint (often lopsided, thanks to poor lighting and the ship's motions).

One of those was Mrs Nunnally, whose preoccupation with the middle-aged pirate David freed young Edith to cultivate a friendship with Jack. Edith was happy to find someone with whom 'she' could hunker on the decks with dice or a pen-knife.

Among the pirates I slowly became aware of some facts. I knew that La Rocha, Samuel – Selim – and Gröhe all spoke Arabic, although with a different accent from what I had learnt in Palestine. Over the next days, despite Samuel's constant presence that had the sailors guarding their tongues and their actions, several of the men let slip a word here, a phrase there, betraying their knowledge of the language. Adam and Jack were the first two I overheard, followed by Benjamin, then Earnest.

And not only linguistic clues emerged: On our third morning, Adam spotted Annie in conversation with one of the constables (not, as symmetry might suggest, 'Alan', but her other attendant, Bert) and he took objection. Shouting soon escalated to jostling, but to my surprise, Annie did not perform the requisite girlish mock-protest that serves to feed tensions to the point of open violence. Rather, she shoved herself in between the two young cockerels. With her there, no punches could be thrown, and in a flash others had intervened to separate the would-be combatants.

I watched closely as Adam slid his knife back into its hiding place – then Samuel had the young pirate's collar in his fist, to drag the lad off to the side and give him hell and a couple of hard shakes. When he let go, Adam staggered against the railings. Samuel snapped out a harsh order and pointed at a bucket with a frayed rope tied to its mended bail.

He was setting Adam to scrubbing the deck, on his knees, with a brush. The young man, face red and stormy, snatched up the bucket, upturned it so that a brush fell out, then dropped the pail over the side to fill it with sea water. As he stomped past Jack, the pail sloshing furiously, Jack reached out a comforting hand; Adam threw it off with a snarl. The younger lad shot a covert look at the quarterdeck, saw with relief that Samuel's back was to him, then walked away towards the bowsprit, looking bereft at the rejection of his friend.

As I thought over the motions, the postures of long familiarity between the two, an odd notion took root in my mind: Perhaps Adam and Jack were *familiar* in more than the abstract? If one looked closely and discounted the difference in years, one might say there was a degree of resemblance between them.

Almost the resemblance of brothers.

CHAPTER THIRTY-ONE

GIRLS: Piracy their dreadful trade is –
Nice companions for young ladies!

As GEOFFREY HALE's assistant, one of my tasks was to ensure that the crew remained more or less content, letting the film go ahead without disruption. As *Harlequin* worked her way southwards, with fifty-two individuals spanning the variations of age, background, interest and gender, keeping everyone placid proved an increasing problem. My only reassurance was that, given the tight quarters, all these burgeoning relationships – both affectionate and war-like – would find consummation difficult until we had made landfall.

The changing tide from the quarterdeck was most worrying of all.

Before leaving Lisbon, La Rocha's attitude towards Fflytte and Hale had been condescending but amiable: Apart from the one uncomfortable outburst in the first hour, La Rocha had listened

279

politely to the requests and demands of his English employer, albeit with the amused eyebrow of an expert faced with the enthusiasms of an amateur.

The farther south we went, however, the further Fflytte and Hale were demoted towards the ranks of the actors. Fflytte seemed to have forgotten that La Rocha had come inches from killing him with the belaying pin. Instead, when not actively engaged in filming, our director either ignored the quarterdeck entirely, as if having that portion of the ship – *his* ship – forbidden to him was no more unusual or irritating than being barred from the parrot's perch atop the mainmast, or else he approached that *sanctum sanctorum* with bows and scrapes, to ask our captain's thoughts on some twist of the picture's plot, to enquire of Samuel what the function of that line there might be.

Holmes and I were not the only wooing being done on *Harlequin*, not by a long shot.

Hale approached the demotion of Englishmen by going quiet. He watched the captain and his lieutenant as they came and went, studied their interactions with the crew, and rarely spoke directly to them. He stopped what he was doing whenever Fflytte approached the ship's masters (which was rarely when they were on the quarterdeck), and frowned at his cousin's subservient posturings.

He did not have to say aloud what he was thinking: *Why is the ship's owner given no say in the running of his vessel?* One might imagine that La Rocha not only ran, but owned *Harlequin*.

The thought went far to explain Hale's outburst during the night.

As we neared the coast of Africa, the attitude of the two pirates shifted from patronising to near-scornful. And not just La Rocha and Samuel – I noticed Adam turning away from Fflytte with a faint sneer; later that day, young Jack did the same.

It was worrying.

It would have been positively alarming had the pirates demonstrated the same low-grade aggression towards the girls. But towards all of us women, they held an air of distracted kindliness, as if we were pretty toys who were not to be played with too energetically. An attitude I found personally infuriating, but it was preferable to most of the alternatives.

That last afternoon at sea, Holmes and I managed another brief conversation without having to perch fifty feet in the air. The coast of Morocco was approaching, and all those not actively engaged in running the ship were gathered along the port-bow to watch. So long as we kept our voices low and our expressions those of two people murmuring sweet nothings at one another, we should be all right: there were no port-holes underneath us, and not even Samuel or Annie, between them omnipresent on board, could come upon us from seaward.

We sat shoulder to shoulder on the starboard rail; there was no need to feign my welcome of his physical proximity.

'They're up to something,' I said, fluttering my eyelashes.

'La Rocha and Samuel, with Adam, Benjamin and Earnest,' he replied with a smile.

'And Jack.'

'Adam's younger brother.' He said it as if it were obvious, although he couldn't have figured it out much before I had.

'Samuel's sons, you think, rather than La Rocha's?'

'Adam looks more like Samuel than Jack does, but they all have much the same accent. However, I agree, they're probably both Samuel's.'

'Gröhe must know as well. If it was so urgent they had to sneak him in under our noses, he has to have some purpose. But what?'

'Were I to venture a prediction,' he said calmly (heaven forbid he should be caught out in a guess), 'I'd say we're about to be kidnapped.'

A cold finger ran down my spine: Robinson Crusoe had it easy, when it came to piratic captivity. 'There are some real horror stories about Moroccan prisons.'

'This is 1924, not 1624,' he said, without a trace of doubt in his voice. Which made me lean into him a touch more, in gratitude. 'And although La Rocha is unstable and capricious, I'd say he lacks the mental pathology needed to put a collection of blonde girls into chains.'

'I'm not sure I'd say the same about Samuel.' I gave a shy duck of the head, for the sake of our onlookers – which, considering our topic of conversation, felt even more lunatic than usual.

'Were Samuel in charge, Russell, I should be worried indeed. But La Rocha will take care to leave us in cotton wool, for the time being. Don't worry, holding captives for ransom is a common enough occupation here.'

'Is it?'

'Oh yes. Sir Harry Maclean, who later became the Sultan's commander-in-chief, was held ransom for a time. Twenty thousand, I believe they got for him.'

'Francs?'

'Pounds.'

'Ouch. I can't see anyone parting with that much for this lot in a hurry.' I thought of having to spend months locked up in the company of Bibi and Annie and Edith . . . 'What do you think about taking the ship?'

He smiled – his own smile, not the smarm of the Major-General. 'Have I mentioned recently, Russell, that I find your confidence anodyne to an old man's doubts?'

I snorted. 'The day you doubt yourself is the day I sprout wings and fly with Rosie. You and I could take the ship if we wanted.'

'Not by direct action.'

'We can't put the others at risk, I agree, even though low cunning outdoes open warfare any day. Still, two against sixteen . . .'

'Three if—'

He bit off what he had been about to say, and I turned to him a face that, had anyone been nearby, would have cast our affectionate act into serious doubt. 'Let me guess: You were going to tell me that Mycroft has a man on board.'

'I think he may.'

'So why didn't he tell you?' I demanded.

'Kindly don't look so murderous, Russell, we're supposed to be love-making here. That's better, if a trifle sickly. He didn't tell me because I haven't talked with him.'

'You haven't—' I closed my mouth, pushed away from the railing, and stalked across to the other side, staring unseeing towards the brown line across the horizon. When I went back to him, land was a mile closer and things were somewhat clearer. 'You didn't actually say that you came to escape Mycroft. He never got to Sussex, did he? There were no builders in. Yet he made arrangements for you to come here?'

'My brother may not be aware that he made the arrangements. He kept sending messages to say he'd been delayed, that he would arrive the next day. I thought nothing of it – I've had sufficient experience with British builders to expect that any dealings with them will go awry – but when I received your letter on Wednesday and telephoned to his flat, there was no answer. The building's concierge said he'd been gone for days. I don't know where he is or what he's up to, but I didn't want to wait for him. I forged a document and commandeered his resources.'

How jolly: another warrant for our arrest.

'But you agree that he has a man here?' I asked.

'I'd say the machinations for your getting on board were too complex for Scotland Yard. They carry the aroma of Mycroft.'

'Well, his agent is unlikely to be one of the pirates, since La Rocha brought them. And the film-crew have mostly been with Fflytte for a while. That leaves the constables, of whom Clarence and Donald are regulars. What about Alan? He has the watchful air of one of Mycroft's men.'

'Even if all four of the remaining constables are with us, there are too many innocents standing in the way of harm.'

Plus, La Rocha and Samuel had no small degree of low cunning themselves. And more ruthlessness than either Holmes or I could summon.

'Are you suggesting that we let them continue with their kidnapping?'

'I think it would be more dangerous to move against them now, when they are clearly braced for challenge, than later when they feel secure at their success.'

'Holmes, I hope you know what you're doing.'

'If nothing else,' he mused, 'it will be a novel experience. I have been abducted before, but never within the setting of a Gilbert & Sullivan play.'

I considered our situation, and was hit by a thought that made me chuckle.

Holmes looked at me sideways. 'I should be glad to hear any aspect of the situation that is merely humorous.'

'A moving picture based on a story of fictional pirates taken over by real ones, and the picture itself hires false pirates to play pirates, who turn out to be real? Fernando Pessoa would die with happiness.'

* * *

We, however, in the absence of our walking conundrum and translator, could only wait with interest for the announcement of our abduction to be made. The handful of pirates that we had decided were in on the plot became ever more tense as the coastline grew before us. The girls began to bubble with the thrill of the adventure. The rest of the pirates happily demonstrated their skills in the rigging to the girls below and to the other ships in the vicinity. The tan horizon line became a shaped coast with long white breakers and a tight collection of stone walls and flat rooftops.

No announcement was made.

We came within shelling range of the city, then rifle shot, then bow-shot, without being informed that we were prisoners.

Finally, the water curling back from our hull took on a tinge of brown, from the waters of the Bou Regreg river that divided bustling modern Rabat on the south from the enclosed and xenophobic Moslem Salé to the north. In its heyday, the river had provided a neat refuge for shallow pirate hulls, while keeping at a distance the deeper draughts of the royal navy. Over the generations, the river had silted up, permitting the passage of small fishing boats and ferries – until the French occupation began, and improvements were made.

The French and English Governments would no doubt be thrilled to learn that their European modernisation schemes had enabled the latest generation of Salé pirates to bring thirty-four European prisoners up to the city gates in modesty and ease.

BOOK THREE

In the Kingdom of Bou Regreg

November 27-30, 1924

CHAPTER THIRTY-TWO

PIRATES: So stealthily the pirate creeps,
        While all the household soundly sleeps.

MEANTIME, THE STEADY *breeze serenely blew / And fast and falcon-like the vessel flew...*

Morocco grew near. The girls grew more excited. Holmes and I grew tense with waiting. The odour of sea and ship changed to dust and donkeys, but no word was said of our change in status from film-crew to hostages.

The closest we came to a formal announcement was the look of hard triumph La Rocha shot towards Samuel when the *Harlequin's* anchor rattled down.

That, and the cock-a-whoop yells of the two boys, both of them up in the rigging and thus temporarily clear of their father's admonitory fist.

Anchor down, sails furled – and the whimsical pirate flag long stowed away – I wondered yet again if we were making a terrible mistake. Morocco had risen up against Christians a dozen years earlier. Salé was the country's most closed town, mistrusting of foreigners, with a long history of encouraging pirates.

It did not help that the view in front of us was dominated by a cemetery. Ochre city walls rose up on both banks of the blue-brown river, wrapping a town of pale buildings, domes and minarets on the left – Salé – and of tawny colour – Rabat – on the right. Both were attractive enough on their own, pleasingly exotic, and girt by olive and fig trees. However, the ground between the Salé walls and the pounding Atlantic breakers was occupied by the dead, paved over with thousands of tombs and gravestones, pressed against each other like a gorget necklace of the dead around the town.

I seized myself by my own metaphorical collar. *Oh for heaven's sake, Russell, don't be ridiculous. This is Gilbert & Sullivan, not Fritz Lang.* 'Weary Death' could surely have no place beneath this gorgeous sun and those white, curling waves.

Boats had already begun to approach, a veritable queue of brightly painted waterborne taxis coming to gather us away. Such efficiency was unexpected, but I refused to find it ominous. Holmes and I exchanged an eloquent glance, then I allowed myself to be shepherded with the rest of the women-folk, piled into the boats, and rowed ashore.

The girls were thrilled by the whole enterprise, and although some of the maternal chaperones seemed taken aback at their surroundings, none of them thought it odd that no European figures waited to greet us, just as once on *terra firma*, none remarked on the sensation of enclosure. I looked at the city gate, and saw a gaping mouth. They looked at the city beyond it, and saw a great adventure. The palm-trees were exciting, the donkeys charming, the men in night-shirts and turbans amusing. They even interpreted the large armed men at our sides as servants – although one had only to follow the direction of the men's gazes to see that they were watching us, not watching out for us.

Every step, every turn, made me less pleased with our decision. But short of digging in my heels and forcing open confrontation here and now, it was too late. We were inside the city; soon, we were inside our prison.

I had thought my companions giddy as we were closely escorted through the narrow labyrinth of the town, zigging and zagging past weavers of mats and sellers of leather slippers, sidling around lengths of embroidery thread strung between a tailor and his child, admiring the heaps of red onions and trays of flat bread and buckets of glistening olives and heaps of fly-specked sweets, breathing in the odours of cardamom and chilli and leather and wet plaster and *kif*, ducking under the hairy goatskins of a water-carrier and exchanging curious glances with women covered head to toe in ash-coloured drapes, passing under the reed-thatching that turned the streets into mysteriously dim tunnels and by a hundred heavy nailed doors and house-fronts, their few windows high above street-level. The town struck me as relatively quiet, as bazaars go, but it thrilled the girls. However, their excitement as they walked, and the difficulty of keeping them from straying, was nothing compared to their reaction once they were ushered into the place that was to be our prison.

Their cries of astonishment would have drowned out Rosie.

Even I had to admit that as gaols went, it would be difficult to imagine one more comfortable. The word *sumptuous* came to mind.

Arabic architecture turns its back on the world, to create a cool and cloistered universe inside each set of walls. I was standing in a tiled garden. The house rose on three sides, layers of galleried passages that gave both a sense of intimacy and a plenitude of fresh air. Three levels up, a honeycomb of silvery wood turned the sky into blue tessellations, mirroring the fine blue-and-white designs beneath my feet.

The gallery railings were bleached by time, the complex amethyst and vermilion designs on the ceilings had sheltered generations of inhabitants, the gilding was a faded glory, all the more pleasing for its age. Over the intricately carved double doors leading into the house itself, mother-of-pearl inlays teased the eye inside.

The mosaic paving stones of the courtyard climbed up along the sides to form tiled benches scattered with rich cushions, and at the back into a splashing fountain surrounded by garden – this style of house, *riyad*, means 'garden'. A pair of lemon trees were espaliered against the courtyard's fourth wall, growing tall towards the sky-light; one could smell, if not see, the blossoms. Tiny birds that had been startled by the influx of noise now began to venture from the branches.

A head popped over the carved railing on the first floor, looking down at us: June, who cried, 'The beds are *so* pretty!'

Above her, another head appeared – Kate, adding, 'There's a marble bath in here!'

And at the very top, her face visible through the holes of the wooden roof-grate, was (who else?) Edith: 'There's chairs! On the *roof*!'

At the thought of children on the roof-tiles, all the mothers gave exclamations of dismay and scurried for the stairs, followed less urgently by the others.

I remained in the courtyard. A bird's chirp punctuated the voices of the innocent that were now ringing out from all the nooks and crannies of this open-sided house. Prison? Hah! Holmes and I were mad. We had drastically misread the intentions of La Rocha and his companions. The insane logic of W.S. Gilbert had infiltrated our brains and turned them to blancmange, making us see pretend pirates as real, fictional threats as actual.

It would appear that this entire affair was instead aimed at wringing every last possible franc, pound and *rial* out of Fflytte Films: The cost of hiring the most luxurious available house in Salé; the cost of hiring large and probably unnecessary guards; the price of the luscious odours trickling from a kitchen somewhere in the hidden depths; the cost of the logs stacked high beside the burning fire and the price of the army of cleaning women who had recently got the house ready (carpets still slightly furled at one edge; the faint trace of cleaning fluid beneath the saffron and lemon blossom) and no doubt the repairs to plumbing, wiring and roof that had been tacked onto the rent for our benefit, along with tuning the decorative French spinet piano and replacing the bed-coverings and sprucing up the wall-hangings and . . .

How long before the door-bell rang and the first in an endless stream of carpet-sellers and slipper-makers and *kaftan*-fitters and knick-knack vendors came to ply their wares to the unwary?

Only one way to find out.

I went back to the door and grasped the handle. It did not open. I rattled it a few times, in the event it was simply stuck, and was about to bend to examine the mechanism when it flew in towards me. I gave a wide smile to the two large men standing without, then made to step down into the street.

And they stopped me.

I brushed away the large hand spread out before my face, but the other man moved in front of me as well. Which made for a lot of man in a little doorway.

'I need some items from the shops!' I said, assuming all the effrontery of an English lady. 'Shops, you understand?' Clearly they did not. 'Mercado? Bazaar? *Suq*?' They understood that last, it being Arabic. However, I did not care to reveal that my grasp of that tongue went beyond a handful of words. 'What do you call it – the medina?' I leant forward, touching my fingers to my sternum and speaking as if to a deaf man or an idiot child. '*I* . . . need to *go*—' I directed my fingers in a walking motion, then pointed: '— to the *medina*.'

He shook his head and jabbed his own grubby finger towards the interior of the house. When I did not move, he pointed more emphatically; had I been a man, he would have given me a shove and slammed the door in my face.

Being a good Moslem, however, he hesitated to touch a strange female. That did not mean he was going to let me pass.

Then the marginally smaller of the two spoke up, in the same accented Arabic I had heard on the *Harlequin*. '*You're sure this is not a man?*'

'He *would not make that mistake.*'

'*If she were my sister, I would beat her for wearing those garments.*'

'Don't speak to me in that gibberish,' I snapped, offering up a mental apology to the two cousins who had taught me the glorious language of the *Qur'an* and of Ibn Kaldoun. 'I demand you permit me outside.'

The first man loomed into the threshold, forcing me to move away, then dropped back again to the street and yanked the door shut. I slapped at its solid surface a couple of times for effect, but I had little need of further conversation with the two.

No: not the fevered imagination of a pair of detectives. We were prisoners, in a delicate-looking, highly effective, exotically beautiful, golden cage of a cell.

What an interesting situation.

I spared a moment's thought for Holmes and the others, hoping that the male prisoners would be treated with as much care.

But as things now stood, I was the sole protector of a score of British females, plus Edith.

The most urgent order of business, therefore, was to claim a bed before all the good ones were taken.

A closer look at the house suggested that it was – or, had been – the home of a wealthy Moslem Francophile. In an upstairs storage room were dusty tea-chests filled with the good china, the good linen, and an assortment of Moroccan *galabiyyas*, *kaftans*, wraps, and footwear sufficient for a small village, but underneath the top-dressing of French paintings, French piano, and French side-tables lay the furnishings of a traditional Arab home.

Once I had claimed a bedroom, I snooped through all the other rooms within the fortress-like outer walls. The timber grid covering the inner courtyard was, I was relieved to see, both closely built (its holes would permit the tiny birds to pass, but exclude neighbourhood cats) and sturdy enough to keep a small person – an Edith-sized person, say – from tumbling thirty feet to the tiles. There was even a canvas cover, furled out of the way, designed to exclude rain and keep in warmth. Around this weather-silvered sky-light was a veranda, open to the air and furnished, as Edith had said, with chairs and divans. The roof, too, was walled.

Three of these upper walls were chest high. Two of them looked down over sheer drops to the street, the third onto a heap of rubble where a house once stood, its stones now in the process of being pilfered down to its foundations. The fourth wall, to the west, was higher than my head. It suggested that something lay on the other side.

While the others enthused over the intricate mosaic of domes, minarets, laundry lines, palm-trees, and the pot-plants and divans of neighbouring rooftops, I dragged a bench over to the high wall, chinned myself on the wall-top to peep over – then fell with a squawk when a man on the rooftop twenty feet away snapped a shotgun to his shoulder and pulled the trigger.

Twenty women squealed and clutched each other. They stared, goggle-eyed, at me, sitting at the base of the wall. I stared goggle-eyed back at them, standing in a knot.

'Er,' I said when I found my voice. 'I'd say our neighbour doesn't wish us to look over that wall.'

'Someone *shot* at you!' half a dozen of them exclaimed.

'If he'd been shooting *at* me, he'd have taken a big chunk out of the wall. I'd say it was intended as a warning.'

The mothers gathered their chicks together and clucked their way to the stairs. Annie looked at the high wall, at the bench, and at me.

'Our neighbour has a shotgun?'

'A Purdy, by the look of it.'

She blinked. 'You had time to see the make of gun?'

'I do a bit of shooting.' No point in telling her I'd had a Purdy pointed at me before. No point in telling myself that, either – only time quiets a racing heart, not logic and reassurance. I brushed myself off, and dragged the bench back to where I'd found it.

Still, the fellow's presence confirmed my suspicions: The men's prison was adjoining our own, and care was being taken to ensure we remained apart.

Not enough care, of course – but just as our earlier decision to delay rebellion was tied to the presence of innocents, so now was my ultimate freedom of movement linked to my fellow prisoners. And although the indomitable Mrs Hatley might wrestle her length over one of these walls to be lowered by rope, the more buxom mothers of Isabel and Fannie would never make it.

> In the high chamber of his highest tower
> Sat Conrad, fetter'd in the Pacha's power.

The first muezzin began his sunset call to prayer from a nearby minaret. Fettered in the pirates' power, I propped my arms and chin on the southern wall, listening as other voices joined in from both sides of the river, drowned out regularly by the boom of waves.

This was a quiet, snug little town around my feet. Salé marked the farthest reaches of the Roman Empire – Sala *Colonia* – long before the pirates established their republic. The present rulers, the French, lived mostly in the modern European community, across the river in Rabat. Although Salé's former violent xenophobia had been suppressed by the French, and manacled Christian slaves no longer worked in the gardens and fields, this town kept to itself, thinking its own thoughts behind its pale walls.

There would be no helmeted police constable strolling past on the street below.

This meant that I should have to cultivate an Irregular force from within.

I followed my nose, down the stairs, past the courtyard (tea had been laid out – Moroccan tea, steaming glasses stuffed with mint that instantly transported me back to a goat tent in Palestine – along with trays of sugar cakes and nuts and fruit and crescent-shaped biscuits) and through a sitting-room followed by a dim, heavily draped dining room with a table big enough for us all, past a small office space (no telephone – I would have been astonished to find one) and to a swinging door.

The kitchen was occupied by one woman in simple green Moroccan dress, two young girls similarly robed, and our resident snoop, Annie. Other than Annie's anachronistic frock and uncovered hair, they might have been occupants of a medieval alchemical laboratory, furnished with retorts and alembics. The woman disappeared in an explosion of fragrant steam; the girls took one look at my trousers and short hair and covered their mouths to giggle; Annie gave me a grin.

'Doesn't this smell absolutely fabulous? I've been trying to get them to tell me what it is, but we don't seem to have a language in common.'

The odour spilling out of the pots was, truly, intoxicating. My very soul opened to the spice-laden air, and I found I had moved closer to the cook, to stand within the penumbra of steam. I smiled, to show that I meant no harm.

'Are we to have dinner, then?'

Of course she did not understand, so I handed out another of my miser's stash of Arabic: '*Dinner soon?*'

It took no pretence to stare blankly at the flood of heavily accented Arabic that washed over me, but it seemed to be positive, and I began to leaf through my other languages to ask, '*When?*'

French, of course – although the cook, who had understood the question, spoke little of the tongue, and that mostly monosyllabic. But she got across the answer, which was that dinner would be served in two hours.

Then she made a gesture that clearly invited us to take ourselves away.

Outside, Annie said, 'Well, it's good to know that we don't have to produce our own meals in that kitchen.'

'It is a bit primitive,' I agreed.

'I didn't know you spoke – Arabic, is it?'

'I know about ten words, picked up on a trip to the Holy Land. *Bazaar, dinner, bread, please, thank you,* ma'alesh – which is sort of like, *oh well* – and *How much is it?* I'll need to arrange for a Moroccan Mr Pessoa, to help with trips into the bazaar.'

'Oh good,' she said. 'They've left us some tea. Ooh – mint?'

I drank my syrupy tea and checked on the arrangements for beds. When the door opened an hour later and our trunks and cases were unceremoniously tossed inside, I said nothing to draw attention to the sound that followed: the door being wedged shut from without. When dinner came – magnificent heaps of exotic foods that the cook told us were *couscous* and *tagine* (a rice-like dish, and lamb with dried apricots cooked in a massive low crockery bowl topped by a sort of Chinese hat) with shredded salads and plates of pickles and relishes that had the mothers making dubious noises even as they helped themselves to second servings – I said nothing to dispel their easy assumption that the following evening we would share such foods with the men. And when yawns began to creep in and the women creep away to their richly furnished beds, I wished them sweet dreams, and said not a word about the guards on the door.

Permit them a night's peace, before anxiety moved in.

The room I had claimed as my own was small and dark and although it was clean, it had no decoration on its whitewashed walls. A servant's room, conveniently placed for a shouted summons from one of the ornate bedrooms nearby. A servant's room, with little but a mat and blankets for sleeping. A servant's room, with a window too narrow for most European frames.

All the windows in the house were firmly shuttered, either by decorative wood latticework or, in two of the lower rooms, workaday iron bars installed so recently the black paint was still tacky. This, too, went with the Moslem architecture, and the others did not even question it, since the inner walls were so patently free and open to the lightest breeze.

I dozed, waiting for the household to succumb to sleep before rising from my servant's cot and turning my attentions to the window.

Being on the upper floor, this was a window not formerly barred. The mortar holding the bars was thoroughly set, but not as deep as it might have been on a real window.

And being women, no-one had given us, or our possessions, a more than cursory search.

I divested myself of the hardware I had worn about my person all that day, ending by loosing my trousers and unwinding the length of silk rope that had saved my life more than once over the years (although it did have a way of making me look rather stout). I held a small looking-glass out between the bars to be certain that the street below was empty, then unfolded my pocket-knife to the blade used for prising stones from a horse's hoof, and set to.

By three in the morning, the bars were down.

By five minutes after three, I was dressed head to toe in garments borrowed earlier from the house's lumber-room, my spectacles tucked into a pocket, my face and hands darkened with dust from the window-sill.

By ten after three, I was on the street.

It is one of my favourite sensations, that of stepping out of doors without leave. The very air smells sweeter – as every child knows and most adults forget – whether in London or Morocco. I paused to savour that aroma of freedom. And also to orientate myself in relation to the muted sound of a violin that had begun to play some hours before.

In my borrowed *djellaba*, spectacles off and blonde hair covered, scuffing along in run-down and overly large sandals and with a moon too small and street-lamps too sporadic to give me away, I was taken for a local boy. As I went past our two guards, who spent their night pacing up and down the exposed sides of our prison, I greeted them in an Arabic onto which I had fastened something resembling the local accent. I did the same when I came to the guards outside the men's prison.

'*Good evening*,' I mumbled politely.

'*What are you doing out at this hour?*' the shorter man demanded.

'*My mother needs something from her sister.*' A speech I had prepared earlier, in case.

'*The boy's running errands for his mother,*' he called to the taller guard.

'*Must you listen to that noise all night?*' I asked, with a gesture upwards: Holmes, too, had managed a room over the street, although his window was so narrow as to be impassable.

The man answered with a gutter curse, a new one to me. '*When I go in tomorrow morning, I'm going to put my foot through the accursed thing.*'

'*You will do a service to us all,*' I noted sweetly, and went my way. When the violin came to the end of its song, the music did not resume.

For two hours, I quartered the compact walled city, locating the gates, committing to memory the thoroughfares (some of which were wide enough for a motor car) and the lanes (in which anything but a motorcycle would stick fast). The odours and débris underfoot told me which streets held leather-workers and which sold vegetables, which stalls were coffee-houses and which belonged to barbers. The pound of the sea was the loudest noise I heard, apart from one yowling cat, the clatter of dropped pans from a baker's shop, and a vicious-sounding argument from an upper room between two women in a language I did not know.

Almost the entire time was spent on paving stones where the buildings came near to touching overhead, or where the sky was kept out by reed thatching. At half past five, with the sky growing light and my heart pounding with the conviction that I would not find the correct house in this mole's maze, I succeeded in retracing my steps to my lane, to my rope, and to my window-sill. Inside the servant's cell, I scrubbed off the dirt with a cloth I had wet earlier for that purpose, and set the bars and mortar back into place.

I fell into bed just as the day's first call to prayer rang out, well pleased with my outing.

Chapter Thirty-Three

Girls: At such a time of night as this, so very incompletely dressed . . .

Fortunately, a house full of young women does not wake early. I managed a solid three hours of sleep before the sound of voices roused me, and I dressed – wearing a skirt today – to go downstairs.

A banquet of breads, fruit, various spreads and boiled eggs had been laid out in the courtyard. The air smelt of baking, of oranges, and of fresh-watered soil. The fountain was playing, the small birds dipping in and out.

My companions noticed none of it; clearly, one of them had attempted to leave, and met the same treatment I had the previous afternoon.

I came across the blue-and-white tiles – Miss Mary Russell, the firm's fix-it girl – and they pounced on me, all talking at once.

'We're being held prisoner!'

'Annie felt like going for a walk and—'

'—wanted to see the medina—'

'—see the river—'

'—the market—'

'—tried to go out and these *rude* individuals at the door—'

'—terribly rude, they positively *bullied* her—'

'I'll admit, I did feel more than a little threatened.'

'—no English, of course—'

'What *was* Captain La Rocha thinking, to give us—'

'—none of the servants speaks a *bit* of—'

'—surely someone in this town—'

'—she tried to insist—'

'—*pushed* her, just put his hand—'

'Imagine!'

'—native person, acting like—'

'—really *most* threatening—'

'Miss Russell, you must—'

'—we insist—'

'Please, tell us you'll—'

'—*have* to talk to Mr Fflytte—'

'—have to *do* something—'

I raised one hand. Like a conductor with his orchestra, the chorus of outrage went discordant and trailed away.

'Thank you,' I said. 'I hope you slept well?' The chorus threatened to break out again, so I waved my outstretched palm, and continued, 'I personally did not sleep very well, I suppose the lack of a ship's soothing motion seemed odd, so I should like some coffee before the day gets much further along. However, yes, I am aware that we are not being encouraged to leave here just at present. I shouldn't worry about it if I were you. Mr Fflytte chose to film these portions of the movie in Salé rather than Rabat, for the sake of realism. Had it been Rabat, which has a large European community, you should have been quite secure walking about at all hours. However, Salé is a small town with a high degree of suspicion regarding outsiders. I imagine that Captain La Rocha did not wish us to be made uncomfortable by the attentions and curiosity of the inhabitants. I'm sure that when we go out, he will provide us with bodyguards. In the meantime, you'll have to admit that we are most comfortable here. Now, can anyone tell me, is this coffee as good as it smells?'

My phlegmatic attitude, more than my words, gave my fellow prisoners pause for thought. Twenty pairs of eyes followed me to the richly laden table; twenty pairs of ears heard the ting of silver on porcelain as I stirred in the cream; twenty stomachs decided that they might deign to try one of those croissants and some of that pale butter.

Annie seemed to have got over her affront at being ill-treated by the guards. She loaded a plate and filled a cup with tea, then brought them over to where I was sitting, on the wide decorated edge of the fountain.

'I'm sorry you were frightened,' I told her.

'I was more angry than anything else,' she said. 'And it's frustrating, to not be able to speak to anyone. Even the maid and cooks just stare at one blankly when one asks for another bath-towel.'

'I'd have thought an actress would be skilled at making herself understood.'

'True, but some things are a touch embarrassing. And more complicated forms of communication, such as asking *why* one is not permitted to leave a door, can be difficult.'

'Yes, I'm sure we'll find that this is all merely an oversight on Mr Fflytte's part. Just as he overlooked the problems of arriving on the eve of the Moslem Sabbath.'

'Do you think so?'

I can turn a bland face on anyone short of the Holmes brothers and have it believed. 'What else could it be?' I asked mildly. Before she could answer, I went on. 'I for one intend to make the most of our paid holiday here, and gather the sun's rays on the rooftop. And perhaps I ought to take a glance at those French novels in the sitting-room, before the younger girls spot them.'

I abandoned my empty cup and plate to do as I had announced – and did in the end notice one or two books that might be inappropriate for young girls, although I should have to read them to be certain. I carried them to the rooftop and made a show of setting up for a leisurely day of relaxing in the sun. The others, after some hesitation and grumbling, decided to throw over their complaints and take my lead.

By mid-day, we had a ladies' salon going atop the house. In one corner, Bonnie and Harriet were taking turns translating one of the more innocent French novels aloud to an audience. Some of the mothers had uncovered a supply of embroidery floss and were teaching two of the girls (who in the normal course of events would have nothing to do with needlework) to pick out a design, an experience that became more enticing when I descended to the kitchen, figured out (using gestures and raised eyebrows) which of the inhabitants had been responsible for some of the towelwork, and dragged her up to demonstrate Moroccan designs. Celeste and Ginger were to be in a stage-play when we returned to England and were helping each other with their lines; Edith was teaching Kate and June how to whittle; and Fannie and Linda, looking like a pair of schoolgirls, were playing a cut-throat game of *chemin de fer*.

Several times during the day I wandered down to the kitchen, hoping, if not to find fodder for a band of Irregulars, at least to forge some kind of relationship with the ladies there. Each time, either Annie was already in residence (scrubbing vegetables and stirring pots and laughing merrily at the impossibility of communication while creating a language of hand gestures and facial expressions) or she would appear a few minutes later. In the end, I abandoned the kitchen to her. Which was probably for the best, since she seemed less likely than I to burn down the house or be the cause of an epidemic of food-poisoning.

Lunch was brought to the rooftop, served to us like a picnic without the champagne or the ants. Afterwards, Doris excused herself to go wash her hair, and when she came back up, she carried the looking-glass from her bedroom wall, that she might better primp and admire the fall of her thick, wavy locks. One glance, and six of the others rushed for the stairs; soon, our tiled picnic grounds more resembled a boudoir.

When the two kitchen girls climbed the stairs with a tray of mint tea, shortly after the mid-afternoon chorus of muezzins, they lingered, glancing disapprovingly at the cigarettes but frankly gawping at the sea of yellow hair. Doris spotted the two girls and waved for them to come over. Soon, she had them brushing her hair and giggling behind their hands at the way it sprang back under the comb.

They left, heads together and talking far too quickly for me to follow their exclamations, then returned a few minutes later with a basket full of paraphernalia, followed by the cook.

The cook searched the rooftop of Europeans at play until she spotted me. I did not understand most of her words, but using a handful of French and grabbing my hand for a demonstration, she managed to get across the gist of her message. I explained to the others.

'They're offering to do henna painting on us. See that goo that looks like mud? That's pure henna. When you trickle it onto the skin and let it dry there, it stains intricate patterns. It's not permanent,

307

one scrubs it away after a few days. I've seen it before, done for weddings and such. It's pretty. Anyone interested?'

June jumped forward, but her mother said she could not; as they were arguing over the child's right to be a canvas, Linda stepped up, and Bonnie.

We kept the three ladies of Salé busy for a couple of hours, trickling arabesques of mud onto hands, arms, and ankles. When the trio descended below to their labours, leaving a bevy of Europeans oohing and aahing over the orange-brown tendrils woven over their pale skin, I looked around and was hit by a startling thought: I was in a harem.

And if I stayed here much longer, I should die of boredom.

The weather stayed remarkably warm, considering it was nearly December. The wind died away, permitting us to take our evening meal down in the open courtyard, and if some of the girls and all of the mothers grumbled at the food, which again was spiced and coloured and possessing unrecognisable components from the soup to the dessert, some of us enjoyed it immensely. I polished my plate and sat back, replete.

The courtyard was lit by small lamps, above the table and in the trees; the earlier brilliant crimson sky had given way to a panoply of stars.

'Shall we take our tea on the roof?' someone suggested: I was surprised to find it had been I.

The cook-housekeeper studied our charades of climbing stairs and sipping cups, and nodded her agreement. We gathered armfuls of cushions, and carried them up, and up again, covering every surface with padding. We lay there with tea and coffee, the lamps shut down, and counted stars.

A short time later, the violin started up, clear despite the distance.

This time, the melancholy squealing was replaced by a lively tune. Twenty-one British women heard the tune; half of them shot upright and exclaimed, 'The Major-General's song!'

And so it was, the proud proclamation of the father of thirteen blonde daughters, declaring his knowledge of matters vegetable, animal and mineral. The jaunty tune rang out over the dusty pirate town, hushing its inhabitants and its prisoners alike, and when it was finished, the instrument started in on Mabel's song to Frederic, 'Poor Wandering One'. To my astonishment, a woman's clear soprano rang out in accompaniment, and we looked around to see Bibi singing to the heavens. I hadn't known the woman could sing a note, much less knew the score of the comic opera.

After that, those who knew the words followed Holmes' violin into a variety of the chorus numbers, and although I neither joined in nor appreciated the musicality, I did enjoy the sensation of hearts meeting across the rooftops.

There came a pause, while Holmes took a drink or tightened his strings – or silently fought off irate guards, for all I could tell – and Annie sighed. 'One might wish for a number of strong men to bring up that piano from the sitting room.'

Again, I spoke without thought: 'Who needs men?'

Of course, once the idea was out in the open, the others fell on it, and although I tried to withdraw the possibility of hauling the thing up the stairs, nothing would do but we all trooped down to examine the possibility. And, in fact, the instrument had legs that could be detached, so with a series of mattresses to turn the stairs into a ramp (a bump-filled ramp, true) and a quick transformation of bed-sheets into hauling ropes, the project was on.

It was heavier than it had looked, but not so massive that we couldn't shift it. The turns in the stairs meant several great gouges out of the plasterwork, and I had a bad moment when I (on the downhill side, steadying it with a shoulder) felt the load wobble and gather itself for a rush towards the ground floor – one of the bed-sheets had slipped. But the weight did not crush me, and the other ties held, and in the end, we made it all the way to the top. There we reattached the legs, and set the instrument with its back to the opening over the courtyard, so that the sky-light's canvas tarpaulin could be extended to protect it against the night mist.

The piano's arrival on the rooftop brought a great outburst of feminine triumph that silenced the violin, and no doubt made for a number of puzzled male expressions behind barred windows. Annie pulled up a stool, and began to play.

Separated by walls and armed guards, the violin and the piano combined, joined by a chorus of women. I waited tensely for the guards to storm in and quiet us, but either they were lovers of music themselves, or their instructions had not covered what to do if the *firengi* women next door burst into song.

And then a little after ten o'clock, the violin stopped. The women valiantly kept going for a song or two, but in a pause, Mrs Hatley sighed and said that she was tired. Annie's hands remained at rest in her lap, and within the quarter hour the piano was shrouded, the pillows gone, the rooftop lay empty and silent as the city around us.

I could only hope that the silencing of our other half had not been too brutal. I needed to speak with Holmes, which would be difficult if he'd been knocked unconscious.

CHAPTER THIRTY-FOUR

SAMUEL: Your silent matches, your dark lantern seize,
Take your file and your skeletonic keys.

I HAD SPENT much of the day dozing in the sun, so as to be fresh for the evening's activities. Holmes' violin the night before had given me the location of his room; tonight, there was no need for the street. I waited impatiently for the house to grow still, then changed into my boy's garments and eased open the door.

As I'd hoped, a cautious venture of my head over the high wall confirmed that the neighbouring rooftop was deserted, the guards safely indoors with their prisoners. I padded over to look at the door, finding to my irritation that it was bolted, not locked. It is difficult to pick a bolt. Fortunately, I had other means of reaching Holmes.

I looped my rope around a convenient sturdy lump – not as convenient as it might have been, unfortunately, placing me a good three feet to the side of where I wished – and walked backwards down the wall, as silent as I could be although the outside guard was nowhere in sight. As I came even with Holmes' window, just ten feet down from the roof level, a pale hint of motion came from the side of the metal shutter: his waving fingers, confirming his presence.

I made myself as comfortable as one can be on a thin rope dangling twenty-five feet above cobblestones, and reached to slide my fingers through the narrow gap.

Two warm and oh, so welcome hands swarmed up to take possession of mine, and I felt happy for the first time in days. Well, perhaps *happy* is not the exact word, but I no longer felt quite so alone. I scooted over, searching in vain for an external anchor that would take some of my weight, and ended up stretched across the stones to hold my face to the window covering.

Before I could speak, a voice as much felt against my face as heard by my ear recited, *"'What is that form? if not a shape of air, / Methinks, my jailor's face shows wond'rous fair!'"* Perhaps Holmes, too, had once laboured under a Miss Sim?

'Thank you, Holmes.' I, too, breathed the words into the blackness within.

'Good evening, Russell. I regret having to ask you to seek me out.'

'All in a night's exercise, Holmes. I could see that your windows are considerably more secure than ours.'

'A number of the fittings of the house make me suspect that this was at one time the harem. And, as you no doubt could infer, the search of our bags was scrupulous.'

'Well, they seem to be concentrating on you men – we have no inside guards beyond the housekeeper and her two maids. It would appear that our pirates meet few females with a streak of independence.'

'And a climbing rope,' he added.

'Extraordinary, isn't it? The only thing they removed from my bag was the revolver. They must have thought my pick-locks were a manicure set.'

'You have your pick-locks?'

'Indeed I do. Shall I—'

'That would be a great service.'

I worked the leather pouch of tools from my pocket without dropping it, thumbed out a tool by touch, and slid it through the metalwork. He thanked me, and got to work.

'I heard a shotgun yesterday,' he remarked.

'A warning shot, literally, to let us know we were not permitted to look over the wall that separates our house from yours. They seem to have decided that the lesson was well learnt, because there's no-one on your roof tonight. And you, are you all well?'

'Mr Fflytte is nursing a sore head after protesting against our confinement – not that the situation itself seems to trouble him, oddly enough, but he grew increasingly restive during the day, and when the guards finally opened his door he expressed his outrage, that our confinement will interfere with the making of his film.'

'That sounds like him. Do you have any—Aah.'

The lock mechanism gave its whisper of release, and I shifted so Holmes could push the shutter out. I studied the resultant hole.

'I believe I can get inside,' I told him.

'But the process will be slow, and I would not wish you trapped here.'

However, the open sill meant that I could transfer a portion of my weight onto the sill and off my hands.

'You were asking me if I had something?' he prompted, when I was settled again.

'Yes, do you have any of the pirate crew with you?'

'I think not, although our only communication has been brief tapping on the walls – someone knows Morse code, although three others only imagine they do, which rather confuses matters. La Rocha and Samuel were in the house earlier – my first inkling of their presence was a shriek that made my blood run cold until I realised it was that accursed bird. In any event, Hale was brought out to speak with them, for quite some time, but the conversation took place behind closed doors in a room on the ground floor. After the two men left, Hale's voice shouted out that if we are obedient tomorrow, we shall be permitted to gather in the courtyard during the afternoon. That is the only thing I have heard from any of them.'

'Carrots and sticks.'

'Precisely. What have you learnt?'

'The town is small and its walls and gates maintained. As you may have seen when you were brought here—'

'We saw nothing: Sacks were drawn over our heads. A certain amount could be discerned by hearing and by—'

'Holmes,' I interrupted happily, 'I shall never again complain about men who believe in the incompetence of women. Thanks to my freedom, I can tell you that we are in the north-east quadrant of Salé, about a hundred metres in from the walls.' I described all I had found during the previous night's wanderings: gates, walls, guards, the road out, the ferry; the layout of our house, the orientation of the adjoining streets, the heap of rubble to the side. I gave details of house and inhabitants, the distribution of the bedrooms.

Then I came to the more complicated part, which concerned the characters acting out their parts inside our tight little stage.

Four sentences into my analysis, however, Holmes stopped me. 'Perhaps you had better go through that more slowly.'

The section of my body resting on narrow stone had lost sensation and my arms ached, but I could not bring myself to be impatient with him, since it had taken me hours with mental graph paper to map out the permutations of all that I had gathered on the rooftop harem that day.

'We knew on the *Harlequin* that Adam is smitten with Annie,' I began. 'However, paying close attention to her concerns during the day, she responds to remarks concerning Bert-the-Constable with approximately the same ratio of interest as she does to remarks about Adam-the-Pirate, even though I'd have said that Bert was more intent on a friendship with Jack than on reciprocating Annie's affections. Jack, on the other hand, would rather follow Edith about, being unaware that Edith is a boy.'

'Edith is a boy?'

I was pleased to find *something* he'd missed. 'Didn't I mention that? Yes, I found Mrs Nunnally plucking her child's emergent beard. Beyond those specific links, various of the girls are interested in the young pirates and the young constables interchangeably – any young male will do – but I should say that Mrs Hatley—'

'Mother of June.'

'Right. Mrs Hatley appears to retain both affection and hope regarding Geoffrey Hale – although it could as easily be a sort of psychic contagion spilling over from her rôle as the pirate's nursemaid, Ruth, since she also pets Daniel Marks, her Frederic, at any given opportunity.'

'And yet I should have said that if Geoffrey Hale is interested in anyone, it's his cousin Fflytte.'

My numb hands jerked along the rope and nearly spilt me to the paving stones.

'Russell? Are you there?'

'Yes, Holmes, merely startled. You think . . . ?'

'They would not be the first aristocratic cousins we have known in . . . that situation.'

'Except that Fflytte has a reputation as a womaniser. And is currently – well, not currently, but until *Harlequin* intervened – associated with the picture's choreographer, Graziella Mazzo.'

'Which association appears to trouble Hale considerably.'

'But, Mrs Hatley, and June . . . ?'

'A man's tastes may change. Or they may be, shall we say, inclusive.'

I thought about that, about one or two times when I had found Hale studying his cousin with an expression difficult to analyse. 'You could be right. But what about La Rocha and Samuel?'

'You suggest they may have a similar, er, affection?'

'No! I mean to say, I hadn't thought of . . .'

'I should think more along the lines of the Barbarossa brothers,' he said firmly.

'The sixteenth-century pirates.'

'Aruj the elder – called Red Beard by Europeans – and his brother Kheir-ed-Din,' Holmes mused. 'Aruj was a brutal fist of a man, and became the virtual ruler of Algiers. When he died, his brother took over, and consolidated their base of power. He was every bit as merciless as Aruj had been, but he was also a sophisticate, educated, capable of seeing beyond the reach of a pirate ship.'

'Holmes, the length of time I wish to linger out here is limited.'

'I suspect that we may be caught up in a re-establishment of the Barbarossa empire.'

'What, in this little place? The smallest gunship of the British Navy could flatten Salé in an afternoon.'

'With thirty-four European citizens within its walls?'

He had a point. 'So how do we remove His Majesty's citizens from harm?'

'Having had a plenitude of time in which to reflect, I believe I have identified Mycroft's agent here.'

'You don't sound terribly pleased.'

'It's Bert.'

'Really? But that's good, isn't—Ooh. Bert, who may be fond of Samuel's younger son. I could be wrong,' I offered.

'I, too, have seen reason to believe that there are emotional ties there, ties that could make Bert less than wholehearted in his support of an escape.'

'If he's Mycroft's man, he'd never side against his countrymen.'

'Not consciously, I agree, but a slip of the tongue? A moment's hesitation?'

I dangled glumly and had to agree: Mycroft's undercover agent had best be considered a broken reed, and should not be brought into any plans. 'For my part, the only person on my side of the wall with a degree of native wit is Annie, and I consider her judgment clouded by affection for Adam. Certainly, she seems to have a suspect degree of curiosity about the actions of others – you saw how every time one turns around, there she is, blinking her pretty blue eyes.'

'It is true, beauty and reliability rarely go hand in hand.'

Which rather trod underfoot the compliment with which he had greeted me. 'Thank you, Holmes,' I muttered.

'Beg your pardon?'

'I said, it looks as if it's up to the two of us, yet again.'

I remained at his window for another ten minutes or so while we discussed options and signals, then reluctantly I told him that I had to go or risk falling. He ordered me to give him one hand, which he massaged back to life, then the other. Feeling restored, I dug out my pocket-knife and held it into the inner darkness, then set about climbing back up the wall to the rooftop. Behind me, the metal shutter swung shut on silent hinges and I reflected that Holmes had contrived to grease them, probably with a pat of butter from his breakfast. That he had done so spoke of his confidence in me.

As I set my hands upon the rope, there came a melodramatic whisper:

"'And noiseless as a lovely dream is gone. / And was she here? And is he now alone?'"

I nearly fell off the rope laughing.

Warmed by his hands and his attitude, I walked up the wall to the rooftop. There I hung for a couple of minutes, peering over and waiting for motion, but the area was still deserted. I swung up and onto the rooftop, retrieved the rope and bound it around my waist, then clambered to the top of the high dividing wall to stretch my foot down for the bench, left against the wall.

Except that it was no longer there. Dangling, I craned to look over my shoulder, and saw two figures stand up from their seats on the bench, now ten feet distant.

They did not rush to seize me. After a moment's thought, I let go and dropped to the roof, then turned to face my captors.

There came the scrape of a match, and a flame gave light to our tableau: Annie holding the flame to a candle, with at her side a smaller person. Oh, God: Edith.

All in all, I'd rather have confronted a pair of armed guards.

CHAPTER THIRTY-FIVE

SERGEANT: This is perplexing.
POLICE: We cannot understand it at all.

EDITH HAD DISCOVERED me missing first.
     She, or he, had been lying awake in the room she shared
– or, he shared . . . oh, dash it all, call the diabolical brat a female
– in the room she shared with her mother, lingering over the day's
events and the basic dreadful pain of adolescence heaped high with
the unutterable shame and anguish of being a boy in a dress, when
she heard a faint whisper of sound from the hallway. By the time
she dressed and figured out the person had been going up rather
than down, I was no longer on the roof, and she was too short to
reach the top of the wall from the bench-top.

     Annie, whose attention had been caught by the sound of
Edith going through two doors and up the stairs, caught the child
arranging a chair atop the bench. And although Edith tried hard to
convince her that it was the only place the mysterious person could

have gone, Annie had the sense to keep Edith from throwing herself on top of the wall and, for all either of them knew, into range of that Purdy shotgun.

She tried to convince Edith that she had been hearing things, that there was no sign that any intruder had passed here, that the bench had, in fact, been against the wall when they went to bed (even though Edith was adamant that it had not been, and Annie herself not at all sure). In the end, she offered to sit with Edith and wait, thinking that half an hour of staring into nothingness would be enough to convince the child to return to bed.

But Edith was made of sterner stuff; although I had been gone over an hour, she'd been determined to wait me out.

'And so you did,' I told her in that jollying voice one uses towards children, which had about as much impact on her as it had on any other child.

'I'll rat on you.'

'Edith, what kind of English is that! You're not going to give me away.' The warning note was clear in my voice – although, with Annie standing there, I could not very well be more specific about my own side of the threat.

'I don't care, tell them if you want, I'll do the same on you.'

'Now, why would you do that?' I chided desperately. What could I use on the child to keep her mouth shut? I really did not want the entire household to know that I'd shinned down the walls at night. For one thing, half of them would promptly demand that I take them along the next—

Ah.

'Do you want to go out?'

Her expression made for a sharp contrast to the warm little light Annie held, being cold and very adult. *Idiotic question*, she might as well have said aloud.

'I'm not going to take you over to the men's house, because there are armed guards over there who might come at any minute. But the next time I go down into the town at night, you can come. If, that is, you don't mind dressing up as a boy.'

'I—' She caught her tongue before it gave her away to Annie. 'No, I don't mind. When?'

'Probably not tomorrow night, but possibly the next.'

'That's too long!'

'Sorry, but I'm not going to put everyone else in danger just to take you on an outing.'

'You'll probably go without me.'

'I promise,' I said, and when the young face continued to eye me with mistrust, I added, 'I give you my word as an Englishwoman.'

'The next time you go down to the street, you'll take me, too?'

Annie started to object, but I put up a hand to stop her. 'I will take you.'

'Then I won't tell that you went away tonight.'

I put out my hand, and we shook on it.

'Now, you must go back to bed,' I told her. 'And make sure you don't go dropping large hints to the others tomorrow about adventures you're going on. If they find out, I won't be able to take you.'

'You have to come to bed, too!'

'I need to have a word with Annie.'

'But—'

'Go.'

Drooping and dragging her slippers, Edith slumped across the rooftop and through the door. I waited; eventually, it clicked all the way shut.

Annie, too, had stood waiting, and now she chuckled, and dribbled a bit of wax onto the bench to attach the candle upright.

She settled herself across one end of it, and I straddled the other, wondering what I was going to have to promise this older foe.

'Don't tell me you want to dress up as a boy and walk through the bazaar at night, too?' I asked her.

'You're not as bright as I thought you'd be.'

'I *beg* your pardon?' My husband had back-handedly referred to my lack of beauty; now an actress was questioning my brains?

'I figured you'd have this all sorted in nothing flat, and we could all go home, waving the flag and cocking a snook at His Majesty's enemies.'

'I—' I stopped. Oh Lord. She was right, I was being exceedingly stupid. '*You're* Mycroft's operative.'

She made the gesture of smacking her forehead, and gave me a grin that made her look both younger and more competent. 'One of them.'

'Bert?'

'At least you caught that. Or should I feel proud, that I'm better than he?'

She was right: I was every bit as guilty as the others, overlooking this person because she was a woman – a very pretty woman. Still . . .

'How do you know who I am?'

'I recognised your husband. And I had heard about you, so when the two of you appeared, well, I figured you were on the same track as I.'

'Perhaps you should explain why you are here?'

'I've been working on this case for six months, so that—'

'Which case is that?'

'What do you mean, which case? La Rocha and his brother, of course. What other case is there?'

'You'd be surprised.'

'So you're not here because Mycroft sent you?'

'Just at the moment, I don't know that I would cross the street for Mycroft. No, I'm doing a favour for a Scotland Yard friend.'

'Extraordinary.'

'*Extraordinary* doesn't begin to describe it. But you were telling me why you were here.'

It was a typical Mycroft assignment – if any of Mycroft's assignments could be called 'typical'. In early summer, Annie had been told to look into the activities of La Rocha and the man I knew as Samuel, with no suggestion as to how she might go about doing that. Taking up residence in Lisbon, she had spent several months in disguise, doing what amounted to keeping her ears open. Then a few weeks ago, a rumour circulated through the Lisbon hills that Fflytte Films was coming to do a film about – aha! – pirates.

She made enquiries and discovered the name of Fflytte's local liaison: Senhor Fernando Pessoa, the man of many personalities, who clearly had played an appropriately diverse number of rôles in this unscripted little drama of ours. Annie arranged to fall into casual conversation with the translator one evening at his favourite drinking establishment, loosened him up with poetry and port, and steered him towards the topic of pirates, and *Pirates*. Once she understood the set-up (*The Pirates of Penzance*; filming on location; casting in London and in Lisbon), she took care to remind her new friend of a bit of local colour that might interest his English clients: Captain La Rocha.

With Pessoa hooked, she booked passage to London, flung off her false spectacles, bohemian clothing and black wig, and got there in time to try out for a rôle in the picture.

Although she admitted to me that she was not much of an actress, she got the part (of course she got it, with her perfect skin, snub nose and big blue eyes – had Bibi been at the casting things might have gone differently, open competition not being a welcome sport among actresses). Once back in Lisbon, she took care to keep away from Pessoa, and no-one recognised the sweet-faced English blonde as the town's dowdy but competent part-time typist.

'I assume Bert came about his part in the same way?'

'I think he bought off one of the constables who'd already been hired, and took his place.'

'There's a lot of that going around,' I remarked, but shook my head at her look of enquiry. She went on.

'I was surprised to see him – "Bert" – on the steamer in Southampton; the last I heard he was in Ankara. But you – if you're not after La Rocha, why are you here?'

I could see no reason not to tell her. 'I'm looking into Fflytte Films. Everywhere they film, they're followed around by criminal behaviour. They make a film about guns, and no sooner do they move on than a dozen revolvers go onto the market. A film about cocaine, and the drug is suddenly available. A movie about rum-running, and the world's most famous rum-runner is arrested.'

'And after *Hannibal*, were there elephants all over—'

'Please, I didn't say I believed any of it. But I have to agree, the disappearance of Hale's assistant requires looking into.'

Annie looked at me sharply, so I gave her what I knew.

When I was finished, she shook her head. 'I'd be happier if they'd found a suicide note.'

'Wouldn't we all? What's also troubling is the suggestion that Geoffrey Hale makes a habit of seducing his employees. We believe that Anne Hatley – the child playing June – is his. Myrna Hatley is a robust personality, but if this assistant was a more fragile type, or more vulnerable . . .'

'If she was pregnant, she might have seen suicide as the only escape. On the other hand, if she chose to assert her rights and make a fuss . . .'

I admired the way this woman's mind worked. 'Then Hale might have decided to remove a problem. Either way, he was involved. As now he may be involved with the current situation. Last night, he spent some time in private conversation with La Rocha and Samuel, and afterwards was given leave to impart the message that the men would be permitted a degree more freedom tomorrow – today, rather – if they spent a quiet morning.'

'Internal tensions in the film world?'

'Of course, I've also had my suspicions of Will-the-Camera. And of you, for that matter.'

'An embarrassment of riches when it comes to shady types.'

'Speaking of shady types, what of our pirates? Holmes and I are operating under the assumption that we're to be put up for ransom. You've been investigating La Rocha for months, do *you* have any idea what he's up to?'

'Well, for one thing, I'm not altogether certain that La Rocha's the centre of this.'

'Samuel?'

'As you know him, yes.'

'He's both more intelligent and more cold-blooded than La Rocha, a dangerous combination.' I thought of the first time I'd seen Selim, standing behind La Rocha: the power behind the throne?

'And his sons?'

'Adam and Jack,' I replied: This was beginning to feel a bit like one of Holmes' examinations.

'I don't think that Adam altogether approves of his father's . . . work.'

The wistfulness in her voice did not sound like the judgment of an experienced espionage agent. It sounded like the wistful desires of a besotted young woman.

I sighed. 'You know, if we'd been working together on this from the beginning, we might be heading home by now. Mycroft's mania for keeping his left and right hands from communicating leads to more confusion than one requires.'

'Would you have come if your brother-in-law asked?'

'No. But you don't seem—'

'I'm glad you're here,' she cut me off.

'Oh. Well.'

'How much do you know about La Rocha and Samuel?'

'Not a lot.'

'Well, I had some months to build a dossier. You've probably figured out that they're brothers – or, rather, half-brothers? They believe themselves descended from Murad Reis. You know who that is?'

'Dutchman. Salé Rovers, English captives.'

'Converted to Islam in 1622, made Salé his centre, brought slaves from as far as Ireland and Iceland. When the Sultan tried to take the city and failed, he just made the Dutchman governor and married him to one of his daughters. Another sort of conversion, you might say.

'He had a number of children by his two Moorish wives, and there seems to have been some kind of a pirate in each generation. La Rocha's grandfather was hanged for killing a man in 1860, when La Rocha was four. La Rocha started his own career before he was twenty, boarding merchant vessels and robbing them, then slipping away. He seems to have paid for his brother to go to university in France, while also buying up holdings that had belonged to earlier generations of the family and been seized as reparations after they were gaoled or hanged.

'It wasn't until Selim – Samuel – graduated from university and came into the family business in 1895 that things began to get vicious. Victims would be thrown overboard and their ships stolen, other ships set alight with their dinghies stove in. Women passengers would disappear entirely. Over the next twenty years, the brothers created a network of informants and occasional partners to supplement their crew. During the War they went dormant, because of the number of warships in the Mediterranean, but they did manage to board a small ship that was removing gold from Turkey. A lot of gold. They lay low after that until the gunships retired, then after the War, started up again. In 1920, they made a raid on what looked like an easy target, and was not. Their ship went down, hands were lost, La Rocha and his brother were very nearly caught.

'After that, they seem to have taken a hard look at themselves, decided that they weren't getting younger and the modern world was inhospitable to their profession, and more or less retired to Lisbon.

'At any rate, La Rocha did. In recent months, there have been signs that they may be rebuilding the old alliances. Several of the pirates Mr Fflytte hired, for example, are the sons or grandsons of the original crew.'

'Restoring old grandeur? But surely they can't believe that they can rebuild their pirate kingdom here in Salé, under the noses of the French?' I asked.

'I imagine that Salé was a symbolic choice, just as the *Harlequin* was seized upon to evoke the heyday of piracy. Once they've finished with the ship and the city, they may slip away.'

'So you'd say that after selling us back to the British, they'll take the ransom monies – where? Somewhere out in the Sahara?'

'A startling amount of this continent is beyond the reach

of British guns. The Rif mountains have already declared independence – one can reach them in a day. And,' she added, changing her voice as if to mimic a textbook or lecture, 'the giving of ransom is no guarantee of the getting of hostages.'

The candle suddenly danced; it was down to its final inch. 'You'd say they're not planning on freeing us, then?'

To my astonishment, she began quietly to sing, in a sweet contralto:

> *Here's a first-rate opportunity,*
> *To get married with impunity . . .*

The smile on her shapely mouth contained no humour whatsoever. 'After all, what is the Gilbert & Sullivan opera about, ultimately, if not the *permanent* abduction of young English women?'

CHAPTER THIRTY-SIX

GIRLS: We have missed our opportunity
     Of escaping with impunity.

I GAPED AT Annie as if she'd begun to speak in Pashtu (while the ghost of Miss Sim whispered urgently in my ear: '*Oh! burst the Haram – wrong not on your lives / one female form*'). I hastily pulled together my thoughts. 'I refuse to believe that La Rocha's pirates are in fact English aristocrats fallen on hard times who wish to marry English wives.'

'That's rather too much to hope for. And I wouldn't count on a declaration of loyalty to the Crown to soften their hearts, either – I think Adam and Jack have already picked out me and Edith for their respective harems. As for the others, no doubt a bouquet of young yellow-haired English roses would fetch a high price on the open market. Some of the mothers perhaps not so much.'

'You've seen *The Sheik* too many times. Read too much Ethel Dell.'

'Perhaps. But can you honestly tell me that such things do not happen?'

In all honesty, I could not.

'And . . . the men?' I asked.

'If they're out to re-establish the Pirate Republic of Bou Regreg, slaves are a necessary detail. Although they may simply decide that females are so much easier to move and to hide than men are.'

I took a deep breath, then another. The candle guttered, nearly spent. 'So we can't get just the women away.'

'That would not be the ideal solution.'

'How long do you suppose we have?'

'A few days. No more than that. The message will have to be delivered, a response given. If the European officials who receive the demand have any wits at all, they'll require some proof that we are both here and alive. Perhaps La Rocha will free someone, to carry the word.'

A pleasanter thought than his sending the word with a corpse.

With that cheery notion, the candle went out. We sat, two women on a darkened rooftop, in a city of pirates, in a country where Europeans had the most tenuous of holds.

Oh, Holmes: What have you got me into now?

We went down to our beds a short time later, periodically illuminating our way by Annie's matches. I do not know about her, but I slept little, feeling pressed around by responsibilities and ruthless men.

The next day, heavy in spirits and heavier from lack of sleep, I forced my feet to take me downstairs to break my fast with the others. I was grateful for the strength of the Moroccan coffee.

Mrs Hatley was the first to voice the uncomfortable question on every woman's lips, as if placing a bowl on the table before us. 'Are we still being kept in?'

Annie responded before I could, putting on an act of severe irritation that drowned the apprehension in the older woman's voice and set the tone for the day. 'Oh, isn't it vexing?' she declared. 'I mean to say, I adore Mr Fflytte and have nothing but respect for his work – and I'm hugely grateful for the job, of course – but one would think that he and Mr Hale might have made the arrangements for our filming in good time. Haven't they filmed in *France*, for heaven's sake? They should have known how mad the French are for bureaucracy. Forms for everything, passports if one wants to travel to the next *ville*, permission to paint one's front door – I imagine he's having to put up monetary assurance in case we chip the paint on some wreck of a building! Why, I remember—'

And as she picked over the croissants, rejecting several in dissatisfaction, she recounted a tale of bureaucratic excess encountered by a troupe of visiting players in the wilds of rural France. When Annie had finished her much-embroidered story, Edith's mother chimed in with a similar complaint. Celeste contributed a pointless but impassioned history of a job she'd had in a French production, when the producer had withheld a portion of her pay due to a tax question.

Soon, the cold dish of impending prison had given way to a nicely heated stew of resentments. Then, before it could boil over into action, Annie rescued us again. 'I say, I know just what we should do with this extra day we've been given! If we can't rehearse with our pirates, why can't we rehearse without them? We know their scenes as well as they do – half of us can dress as pirates, the rest of us can practise around them. What do you say?'

With the alternative being another day of polishing nails and reading aloud, the actresses welcomed the opportunity. And I was not in the least surprised when someone suggested – Annie again – that we might as well be in costume.

The house-keeper and her two maidservants were alarmed when

we stormed the upstairs lumber-room and began to hurl garments into the air. In suitably fractured French and one or two words of Arabic, I made her to understand that we were making a stage-play, dressing up, *non*? And although I could see that the three of them were shocked by the sight of young women in the dress of native men, honestly, what could one expect from the English?

It did, however, mean that we should be prepared, were we to need to leave the house disguised as so many males.

I participated in the action, since having the mothers, the seamstress, the make-up girl and me in the stead of pirates let more of the girls act their proper rôles. But after lunch, when the sun grew warm, most of us curled up on our sunny cushions and slept.

I came sharply awake just before three o'clock, hearing men's voices. And not just men: Holmes. I sat upright, and saw the others doing the same.

June listened, then jumped to her feet and started to shout out a greeting to our neighbours – and three of us hushed her instantly: Annie, Edith and me.

I hastened to explain. 'They may not wish for us to talk to each other over the fence,' I told her. 'Moslems, like the people whose house this is, are very fussy about keeping boys and girls separate.'

A ridiculous explanation, but one they seemed to accept. After all, who knew what sorts of rules heathens might have? So voices stayed down for a while, on both sides of the wall, until Annie (what a very useful associate!) sat down at the piano and began to play. The girls joined in, with that most English of Gilbertian odes, sung in the opera when propriety and sympathy conflict and the only option is to talk about the weather:

> *How beautifully blue the sky,*
> *The glass is rising very high,*

Continue fine I hope it may,
And yet it rained yesterday.

Annie continued on to various songs, concentrating on the girls' choruses. When she ran out of those, she hesitated, but rather than repeat herself, she started one of the duets sung by Mabel and Frederic. Bibi's voice rang out, strong and high, and after a time, we heard Daniel Marks from the other side of the wall, hesitantly, then more surely as the guards gave their tacit permission by not raising their guns or their fists.

It made for quite a cheerful matinée, Sullivan's tunes and Gilbert's words spilling over the scruffy and no doubt bewildered little town. Annie avoided the piratical songs, and the constables joined in with gusto on their song about the policeman's lot—

> *When the enterprising burglar's not a-burgling,*
> *When the cut-throat isn't occupied in crime,*
> *He loves to hear the little brook a-gurgling,*
> *And listen to the merry village chime.*

– although I had to wonder if her playing did not hold just a touch of spite as she crashed into the chords of the policemen's other song:

> *When the foeman bears his steel (Tarantara! tarantara!)*
> *We uncomfortable feel (Tarantara!)*

It may have been my imagination that heard a slight falter in Annie's hands on the keys at the words *Go to death, and go to slaughter.*

The moment that song's chorus of blood-thirsty supporters and highly reluctant police ended, a violin swirled into life, sawing madly through the double-time tune of the Sergeant-Major's song.

Annie didn't even try to catch him up, and when Holmes started to sing at the end of the verse (his accurate if nondescript voice was suited to the song's limited range), he delivered the words at a rate nearly as fast as the instrument's playing. The audience on both sides of the wall listened intently to the feat, although a few smiles of appreciation gave way to faint frowns as some of the words seemed to go awry.

He ended the tune with another round from the violin, and applause broke out.

'Didn't the words—?' Isabel's mother began, but her next words were drowned out by Annie as she launched into one of the songs from *Pinafore*. Which, being English, they all knew as thoroughly as they knew those from *Pirates*.

I left the smile on my lips and continued my slightly off-the-beat nods of the head (were I to join the chorus, it might set the dogs to howling, and drive the more sensitive souls from the rooftop) as the matinée edged into soirée and the cool sea air began to move in. In the middle of a song (this one from *Gondoliers*, a heartfelt rendition of *And if ever, ever, ever they get back to Spain, they will never, never, never cross the sea again, they will never, never, never, never, never, never, never*—) the voices from next door broke off in a series of protests and then shouts.

The piano stopped, the women's voices dribbled into silence, as we waited, hearts in throats – but there were no gunshots, no cries of pain, it was merely that the guards wanted their supper.

Being a more civilised household, we took afternoon tea instead, but the meal that followed soon afterwards was not spurned as being too early. A day of excitement and fresh air took its toll on the younger girls and on their mothers, and to my relief, Holmes' added words to his rapid-fire recitation had been forgotten.

Except by Annie.

When the *tagine* had been polished off (chicken this time, with pistachios) and the mint tea drunk, when conversation had lagged, lamps had been shut down, and everyone had retreated to their beds with a selection (carefully vetted by the mothers) from the book-shelves, a faint tapping came at my door, and Annie stepped inside.

Her eyes went to the window, although she had to look closely to see how I had removed and replaced the mortar. She sat down on the stool and gathered her hands in her lap.

'The words in that song were for you?' she asked.

'Various code-words and references, yes. Which, being Holmes, means I've probably missed half of them and got the meaning wrong of others, but the general gist of it seems to be that Hale may not be in league with La Rocha and Samuel, that La Rocha is delivering the ransom demand this evening, that I need to be ready, and that I'm not to stir from my room tonight.'

'You got all that from a few words?'

'And the way they were sung. There's a mathematical—Ooh, never mind, it would sound like lunacy, and probably what he meant to tell me was that they're all hale and hearty, that they're eating raisins, and do I have a pen he can borrow?'

'The communication of true minds, I see.'

'I take it you've never been married? If the ransom demand has been delivered, I shouldn't imagine it will be long before the government's machinery gets under way.'

And indeed, the government's machinery presented itself in our drawing room – or the Moorish equivalent, the courtyard – bright and early the next morning, in the form of two diplomats in their full battle regalia of high collars and chest-medals.

Any plans we might have laid went over the edge seven minutes after they were shown in.

CHAPTER THIRTY-SEVEN

MABEL: Young Frederic was to have led you to death and glory.
POLICE: That is not a pleasant way of putting it.

'You've what?' I cried in horror.

'Oh, *good!*' exclaimed the others, along with 'Too right!' 'That shows him!' 'God save the King!' (for some reason), and even 'Alan and Bert will rescue us!' (from one of the more excitable girls, momentarily forgetting that our police constables were fictional).

The two diplomatic persons had disturbed us at our breakfast, with half of us still in our dressing-gowns and the other half wearing various of the exotic dressing-up garments from the day before. However, such was the urgency of their mission, they merely cast their eyes away from our state of *déshabillé* and spoke in the direction of the lemon trees.

Clearly, the two had concluded their negotiations over who would speak first before they came here, because once the introductions had been concluded, the French gentleman cleared his throat (this being, after all, a country governed by France) and informed us that ransom had been asked for our safe return to the English community, and M. Dédain and Sir Morgan Brent-Williams had been dispatched (hastily, to judge by Sir Morgan's poorly shaved chin) so as to bear witness that we were well. (In other words, that we hadn't already been tipped into the sea.)

This was the first inkling the majority of the women present had that our prolonged presence within these four walls was not merely a side-effect of Randolph Fflytte's inefficiency. Mrs Hatley set down her tea-cup with a clatter and said sharply, 'Young man, don't be absurd. We're not being *held* here. We are—' but her admonishment was drowned in the voices of the others, shocked and eager and in the end acknowledging that, indeed, we had not been permitted to leave. I kept a close eye on young Edith, lest she blurt out that *one* of us anyway had gone a-wandering, but she had her lips mashed together so tightly, the words stayed in.

Sir Morgan then cleared *his* throat to request silence. His own speech repeated much of what M. Dédain had said, which suggested that his frown during M. Dédain's monologue was not due to disagreement, but because he was hard of hearing. His audience was beginning to grow restless in its desire for originality when he drew a piece of paper from one breast pocket, a pair of reading spectacles from another, and began to read off our names, pausing after each to locate the respondent. The last name was Graziella Mazzo, and it took a while to convince him that she had left the crew under her own authority back in Lisbon. The news caused some consternation and shaking of heads, but it was finally admitted that neither English nor French citizens could expect to have any control over an Italian *danseuse*.

At the end, satisfied that we were all (with the regrettable exception of La Graziella) alive and present, he folded away his page and said, 'I understand that the men of your party are being kept in separate quarters. We shall go there next. But rest assured, ladies, that we shall soon have you away from this foul and dreadful place.'

The songbird in the tree chose that moment to launch into a gentle ripple of notes, rather belying the keenness of our suffering, but the King's representative went on, undeterred (or perhaps unhearing). 'These rascals imagine that they can play fast and loose with British citizens, but we shall show them otherwise! We have already taken their chief into custody – a rough-looking type with a scar, can't imagine how you ladies stood having him near.'

'You've *what?*' I cried in horror.

'Oh, *good!*' exclaimed the others, and our contrary opinions filled the courtyard. I stepped over the chorus of dissenting opinion to seize the man's arm. 'You mustn't do that. If you arrest him, it will make the problem far, far worse!'

His stout expression wavered as his eyes drifted to his companion, and I was not surprised when he said, 'Madam, I might have agreed with you, had it been my decision, but as M. Dédain explained to me, the French have their own way of dealing with such things.'

It was on the tip of my tongue to point out that 'their own way of dealing with such things' might well duplicate the bloody Fez uprising of 1912, but voicing my apprehension risked plunging the gathering into the tedium of hysteria. Instead, I permitted him to go on with his little speech, his awkward enquiry as to whether we had any . . . particular needs (to his patent relief, the needs expressed were no more intimate than fresh cow's milk and a packet of English biscuits), and his promise to convey any letters we might wish to send home with utmost dispatch, ending with a heartfelt declaration that His Majesty's Government – and that of France, but perhaps not that of Italy – would not rest until we were safely in the bosoms of our families again. And that he would be back on the morrow.

The women, naturally, erupted with questions.

'How much ransom are they demanding?'

'The picture will still go ahead, won't it?'

'Will we be paid for our time here?'

'Mr Fflytte wants—'

'Mr Hale said—'

'My agent won't—'

'My family will—'

'I can't possibly go into—' Sir Morgan protested, blanching at the thought of discussing finances with ladies.

'I'm sure they're asking more ransom for me,' Bibi said.

'*You!*' Mrs Hatley was outraged. 'They'd throw you in for nothing.'

'Why, you—' Annie and three others dove in to separate the two furious divas, allowing the alarmed diplomats to beat a hasty retreat for the door, with me foremost among those in their wake.

I hated to do it – oh, *how* I hated to do it! – but with this many innocents being caught up in a well-meaning but potentially catastrophic process, I had to speak up. As Sir Morgan turned to pound on the door, I thrust forward to murmur as loudly as I could into his ear, 'You need *urgently* to consult with Mr Mycroft Holmes in the Treasury Office. Urgently!'

Not that Mycroft would be in time to stop the gun-boats entirely, but he might possess a spanner sufficient to slow the works, and permit us time to work.

The door closed; a hubbub of outrage and tears and *How dare they*s and *I knew there was something wrong*s shocked the little songbirds into silence. But as if to speak up for its fellow creatures, a terrifying but familiar scream ripped away the clamour of the mere humans; our chins jerked upwards to the shape on the rooftop grate.

'The people will rise!' it roared, adding darkly, 'She was a phantom of delight.'

There above us, its head descending through a square too small for the rest of its body, perched La Rocha's parrot, in search of its gaoled master. Lesser voices held their silence for a moment, then as one burst into the relief of laughter. When conversation started up again, the panic had retreated, although talk was no more coherent than at their first reaction.

Annie calmly went to fetch herself coffee, and brought it back to sit at my side.

'This makes matters considerably more serious,' she murmured around the cup.

'We have to get them out of here.'

'And abandon the men?'

Our presence might be the only thing keeping the men from slaughter. 'No, we have to get them, too.'

'I'd say we have at least three or four days before . . .'

'I agree. I'll talk to Holmes tonight, and co-ordinate our resources. I gave him a pen-knife. I wish I still had my revolver.'

'I have one.'

'You do? How did they not find it?'

'Do you really want to know?'

'Probably not. But you only have the one?'

'I'm afraid so.'

'Pity, it might have given the men's side an edge.'

'We could let them have it. Just barricade ourselves behind the door and trust that His Majesty will reach us before the pirates break it down.'

'We may have to.'

'If you want to take it with you tonight, let me know.'

'What are you two talking about?' Edith demanded.

Not missing a beat, Annie said, 'We were agreeing how smashing you look in that garment.'

Men in this place wore long robes (not, in fact, night-shirts) called *galabiyyas*, with or without hoods, of plain fabric but often with elaborate embroidery down the front. The women's garments, called *kaftans*, were nearly identical – to an outsider. Edith's *galabiyya* had been made for a taller person, but we did, after all, have an official seamstress with us, for whom it had been no task at all to raise a few hems.

Edith looked unconvinced, but couldn't help glancing down at the thick intertwining pattern decorating the front of the otherwise plain brown garment. 'I need a belt for my knife.' Somehow, the child had adopted (and what was more, managed to retain) one of the pirates' dummy knives, impressive but useless for anything more demanding than cleaning beneath one's fingernails.

Annie stood up. 'Lots of men wear their weapons in a sort of sash. I'm sure we can find something that will do.'

And thus the long day began, with the worst possible news and a dive into the dressing-up box. Many, many maddeningly long hours later, during which every possible permutation of our captivity and rescue had been mooted, I finally took up my climbing rope and Annie's revolver and made my escape over the wall.

Holmes was expecting me, the shutter-latch already open. The odour from within suggested that a candle had recently been extinguished, lest it outline my figure dangling outside, but the room remained dimly illuminated by the light seeping around the door. His hand came out, reassuring and warm. I adjusted the rope so the pressure was to the side of the previous bruises rather than directly on top of them, and greeted him.

'Were you permitted to converse with the two diplomatic gentlemen this morning?' I asked.

'Briefly, but enough to see that they are working hard to shape a disaster. You caught the messages I embedded into the song?'

'That Hale is not a villain?'

'When La Rocha and Samuel came for Hale the other evening, it was to compose letters to the British and French authorities. Ransom has been set, two thousand guineas a head in British or French currency, to be paid the day after tomorrow.'

'Hale told you this? And you believe him?'

'I think him an unskilled actor. In any event, his claim is verified by Maurice.'

'The cook?'

'He is French, so Samuel handed him the letter and had him translate it aloud into English, or enough of it to satisfy him that it was as he had instructed.'

'Two thousand guineas a head,' I mused.

'They must be in a hurry to conclude the business, else they'd have asked for more.'

'Well,' I said, 'Annie thinks – oh, that's right, you don't know – oh, for heaven's sake, Holmes, if I try to tell it all out here, I'll never make it up the rope again. Move back.'

Between my wriggling and Holmes' tugging I got inside without a huge amount of noise or loss of skin, and I was alone with my husband for the first time since Lestrade's bombshell of a letter had arrived in Sussex. He relit his candle and we sat, shoulder to shoulder, as I recounted the events since last we had met.

'When I returned to the rooftop the other night,' I began, 'two of the girls were waiting for me. Though one is a boy, and the other is Mycroft's man.'

He reached into his garment and came out with his tobacco

pouch; clearly this was a tale requiring thought. His hand went still when I told him Annie's theory about white slavery, and although I tried to keep it light, by that time I more than half believed it myself. The grimness with which he continued filling the pipe bowl suggested that he did, too.

When I had finished, he asked a question that seemed to have nothing to do with it.

'Am I correct in thinking that from your side, there is no view of the water?'

'A slice to the south and another to the north, but you're right, the wall they put up to separate the two houses blocks most of it.'

'Then you will not have seen the British gun-boat, lying offshore.'

To that, there could be little response but an expletive. I readily provided one, adding, 'Do they think they can shell the town?'

'I shouldn't say the verb *think* applies in this case.'

'And Holmes, they've arrested La Rocha.'

'That explains why one keeps hearing the parrot.'

'Searching for his master, yes.'

'A person would imagine Lestrade was in charge here,' he muttered.

'Sir Morgan intends to come back tomorrow with biscuits and fresh milk, and to take away any letters we wish to send home.'

'They won't permit him inside the city wall.'

'I agree.'

'Tell me the rest of your day.'

My story took some telling, but eventually I came to the distasteful admission of my surreptitious message to the English envoy. I added, 'I have to say, however, that the name seemed to have no effect on him. Either he is ignorant of Mycroft, or so hard of hearing that he missed the message entirely.'

Holmes drew thoughtfully on his pipe, although by this time it no longer contained any combustible material. 'One must indeed speculate over the relationship between La Rocha and his brother. If they are close and Samuel is content to be subordinate, he will do all he can to free La Rocha. Which would include physical threat to his prisoners. On the other hand, if your new friend's speculation is correct and Samuel is making a bid for control, then he will leave here as soon as possible, now that the British have confirmed the state of those to be ransomed.'

'You don't think he'll wait until he receives the ransom money?'

'He may. He may also leave us men here, under guard and with an agent, until the British monies are transferred, while he heads into the Atlas mountains with you women. Or he may simply dispose of us as superfluous burdens. I should say it would depend on whether or not he has a trusted agent he can leave behind.'

'Like, a son.'

'Precisely.'

'And yet, I'd have thought Adam too squeamish for killing and abductions. He's more than half in love with Annie.'

'He is also the age at which young men need to prove themselves to their fathers.'

I found that I had been leaning against him, firmly enough that his arm was now around my shoulders. I relished the heavy security, the sense of being under protection. Then I noticed what I was doing and sprang to my feet, suddenly furious.

'Holmes, I have no intention of permitting any of those girls to be put into a harem, even temporarily. We can get everyone away. We simply have to.'

He withdrew his pipe from his lips; his grey eyes sparkled in the candlelight. 'That's my Russell,' he said. 'How?'

CHAPTER THIRTY-EIGHT

POLICE [*pianissimo*]: Tarantara, tarantara!

I SPENT HOURS in Holmes' cell as we shared what we knew of the city, of our captors, and of our fellow prisoners. We agreed that Fflytte and Will were our weak points: Will would refuse to abandon his reels of exposed film; Fflytte would refuse to abandon his dreams. In the end, we decided that Hale would just have to tuck his cousin under his arm, while Bert and one of the other pseudo-constables could deal with Will.

We would go at midnight tomorrow, an hour that in Lisbon would find half the city still moving around, but here found even the dogs asleep. Using the pick-lock I had given him, Holmes would let himself out of his cell and, when he had overcome the closest guard, loose his fellow prisoners.

At one a.m., we would assemble on the street outside, men and women alike, and move fast through the streets of the medina to the gate.

The success of the venture rested on the element of surprise: By the time anyone could decide to shoot at us, we would be upon them.

We sat on his hard cot, staring at the candle – wearing, no doubt, identical expressions of dissatisfaction. Holmes glared at his stone-cold pipe. 'There are too many uncontrollable variables.'

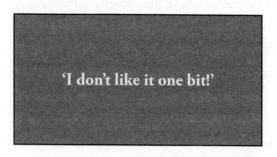

'I don't like it one bit!'

Get a grip, Russell. 'I agree, it stinks of the stage. One of those plays in which every turn is thwarted by disaster. I keep expecting some unforeseen twist that will throw everything into confusion. Oh, I'm sorry, Holmes,' I said. 'I've been surrounded by actresses too long.'

'Never mind,' he said. 'I've spent much of my life being thought of as a fiction. One grows accustomed to it.'

Time for me to leave.

I stood up and removed Annie's revolver from my pocket. 'I think you should have this.'

He shook his head.

'Holmes, you have armed guards, we have one housekeeper and a pair of adolescent house-maids. We are valuable property, you are easily disposed of. We have more knives and blunt implements than we can hold; you have your hands. Until we join forces, you have greater need of armament than we do.'

He pressed the weapon back into my hand. 'The pocket-knife is sufficient. If I succeed in overcoming the first guard without noise, then we will have a gun. If I do not, those on this side are lost in any event, and you will need your gun to get out of your front door.'

Reluctantly, but in agreement, I returned the weapon to my pocket, and went to the window. When he had snuffed the candle, I put my head out, waiting until I was certain there was neither guard nor traffic before I inserted myself into the narrow slot and permitted Holmes to shove me steadily outward.

'Until midnight tomorrow,' I whispered.

'*Insh'allah*,' he returned, that Arabic phrase and philosophy that I had learnt (and lived by) in Palestine: *If it be the will of Allah.*

Indeed.

Annie and Edith were on the rooftop again. This time, they had wrapped themselves in their bed-coverings, and were fast asleep.

I would have left them where they sat, propped upright against each other, but their backs were to the door and I did not feel like finding an alternative route downstairs. I laid a hand on Annie's shoulder, and found myself looking into the gleam of a knife in the low lamp-light. I went still; she blinked; the blade went away. She threw off her bed-clothes and stood.

Edith did not wake – or did not appear to – but still I turned my back on her before I retrieved the gun and handed it to Annie. 'He didn't want it,' I said. She thrust it without hesitation into her waist-band, then squatted to pick up Edith. I tucked cotton and eiderdown under one arm, held up the shielded lamp, and followed the two of them down the stairs.

Despite the misgivings I had shared with Holmes, no unexpected disaster met us on the stairway, no twist of wicked fortune roused us from our beds.

The Fates waited until we were up and around the next morning before throwing out their threads and entangling us all in catastrophe.

CHAPTER THIRTY-NINE

PIRATES [*very loud*]: With cat-like tread,

Upon our prey we steal;

In silence dread

Our cautious way we feel.

IN THE THREE days we had spent here, the outer door had
opened precisely six times: once to receive our luggage, twice
for the diplomats the day before, and once each afternoon during
the quiet time between lunch and tea, when the cook's two girls
collected the baskets and string bags of supplies, and gave any
requests for the following day. Apart from that, it was closed and
locked.

Which meant that when the door was pushed open that
morning, it took a moment to identify the noise. Confusion lasted
but an instant, replaced by alarm as the sound of multiple boots on
tiles echoed down the entrance-way.

Half of us were on our feet, and of those still seated, most had
a hand at her throat when Samuel marched in, two armed guards
at his back and a look of open triumph on his face. It was the sort

of situation in which women traditionally swooned; actresses, it seemed, were of sterner stuff.

Mrs Hatley, one of those who had stayed in her chair, forced her hand away from her throat and brought her spine upright. 'What is the meaning of this?' she demanded, her voice very nearly under control.

'Meaning is, time to go now.' He leered; that is the only word for that expression.

Everyone but Mrs Hatley and I were on their feet now, the girls drawing together in uncertainty. 'You mean,' Fannie asked, 'we're free to go?'

'Oh, at last!' Isabel cried.

June's head came over the upstairs balcony. 'We're leaving?'

Doris's pale curls appeared directly above June. 'Have I time to wash my hair?' A third golden mop was just visible above hers, on the other side of the wooden grating – someone had gone up early to the rooftop. No head was still on its pillow; all ears were hanging on the pirate's words.

Edith, who had just come into the room wearing her Moroccan pirate's gear, looked from the men to me and asked, 'Shall I change back into my frock?'

'No,' I said in a loud voice. The criss-cross of talk stuttered and died. With all attention on me, I faced Samuel across the courtyard. 'He doesn't mean we're free to go. He means he's taking us elsewhere. Somewhere very secure and impossible to escape.'

He ignored the ripples of distress that swept the house and had the guards tightening their grips on the guns. His gleaming boots padded across the tiles. With every step he grew larger, until he came to a halt a hand's breadth from my knees and stared down, willing me towards retreat. But I had no place to go, literally or figuratively, and I fingered the knife I had secreted in my sleeve, waiting for a distraction that might give me a chance against those lightning reflexes.

'What is this, Parrot?' he asked.

Being a tall woman leaves one ill prepared for the sensation of smallness. I felt myself shrinking with this cruel figure towering over me, growing small, and weak.

And he knew it. I saw in his eyes the dawning of cruel delight. His lips parted, but—

'Edith, *no!*'

Samuel whirled away – God, he was *fast* for a big man! – before my arm could move. Edith, sprinting across the tiles, skidded to a halt not because of her mother's command, but because of the blade in Samuel's hand.

Seeing the threat was nothing more than a little girl in a boy's kaftan, Samuel straightened, and said something to the guards. They laughed; Edith flushed; Mrs Nunnally gathered her child in. The pirate's lieutenant turned back to me – and the sky fell in.

That was what it felt like. Impossible motion from the upper reaches of my vision, a sound like a roomful of teeth crackling down on a million tiny bones, and then a huge hand smashed out of the heavens. All the musical notes in the world shouted at once; as I cowered down, my hunched back was pummelled by a rain of sharp, dry objects.

Things stopped falling. My head beneath my arms seemed to be in one piece. I tentatively raised one arm – then remembered Edith, and staggered upright.

The child stood, her mother at her back, both of them untouched but gape-jawed with shock. I, too, was aware of that familiar swaddled sensation that accompanies a severe blow. I bent to pick up a length of silver-dry timber that my foot had kicked. There seemed to be quite a bit of the stuff scattered around. Numbly curious, I looked upward, past first one, then another blonde girl, both wearing the same flabbergasted expression as Edith. Beyond them a third face looked down, from the roof-top. Yet I could see her clearly. For some reason, the wooden grating seemed to have a hole in it. A large hole. Through which I could see Annie. Her big blue eyes were wide, too – but not with shock, or horror.

With triumph.

Unwillingly, I made my gaze descend, to see what caused that expression.

And saw an overturned piano.

From under its edges protruded a pair of shiny black boots.

Isabel's mother broke first, with the sort of dangerous giggle that pleads for a slap. Fannie and June followed, their laughter freer, as if this might be one of Mr Fflytte's clever tricks.

The guards put an end to it. No-one but me understood their urgent command for silence, but all grasped the intent of those weapons.

The house shuddered into silence, broken only by the whimper of Isabel's mother.

The larger of the two men walked over to his engulfed boss. Samuel's disbelief had frozen him to the spot for one crucial second; now the instrument neatly covered all but a few inches of his footwear. A glance under the other edge convinced the man that he did not want to see further. He told his partner, '*He's dead.*'

The man gave forth a rich curse, and followed it with, '*What do we do now?*'

'*We hold them until someone comes.*'

'*No-one will come.*' I spoke in Arabic; the guards goggled as if the fountain had made a pronouncement. I went on, my voice inexorable, speaking a language designed for pure rhetoric. '*No-one will come but the British and the French armies. They will find you here and they will kill you. They will fall on you and they will arrest you and they will arrest your families, then they will stand you before a line of men with rifles and they will shoot you dead, your sons and your brothers and your mothers, if you do not leave us this instant, if you—'*

I'll never know if my words alone would have broken their will and sent them bolting for the door, because instead of the Army falling on them, an *afrit* came down, a ghost or perhaps the spirit of their dead leader: A great billowing white cloud filled the air over their heads, giving out a ghostly moan. Both men snapped up their shotguns and fired, both bores. The next moment, as one panicked guard was beating away the shredded bed-sheet, a regiment of harpies fell upon him, pounding at him with flower-pots and broomsticks and the upper half of the *tagine* crock, descending on him like the Red Queen's deck of cards, screaming and pummelling him to the ground. The other guard dropped his empty shotgun to rip at the revolver in his sash, and my hand threw the weapon it held – except as it left my grip I realised it was not my knife but the scrap of wood. I scrabbled for my blade. His gun went wildly off, once, before the blade reached him and he grabbed his shoulder and went down, the revolver skittering across the tiles to Edith's feet. She picked up the heavy weapon and pointed it at him, her hands wavering but determined.

Panting and wild-eyed, twenty-one English women in dressing gowns and *galabiyyas* surveyed a tableau of ruination. The lovely tiles were buried under blood, death, dirt and débris.

I thought my heart would burst with pride.

The man with my knife in him groaned – reminder that the battle was by no means over. I flew to the kitchen, where the house-keeper and her girls cowered in one corner. The younger one cried out when I appeared but I ignored them, upending drawers and overturning jugs to gather all the knives I could find. Back in the courtyard, I distributed the blades along with a couple of sturdy pestles, and we waited for the next phalanx of guards to pour in. We waited, as the pounding of our hearts gradually slowed. We waited, until we could hear over the heartbeats. Hear the boom of the surf, the nervous cheep of a bird, and some peculiar noises coming from above.

Annie's head vanished from the ruins of the sky-light; I stepped forward to relieve Edith of the guard's revolver. In three minutes, Annie burst from the stairway. 'I don't think they heard! The men are doing some kind of bashing about – they had just come out onto their rooftop when I . . . did *that*.' She gestured at the entombing piano.

We waited, collective breath held. Incredibly, the violin started up, and with it, our hopes.

'Tie them and gag them,' I said. 'Use bed-sheets. And the cook and her girls, we'll have to tie them as well.' I roughly bound the knife wound on the one guard, more to save the tiles than him, and ordered my fellow Amazons to get their shoes and to bring all the clothes from the dressing-up box to the roof.

'Don't stop to fuss with your hair,' I called after them.

'What shall I do?' asked Annie at my elbow.

'Get the girls singing, and have Maude put brown make-up on everyone's faces and hands. And see if you can think of a distraction. Holmes heard the gunshots – that's him covering up our noise – but if we can divert their guards' attention for a moment, it'll give the men a chance.'

'I may be able to think of something,' she said.

I returned to the kitchen, dropping to my heels in front of the bound cook. '*I am sorry we had to tie you up,*' I told her in Arabic. '*Once we are out of the city I will have someone come back to set you free. And I will leave a knife in the courtyard, for you to cut your bonds. Thank you for all your service, these past days.*'

The Arabic startled them into stillness, the coins I placed on the table widened their eyes. I laid a small knife on the ground near the fountain: It would take a while for one of them to reach it, but I would not wish them helpless for ever.

I snatched up various table-cloths and towels on my way to the roof, where I found the girls valiantly singing along to Holmes' tunes, mixing up the words but belting out the music unabated. Maude had her lips pursed as she smeared brown paint onto pink faces, assisted by Mrs Hatley and Bonnie, both of them old hands at the make-up box. I turned to Annie, who was waving the girls into greater enthusiasm. She was wearing a tan *galabiyya*, the hood thrown back so that her pale hair and English skin shone out.

'You need some face paint,' I noted. 'Did you come up with a distraction?'

'I need more than face paint. *I'm* the distraction.' She yanked off the voluminous garment, revealing a sight that had the girls strangling mid-song. She whirled around, tassels flying, to wave them back into full voice, although in truth they found it difficult to produce music past the choking laughter in their throats.

'A *belly dancer*?' I exclaimed. 'Where on earth did you find that . . . costume?'

'It was in one of the boxes. Mrs Hatley didn't think it was appropriate for the girls, so we hid it away. Do you think it's distracting enough?'

The question was, would it be so universally distracting that it would turn every man over the wall to stone, prisoners and guards alike? 'Well, if we put you at one end of the wall, I can go across at the other end and simply tip them on their faces. Maude?' I called. 'I hope you have a good supply of paint.'

I distributed the various scarves, cloths and towels to the girls whose garments lacked hoods, demonstrating how they could be wrapped. I hid Annie's platinum locks under the folds of a brightly embroidered table-runner, then stood back to study the result. I could only hope it didn't give any of our men a heart attack.

I motioned the girls to come together around me, and when the song came to an end, I quickly explained, 'Annie's going to catch the guards' attention so our men can overcome them and get their weapons. Once the men are free, they'll come here and we'll all go down together and make our way to the nearest city gate. We will have guns at the beginning and at the end of the group, so you need to stick together between them. If there's any shooting, jump into the nearest doorway and get as small as you can.

'Ready?'

They weren't, of course – what normal person considers herself ready for a daring armed race through a strange and hostile city? But none of their protests were of any import, so when the next song got under way – the oddly appropriate pirates' song that begins, *With cat-like tread, upon our prey we steal* – I waved my hands and glowered at the chorus until they began to chime in, and were soon singing as if their very lives depended on it.

Annie and I took up positions at opposite ends of the dividing wall. We had heaped a table and bench on top of each other, to give her the height to display her . . . self, while at my end I had another bench, sufficient to help me scramble over. She knelt in place. I looked at her, and nodded.

She stood. The girls were singing their hearts out – *the household soundly sleeps* – and Annie rose from above the parapet, stretching her arms high, moving to the tempo. She was too thin for a proper belly dancer and had no clue how to mimic the sinuous sway of the original, but somehow I did not imagine that would matter to her audience.

I began to count, and got as far as 'two' before the violin descended into a parrot-squawk of discord. I raised my head above the stones, saw nothing but the backs of many heads, and swung myself over.

Holmes recovered first: A heart-beat before my feet hit the rooftop, his hand was swinging the violin hard into the face of an open-mouthed guard. As it made contact, I leapt for the back of another. In an instant the roof was a battlefield tumult of shouts and cries and grunts and bellowed commands and the single blast of a revolver as the pent-up masculine frustrations of twelve British citizens and a French cook exploded on the heads of the four guards.

In thirty seconds it was over. Daniel Marks continued to batter the man at his feet with – oddly – a fringed velvet pillow, but the man's unconscious sprawl suggested that some more solid implement had gone before.

'Are there other guards?' I demanded.

As if in answer, the door crashed open and a big man came through it, moving fast, shotgun up and ready. Holmes stuck out a foot; our chief constable caught the falling guard with a tea-pot as he went by; Bert delivered the *coup de grâce* with a flower-pot: as neat a piece of choreography as I had seen off the screen.

Except: The shotgun went off as it hit the ground.

And a wail of pain rose up from the women's side.

I launched myself over the wall, seeing nothing but a scrum of *galabiyyas* and dish-towels. I hauled away shoulders until I had uncovered the victim, and saw – oh God, I knew who it would be before I got there – Edith, huddled over, one hand plastered against the side of her face.

She was breathing. 'Edith, let me see. Is it your eye?' *God, I should never forgive myself, if—*

Annie enfolded the panicking mother's hands in hers, and I gently peeled away the child's bloody hands, expecting a terrible sight.

But an eye looked back at me, stark with alarm but undamaged. And the blood seemed lower. I wiped my sleeve across the young cheek, and went light-headed with relief at the neat straight slice across the top of the cheekbone.

Around me, nineteen females drew simultaneous breaths. 'Someone give me a handkerchief,' I requested, and dabbed at the wound with the delicate white scrap. The ooze was already slowing.

'Ooh,' groaned Mrs Nunnally, 'my poor baby, look at that, there's going to be a *scar!*'

Mrs Hatley tried to assure her that, no, it would heal nicely, but I had seen the flash of hope behind the blood. 'No, she's right,' I said. 'That's almost certain to leave a scar.' The expression on the child's face was undeniable: pride. I gave the wounded warrior a hand up, and said solemnly, 'Yes, you're going to have a nice handsome scar. People will ask about it for years.'

The men began to spill over the wall. As they came, each was led to the small mountain of clothing we had brought up from below, and each was draped, painted and covered to give him a semblance of belonging here. The last one over was Bert-the-Constable, holding a familiar Purdy shot-gun; Annie grabbed his hand and pulled him to one side for an urgent briefing.

As the trickle of scrambling men slowed, I climbed onto the bench to peer over the wall. Five guards lay trussed and gagged, dragged into a shady patch. Two were conscious and angry, two were half-conscious. One would be lucky to live 'til evening.

I went back to where Annie was handing Bert a cloth and Holmes was making a head-wrap out of a length of curtain. As I pawed through the much-diminished pile of clothing, hoping to find something other than one patched *galabiyya* the colour of goat dung, Bert's Cockney voice stated the obvious. 'That shot will bring attention. We must go.'

'You two bring up the rear,' Holmes ordered the two agents. When they protested, he simply picked up the shot-gun he'd left leaning against the wall and disappeared down the stair-way. I dropped the disgusting robe over my head, checking that I could reach through it for my weapons, then turned to this singular assortment of lovely young women and comically ugly men.

I overrode the gabble of conversation with a trio of brief declarative sentences, capped by a pair of imperatives. 'We have to hurry. We'll all go together through the city to the gate. Once we're outside the walls, the Army will see us and we'll be safe. If shooting starts, get into a doorway. And don't say a word to anyone.'

Then I stepped through the doorway before the questions could begin, although I heard Fflytte's voice behind me, raised in protest that a mere assistant should give the orders, and why were all the women in men's dress? But Hale shut him up before I had to, and we poured down the stairways to the courtyard. Male exclamations and female explanations rose up at the sight of the boots, the piano, and the two tied guards, but I turned and brutally squelched it.

'If you want to live, do as you're told, immediately. Do you understand?'

They understood.

Holmes and I led the ungainly procession; Annie and Bert brought up the rear. Holmes ventured out first, checking the narrow street for guards, then continued to the next intersection before giving a signal that we could follow. One after another, our charges stepped over the threshold onto the dusty stones: Fflytte and Hale, Will and Mrs Hatley, mothers and daughters and fictional sisters, with six constable-actors, a make-believe sergeant and a cook mixed among them. They looked as much like Moroccans as a group of painted storks might have, but from a distance, in the dim, thatched recesses of the Salé medina, each of us swathed in the same anonymous hooded *galabiyyas* the rest of the population wore, moving fast, we might not attract too much of an audience.

I was the only one who had been out here, so I went first – with a frisson of terror, sure that I had forgotten the way. But my feet remembered, even with the distractions of day versus night, and we trailed along, stretching out more and more as we left the quieter sections and came to the bazaar proper. Soon, we were forced to edge past laden donkeys and men with carpets and sellers of oats and spice and the occasional flayed goat or camel hanging before a butcher's.

'I hadn't realised how crowded it would be,' I hissed at Holmes. He raised an eyebrow in agreement and stepped to one side in order to survey the long – too long – trail of foreign shapes, moving at a snail's pace in our wake. I shook my head in despair, edged around a donkey (four legs and two ears sticking out of seventeen baskets of yellow slippers), and looked into the lane beyond.

To come face to face with a band of enraged pirates.

CHAPTER FORTY

PIRATE KING: Let vengeance howl;
　　　　The pirate so decides.

I LEAPT BACKWARDS towards Holmes and collided with the donkey. The creature blatted; a rope parted; a yellow tide of leather spilt into the lane; the shoe-maker began to bellow. 'Go!' I shouted at Holmes, but it was too late. On the other side of this four-legged cork the slow moentum of my fellow countrymen continued to pile up. Holmes, who was tall enough to see even over a laden donkey, spotted the pirates as they pounded around the corner at my back: Adam, Jack, the beautiful Benjamin, the Swedish accountant Mr Gröhe (in whose hand a knife looked simply bizarre) and an uncountable number of others (in whose hands the knives looked far too comfortable). Holmes turned to shout at the escapees; those who heard him did attempt to reverse their tracks and flee, but by this time the column had come to a halt, thoroughly wedged between the pressure from behind and the irritated quadruped.

The howl of pirates filled the alleyway; the donkey's ears twitched its displeasure; those on the other side would have milled about if they had not been stuck fast; I turned towards my pursuers, and came face to face with Adam.

'*Why are you here?*' he demanded in Arabic, then remembered, and paused to assemble a translation.

'*We wish to leave,*' I replied in his tongue.

He started to answer, realised what I had said, started again, paused a second time, and then looked past me and saw the others. Including Annie, who had climbed on a greengrocer's display to see what the problem was. Adam's words died away as he and Annie regarded each other above the crowd. They were both unaware of the growing turmoil, the shouts of the donkey's owner, the cries of other would-be pedestrians in three directions.

The owner of the slippers swam upstream towards his four-legged lorry, bawling a constant stream of '*Bâlek! Bâlek!*' ('Give way!'), although the additional pressure only forced the creature backwards, onto me and the pirates. In a minute, the beast would start to kick. Adam shouted. The man shouted back, until he came to a clear place and caught sight of his foe. His mouth went wide, then snapped shut. Without a glance at his lost wares, he grabbed the creature's halter and hauled furiously away. A receding wave of cries, protests and curses traced his retreat; the sardine-tin sensation grew less marked.

Adam turned at last to look at me. '*You speak Arabic.*'

'*I do. The others do not. You must let us go. This will bring war onto your city.*'

His dark eyes did not react, although a slight tilt of the head made me aware of the men at his back. A dozen or more large, armed, ferocious-looking men, hungry for a fight.

'*We will return to the house,*' he said.

'No!' I looked at his younger brother, Jack, and thought of those shiny boots sticking in such awful absurdity from under the piano. No child should live with that image in his memory. '*Your father is dead there.*'

Reaction rippled back into the men, with a burst of cross-talk. Adam seemed oblivious, but Jack took a step closer to him.

'*You lie,*' the younger boy declared.

'*I do not. It was an accident,*' I said – which, granted, was not exactly true, but ... '*He lies in the courtyard.*' Then I added in English, 'Your brother does not need to see it.'

Adam's black eyes studied me for the longest time. With the donkey gone, Holmes and the others had come together, and I could feel him, three feet from me, ready to pull his revolver from its inner pocket and go down shooting.

'Dead.'

'I am sorry for you.' I had no idea what he was thinking, how he was going to react.

'And my uncle?'

'As far as I know, he's still under arrest. The French—'

'The guards?'

I switched back to Arabic. '*Your men are tied. Two are injured badly, the others merely bound.*'

'*And my father is dead.*'

For God's sake, was he about to gut me? Hug me? Turn his head to the wall and weep? '*He was a brave man,*' I ventured.

'*He was a—*' I was not familiar with the word, but his inflection made me suspect it was not a term of endearment.

He took a tremulous breath, then seemed to grow two inches taller and ten years older. For the first time, I saw a resemblance to Samuel. He looked towards the back of the crowd – towards Annie – and then whirled about to face his compatriots.

'*You heard this foreigner!*' he shouted at them. I thrust my hands into the *galabiyya* to grab my knife in one hand and the revolver in the other. Holmes pushed forward, and a sudden caterpillar of motion from the rear suggested that Annie and Bert had done the same. '*My father is dead. My uncle is in the hands of the French. Who will deny that I step into my father's boots? Any?*'

The lad's fury brought the others up short, stopped me in my place, made Holmes raise one hand to keep those at his back from shoving into an uncertain but clearly perilous situation. The pirates looked at one another. Jack wormed his way around to take up a position at his brother's side. Benjamin stared, first at them, then at Mr Gröhe, and finally craned to look into the foreign faces, but Celeste was not to be seen. He shifted, looking as if he were about to move away – when a scream rent the air.

Everyone ducked. A gun went off, although the shutter it destroyed was a good ten feet from the bright visitor that swooped through this urban canyon, beating its wings to perch upon a frayed clothes-line strung between buildings. 'She is MINE!' the bird screeched.

The street blinked, and began to breathe again. Benjamin lowered his eyes to the two brothers and, as if Rosie's words had been meant for him alone, stepped forward to side with Adam. The remaining members of the crew exchanged another round of speechless consultation; their weapons stayed up, but their shoulders lost a degree of belligerence.

Adam kept his chin raised, as haughty as if the question of succession had never been in doubt. '*You take me as leader?*' he demanded. '*You agree that I am my father, in your eyes?*'

No-one openly denied it; in fact, a general shrug of acceptance ran through them as if to say, *Well, why not?*

I shot Holmes a glance, warning him, and then Annie at the back – because, in truth, whether it be Samuel or his son giving the orders, our position had changed little. We had to fight here, or risk abduction into the distant inland, never to return.

Should I attack first, before Adam could give the order? The confusion that followed would free the others for a panicked flight – *some* of them might find their way to safety. I eyed the young man's back, tightening my fingers on the knife in my sleeve. *If I go in under his ribs with a sharp push to the right, my knife will clear as he falls into Benjamin and that big fellow, after which—*

'Then I say, we let them go!'

—my right hand is clear to shoot the Swedish accountant and . . . Wait. What?

The pirate crew were looking every bit as puzzled as I.

'*No!*' one of them finally said, although the word grew elongated and ended in a distinct question mark.

'*Yes!*' Adam shouted. '*You said you would follow me. And I will lead you, and I will provide for you and for your families. This I vow. But I will not have you living off the takings of a wicked act. I will not feed my men off the suffering of women.*'

Good God: The subversive sentiments of W.S. Gilbert had converted this hereditary Moroccan cut-throat into a Frederic of morality. I had never before thought of the Savoy operas as a tool of Anarchic philosophy.

'Noble lad!' Holmes murmured.

But the pirates were not convinced. Indeed, judging by the spreading grumble of dissatisfaction, if something was not done quickly, this would be the briefest reign in Salé's history.

I raised my voice. '*I know you men were looking forward to your share of the ransom monies, but there remains much money to be had, and without the disruption of British cannonballs or the inconvenience of French gaol.*'

That caught their attention.

'*The small man, in our company – Randolph Fflytte? He is a man who lives for the privilege of giving money to others. He points his camera, and it makes a man wealthy. And he may be small in stature, but in my country, he is huge in authority. If he says "Come", many will follow – all of whom will have busy cameras and equally large purses, and an equal desire to share their wealth. Think for yourselves, O men of Salé: A single payment'* – (What the hell was the Arabic for ransom?) – '*now, followed by years of grief with your families huddling in the far mountains? Or a moment of generosity that opens the doors to long years of gentle thievery? The choice is yours.*'

The men knew all about Fflytte; even those who had not received his money personally had heard that he could certainly throw it around. It was not a far reach to believe that he might cause a tap of gold to flow. They thought about it, and the weapons in their hands sagged a fraction.

'*Your pride is your country,*' I persisted in a gentle voice. '*You can conquer the world from within.*'

None of which actually meant anything: I was merely offering a stall and a distraction, desperately gambling that their blood might cool and dilute their single-minded intent.

Adam stepped forward. '*My friends, the days that my uncle and my father were trying to remake are gone. The wind has shifted. If we deny this, if we shake our fists at the sky and tell ourselves that the wind is still at our backs, we will end up wrecked upon the shore, or worse, becalmed. If, however, we trim our sails and run with that new wind, who knows where it will take us? Us, and our sons and grandsons, bearing the blood of our noble ancestors.*

'*The pirate way gives all an equal voice and an equal share. The pirate way demands that the king be chosen. I ask that you trust my father's blood, and follow me.*'

When he ended, I half expected the film-crew to burst into

applause – then remembered that they did not understand Arabic, and in any event, had their hands full with knives. Adam's followers, more inured perhaps to flights of Arab rhetoric, were not so instantly convinced, but they could not deny that a boy who could talk like this might be just the fellow to deal with the French authorities.

Gröhe felt the shift in the metaphorical rigging first, and gratefully worked the unaccustomed blade back into its scabbard. One by one, others did the same. Three men at the far end looked at each other, looked at the guns they carried, and put them up.

Adam nodded, and gave a brief command that I did not hear, but that sent one of his men off at a run. When he faced us again, he was no longer a boy.

'Come,' he said.

We came. Through the medina we passed, the streets gone silent as word spread like a fire through dry grassland. Donkeys miraculously vanished, heaps of merchandise no longer filled the way, and I pushed the hood from my robe, allowing my European hair to shine out. When I glanced back, I could see the others doing the same.

Full points to Adam, the new pirate king of Salé, parading his foreign captives through the streets of his realm.

He led us, not to the closest gate in the walled city, but to the river entrance we had come by, half a lifetime before. Boats were already waiting, summoned by the new king's runner. By the time the first of the boats had crossed the Bou Regreg – laden with the younger girls and their mothers, despite Edith's furious protestations that she wanted to stay behind, to be a pirate, with Jack – a crowd had begun to gather on the Rabat side.

Finally, a small knot of us remained: Holmes, Annie, Will and I, talking to Adam as we waited for the last boat to come back for us.

Or so I thought.

'I'll send the film over with the luggage,' Will said.

Annie looked puzzled, Holmes (although he later denied it) did, too. I, however, merely asked, 'What about the cameras?'

'I'll keep one. They'll be hard to find here, and Mr Fflytte owes me that much.'

'Will!' Annie protested. 'You're surely not thinking of staying behind?'

Holmes had caught up quickly. 'I believe you'll find that Mr Currie is concerned that if he comes within reach of the British authorities, he'll find himself behind bars.'

'What? *Will!* No, not you – tell me you didn't kill the poor girl!'

'Kill? Who? Me? I didn't kill anyone! What are you talking about?' He looked confused, and frightened.

'Lonnie Johns,' I said.

'What, Lonnie? Good heavens, has she died?'

I remarked to my husband, 'He's a cameraman, not an actor.'

'I agree.'

'When did she die?' Will asked.

'No guilt in his eyebrows.'

'No avoidance of the eyes.'

'*How* did she die?'

I took pity on the man. 'We don't know for certain that she's dead. The police suspect it.'

'They're usually wrong,' Holmes commented.

'I wouldn't say "usually", Holmes,' I chided.

'Then why the hell did you tell me she was dead? *Accuse* me of killing her?'

'To see your reaction. You smuggled guns, and drugs. If Miss Johns had discovered it, perhaps you'd have killed her.'

'I never!'

'But you did sell the guns and the drugs.'

Now he looked down, kicking at the dust with his boot. 'Well, yeah. But it was just . . . lying there. Hale got all that stuff, for Fflytte. Nothing would do but that we had the real thing, for the camera. Insane, but it's what he wanted. Only the three of us knew, the others thought it was washing-up powder or something. And then when we moved on to the next project, someone had to tidy after them.'

'And you always resented, just a little, that Fflytte's name alone was on the credits.'

The Welshman's face lifted, his eyes bitter and defiant. 'Without me, Randolph Fflytte would still be scratching his head over that first camera. So yes, I will admit, I thought that picking up a little extra on the side might make up for it, just a bit. But I never hurt anyone.'

That was, I supposed, debatable. But I for one did not intend to tackle him and truss him for the next boat across the river. 'You want to stay here in Morocco?'

'It's warm. I like the food. The French can't arrest an Englishman here. There are worse places to retire. And, somebody has to let these boys know how to deal with the actors and directors they'll be meeting.'

Adam decided we had finished, and said to Holmes in English, 'I will return your things by morning.'

Holmes replied in Arabic, '*The ladies will be glad for their clothing, certainly. And do not forget your guards on the roof of the house.*'

'*Or those in the ground floor of the women's quarters,*' I added.

'*The punishment for the men should be light,*' Holmes suggested. '*They were overcome by the artistry of women, a mistake they will not make again.*'

'*We are all overcome by women,*' said the young pirate ruefully, and turned to the yellow-curled source of his overcoming (and of his guards' overcoming, which I was glad he did not know). 'Would you stay?' he pleaded. Holmes and I studied the river, although we did not move out of earshot. Neither Adam nor Annie seemed concerned with privacy; why should we be?

'I cannot,' she replied, her voice low with emotion. 'Your people, your country, are beautiful, but they are too different from what I know. My heart tells me to try, but my head tells me that in the end, that difference would come between us. And I would not hurt you, not for the world.'

'I will come to you, then. Let me help my people for a few years, and then I will return to you.'

'No,' she said – just the tiniest fraction of a second too quickly. 'Your people need you. I see that now, and I rejoice for them, even as I sorrow for myself. I can live with the hole in my heart, knowing that it is for a good cause.'

I couldn't help giving her a quick glance, then looked away again, astonished: I'd have sworn her eyes welled with unshed tears.

Adam seized her hands, a shocking public demonstration for a Moslem male.

'You are as noble a woman as any man could desire, and I can only say, if your heart aches too much, when you are home, if you wish to return here and become my wife, I will be here.'

'You must not wait for me,' she answered firmly. 'You must marry and have sons of your own.'

'Oh, I will. But I will always welcome you as another wife.'

I shot her another glance, but fortunately her head was down, studying their entwined hands, and when she raised her face, any reaction was hidden away.

'I will always remember you,' she told him.

'And I, you,' he said.

And with that she retrieved her hands and walked away, head

bent, to the last boat. I got in behind her, with Holmes last. She kept her head down as we crossed the muddy river, and when we climbed out, she kept her rigid spine to the pirate town across the water.

We pressed our way into a noisy crowd made up of British soldiers, French soldiers, film personnel, half-naked bathing children, donkeys, sheep, a camel, some bewildered tourists, and a parrot. A half-naked water carrier with a bulging goatskin slung over his shoulder was selling cups of water to an audience of delighted locals who sat atop the wall, kicking their heels and passing around small baskets of pistachios and dates.

Hale was pointing at the figures on the northern shore and shouting about his camera, his film, his—

Fflytte was in full bore to an uncomprehending *poilu* about the interruption to his schedule, his urgent requirement for a local assistant, someone to help him hire replacement pirates—

Mrs Hatley and Isabel's mother had set the sails of their bosoms, despite their enveloping *galabiyyas*, and had cornered a British officer to demand that they and the girls be taken to the best hotel in Rabat, that very instant, because heaven only knew what sorts of vermin these costumes had in their folds, and they hadn't seen a proper tub in days, and—

Bibi, with her customary skill at arranging the scene around her, waited for a camera to appear before she gracefully fainted into the not entirely willing arms of Daniel Marks, who staggered and permitted her to slump to the filthy paving stones, which revived her into a cry of disgust recorded by the camera and—

The parrot decided in the end that we were not where fate had intended him, and flew away across the river in search of his pirate king, shouting all the while, 'The people will RULE! Golden daffodils! SEIZE the—'

A perplexed and red-faced Mrs Nunnally was trying to quiet the tear-streaked Edith, who was demonstrating several new additions to her vocabulary and declaring that the instant she turned eighteen she would return, and that she would never wear a frock again, and that she wanted a hair-cut immediately, and that—

With all this going on, I nearly missed the sound Annie made. My first thought, seeing the rhythmic heave of her body, was that she was sobbing at the loss of her one true love. Then she shot a look over her shoulders, back across the river where lingered the newly crowned pirate king of Salé, and I saw the dance of her dry eyes and the quirk of her lips.

And the woman had claimed she wasn't much of an actress.

CHAPTER FORTY-ONE

PIRATE KING: . . . with all our faults, we love our Queen.

I DID NOT know if Mrs Hatley and Isabel's mother got their baths
that day. I did not know if Edith – Eddie – was granted his
hair-cut. I did not discover until some days later whether or not
Hale got his film back, or if Bibi arranged a more satisfactory news
photograph, or if Fflytte found a local capable of working the ropes.
And some things I never did learn: if Hale knew that June was his
child; if the girls found a source of chewing gum in Morocco; if
Rosie screeched for ever in the air above Salé.

Two things I knew, when I staggered into my own very small,
very dim hotel room, very late that night. First, a telegram from
Scotland Yard informed us that Lonnie Johns had been found,
alive and well, having returned from an illicit holiday in Barbados
with a Member of Parliament she'd met in the course of making
Rum Runner. And second, that I was wearing the same goat dung-

coloured robe I'd put on that morning; the itching from the wool (I prayed it was only from the wool) was driving me mad.

I tore it off and threw it into a corner, replacing it with a dressing-gown I had chosen from a heap of cast-off clothing Rabat's European community had hastily donated to their filmic refugees. The garment might have been designed for Randolph Fflytte, but modesty was not high on my list of concerns. I tied its belt, dropped into the armchair that was wedged between bed and wall, kicked off my boots, tipped back my head and closed my eyes.

'Just so you know,' I said, 'I plan to murder Lestrade when we get home.'

There came a ting of cut-glass carafe against tin mug, then the tap of my drink being set atop the small deal table tastefully decorated with cigarette burns.

'I may be too tired to swallow,' I groaned.

I heard another movement of clothing, then the cup nudged my hand. My fingers wrapped around it: perhaps I was not too tired to swallow, after all.

'A most successful day, Russell. You overcame a band of ruffians with minimal bloodshed, freed thirty-two British captives and a Frenchman, and prevented a war. You oversaw the peaceful change of régime of a criminal gang into the hands of a young man eager to promulgate the noblest sentiments of Victorian England. You made your erstwhile employer – he is, I trust, erstwhile? – happy by finding a source of what might be described as Moroccan actors, and in the process not only salvaged the economic future of the British film industry, but saved king and country from scandal.'

'However,' I told him, 'scandal there will be, enough to keep Fflytte Films in the news for some weeks. To begin with Edith keeps trying to sneak across the river. Her mother caught her the first time. The second, she was returned by Benjamin.'

'The pretty pirate?'

'Yes. Who brought her into the dinner where the entire crew was gathered – her mother had thought she was sleeping – and asked M. Dédain for assistance.'

'Asking for asylum?'

'Asking for marriage.'

'Celeste, wasn't it? Well, at least someone is happy.'

'Celeste is not happy. Oh, she was when she first saw him. But after a short time, the pretty young man contrived to be sitting next to Daniel Marks. Celeste swore she would talk to every newspaper in England.'

'I see.'

'Daniel removed himself to sit with Bibi, which made everything settle down nicely. Although as I came past the hotel tonight, I saw Benjamin going in through the service door. So everyone except Celeste should be happy.'

'And thus is Fflytte Films hauled from the rocks of scandal. In addition – although I do not for a moment suppose such was your intent – you appear single-handedly to have shaped the basis for a future Moroccan tourist industry, by giving the country's hereditary buccaneers an outlet for their innate drive for plunder.'

'I've certainly left Fflytte Films open to plunder, at any rate.' My final duty that evening had been a long and brain-wracking English-and-Arabic, legal-and-criminal conversation with Captain La Rocha in his gaol cell, arranging for the hire – at rates just short of extortion – of the *Harlequin*, which (it turned out) was still registered in his name. It had been my offer to restore to its hull the ship's previous name, the *Henry Morgan*, that sealed the deal with the former pirate king. 'As for my employ, I've given Geoffrey Hale notice that he needs a new assistant.' I took another mouthful, relishing the sensation as the young cognac seared its way down my very empty gullet. I looked past the glass at the pair of filthy, blistered feet propped on the bed-covers.

'However, Holmes, I'm afraid there may be a slight delay in our departure.'

My cheeriness gave him pause. After a moment, he ventured, 'Yes?'

'It would appear that while Randolph Fflytte does not mind having been taken hostage by his actors, Geoffrey Hale is not so forgiving. He firmly decrees a new set of pirates. And although I don't imagine there will be a great problem in locating a sufficient number of dark-complexioned gentlemen here in Rabat to fill the rôles of the pirates, it will take some days to teach them their parts. During this time, Fflytte Films will be paying the cast and crew – girls, mothers, Sally, constables, Marks, Maude and Maurice – simply to lie about in the sun.' While I talked, I had set down the empty mug and noticed the state of my hands – the morning's brown paint had mostly worn off, but the edges were quite disgusting. I stood, easing a crick in my back, and limped over to the room's sole luxury, the cold-water basin in the corner.

'Yes?' The wariness in his voice was stronger; I could feel his narrowed gaze drilling into the back of my head.

'Well, instead of supporting them at their leisure, he proposes to employ them in an interim project. He is, even as we speak, madly penning the script for a new picture, to be filmed while his substitute pirates are in training.'

I looked into the speckled mirror, grimacing at the ravaged face and hair that met my gaze.

'Why does this concern us?' Holmes' voice now contained outright suspicion. And rightly so.

'Because,' I said, turning on the tap, 'we do have a means of lending assistance to the British film industry and to the House of Lords, if not the Palace itself. It seems that Mr Fflytte was inspired by today's passage through the medina. He envisions a tale weaving together said passage with elements of Byron's epic poem, *The Corsair*. Particularly the scene in which the pirate, Conrad, is rescued from a sultan's dungeon. By a woman.'

I lifted my scrubbed face from the now-grubby towel, and met my husband's eyes.

'He proposes to call the new picture *Pirate Queen*. Starring Mary Russell.'

'When stern duty calls,
I must obey . . .'

ACKNOWLEDGEMENTS

Fernando Pessoa, beneath his seventy-five or eighty heteronyms, was a real person: famous though nearly unpublished during his life; a reluctant traveller whose imagination wandered the globe; author of an 'autobiography' rich in content (and pages) yet so formless, readers may shape it as they like. I am grateful for the work of Richard Zenith, tireless editor, translator and commentator on the Pessoa manuscripts – of which more than 25,000 loose pages were left to entertain posterity. Any person travelling through Lisbon must by all means visit the Pessoa museum, where his variations on one single poem cover all the walls.

With thanks to Nina Mazzo, who donated to the Friends of the San Francisco Public Library and the 826 Valencia writing project during BoucherCon 2010, and to Lonnie Johns-Brown, who gave to Heifer International's Team LRK during the spring of 2010. The generosity of both ladies won them (or in Nina's case, her mother) namesakes in this book.

I am grateful for the guidance of Mark Willenbrock (madabout morocco.com), whose unique view of his adoptive home brought a whole new dimension to Morocco. (May I underscore here Miss Russell's own assertion, that this story should be regarded as a work of fiction? One will in fact find the country of Morocco, and its city of Salé, warm and welcoming, being neither xenophobic nor infested with pirates – filmic, Muslim, or otherwise.) And thanks again to Louisa Pittman, whose skill in the rigging is only excelled by her willingness to give countless hours to help a landlubber writer.

The chapter headings are from *The Pirates of Penzance*, by W.S. Gilbert, except for chapter 14. 'I need truth, and some aspirin' is the sentiment of Álvaro de Campos, one of the faces of Fernando Pessoa, in an untitled poem dated 14 March 1931, found in the collection edited and translated by Richard Zenith, *A Little Larger Than the Entire Universe*. The lines from Pessoa's 'Maritime Ode' in chapter 19 also come from Zenith's translation.

The good folk at the Hollywood Heritage Museum, along with Shelly Stamp, professor of film and media at the University of California, Santa Cruz, helped me get the cameras turning. Although thus far we have not been able to unearth a copy of that great lost film of the silent era, *Pirate King*.